What
the
River
Washed
Away

What the River Washed Away

Muriel Mharic Maclcod

ONEWORLD

A Oneworld Book

First published by Oneworld Publications 2013

Copyright © Muriel Mharie Macleod 2013

The moral right of Muriel Mharie Macleod to be identified as the
Author of this work has been asserted by her in accordance with the
Copyright, Designs and Patents Act 1988

ISBN 978-1-78074-234-2
eBook ISBN 978-1-78074-235-9

Text designed and typeset by Tetragon, London
Printed and bound by Page Bros Ltd

Oneworld Publications
10 Bloomsbury Street
London WC1B 3SR
England
www.oneworld-publications.com

Stay up to date with the latest books,
special offers, and exclusive content from
Oneworld with our monthly newsletter

Sign up on our website
www.oneworld-publications.com

For my father, Callum an Ach,
and my mother, Ishbel.

My name is Constance Laing, but I have another: it is Arletta Lilith Johnson. I have been in Africa most of my life but I was born near Brouillette, Louisiana, in 1901, and I have not seen my country for over half a century. Africa gave me a life I could not have had in my own country, not because I am a black woman, but because I am a brave one.

I have spent each evening of the last few weeks at my desk listening to Louis Armstrong sing as I recall so well from days gone by, and telling you, my confessor, why I came to Africa these many years ago, when they permitted unmarried women to take up auxiliary missionary posts. Here I was able to be among my own kind, and I was able to satisfy what I believe was my vocation; I became a teacher. I had my own classroom and my own house, which I built shortly after I arrived.

Here in Africa I never leave the house without a hat; in fact, I am never seen in public without a hat and lace gloves. I have forty-five pairs of lace gloves. I bought my first pair when I arrived here in the 1920s. I saw a small advertisement for them in the paper and ordered them right away to hide the scars of my past. I have a habit, you will see, of reading every word in a newspaper.

In America ladies nowadays wear lace gloves only at weddings and funerals. They do as they please without fear. Be glad that America has changed.

Here I give up the secrets of my life for you to do with as you please. I have never regretted the actions you will read about. It has not been difficult to tell a stranger; it would have been impossible to tell a friend.

One

H e's a bad man.
I scrub myself clean after he's gone. The water is shivering cold. He says my feet feel soft like a baby's, but blood flows from where I scraped them raw on the slab beneath the pipe.

'Arletta!'

That's Mambo. She can scream. I'm gonna get thwacked for sure. As if I ain't sore enough.

'Arletta, feed them chickens, and feed them good. Arletta, what the hell ya doing? Don't go washing ya hair in the evening time girl, that's how ya get chilled all the time and what do I get? A poorly child!'

Thwack.

'How many times I tell ya girl?'

'All times, Mambo.'

Thwack.

'Well, one of them times it gonna be real fine if you just do as ya told. Go on now. Feed them chickens and then get y'self right on off to bed. Ya hearing me, Arletta?'

'Okay, Mambo.'

'And come on in here, so I can dry that hair. Come on now.'

Mambo's fresh home from wherever she's been and it ain't long before she's taking right off again. She's wearing her fine dress, off meeting some new beau I s'pose, now her old one found me and don't want her no more. Times I feel I got a Mambo who don't seem to care for me at all. She don't seem to care what he's doing to her daughter. I tried telling her about the first time he come at me with his doing, but I got me a thwacking and tell't not to be telling lies 'cause of him being white folks, and right high and mighty and all she says.

'He's a man with what they call a profession Arletta, that's a right high and minded kinda job. Ain't no messing, and y'all need a be washing ya mouth out. Go on! And I'm gonna rub that block of carbolic on ya tongue if ya start talking bad on folks. Where ya get that from, Arletta? Ya know somebody got a daddy meddling with them or what?'

'No.'

'And them whites ain't gonna give us no say-so at all if they hear ya talking that way. Ya knows that, don't ya?'

'Yes.'

'Then just quit with them kinda stories Arletta. We gonna be in a fine set of trouble if folks hear that talk. I don't know what ya thinking.'

'But he ...'

'I'm tellin' ya, Arletta, Mr McIntyre's got one good and proper job. He's working in a bank and all, and even running it now, from what I'm hearing. And look what ya doing to what folks think on him. He's got what folks call a reputation. Ya know what that is?'

'Well, no, I ain't know nothing about that. I ain't know nothing except he's a bad man, Mambo.'

'Enough girl, or ya gonna find y'self stretching from the branch of a tree, and me dangling 'longside ya, and all them white folks thinking they's having themselves a picnic.'

She sure ain't listening to me, so I'm just glad Mr McIntyre's gone and got himself all spent out already for today and won't be coming back as soon as she takes off again.

She's wearing a bright red bandana wrapped up on her head so high like she means business. She's got pink flowers pinned down one side, says it's the fashion, and she's wiggling off down our track in that tight dress, the one I says gotta be a size too small and showing off everything she got. Up top that looks like plenty after she's done shoving them up, this way and that way, and pulling that frock down so a nipple pops right out first stretch she makes.

'Oh my,' she always says, 'just look at that. Pardon me, won't you now.' And she reckons that's fine for getting folks giggling.

I sure hope I don't get like my Mambo when I grow up.

'Arletta, feed them chickens, ya hearing me? And be good to that cockerel. He'll be needing special attention now, 'cause I'm wanting him well fed and wild this Saturday.'

She knows I'm watching her wiggling off to parade herself, half-dressed and rouged all over. 'Cheap devil Mambo and no panties,' that's what Pappy used to say, and about his own daughter, too.

Ain't nobody ever put no stop to Mambo when she's planning on getting wild.

It's gonna be a dark moon this Saturday, that's what she's talking about. She's gonna get outta that tight frock of hers and get herself all done up in sparkling white. Ain't gonna be nobody like her. I hear folks say ain't never been anybody like my Mambo.

Out on the front step of our cabin I finish drying my hair with a cotton rag and stop sniffling on account of Mambo leaving me here by my lonesome again. Sniffling ain't any use anyways. She's off parading herself just like Pappy said she's good for, hanging out and dancing all night in one of them juke joints, and coming home to our cabin when she feels like it. Ain't got no mind about me.

We got two rooms in our old cabin. One we live in, though ain't much in it, just our table and two wooden stools Pappy made a long time ago when he was able. We got a beat-up old Tilley lamp – Mambo says it was once as blue as the sky, but now it's got all over with rust. What food we have is laid out on the other end of our table – ain't ever much – and down below is where we keep kindling for the pot. We got a big shelf stuck up above the fireplace – ain't much on that neither, except the gourd we use for washing, Pappy's Bible, real worn out with reading, and a box of matches I ain't s'posed to touch. We got an old bucket placed outside of our back door that's all chipped on the edges now, and four tin mugs, but one gets used for tallow since

Grandma passed away. And wooden bowls Pappy sliced off a tree and whittled down good till he says they got fit for using.

Pappy's rake and spade are laid out across the rafters now, gathering dust and mighty cobwebs, 'longside a rusty old wheel he was gonna use to make a handcart one of them days. Mambo keeps his saw and box of nails up there too, but she ain't never opened that box and there's a lot that needs a nail round here.

The threadbare chair we got in the corner needs fixing up too; don't s'pose it ever will be, now Pappy's gone. That's where I curl up when I need to be remembering him, even though that horsetail sure is prickly coming through all them holes. Pappy said, 'When ticking need new stuffing, that's called upholstering, Arletta,' but ain't never get done. Only other chair we got is his rocking chair out on our leaky porch.

Mambo and me share the other room in our cabin for sleeping. We still got Pappy's old closet in there, and a dresser with proper drawers down below and a big mirror on top that she got from one of her fancy beaux 'cause his folks were turning it out for burning. He brought it over here himself on the back of a cart and stayed for two days. Mambo paying it off I s'pose, with all that giggling. She's got Pappy's bed now and the cot we used to share been moved into the bedroom as well – seems just to stuff the room up. We got too much in one room and not enough in the other, but I ain't saying nothing.

When it's fine we cook out back under the boards Pappy nailed up a long time ago. It leaks bad when it's raining though, and we take the cooking grate in every night 'cause we're feared it might get taken. We share a toilet with everybody else round here – and the flies – which the gov'ment s'posed to send a truck for emptying every week. We get water from the pipe on the side of the road, same as everybody else. When Pappy was still living, he'd haul water from the pipe to our washtub out back every day and wash me first. When it got cold he'd heat the water, but Mambo says that time gone now and I gotta be doing for myself.

We're lucky having our cabin, Pappy used to say, and lucky we don't have to be sharing it like in the old days. He says it got built bad, but he fixed it up good and gave it a proper chimney and now it's gonna stand for a hundred years. He planted plenty sweet potatoes and corn out back, an orange tree and two fig trees on the side. Sometimes that orange tree don't give good fruit if winter's been real cold, but we always have figs in summer 'cause he'd keep them wrapped up from frosty mornings. He was soft on eating figs, my Pappy.

One thing my Mambo can do for sure is look after out back. Once when he got mad at her, Pappy said the way she was acting would make folks think she ain't good for nothing at all. But then he said he was sorry for talking like that. She said he oughta pay it no mind. He said he was glad she was good out back and always been a fine help about the place, and he was right proud of it too. Pappy and Mambo just fight all the time.

I used to go with him for chopping thin branches out back of our cabin. He said he needed a hundred and I gotta learn my counting, so he'd be sure on getting enough. We stepped out and got ten each time, so I learnt easy. Then I had to count how many he trimmed up, and how many he whittled down for sticking in the ground. That's how we got a fence out front of our cabin, like nobody else, 'cause Pappy was busy teaching me my numbers. He always said he was gonna put that fence all round his land and I'd learn half a thousand, but he got old. Grandma and Mambo just laughed.

'What land? Ain't ya land, we just dammit lucky ain't nobody come on over here throwing us off. Ain't nobody round here own nothing. Ya just nothing but an old fool.'

Once he was gone, Mambo grabbed his stack of old newspapers and started covering up the walls of our cabin. Mixed a paste of flour and water and set about sticking them all over. Pappy always got a hold of old newspapers for learning me my letters and teaching me my reading. We were always reading news when it ain't news any more, and I know every story on them walls near enough word for word.

'Don't go pasting them up any old how Mambo. Put this here, 'longside of this. See? Them's the same story, so put them pages together, so's folks can read all about it.'

'Lord, girl. If ya head ain't just full of what nobody care nothing about. Ain't nobody coming over here reading them walls. Folks coming over here don't read nothing.'

'But they's oughta Mambo, and they's oughta learn anyways. I can teach them Mambo, just like Pappy teach me. Ain't hard Mambo. Look, they's talking about the fire down in New Orleans here, and here, so put them right next to one another so everybody can read what happened to folks and how they all get hurt, and all them houses, how they burned down, and how they's gonna raise them up again. Over here Mambo, look. Look at it, that's a real story, it really happened to folks. It did.'

'Stop with the talking. Just once, stop with the damn talking.'

'And this here's about all them trees they's gonna take from round here, Mambo. They's gonna do it, take them for the railway line and for one of them mills, 'cause cottonseed got oil, that's what they say. Listen, this one says — it's from Mansfield, that's over Desoto parish way—'

Thwack.

She wants to be throwing out his magazines, too, but I screamed every word I ever heard him call her. 'Whore, daughter a Babylon, voodoo queen just like ya ma, slattern,' and I don't know what else, till she dropped them magazines right in the middle of our cabin floor and thwacked me plenty. Then she washed my mouth out with the carbolic. I got to keep my magazines though. Seems she's so upset with my mouth she forgot what she was thwacking me for, I guess.

Pappy was always telling me to get all the reading I can, 'cause when he was young, coloureds ain't ever get any reading at all, they ain't never allowed that. I keep all them magazines under my cot now and study them over and over again. I've read them a hundred times. I touch them just the way Pappy said, with a gentle care, so no page gets torn, 'cause the way I see it, that's the only reading I'm ever gonna get now he's gone. Except maybe the paper coming wrapped round crawfish somebody give us 'cause a mambo don't always take dimes. I read them too, so I know what's going on, even though Mambo ain't ever take me anywhere. She's too busy having herself a good time.

Since Pappy died I ain't been nowhere. He used to take me to the fairground when it pitched up a ways outside of Marksville and he'd get himself a job selling tickets. Even got me some rides, 'cause he knows most folks getting fair work too, and he'd take me to Mardi Gras down the Cheney dirt road every year. He'd take me hanging out with his old Creole pals for a smoke after they'd pull bass out of the bayou, and they'd always be singing on the way home in the back of Bobby-Rob's cart. Took me to see the lake once too; that's a fine sight when the sun's going down. But since he's been gone, ain't nobody taking me nowhere.

I'm scared of Mambo and all her mumbo-jumbo sometimes, that's what Pappy called it. He called it mumbo-jumbo on account of him being God-fearing and the Church ain't got no truck with them old ways. I'm scared Mambo's doing devil's work for real. Now Pappy's gone, all that ju-ju stuff sure is all over the place too, even inside of our cabin, and that's something he ain't ever go for at all. Grandma and Mambo just about covered hereabouts with bad stuff and vengeance, he always said. Sometimes he'd take me by the hand and we'd go on out finding that bad stuff, dig it up and he'd teach me how to pray to God Almighty so nobody got hurt on account of it. I don't know nothing about God Almighty, or all that ju-ju voodoo talk – all I know is it sure has caused me trouble every day.

I'm reading one of my magazines, thinking about how much I miss my Pappy. The sun's slipping down the sky, but it still feels hot, and it sure is making me feel sleepy. The dogwood under the trees out back are spread all over with flowers that smell real strong. Pappy always liked that. Once it's dark the only light's gonna be from Grandma's old tallow tin cup so I can read. Then I hear the wooden boards on our front porch start creaking.

'Sweetpea?'

Mr McIntyre! I done him already. I ain't able for no more, I'm just a kid and sore and …

'Sweetpea. I have a new friend for you, Sweetpea.'

'Go away.' I crawl under my cot. I'm so scared of Mr McIntyre that I know sure as anything that I'm gonna be scared as hell of his friend.

'Come on out of there, Sweetpea. Come and meet the nice Mr Seymour. Come on now.'

'No! I done with ya already, Mr McIntyre, and I ain't doing ya no more! I done already and I don't wanna see no friend. Go away!'

'Come on out of there or I'll whip you, girl. You'll do as I tell you.'

I hold onto the bed frame tight and whisper to Pappy.

'Pappy, please help me. Please.'

He starts pulling at the cot and I start yelling.

'I thought you said this was all sorted,' says his friend. He sounds terrible angry. 'I'm getting out of here before a whole darned squad of niggers turn up.'

I hear his friend stomp right out of our cabin and onto the porch, with Mr McIntyre following fast behind him. My heart feels like it's gonna bump right out onto the floor.

'Nobody's ever going to turn up here. Look at the place, it's the back end of bloody nowhere, there's nobody around here for half a mile and I bet most of them don't even know that little whipper's alive.'

'Well, you get her to quit yelling, that's the deal.'

They take off. I hear their footsteps fade up our track, but I just lie there with my heart pounding so hard and so fast I can even hear it thumping inside of my ears.

I'm so scared I just stay under my cot hugging Pappy's magazines right up close. I think about his old face, all wrinkly and brown under the felted hat he used to pull down to shade his eyes. I think about the only tooth he had left, sticking straight up outta his gum – last man standing, he called it – and how he used to stop and lean on his cane for laughing. Pappy couldn't walk and laugh at the same time. He's been dead just about a year now, I think, but I can still smell him, that nice baccy smell of his, especially on his old chair.

In the morning my legs are stiff from how I been stuck underneath the cot all night. Mambo's bed is empty. That means she's gone and met a new beau. I'm glad about that, 'cause she's happy when she's got a beau.

I eat stale cornbread from the skillet for breakfast, softened up in cold sweet tea, but I'm terrible hungry. Mambo paraded herself off last night; ain't no thinking about cooking for me when she sets her eye on a beau, and I was just too scared to come out from under my cot once Grandma's tallow gave out. I was sure as hell Mr McIntyre and his friend were hanging about someplace waiting to get a hold of me for their doing. I find rice and dry spice, one sweet potato, though it's gone mouldy where Mambo's taken slices off, and I fetch three eggs from our hens. I light a fire under the cooking grate – ain't s'posed to, but I learnt how to get good at that when Pappy passed away and my Mambo forgot to be getting herself home and looking out for me.

Kids from across the fields round here are making a right noise out there on the gov'ment road where it passes near the end of our track. They're on the way to catch the school bus that gets them in to lessons on time. I hear they're right strict about getting in on time, and I hear folks say they're glad they got a bus out this way now so kids don't have to walk like they used to. White folks' kids always got a bus, they say, but coloureds had to walk before they got a bus of their own. I don't rightly know why Mambo ain't letting me go for schooling. A lotta folks hereabout don't send their kids in for it at all, and I hear other folks say that ain't right. We s'posed to go for schooling, gov'ment says, but they don't do nothing about getting us there.

I place the rice in our black iron pot with fresh water from the bucket and then I put the three eggs on top. I creep through the trees at the side of our track to watch them kids on their way to school. They sure do look nice fitted out in clothes they ain't allowed to wear for nothing else, just school. And they all look the same, real neat, I call it. I wish Mambo was sending me to school too, and I was walking right 'longside them. Pappy taught me my reading and Mambo says that's all I need, but I know I'm gonna need more than that. I reckon I'm gonna need to know about math, and I'd sure like to know what it's like living in all them fancy places I keep reading about in Pappy's magazines.

Mambo says she's gonna teach me everything I need to know, 'cept I don't wanna be like Mambo. I wanna be like all them other kids, instead of always hiding and worrying about how they're gonna be laughing at me and hollering 'Po'bean' like they do. That's what they call me. Po'bean. Ain't nice. I hide behind the trees till they've gone, then I go sit on the back step of our cabin on my own. I watch the hummingbirds flutter at flowers – they need breakfast too, I guess – till I think my eggs gotta be done. I lift them out with a spoon and set them down for cooling off. Then I pop spices in the rice and take it off the grate so it don't get no more heating. Pappy says that makes the best rice.

'Just let it rest in water that boil for about four minutes. That's all there is to it, Arletta.' It was always right fine when he made it, but I don't know four minutes.

I eat one of my eggs right away and get to thinking I'm gonna have me a walk by Sugarsookie Creek. I feed the chickens, 'cause I never got around to that with Mr McIntyre and his friend and all, and watch that cockerel strutting about the place, lording it over the hens. He don't know what Mambo's got coming to him as soon as the moon gets to its darkest night.

I roll the rice in newspaper along with the other two eggs and head off. Pappy and me went sitting down by Sugarsookie Creek all the time to watch it flow on its wise old way. I watched him smoke his pipe and listened to all his old stories about days gone by that he was right fond of talking about. I listened good to anything my Pappy ever had to say in his deep, slow, drawling voice that sounded as warm as fresh-made steaming pie. I kept hold of his pipe after he was gone, so when I get to feeling real sad I can suck on it and remember him like he's still right here and smoking it himself. I do that when there ain't nobody around to see me acting like I'm crazy, smoking an old pipe with no baccy in it at all.

'What the hell he do with that pipe of his?' screamed Mambo, turning the place upside down after he was gone. 'I promised that pipe to Louis Marquez. He says he loved the look of that pipe and I says he could have it because of him being right fond of Pappy.'

'He ain't love it and he sure ain't never fond of my Pappy. You owe him money, is all.'

Thwack.

It's my pipe now and I got it hidden away in my green tin buried way back of the treeline at the bottom end of our track, away from the gov'ment road. Ain't nobody ever see me go there, 'cause I take good care they don't, and I never go near it in daytime at all. More than the magazines he left me, Pappy's pipe is my most precious thing, it's my own treasure, safe and hidden in the beat-up old tin with the face of the King of England on the lid. Pappy gave me that tin and said I ain't never to open it unless his pal Jeremiah was right there with me. Jeremiah passed away not long after Pappy though, and I'm so scared Mambo is gonna find his pipe and give it to Louis Marquez that I open the tin anyways. Pappy ain't gonna mind that. Just some 'sentimental old papers' in it, he said when he gave it to me, and I've gotta hold onto them 'cause they're mine and mine alone. That's what he said, I remember it clear as day. I wrapped them sentimental old papers in the only handkerchief he ever had, placed his pipe on top and asked Lord Almighty to tell him I'm gonna keep them safe till he rise up.

I ain't saying I know for sure how Mambo paid off Louis Marquez, but I got a pretty fine clue, since she got herself all smiles and pushed-up bosoms when he came for it. I took off as soon as he walked down our track, so I ain't rightly sure about it.

Cicadas are settling down 'cause the day is getting hot, and down on Sugarsookie Creek the water seems just too lazy to make a sound. I soak my poor sore feet, 'cause they've started bleeding again from walking, and I'm still hurting bad from Mr McIntyre and his doing to me yesterday. But it feels better if I hug my knees up tight close to my chest and watch the water flow. Pappy always said a river remembers everything in its water. All the dirt it took from the hands of poor hard-working slaves, and all the sweat of the cotton fields soaked in the only clothes they got. The river remembers the sound of them all singing in praise and pain, and every scream they had from a master's lash. The river remembers the blood on their backs because it had to wash it away.

I hear a noise, like somebody is close-up by. Sounds like they're singing a sad song, slow and full of mourning.

'Somebody there?'

My voice is just a whisper asking, 'cause I'm fearing Mr McIntyre and his friend have followed me out here.

'Somebody there?'

The singing voice is deep and low. But it's a woman's voice. I'm glad about that, anyways.

> *I never laid down my load, Lord*
> *I never gave Jesus my yoke*
> *And on both sides of the river*
> *Blood fed the roots of oak.*
> *Deliver, deliver, deliver my soul*
> *Rest my head on your pillow*
> *Lord, I never grew old.*
> *Hmmm, hmmm, hmmmmmmm …*

The humming is just about as close as it could be without belonging to someone I sure oughta be seeing with my own eyes. My breathing catches in my throat, 'cause it's full of so much choking fear I can't get any air in.

'Hmmm, hmm, hmm-hmm.'

My eyes start darting all over, but I ain't seeing nothing at all. Then the singing stops. I'm scared as hell somebody's gonna be touching me from behind, so I ain't dare turn round neither. I hold my picnic up close and back my way careful along the bank of the creek. Us black folks always kept fearful, Pappy used to say. The humming starts up again.

'Pappy? Is that my Pappy?'

I don't know why I think it's Pappy; I ain't never hear him sing. But if I could feel him close, I know I would be safe. I sure do miss him.

'Pappy, I'm scared. I'm just scared all the time since ya gone with God Almighty.'

I sit down, lay my head on my arms and start rocking to and fro. I'm talking to Pappy like he's right there, same as always.

'I don't know what to do since ya gone Pappy. I want more than anything in this world for ya to come back. Even if ya gonna be shouting at Mambo, I don't mind. I don't mind that at all. It sure would be better than not having ya here at all. Pappy, please come back.'

'That's ya child and ya gonna do right by her. I'm gonna see to that,' he warned Mambo one time, pointing a smoking pipe her way and she ain't care a thing about it.

'What ya gonna do, Pappy? What ya gonna do that I ain't able to sort out good? Eh? Mamma and me sort everything out good, and I'm Mambo round here now. Ya hear me, Pappy?'

'Bad stuff and nonsense, all of it. Children of the Devil, both of ya, and don't even know it. That's the Devil's way. One thing I gonna make sure about is this here child ain't never gonna practise them stupid ways. Ya mind that good! Ya just a pair of fools. Both y'all just devil's fools.'

I remember Mambo tossed her head back and laughed at Pappy.

'Oh what, Pappy? What ya calling us? We're the fools?' Mambo was always teasing poor old Pappy with that giddy sing-song voice she puts on sometimes. 'And maybe ya not even my Pappy at all. Maybe my mamma lay with that old devil himself. Maybe it was just any old somebody else, any old fool. Anybody but Pappy, old Pappy.'

Mambo made Pappy sad all the time.

'Ya has a child, girl, a child ya bring in this world ain't nobody ask for. Ya gonna do right girl. Ya gonna do right or no good ever gonna come of it.'

That night Pappy sat out on our porch holding me close till I fell asleep in his warm baccy smell and we ain't seen hide nor hair of Mambo for days. That's when she took to staying out all the time and my Pappy died with his heart broke.

Seems there ain't any love at all coming my way from Mambo these days. It ain't even that she's taken to thwacking me since Pappy's gone, ain't even all them ugly dolls and all that root-grinding, or the moaning and groaning. I just ain't feeling safe no more. She ain't here enough anyways.

The humming starts up again. I hear it over the noise of my own sniffling, getting louder and louder.

'Please, who is it? Pleeease, please … don't hurt me.'

'Shush chile. Ain't no cause for crying.'

I jump near right outta my own skin when I hear that talking.

'Don't look for me chile.'

'Pappy? Where are you? Please, I'm scared.'

'Leave Pappy be. His time for resting come now.'

'Who is it? Who is it I ain't seeing?'

'Ain't my time for resting. Nell, they call me, but I'd like y'all to call me Nellie. They called me Nellie when I was just a girl.'

The voice is kinda deep, but it's soft too. It sounds to me only good folks ever gonna be speaking that way, but I'm still scared as I've ever been, hearing it. I get brave enough to swing around fast but I ain't see nothing at all.

'I'm real scared. Don't do nothing, please don't …'

'I see ya crying is all, lonely and far from home for a little one. Ya way out here by y'self, cryin' and all alone. Don't be frightened, chile, ain't no cause. Shush now.'

'Where are you? Please. I'm scared.'

'I'm right here, watching the river flowing too, and I like singing. I gotta say, ain't nobody ever hear me before. Just you, chile.'

'Ya dead and gone?'

'Have no mind on that. I'm just right here.'

The sound of her voice is starting to make me feel easy, though I'm still shaking with fright and losing hold on my legs. The rice from my packet spills out all over the grass and my eggs roll off down the bank. They plop into the creek.

'I don't wanna be hearing no dead voices, I don't wanna be like my Mambo. Please go away!'

'Ya just a chile. And ya ain't like Mambo, not at all chile.'

'D'ya know her? My Mambo?' Fear is beating hard at the side of my throat. This has got be one of Mambo's devils, for sure. I'm gasping for air and swallowing warm stuff.

'Ya … ya know who Mambo is?'

All those years of feeling scared, huddling behind bushes watching Mambo and Grandma slit the throats of running chickens, throwing cursed ashes at folks, dancing and mumbling in the spirit world, sure has got me nervy. Now I'm standing right in front of one of them devils Pappy said they cause trouble with, and there ain't no living soul about but me. And this devil ain't got no more than a voice. Nobody should ever be on the wrong side of a mambo 'cause of how they's able to do bad things. I know, with all that thwacking and leaving me by myself so one of her devils can send Mr McIntyre to be doing his hurting. I sometimes think he's the Devil himself and that sure freezes me up every time.

I open my mouth to scream but no sound comes. Wetness trickles down my leg.

'No. I don't know ya Mambo, but I seen her.'

'Where? Where ya seen her?' I'm just whimpering with fright.

'Oh, I sees her here and there. I can tell ya mother and chile, but ya ain't like her at all. That ya ain't. Ya just a sweet li'l chile, nice as nice can be, and I'm sure glad to know ya able to hear me singing. Sure am.'

She hums.

The sound is real strange, on account that she ain't there I s'pose, but I start feeling something soothing coming on all over me. I fix my eyes on a stick in the middle of the creek, ain't hardly moving at all, and my breathing comes back easy. My eggs have sunk in the deep pool, but my hunger's gone off anyways. I stare at that stick for one long time before it floats off round the bend that's gonna take it to the Red River and the Mississippi. And I keep drying my eyes 'cause it seems my tears ain't never gonna stop running at all. Once that stick is gone I peep around, slow like, 'cause I ain't sure what I'm gonna be seeing, but I ain't see nothing. I just hear water start lapping at the side of the bank with the wind coming up, and the sound of Nellie's humming getting farther away.

Two

When Mambo comes back, she's singing a flighty tune. Must be the latest in a juke joint someplace. I wish she'd take time to teach me singing – she's real good at it. I wish we had one of them phonogram boxes I see in my magazines, ones they say can play music on the end of a needle. Pappy ain't never able to sing a 'blessed note' he said, but Jeremiah and his other pals sure could. They got something special goin' on, folks always say. They'd be clapping hands and shuffling feet, and telling Pappy to keep in time with the bent spoon he used to beat on his knee. He was able to do that fine. Pappy chipped away one time making a couple of wooden spoons for his clapping, but Jeremiah took them over 'cause of him being right musical and able to drum them both at the same time as turning out a fine song. Pappy said he was happy enough getting back to his bent spoon. He always used to keep that spoon in the inside pocket of his only jacket, but I couldn't find it after he was gone. I guess that went the same way his pipe was gonna go if I ain't get to that first.

Mambo brings home some nice fresh cornbread, and she's beaming all over happy.

'Arletta, honey, fetch me something to drink. And cut me some of this cornbread. Come on now, this cornbread real fresh. Just got made.'

She goes on singing and I pick up the bucket from out back for fetching fresh water. As I pass through our cabin, she's standing in front of the dresser mirror stripping off her tight frock and loosening up her corset. That corset is her most precious thing for sure, 'cause if she don't do up all them pins and hooks and padding just right, her breasts flop flat out, ain't no life like Grandma's in them at all. She flicks them up and tells the mirror it's what giving birth to a daughter did for her. I slip out and go fill the bucket, ain't saying nothing.

Since she's come back, Mambo is spending the day lying in bed and grumbling about the heat.

'Mr McIntyre promised me a motor-fan. He promised clear as day to bring one of them motor-fans and get us all wired up. They's getting wired up in Brouillette now. He been round here saying something about a motor-fan, Arletta?'

'No.'

'Well, he said he'd be round. Come and fan me, Arletta. Keep me cool honey. I ain't standin' this heat and ain't even past spring time. Come on now.'

I fan her till she dozes off, then I sit out back thinking about Nellie and her deep, warm humming voice. I recall her easy tune and hum it into the palm of my hand, quiet-like so I don't wake Mambo.

Then I hear somebody knocking out front. There's a young girl out there, about my own age, hopping from foot to foot in our front yard. She's looking kinda scared to me.

'Ya want something?'

I ain't seen her before. She ain't one of them kids I see passing our track for the school bus. If she calls me Po'bean I'm gonna get mad as hell though.

'My grandma says I gotta come on over and get something from Mambo. She says Mambo knows all about it and knows what to give me. She says she spoke to her already.'

'Mambo, a girl out here come for ya.'

Mambo raises herself up off her bed like she's expecting her anyways. She's wearing a thin slip, hands on hips, don't look like a mambo at all, but that girl creeps round the edge of our porch like she's scared as hell to leave them walls. Like creeping gonna be saving her from something.

'Come on in honey, I ain't gonna bite, ya know.' Mambo yawns.

I nod my head so that poor girl knows it's okay to come on in. She nods, sees right away we got two of us scared of Mambo.

Her eyes start darting round our cabin like she's thinking the Devil himself must be living inside of it. Mambo's towering over her with hand stretched out, which don't help none, so when she looks my way again I give her another one of my nods, since looks like she reckons that makes things fine. She places her rolled-up coins on the table, ain't taking no risk placing it right in Mambo's hand at all. I reckon she's even more scared than she looks, and I wanna tell her everything is okay, but I keep quiet 'cause of Mambo doing business and I ain't got no place in the middle of it.

Mambo unrolls the few coins and turns back into the bedroom, rattling them in the palm of her hand. She closes the door behind her. I hear the key unlock Pappy's old closet and my heart sinks low. I ain't ever seen what she keeps inside of that closet, I've always been scared to look and, anyways, she's still using Pappy's big lock on it. Pappy made his closet out of wood from a broken cotton cart off the old plantation long before she was even born and he kept what he called all our worldly goods in it. Ain't ever clear what they were, though. Sure couldn't have been much because I ain't never see much, but he kept it closed up anyways, and the key to that lock was hanging round his neck as long as I can remember. He kept what few clothes we had inside of it, I know that, and he sure was fussy about what he called 'his best', but now Mambo's dresses hang over a piece of string between her bed and my cot and, far as I can tell, all her mumbo-jumbo is filling up Pappy's closet.

'It's all right, don't be frightened. She ain't gonna harm ya,' I tell the girl, 'cause I see she's shaking. Truth is, I don't know if all that mumbo-jumbo does good or harm to folks. Pappy was always calling it devil's work, but I ain't ever wanna think of my own Mambo doing harm to folks, or doing any devil's work at all. That's for sure. She's real handy with thwacking and all, 'cause I'm right there and I'm mouthy, but she ain't bad. No way. She's just scary 'cause she's a mambo and right keen on being off someplace when she oughta be right here looking after me like Pappy said she should be. Don't make her bad. She says it's just 'cause she's young and gotta do what young does.

'Ya living here with her?' the girl asks.

'Yeah, she's my ma.'

'Ya ma!' she whispers from the shadow of the wall she's still creeping round. Looks like she's in some kinda shock that a mambo can be a ma too and I don't bother saying she ain't much of a one.

'I ain't never seen ya round here before. Where ya living? Where ya come from?'

'Other side of the dirt road,' she says. 'We staying out past the new train crossing. We just come. My mom ain't feeling well, so my grandma sent me on over. We come back 'cause Mom ain't well and she knows ya ... uh, she knows ya ... she knows Mambo.'

'What's wrong with her?' I raise my voice, trying to cover the garbling noises coming outta Mambo. 'Ya ma, what's wrong with her?'

'I don't know for sure, but Grandma says maybe she's been accursed.'

'Accursed?' I ain't never hear the word with an 'a' on the front of it before. Seems quite fancy: must be what they say where she comes from. Out here she'll get to know a curse is just a curse, and quite soon too, if Mambo don't get more business.

'Yeah, that's what she says, and she says ya mom can catch a curser good, and I gotta take whatever she gives me and do whatever she says.' Her eyes are wide with fear hearing Mambo mumbling behind that door.

I nod. I hear it plenty. Mambo's mumbling and all that stuff folks say they come for.

'My grandma, she says my mom's gonna stop crying and get better.'

'I hope so.'

'Ya think it gonna work? 'Cause something sure gotta,' she says. 'She's crying and ain't able to look after us kids at all.'

'Yeah. It gonna work.' I chew my lip and think about Pappy telling me I ain't got no business telling lies. I know Mambo is well able to make some things work, but I don't know for sure it always makes folks feel better. I wish with all the heart I got that she's able to make folks feel better.

Mambo gets done mumbling and she's standing in the doorway with a small black wrapping in her hand. That's a piece of newspaper I gotta paint black or red as one of my chores. Nobody but Mambo is ever gonna know what's inside of that wrapping.

'Ya ma need to boil up half of this and drink it right away. Right away, ya hear? Soon as ya gets home. She needs to give the other half to the gentleman in question. Y'all able to recall that?'

'Yes.'

'That's good. Off ya go then, she's waiting. Arletta can write it down if ya wanna be sure on getting it right,' she says and flounces on back into the bedroom.

'Ya's able a write?'

She sure does look right surprised at that, so I tell her how Pappy taught me, and how he taught me to read too. She gets right up in the air 'cause Mambo don't send me for schooling.

'Ya gotta go to school, we're all starting next week 'cause we just get here. Y'all gonna get in trouble if ya don't go. If ya try gettin' in church and ya children ain't in school, they say the Devil's gonna find work for ya hands.'

I get her outside quick before Mambo hears her talking like that.

'She says I got enough to be doing at home and she needs me right here for it. She says I read and write good enough already and half the ones going to that school don't ever get able. And she says them darn teachers are just one bunch of trumped-up do-gooders getting gov'ment money for telling folks round here to do as they's told. Or be scared as hell. That's what she says about it.'

'Oh.'

'Ya want me to write it? What Mambo says to tell ya ma?'

'No, I remember it. My name's Safi. What ya called?'

'Arletta.'

'Ya wanna play sometime? We don't know anybody since we come to live with Grandma. We can meet at the train crossing. That's what we do sometimes, watch out for trains comin' through and blowin'.'

'Yeah, sure, that sounds kinda nice,' is all I say. I don't reckon she'll be allowed to play with me 'cause of Mambo, especially if her folks are sending her for schooling, and them trying for church and all. Once she gets to know folks round here, they're gonna tell her I'm called Po'bean too.

She says there's a train coming through at ten o'clock and we can watch it. Then she heads on up our track. I don't go near that crossing though, 'cause I don't think she's gonna be there and I ain't wanting to be called Po'bean when them other kids catch sight of me anyways. Ain't got no ways of telling ten o'clock, neither.

The weekend comes and the moon gets dark.

Mambo is quiet. All week folks been coming from all over and I gotta leave our cabin every time they come, 'cause of stuff they's telling Mambo ain't no other folks oughta hear about. Some folks stay on a long time and I get left outside till the last one of them leaves, like I'm just nobody. Most times I fall asleep in the rocking chair. One time I got lifted up, like Pappy always used to, and put in my cot, but one time I woke up shivering with cold 'cause of being left outside all night and them folks still talking.

Mambo lays out her white clothes for bleaching under the sun for two days. She's careful to take them in when the sun goes down, keeping them outta the kinda trouble going about when bad folks see a dark moon coming, she says. Every month gone by, since she got her first bleeding, she's been soaking her head cloth in blood mixed with madder root she grows out back. It's got a deep red colour she's right proud of, and the power of Mambo's belly in it too, she says.

She takes to cleaning out every corner of our cabin, except for Pappy's old cartwheel and the box of nails in our rafters. She don't touch under my cot, neither. I ain't ever hear her speak much about Pappy's stuff these days, and I get a feeling that she don't wanna be touching it at all. I ain't saying for sure, but she just might be fearful of Pappy now he's dead and gone with God Almighty. She don't ever say a thing about it, but I see her face get kinda sad when he's spoken about, and that's something folks round here do a lot of the time. They say my Pappy was a fine man and good enough for God.

'Ya getting y'self ready, Arletta, like I tell ya?' she asks, serving me sweet rice and creamy goobers for breakfast.

'No, I ain't.'

That just come straight outta my mouth, so I duck down right away in case the back of her hand comes shooting over my face.

'Ya gonna do as ya told, Arletta, just as I says. Hear me? I need ya up there this morning making sure all them torches get put where they's oughta be. Ya know they's always putting them torches where I ain't able to see folks' faces, and that's something I need to be seeing.'

'I'll go and do that Mambo, I gonna help ya set stuff up, but I don't like no dark moon an' I ain't gonna go up near that place in it. No way, Mambo.'

'Arletta, ya the daughter and the granddaughter of mambos, best round here for miles. Grandma was the best in her time and I'm the best in my time. And my daughter's gonna be too. That gonna happen if ya like it or not. Liking ain't no part of it. Mambos need strong blood, family blood, and that's what's running in ya veins child. Ya's Mambo's flesh and blood, and that's all there is to it. Ya gonna do it.'

'No, I won't.'

'Yes, ya will.'

There's times I know my Mambo is worse than when she's thwacking. She's downright stubborn, Pappy said, and no question of it. That's what always caused a heap of trouble. She's gonna make me stay up late listening to them drums beating and all them voices wailing when bad spirits get a hold on folks. And then our cockerel's blood's gonna get spilled all over, 'cause we already got a new one. Mambo says getting a new cockerel is a sure sign of something, ain't sure what. Some folks gonna be so gone with liquor and spirits getting a hold of them, they's gonna be drinking that blood and saving the rest of it for cursing on other folks. It's gonna be rubbed all over them and all I know is my belly's gonna turn upside down and I'm gonna be feeling like throwing up with fear of it all. Same as always. Sure don't wanna be no mambo.

The day gets along and I start feeling more scared than ever about what's coming with that dark moon. They take away our cockerel and Mambo packs me off to the mule barn to make sure the torches are put where she says they gotta be. Gonna be hell to pay if that ain't right this time, she says.

Lamper Ridge mule barn's been half in ruins for a long, long time; ain't nobody ever lay no claim on it. The walls are falling down and ain't much of a roof left neither. Our mambos been using it since they came to these parts, and my own Mambo says great spirits take care of their own and ain't nobody ever gonna lay no claim on it. I reckon that's just 'cause they scared as hell about what's going on, but I ain't saying nothing.

There's three men up there already and I tell them where Mambo wants the torches. That gets one of them saying my Mambo is real fussy. 'The best there is though,' another one says. 'She sure knows about raising up spirits from the old country better than anybody I ever seen. Best in Louisiana state as I knows it.'.

They're passing round a jug of moonshine and ain't long before their tongues loosen up, like always. One with no wife talking about who he's courting, and even though them other two have wives I knows about, they start spouting about who else they's courting too. They forget I'm there and hearing all that talk. Well, I sure do know all about holding my tongue on that sorta thing, but I'm right ready for running in case they start thinking on doing to me with that stinking liquor making them crazy.

The place is fixed up good though, like Mambo says, and a fire set ready for lighting soon as it's dark. Then the drums come and the ground's marked out with stones. Once that's done, everybody gets real quiet. Women come and set baskets down. One of them says Mambo wants me back at the cabin right away. I'm glad I can leave that place, and I'm thinking there's still time to find some kinda reason I don't need to be coming back after sundown.

Mambo shows me a new frock I gotta wear for the night; she wants to see how it's looking on me. Course, I never knew anything about Mambo getting a new frock for me at all. She never takes me past the end of our track, so how I gonna know, anyways? 'Gallivantin'', Pappy called it. I just gotta take what I get and ain't no say if I like it or not.

Course, everything I ever have is a hand-me-down from someplace. That's all I ever have. My new frock ain't exactly new at all.

'Arletta honey, if ya ain't so damn sulky that darned much of the time, ya'd be real pretty. Look here girl, see how nice this dress is on ya? See how nice ya looking? My, my.' She twirls me round so fast to see myself in the mirror, I nearly trip over my own feet. 'Ya just the prettiest li'l girl I ever seen, and ya's my baby.' She plants a kiss on my cheek.

'It's real fine Mambo. I hope it don't get no soiling, though. I'm gonna be taking real good care with it. It's right pretty and I'm thinking it's just so nice I best not be going up to that old mule barn at all. It sure does get messy up there and I ain't wanting no messing ...'

Mambo ain't hear a word of that, just tells me to go wait outside and calls me her honey. She pops another kiss on my other cheek, so I reckon on doing like I'm told. I don't want no fighting with my Mambo when she's so full of love and kisses.

Outside is real dark 'cause there ain't no moon, and then Mambo even turns out our Tilley. She starts up on her mumbling, and whatever it is she's burning has me feeling about as strange as I ever been. I'm as fearful as any poor soul can be.

Folks start coming, some I know and some I don't, but my mind has me thinking they're all spirits of dead folks passing over to take a hold on my Mambo. Ain't nothing I can do about it. Ain't nothing I can do that's ever gonna stop them making her the Devil's child. Pappy ain't never able to stop it, and he got Jesus, so I sure ain't able to neither.

Inside of our cabin a drum starts beating – I don't even know how it got in there – then somebody lights the tallow tin and I see Mambo's shadow swaying from side to side. The spirits of the old world are taking hold on her good, nothing I can do gonna stop that now. Then somebody I don't even know takes me by the hand. I just follow and do like I'm told.

Mambo's so far gone she needs holding up. Burning torches throw up creeping shadows all over the place and them pounding drums get louder and louder every step I sure don't wanna be taking.

Lamper Ridge mule barn is crowded with folks now. They all give way for Mambo and I take myself off outta sight to hide in the rubble of the wall, same as always. Feet are thumping, hips are swinging, and Mambo's bangles keep time with the drums when she starts stamping the earth. I curl up in the broken-down wall and pray to God Almighty that none of them spirits come over my way at all. I ask Him with all my heart to make sure I get my Mambo back safe.

The crowd are swaying like a ripple on Sugarsookie Creek. The night is hot and the devils' eyes glow red in the fire. Mambo is chanting in the old tongue, calling the spirits of Africa so they know to come. I never learnt any of that old tongue, so I ain't never get what she's talking about when she's off with them spirits. She's been trying to teach me the talk that came over when our own people got dragged outta their own land, but it don't sound right to me, and I ain't gonna say it, 'cause Pappy told me Jesus don't like it at all. Boy, that sure did cause a heap of trouble in our cabin.

Mambo pulls an old mamma into the circle of stones. That mamma's looking right poorly and in need of something doing for sure. They start swaying together and Mambo starts rubbing ashes into her hair. She gets her drinking from one of the little bottles she has swinging from her belt. When Mambo steps back a bit, that old woman starts shaking herself all over like nobody's ever gonna think she's able. Looks like some devil's got inside of her. Next thing, she falls flat out on the ground. She gets up and shakes them skinny legs all over again like it's the most she moved in years. She falls down one more time and there ain't no way she's getting up at all. Her boys, I know them from when Pappy used to go fishing, carry her off to the side of the barn and take good care of her till the Devil leaves her belly.

One after another, folks take to inside of that circle and Mambo gets something going on. There's times they just drink from one of her bottles and get themselves on outta there, 'cause I reckon they still got a bit of sense in them, and times they take to shaking all over with the spirits of the old world taking up in their bellies. Some folks start screeching hard, some start singing, some laugh and some cry. Like they're all crazy as hell, is what Pappy would have said about it.

I see Mambo whip the shirt off a man one time and draw blood with her knife, the one she keeps sharp as a razor for gutting fish and letting bad spirits outta folks. I see her pounding the good earth hard, and stare, wild as a mad catahoula, at a woman till she falls down crying and trembling all over about how she's sorry for all the trouble folks say she's causing.

Those drums sound terrible now, so I press my fingers tight inside my ears. Then two men come struggling with our cockerel. Ain't easy on account of that bird being frightened for his life, and he's right about that.

'He's a big beauty. Plenty spirit in him.'

Ain't gonna be there long.

Mambo's holding her knife high and ready. The crowd close in so that poor bird ain't able to run amok once his head is off and he's done for.

I turn away and cover my eyes. My thumbs are stuffed hard inside my ears 'cause I ain't wanting no part in it. I ain't wanna be seeing nothing and I ain't wanna be hearing nothing, but I know that cockerel is fighting hard for his life 'cause I can still hear him squawking. When it stops, a big noise raises outta that old barn like it's rumbling up outta hell itself and bringing one heap of trouble up with it. By the time I peep out between my fingers, there ain't nothing to see but that poor bird's blood splattered all over white dresses and bare bones. And I sure reckon it's shameful. Like Pappy said, it ain't right.

Blood is splashed all over Mambo's white clothes and I see it's trickling down her neck. Her neck is near as long as that bird's, so there's plenty blood on it. Her dress is falling off her shoulder and two men stand with her 'cause it looks like she's losing the power in her own legs now. Her eyes are fearful white and I'm shivering with thinking about what all them spirits must be doing inside my Mambo.

Everybody is shaking and dancing and wailing, 'cause now business taken care of, they're happy spending time with the spirits of the old country. They say it keeps them strong and able to stand up to white folks. They say the spirits of the old world can cross over and turn white folks' holy spirits back on them, give them plenty of fear with it, 'cause that's the power of Mambo's blood.

They're holding Mambo up so she can pass the spirits over. They call that 'passing the power of kings'. Some folks tremble and fall, some start talking like they're seeing them spirits right there, walking down the bayou road.

All of that's what Grandma taught my Mambo and what Mambo wants to teach me too, but I ain't never gonna do it. I pray to my Pappy and ask him to make sure of it, just like he always said he would.

'Please, Pappy, make it so that I won't never have to do that. Please, please, Pappy, I don't wanna be drinking no blood and have no bad spirits shaking inside of my belly. Please ask God and make him save me. Everybody says ya right close to God Almighty, please, Pappy, please. Our Father, art in Heaven ...'

I say the prayer he taught me over and over till I can hardly breathe. I open my eyes just as Mambo falls to the dusty earth with all her nice white clothes covered in blood and hardly on her at all. She ain't got her corset on neither and her saggy breasts fall out for all the world to see, and I feel shamed 'cause I'm the one who made them get that way. I'm shamed now everybody can see what I've done to my own Mambo. Her skirt rides up and I reckon Pappy would have been thankful she's smart enough to be wearing her panties.

She gets carried off and I watch everybody dancing; spirit or liquor, sure ain't no way of telling what makes folks like that. I'm just glad Mambo's all done and we can get on back to our own cabin.

But I ain't keeping my eye on things and I don't see her at all. I get to thinking some of that blood maybe ain't from our cockerel after all. What if some of that blood is Mambo's own? Maybe one of them devil spirits is doing her harm someplace, making her bleed. I don't know what they're able to be doing inside of her at all.

'Playing with fire, that's what ya doing, playing with the Devil himself and one day he gonna turn on ya. Ya best be watching out, my girl. He gonna turn. Always does.' Pappy used to say that.

I stare into the darkness round the mule barn, feeling sure the Devil's gone turned on Mambo.

'Mambo?'

No answer.

'Mambo, where are ya? Mambo?'

She's gonna be bleeding someplace and needing my help, that's for sure. Fear takes a grip of me all over. I'm just scared as hell all the time, scared of Mambo when she's like this, and scared for what all them spirits are doing inside of her. I'm scared of Mr McIntyre and all his doing to me. I'm scared of all them white folks lynching and burning. I'm scared about what all them bad folks are doing to us poor folks, and ain't nothing we ever able to do about it.

I climb down from the wall and run round the barn, but Mambo ain't nowhere to be seen. I gotta go far from the light of the burning torches, but still I ain't seeing her any place. And one thing I can say is, I'm scared of the dark, always been. Then I hear a noise. It's Mambo moaning in pain. I know she's hurt bad, I saw all the blood, and I'm worried about how bad she's gonna be when I find her.

Her white clothes lie spread out over the ground. Right next to them I catch sight of her legs high up in the air and somebody going at her like he's gonna kill her. I run head first, butting like a bull, with all the strength I've got to save her.

'Leave her alone! Leave my Mambo alone!' I scream as loud as I can and charge full on into the man beating at my Mambo.

He's left with two cracked ribs.

'Leave her alone! Help! Somebody help!'

'Arletta? What the hell are ya doing?'

'Mambo! It's me, Arletta. Ya okay?'

Thwack.

Three

N ext morning it seems to me Mambo's forgotten all about it. I ain't falling for that at all; that's when Mambo sure is up to something.

'Arletta, get up. Come on now.'

'Comin', Mambo.'

'Come on now. I've got a surprise.'

I get up and go out back in my old cotton slip, rubbing the sleep from my eyes. Mambo says she's got a surprise and I reckon I need to be looking out about it.

'What surprise, Mambo?'

'You know what day it is?'

'No.'

'It's ya birthday Arletta. Come on now, don't say ya forgetting it's ya birthday. I've made sweet sugar cocoa and I'm gonna …'

Cocoa? Mambo's made cocoa and I'm all awake now. I ain't hardly ever had cocoa.

'Yup, and I'm gonna be making some real fancy pancakes too.'

She hands me my tin cup full of frothy sweet cocoa and that sure is the best-tasting drink I've ever had. She's all smiles and wiping froth from under my nose with her cloth and I just can't figure it.

'I'm gonna get on into the Brouillette commissary this morning on Bobby-Rob's cart and get some raising agent for putting in flour. Hell, we got plenty eggs, and I'm gonna make some nice special pancakes for ya birthday, real fancy like I seen down in Mamou, with some of our own figs in syrup too, if they's ready. Been hot enough and I reckon they come early. They look good enough for cookin' up anyways.'

'That how ya make pancakes Mambo? And syrup? Can I watch?'

''Course ya can, even help me make it if ya want. Ya like that? Huh?'

I can't exactly get over Mambo being so nice after I charged so hard at her new beau. He got lifted straight off last night to get his ribs strapped up and Mambo marched me home saying how I 'put paid to that one right and proper'. I look her way 'cause it's like she don't remember that at all, but my cocoa tastes so good and sweet, and thinking about having figgy syrup for my birthday is so good and sweet, that I just let it go and finish my cup of frothy cocoa milk.

'Oh, that sure is lovely Mambo. Can I get some more?'

I say it before I think it might be enough to get me thwacked if she gets minded about last night, or even if she don't. I duck, though Mambo's over the other side of the washtub and ain't looking mad at all. I just can't get over how she ain't mad as hell at me.

'And guess what else I'm gonna do on ya birthday?'

Oh ho.

'Guess what Arletta? Go on now. Have a guess.'

Now I'm scared. If I don't come up with guessing something, it sure is gonna go spoiling the whole day, especially with it starting out so darnit nice.

'Well, I guess ya could give me … a … a …'

'I'm gonna be sending ya for schooling Arletta. Seems to me that's just what ya needing. What ya think of that, honey?'

I forget all about cocoa milk and figgy syrup, even how nice Mambo is when she sure ain't got no reason to be.

'Mambo! Ya gonna let me go to school? Oh, thank you. Thank you!' I rush at her and throw my arms right round her whole waist. 'Mambo, that's just the best surprise in the whole world. Thanks Mambo!'

'I knew that was gonna make ya happy Arletta.'

'Well, I'm s'posed to go, I know that, gov'ment says …'

'The gov'ment says?' She laughs in her sing-song mocking voice and starts on about how the gov'ment ain't able to tell us free black folks nothing no more. How they used to stop us blacks having any schooling at all 'cause they didn't think we was up to being educated and how now they're telling us we gotta go.

'Them's just folks saying whatever they feel like saying anytime, day or night, and don't ya be paying them no mind.'

'Well, just as long as I can go.' I'm starting to get worried now.

'Well, them's all what they call Christians at that school, and they ain't thinking much on me at all. They're all like Pappy. Hah! I knows what I am, and I knows a lot of them ain't fine proper Christians neither. But ya just need to be learning, ya ready for it, I can see it's time, and it's fine learning about Jesus helping folks. That's what they's gonna tell ya and that's okay by me. Ya got it Arletta? Ya get on off over to that school and learn what ya can. About time. Ya got it?'

'I got it,' I says, though I don't know what she's talking about. I lost the follow on what she was saying way back and, anyways, I'm still licking my sweet little cocoa lips. I heard the part about them being like Pappy and that sounds fine to me.

'So, what ya think about that then? Ya get y'self into that pretty frock I got for ya, and y'all able to start right away if ya want. Ain't no reason why not. It's time.'

'Well I ain't gonna wear that frock. Ya gotta wear what they's call a uniform.'

'Ya can wear anything ya want.'

Well, that start us off. If I don't say what I gotta say, Mambo is just gonna get me doing stuff all them kids gonna be laughing at and I done had enough of that already. I tell her how I hear them kids talking and I hear Safi Sucree got sent home twice 'cause she ain't wearing no uniform. That mission school is real strict, from what I hear. I hear all them kids talking, and if ya ain't wearing it, ya can't go. That's what they say. That's what they said to Safi and they were right about that, 'cause I saw her bawling about it when she got off the bus.

'Oh, Safi always looks fine. Them's just looking for something else to moan about.'

'Ya gotta wear it, Mambo, the green shirt and the brown skirt. Ya gotta wear it every day.'

'All right! We'll get it, we gonna get it.'

'And ya gotta tell them I'm coming so they knows about me, so they knows I'm coming.'

I know my mouth running off on account of how much I wanna go to school, seems I ain't able to stop it. Mambo slams that pan down hard and throws her hands in the air.

'Darnit Arletta, if ya don't shut up ...'

'Ya can go and tell them I'm coming on the way to Brouillette can't ya, Mambo? They're gonna tell ya all about how it works at school. They got a teacher, she's called Mrs Hampton, she's real hard on them kids about learning, and they say she's tough about keeping them in line too, and she even belted some boys ...'

I shouldn't have said belted.

Thwack.

I get so excited I could jump when Mambo leaves for Brouillette. She's gonna tell the school folks I'm coming. She ain't happy about asking white folks for a hand-me-down uniform, but that's just what everybody's gotta do and I don't know why she's fussing about it, since every darned thing I ever got is hand-me-down from someplace. My mind gets busy thinking about reading real books and learning math that ain't just counting sticks. And I'm gonna feel real special when I get homework. I'm gonna be real good at it too, that's for sure.

I hope somebody will play with me now, and not call me Po'bean like they do when they catch me spying on them through the trees. Well, anyways, I'm so happy I don't care what they do, just so long as I get schooling like everybody else. After I've been at the pipe to wash my face clean of all the cocoa I ain't able to lick, I sit outside daydreaming so much about cocoa and figgy syrup and school, and how this is just gotta be the best day of my life, that I don't even see him coming till his shoes are right up in front of me and he's blocking out the sun.

'Well, hello there Sweetpea. I was on my rounds and saw Mambo get herself a ride on Bobby-Rob's cart. Now, where is she going Sweetpea? Eh?'

I make to get up and run but he grabs both my arms, and then he's dragging me inside. Terror dries up my throat and I ain't able for nothing at all, 'cause I'm already caught and the power's gone out of my legs.

'She'll be just a little while lining up at that mission, Little Miss Thinking-you're-going-to-get-an-education. So let's me and you do what you like best, Sweetpea, before she gets back here and finds out what you really like to do when she's gone.'

'I don't like it, pleeeaase don't ...'

He mocks me with that funny baby voice he uses sometimes.

'Well, it sure don't look like that to me. You look to me like you're having a fine time of it. That's why I have to keep on coming over here. I need to be keeping you a happy little Po'bean. Don't I?'

It sounds like I've only got a whisper for a voice and I sure am about fainting with fear. 'Please no ... please don't make me do nothing.'

Mr McIntyre pushes me into the bedroom and tells me if I scream he's gonna slit my throat and break Mambo in half.

'So you be a nice girl, be a good girl now.'

I nod as he grabs my hair and pulls till I squirm.

'You really are a good girl, aren't you? That's my Sweetpea.'

When he's spent, I throw up. My nice cocoa is up with it, and all over Mambo's clean floor too. I get a thwack round the head and told cleaning up my own mess is something to be keeping myself busy with till Mambo gets home. Then he tells me he'll be bringing his friend back and I've gotta be good to him too, 'cause he's told him all about me and how nice I like to be.

'And guess what?' He bends down right in my face, 'He says he's going to give you fifty cents every time he comes. How about that?'

I retch again.

'Oh, for God's sakes – not on my shoes! I'm in the middle of my working day you know. Clean it up, go on.'

I ain't got nothing to be cleaning it up with, so I just start wiping up with the hem of my frock. He says his friend Seymour don't like all that screaming I did last time he brought him, so I ain't gotta be doing any of it. Not unless I want my Mambo cut in half. He reckons he can snap his fingers and get me and my Mambo burnt to a cinder before we even open our eyes in the morning. He sure can, he says, and I oughta know it.

Then I gotta say thank you to him, like I should be pleased he's coming and doing to me.

'Thank you.'

'That's what I like to hear. Now lie down. Go on girl.'

When he's gone I stay on Mambo's bed a long time before I'm able to get up and fetch the bucket. I go to the pipe for water and it hurts bad. After I clean up my vomit I take off for Sugarsookie Creek as fast as my poor sore legs are able. I strip off and get myself into the deep pool. Wading in right up to my neck, I scrub and scrub all over. I wash my mouth out, over and over and over again, so the water can take his dirt all out of me. I scrub between my legs raw and my blood flows into the creek with the blood of slaves. Still I don't feel clean, but Soogarsookie Creek is washing over me like it's trying and trying, 'cause it knows the pain of slaves.

'Chile.'

It's just a whisper.

'Nellie?'

'Come outta the water chile. It's gonna take ya.'

'I don't care, Nellie.'

'Don't let the river take ya chile.'

'I don't care.'

'I care. Stay with us chile. Y'all need to be staying with us now.'

'I can't make him stop it Nellie, I ain't able to make him stop ...'

'I can tell ya how to make it stop. I'm gonna give ya strength, I'm gonna make ya strong. Then it's gonna stop.'

'Promise me it's gonna stop, Nellie.'

'I promise. Hush, hush. Come on now. Don't let no river take ya good life.'

And even though I ain't thinking my life is any good at all, I climb out of the water and put my frock back on. It's wet, but the sun is hot.

'It's my birthday.'

'How old ya chile?'

'Ten. I gotta be ten years old today.'

'I promise ya gonna have wonderful birthdays chile. Together we gonna make all them birthdays real nice.'

'I'd like that Nellie.'

I cry for a long time on the bank of Sugarsookie Creek. Nobody hears me except Nellie and I'm safe with her singing her song and humming softly. I cry till my body stops shaking and I ain't able for crying no more. When I'm done, I feel worn out all over, but I don't feel dirty no more and that's something.

'Nellie?'

'I'm still here chile. Mmmm-mmm?'

'Nellie, I feel better now.'

'I knows it. Now ain't that one good kinda feeling? Don't that make ya feel strong? It's just as I says now, ain't it?'

'Yes Nellie.'

For a long time it's quiet, except for the sound of water flowing in the creek. Then I tell Nellie I'm gonna be starting school.

'That's good chile, ya's a clever girl and gonna learn quick. Ya gonna make a friend too.'

'A friend? I ain't got no friends Nellie. I gonna get one, ya think?'

'Uh huh. A real good friend. And today I'm giving ya a gift too. It's for ya birthday, remember that chile.'

'Thanks Nellie. What is it?'

'Ya ain't able to see it yet, but ya got it, and ya gonna know it when the time comes along and ya needin' it. It's called ya strength. I said I was gonna make ya strong, and I have chile. Ya got strength now and ya gonna learn how to be remembering it. How to use it, like it's waiting to be used.'

But I ain't even home a day before Mr Seymour comes stumbling back down the track to our cabin. He's tall and blond, and podgy like a fat pig. He smells real bad of stale baccy and strong liquor. He's wearing a cream suit; it was nice once, I guess, now it's crushed and crumpled like he's been in it for weeks and don't even care who knows it. Seems he's got too many teeth to fit inside his mouth and his fat face is flushed pink like a turkey wattle. When he gets close to me I feel sick in my belly with that sour smell of his, and he's holding a bottle of bad-smelling liquor, wrapped in a brown bag, that he keeps slugging from.

'Come on Fifty Cents – have a drink.'

'I don't want no drink.'

I'm so scared I've edged myself stuck into the corner of Mambo's dresser and there ain't no escaping it. Mr Seymour ain't wearing a shirt underneath his jacket and nothing under his pants neither. His belly is hairy and he looks more like a pig with his clothes off than he does with them on. That's the first time I ever saw a man ain't wearing no clothes at all, and it ain't nice either. Mr McIntyre don't ever do that and I'm feeling as scared as I've ever been seeing it. I sure am shaking all over. I squeeze my legs tight so I can hold onto my own water. My eyes squeeze tight shut too.

He grabs hold of my chin and pulls my mouth open with his podgy pig hands. The bad-tasting liquor from the brown bag is burning down my throat when I need to breathe, and I near enough choke to death on it. I'm about as trapped as a wild dog in a Cajun snare. Seems the more I wriggle, the more he likes it.

He's worse than Mr McIntyre. Mr McIntyre is always in a hurry to get on off outta here. That makes him rough, but then he's gone and I'm glad.

After that first time, Mr Seymour starts coming down our track whenever he feels he's got a mind to, and he ain't got no care that somebody might turn up and catch him doing to me, or that Mambo might even come back anytime, though that never happened. He wants to take his time for his doing, leaving me sore, worn out like I'm nothing but an old rag doll.

'You ain't nothing but dirty black trash, little girl, and I'll do what I like.'

I beg Mr McIntyre to stop him coming, but he says it's all natural stuff and I ought to be right pleased somebody like Mr Seymour's finding time to be coming all the way out here to be doing to me. He says he's just able to promise nobody else is gonna come, and they'll both make sure I'm kept safe just for the two of them 'cause I'm special.

'Ain't nobody as good as you, Sweetpea. You're the best we got, and we're safe as houses all the way down this track where we can see anybody coming. You're some kind of find. You're real special. Come on now, be good to Mr McIntyre.'

I don't feel safe at all.

Four

'Now don't go putting her down a class, Mrs Hampton,' Mambo says the day she drops me off at school. 'Ya gonna find it just as I says, she's a right fine reader and writer already.'

'We'll see,' Mrs Hampton says with her tight lips and a funny way of talking I ain't ever hear before. She looks right disapproving of my Mambo and it's plain as day she don't believe her at all.

'Y'all gonna see,' Mambo sing-songs, and wiggles off right pleased with herself. I'm thinking she knows none of her mumbo-jumbo ever gonna work on Mrs Hampton, so when she finds out how good I am at lessons, Mambo's gonna be the one with the winning wiggle. That makes Mambo laugh all the way back on the bus.

Mrs Hampton sure does look strict. She tut-tuts right out loud and hustles me inside like the sight of Mambo's wiggling behind is something no child ever oughta be in sight of. I get stood out front of her class like it's the only thing gonna save me. Well, I'm just about able to be putting up with that, 'cause it feels fine having my uniform and looking the same as everybody else. I'm glad I gave Mambo a real hard time to go get it.

The mission school is built right behind Pappy's church and it's got four classrooms in it, two for starters, one for middles and one for seniors. That's on account of folks letting their kids start school but then find they's ain't able to carry on at it and have to get working or looking after li'l uns. It's built near as tall as Pappy's church, though it looks more like a barn to me.

I'm keen to just slide into that class and sit down quiet-like, but Mrs Hampton holds me back. Some of them boys are sniggering already, and whispering about Po'bean, but I bet they ain't able to read or write like me 'cause it's clear as day already that Mrs Hampton's gone and taken me down to starters, and that I ain't.

She holds me in front of the class and tells them I'm a new girl and they need to be welcoming and kind. They gotta help me with my lessons on account of me being a late starter and I don't go for that at all. But I ain't saying nothing.

'Now, you sit right there in the front, Arletta, and take a look at our schedule here on the wall. This is how we break up the day for our lessons.'

She thinks I'm stupid.

'And we start every day with Bible class, don't we, children?'

'Yes, Miss.'

Mrs Hampton is walking the floor holding a big black Bible up in front of her face. She's wearing a pair of thick spectacles that make her look like she's borrowed her eyes from a frog, and big huge bosoms I'm thinking ain't never seen no daughter.

When she asks who can tell her where Jesus was born, every hand in class shoots up except mine.

'Arletta, you must know where baby Jesus was born.'

But I don't seem to.

'In a stable Miss,' spouts some voice from back of class, and I feel right mad I don't remember that, 'cause Pappy sure told me enough times.

'That's correct, Charles,' says Mrs Hampton. 'Now, who can tell me who built the ark?'

Every hand shoots up except mine again.

'Arletta, tell us all who built the ark. Don't be shy, now.'

'Don't know, Miss.'

I don't know what to think about school at all. I sure thought they were gonna be asking what I know instead of what I don't. Mrs

Hampton is tapping out some kinda beat on top of her desk now, with fingernails so long they ain't never gonna be good in the soil.

'Come now, children, and keep the Lord's beat; He won't be wanting any droning in Heaven. Raise your spirits up for the Lord. Ta-taa-ta ta ta – ta ta tiffy – ta-ta. Ta-ta tiffy ta-ta-ta.'

Them fingernails keep time like Jeremiah gone and take her over. He could keep a good beat too, though I never heard him say nothing about ta ta tiffy.

'Come, children, sing the Lord's own words: "The Lord's my Shepherd, I'll not want …"'

Mrs Hampton sure looks short of a hinge to me.

The class starts singing what I find out is called the Twenty-third Psalm and I'm gonna have to learn it word for word and sing it too.

Then it's time for English lessons and I straighten myself up, real glad we're gonna get on with what Pappy taught me out on our front porch. I'm gonna do fine here. When she asks if anybody knows what the future tense of the verb 'to be' is, the only hand shooting up in class is mine.

'Yes, Arletta, tell us what that is.'

'Future tense of the verb to be tells us what's gonna happen before it happens or before it might do.'

'Very good, Arletta. And do you know how to say that in proper English?'

'I will be, you will be, he, she or it will be. We will be, you plural will be, they will be.'

I get told that's excellent, so I'm hoping there's gonna be more of that, since it's stuff I know. The future tense of the verb 'to be' is gonna be written up on the board and the class have to copy it carefully into their notebooks. They gotta do it nice and neat 'cause Mrs Hampton will be correcting written work and giving it marks out of ten.

I've already opened the first gleaming new page of my red school notebook. They call them jotters. It smells new too, ain't like Pappy's musty papers, and I write down the future tense of the verb 'to be' in the best handwriting I got so Mrs Hampton knows I'm able to do something else right. It's like Pappy's looking over my shoulder, pleased as punch she's gonna be seeing it like he taught it.

'Arletta,' Mrs Hampton says when she notices my writing. 'Would you like to write it on the board for the other children?'

I say, 'Yes, Miss,' but that's a straight-up lie. I don't like to at all but I ain't dare say so. I hear the class do a little tittering when I get up. They think I ain't able to do it.

The chalk snaps right in half first thing and the class get a grilling for giggling. But I get the hang of it after a few squeaky strokes and do my best writing. The class sure is quiet now.

After my slow start with Bible stuff, it's clear as day I already know everything Mrs Hampton's got to be teaching her class of kids about the English language. I take care my notebooks are as neat as can be, my writing just about as perfect as I can get it, so my Mambo's gonna be showing them all off and calling me a pride and joy just like Pappy. Mrs Hampton even asks me to help out one girl with her writing, 'cause she ain't getting it at all. Well, that's real easy for me, since Pappy sure was better at teaching than Mrs Hampton and I just tell her what he told me.

Somebody outside in the yard starts clanging a loud bell that makes me jump. The class shuts their books and sit straight up. Mrs Hampton wants to see if we got posture. She walks up and down correcting what she calls 'exception to perfection' and then we all file out in what she says gotta be 'an orderly fashion' and I ain't got no clue about any of it. It's break time from lessons and it's for a whole ten minutes. That's something I ain't looking forward to at all.

But just as I peel off outta Mrs Hampton's 'orderly fashion', 'cause that's what everybody else is doing, Safi Sucree comes rushing my way.

'Arletta! Ya's in school! Mom said ya s'posed be comin'. Ya like it?'

'Sure, I like it.'

Well, I hope I'll be liking it when I start hearing something I ain't already know, but I ain't saying nothing.

'And the uniform, I really like it.'

I sure like looking the same as everybody else.

43

Safi asks me if I wanna be school friends and play scotch. I don't know scotch, so she says she'll show me.

'Ya ma okay?' I ask. Ain't sure she hears me 'cause them's just about the loudest bunch of kids I hear since carnival.

'Oh yeah, and Pa's come back home too now.' She moves in close and whispers, 'It worked, just like Mambo said it would work.'

I say that's good, and I'm glad to hear it, but I cross my fingers 'cause I don't know for sure if it's good at all. 'No good gonna come of it' is what Pappy used to say. He used to say Mambo's mumbo-jumbo ain't never do no good to nobody, and I feel afraid for Safi and her folks, since she's just come to be the only friend I got.

'Only thing is,' Safi says, 'we got another baby coming.'

Another mouth for feeding is what her pa calls it, but everybody's happy they're all sticking together now. Safi's ma got real sick when her pa took off 'cause he was all done out with looking after them, and they'd be shouting about it all the time. That's when her grandma sent her over to see Mambo.

'I'm glad he's back then, with another mouth and all,' I say.

'And Pa says he's gonna get plenty work on all them new gov'ment roads they's laying down. He says it's just like hard labour and all, but it's gonna put food in our bellies and that's all he ever wants, and that's hard enough. That's what he says, and we're all right glad he's back and Grandma ain't mind, neither. Says she's glad he's facing up.'

I wanna know if she went to the train crossing, 'cause we said we might watch it go by after she came to see Mambo that time.

'I went three days running but I know Mambo ain't gonna let ya off for playing 'cause ya got chores and y'all on ya own. I mean, ya ain't got no brothers or sisters, my grandma says. I got six brothers and three sisters, and we don't know what's coming next.'

'When will the baby come?'

'Too soon, Grandma says.'

Safi teaches me scotch and I like it 'cause nobody wins it. Ya just do the best ya can and that's what Pappy said is all ya can do.

Safi's my first ever friend and I reckon Nellie's gone and done just like she said for me.

Mrs Hampton calls me out of my seat when we get back in class. She tells me to pick up my notebooks and cross over the hall to Mr Parker's class. It's the door right next to hers, she says. I don't like the sound of being in no man's class at all.

'You already know how to read and write, Arletta, so you can go on over to the next class. Off you go, and keep up the good work, Arletta. You've done very well here in school today.'

I take my stuff and hang my head low. My collar feels tight and a terrible heat is busting out like it might boil me over. I'm scared of Mr Parker already. I ain't never meet him before and I don't wanna meet him now, 'cause I'm sure as hell he's gonna be just like Mr McIntyre and Mr Seymour. He's gonna be just like Mambo's beaux. They're all the same, with wanting to be doing. Mambo keeps all our clothes hanging over that string so I ain't able to see nothing, but I hear plenty. That's what all of them do, except my Pappy.

I knock on his door.

'Come in.' He sure got a loud voice.

I'm too scared to even think about crossing over to Mr Parker's desk, and I don't even look up, neither.

'Class, this is Arletta Lilith Johnson. Please go and sit next to Safi Sucree. Thank you.'

Safi! I swing round and see her waving at me from the middle of the classroom. I go sit with her and we're both happy. Then I get a mind to take a look at Mr Parker and all my worrying falls right off. He's just like Pappy. Ain't terrible old like Pappy, and he's dressed real fine with his white collar and neck-tie and all, but he sure is an old man, and Mambo always says, 'Old men stick to what they knows round here or their mamma is on the front step of my cabin to sort 'em out.'

My first day at school is over too soon, I reckon. I get off the bus and rush home to tell Mambo all about it, but she's rouging up and ain't got time to hear it.

'Well that's just fine that ya liking it. And y'all be sticking with Safi, she's a nice girl. She's just like her ma and we been friends since 'fore we were even your age. I'm sure glad ya getting along with Safi.'

'Oh, we getting along all right, and I'm gonna be teaching her stuff too, I know lots she don't know. She say's it's 'cause she's from a big family, six brothers and three sisters, and another on the way, and they don't know what they gonna get …'

Mambo tells me my mouth's running and pushes me out of the way so she can finish scarleting up her mouth.

'Her grandma says the baby's gonna come too soon, but her pa's working hard on them new gov'ment roads, so they gonna be okay, she says. They gonna have food in they bellies, she says.'

Mambo stands up and squirts sweet-smelling cologne over her long neck and pushed-up bosoms.

'Y'all need to be sticking with Safi then honey, like I says, and it's about time ya stopped all that talking to folks who ain't there anyways. Carry on with that shit Arletta, and ya gonna find y'self sitting in a loony bin. Ya stop all that girl, ya hear?'

'What?'

'I hear ya, Arletta, talking all the time and ain't nobody there. That's why I get ya on off to school and all. Y'all needing real folks, instead of making them up and talking to the fresh air. Folks gonna think I got a half-wit for a child. Ya stupid sometimes, but ya sure as hell ain't no half-wit honey.'

'Oh, but that's just Nellie. She's like a friend already Mambo, she's …'

'Y'all as smart as anybody and smarter than a lot I know of. Eat them craws and corn now, 'fore they go off in this heat and don't be waiting up, ya got school tomorrow. Ain't that something, Arletta? My baby's a schoolgirl now, fancy that. Pappy sure would be proud.'

When Mambo's gone I get in front of her mirror and feel real fine looking at myself in my school uniform. All Pappy's teaching is coming in good and gonna make him so proud of me, he might even rise up before his time. I take it off and hang it careful-like over the string across our room and put on my shabby old frock. I'm growing fast and it feels tight, but I'm scared to ask Mambo to fetch another one in case she gets minded to be taking me outta school. I sit on Mambo's bed and spread my new notebooks out where I can see them all. I wanna see how well I've done and what good marks I got from Mr Parker. There's one for

Bible class, one for English grammar, another one for what they call composition, one for geography, history, math and French. Mr Parker says speaking French can help with getting a job in New Orleans. He says folks do real well down there, so I figure I oughta be thinking about doing what he says. He marked me ten outta ten for my writing, says he ain't never done that before in his life and I have the makings of a good student. That's what kids gets called in the classroom.

'Sweetpea, I got fifty cents here.'

Mr Seymour!

I ain't hear him coming and he's already inside our cabin. I hate him more every day, I swear on that, even more than Mr McIntyre. And he's coming out here so much now, I'm sore nearly all the time. Ain't nothing I can do about it. Every time is worse than the last time and I feel my stomach turn over when he walks in. He smells so bad it's like he don't know water.

'I give ya strength,' Nellie whispers after he's gone. 'Ya gotta use it chile.'

I don't care what my Mambo says, Nellie's got a soothing kinda voice that I like to be hearing and it helps me out fine with all the fear and hurting I'm feeling all the time. I don't care if Mambo ain't able to see her, I ain't ever seen Nellie neither. Don't mean nothing and I ain't got no clue why Mambo is making any kinda fuss about it, 'specially since she's the one got all them spirits from the old country taking a hold on her all the time. Ain't never seen any of them neither, and them sure as hell ain't no good at all. Nellie's right there when they're doing to me and when I get to fretting real bad after they're done. I'm sure gonna stick with Safi and Nellie.

But when Mr Seymour's gone, I tell Nellie I'm gonna stop coming to Sugarsookie Creek and get on over to the Red River, 'cause it flows so fast and able to take me. I did well at school and I know I'm gonna like it, but I ain't able to take Mr McIntyre or Mr Seymour doing to me no more.

'Ya don't need to be thinkin' that chile. Remember Nellie is giving ya strength all the time. Ya just gotta learn how to use it, that's all. Learn to use it chile.'

'I ain't never feel any strength at all when they make me do what I don't wanna be doing. And it real nasty Nellie, real nasty.'

I don't even know how I keep it all to myself. Ain't right, but I'm just scared, I guess. And it ain't like I never tried telling Mambo, and she just get on about what's gonna happen when folks find out and we get a lynching for it. Ain't right. Sometimes I reckon I oughta tell Safi, but her ma and Mambo are right close and that makes me scared in case they all end up swinging too.

When I get to thinking about it, I ain't got no clue how Safi's ma and my Mambo are good and close as friends can be anyways. They's both as different as day is from night, but they been together from way back, since knee-high, she says, so I guess that's all there is to it. Ever since Safi and her folks come back this way, we been visiting with them on the other side of the train crossing. Safi and her ma come over our way one time, but they's trailing six li'l uns at a time and them kids get on all over the place and ain't no joy for her ma. She just about went outta her mind. I like it better over their place anyhow, with all them folks talking all the time, seems like they's always cooking something, and Safi's grandma puts me in mind of Pappy 'cause she's real old too. She marches off to prayer meeting like she's all pepped up for courting the Lord, Mambo says. She's got an old felt hat just like Pappy had, 'cept she's got a bunch of spotty chicken feathers stuffed down a hole in the side.

'Must have been the fashion about a hundred years ago,' laughs Mambo. 'And all them still wearing it.'

Safi's ma says her grandma changes that bunch of chicken feathers about every ten years and reckons that makes it good enough as new for another ten. Mambo and Safi's ma are bent over laughing.

'Lord ain't paying no mind, she says, and I reckon she sure gotta be right about that.' Safi's ma ain't able to speak right with laughing over the sight of them feathers.

'Well, I gonna seek out Pappy's old hat and stick me a bunch of feathers in it too.'

'Chile, ya gonna be the belle of the ball looking like that.'

'Well, that sure suits me girl, long as the Lord ain't start thinking I's up for courting his good self too.'

Safi's ma and my Mambo laugh all the time and it's fine to hear, like they're keeping one another cheerful, trouble or no. We're always hearing them out front laughing and hollering and drinking moonshine, when they can get a hold of it, and when they think us kids are bedded down for the night.

I stay awake and listen 'cause I want to hear my Mambo laughing like she's real happy. That's when we stay over sleeping at that crowded shack of theirs so Mambo's able to help with all them kids in the morning. They ain't feeling so good a lot of the time with all that liquor swilling around and giving them giddy heads when they wake up. Safi's pa don't pay them no mind. He's so flat out building roads round Louisiana for keeping them bellies full that he's just glad to be left alone with a wrap of baccy and Safi's ma filling up his moonshine jar till his head nods off and he's gone. He's always fine next morning. Gets up bright as a shiny button and takes off for work on the back of the truck passing right by their cabin to pick him up, 'cause they live on the side of the gov'ment road. Seems he breaks rocks as good as he makes babies. Me and Safi swing out back in an old rope hammock, doing what we're told and looking out for all them kids.

Time goes by and I get to know more folk. Some say Mambo ain't no good, some say I'm a teacher's pet 'cause I learn good and ain't no fun, and Po'bean ain't got no right learning, neither. I just stick with Safi. She takes the same old hollering for being poorer than anybody else, 'cept maybe me and Mambo, on account of them having too many kids. Them folks just mean; ain't nobody round here ever got more than a dime at a time.

'Y'all real smart, Arletta. I wish learning was easy for me too, but it just ain't.'

I tell Safi I'm gonna help her out as much as I can. Ain't that she's not smart enough, it just ain't easy learning with all her kin running around the place all the time. Them's coming and going like nobody's business, and with all kind of things going on, she ain't got no peace for it. One thing I know for sure is ya gotta set ya mind on learning. That's hard to do with kids running and scrapping all the time.

'And I got chores,' she says. 'I get no rest now 'cause of being the oldest after our boys all head off for work and starting out on their own. All I hear is, "Safi take the li'l uns here, take them there. Rinse this out, shell them peas and crawfish." Living round here ain't like down your track. Ya got peace, Arletta, ya got time for it.'

I don't tell her what else I got. I just reckon having all that family round the place gotta be nice. That's worth all the time I got that I rightly don't know what to be doing with.

'Mambo ain't stepping out so much now, is she?' Safi asks.

'No, she ain't.'

Glad to say that's true. I reckon Mambo's taken to changing her ways and staying home, like she's getting some of that sense Pappy always said she was gonna get one day. She's setting down some proper planting too, and it's growing fine, she's got that touch with it. She says, "Arletta, ya go on and stick with ya books and I'm gonna stick with the good earth. That's what my sort do best – always did, always will." Seems that's the way it's gonna be, and it sure suits me fine too.

Me and Safi got to feeling tired swinging out back of her place, one time I recall. It was a real nice time, with everybody dancing and carrying on. I even seen folks there saying they live out near our cabin, but I ain't never seen them. Safi's pa and his pals got a way of smoking hog with jalepeño all day long in the ground before we're able to stuff our bellies so full of that soft and tasty stuff that we ain't good for much else.

I hear Safi's breathing go deep and even, she's sleeping already. The moon is just the way I like it, bright and full, and moving slow across the sky. The only sound I hear is Mambo and Safi's ma talking. Safi's used to having folk around the place, so she pays it no mind, but I lie awake and feel good about listening to folks' chattering, and all the coming and going, with a hush now 'cause all them kids don't need to be wakened. I don't hear much I don't need to be hearing, it's just the sound of life going on in her cabin like it don't go on in mine, and I like to be lying there thinking how it makes me feel safe.

I'm just about dropping off myself, with my full belly, when Safi's pa comes and lifts her outta the hammock. Then Mambo comes to curl up next to me, smelling of moonshine, lime and warm cologne. The night is still, ain't nothing moving out there at all. Mambo holds me close like she used to when we shared our cot before Pappy passed away.

'Get on off to sleep Arletta, ain't no time for li'l uns. Come on now.'

'I'm just listening to the sound of all them babies sleeping. They sure had a lotta babies. G'night Mambo.'

'G'night honey.'

'Ya smell them oranges Mambo? I'm gonna pick some so's all them babies have a nice fresh juice for breakfast.'

She pops a kiss on top of my head.

'That gonna be fine. Ya's a real good girl Arletta, and ya's my baby.'

I love my Mambo. Since Safi's folks come to live with her grandma, Mambo sure has changed. Like she got settled into sense. I reckon Pappy's looking down right proud, 'cept for all that mumbo-jumbo. That ain't changed at all.

I try hard to forget what Mr McIntyre and Mr Seymour are doing and take to studying hard at school. Seems throwing all I got into learning takes the ache right out of me. Safi's over our way sometimes too and that feels fine, like I got somebody of my own. I even see Mr Seymour turn back one time when he sees me and Safi hollering at the pipe 'cause we're so caught up with laughing. We been cooling off with a splashing and I see he about-turns and moseys off like he was just thinking of coming down our way for nothing at all.

Mr McIntyre turns up the next day though, and he gets real rough, telling me I need to be keeping my mouth shut or Mambo's gonna get hurt bad by his people and I ain't never gonna see the light of day again neither. Then Mr Seymour twists my arm till I think it's gonna snap right off and tells me he's taking a mind to be doing to Safi as well.

'She's a beauty. Looks to me like she's just right for getting started.'

'No! Leave her alone! She's got a pa and he sure is gonna be doing a killing if ya start with his li'l girl! I tell ya that for sure.'

'Well, we'll just need you to be keeping me nice and happy all by yourself then, so I don't have to go and be "*doing*" to her.'

'Ya leave her alone, Mr Seymour, ya leave her and ain't never get to laying a finger on her.'

Tears pour down my face 'cause of how I'm pleading for him to leave Safi alone. He says he's finding her growing up pretty and taken a fancy to her. The thought of nasty, dirty-smelling Mr Seymour doing all over my friend Safi makes me feel like I'm gonna kill him myself and save Safi's pa the trouble.

'Well, Fifty Cents, you know I'm thinking things are real special with you and me. You're just as good as can be and if you do right, then we're just as special as it can be. You and me special, that's for sure.'

Mambo and Safi are all I got in the world.

'I ain't gonna say nothing to nobody, Mr Seymour. It's just like ya say. We real special.'

Mr Seymour shrugs like he's simple, and that I reckon he is. Then he starts giggling like we're some kinda buddies.

'That's right. It's just going to be you and me, then. Like you say, we real special.'

He gets hold of my shoulders and leads me out back. Says he don't mind Mr McIntyre doing to me because he's just a little bit of a nobody, what he calls an upstart.

'I hear all about him, just an upstart. You like me better, don't you? We're the special ones, eh?'

My eyes are tight shut. I ain't saying nothing.

'We're special? Go on, say we're special.'

'We's special'

'You don't talk much and I'm taking a fancy to hearing you say, "We're real special, Mr Seymour." Say it now. You don't start talking and telling me how much you like it, I'm just going to go get that friend of yours. She's a talker. I can tell that.'

He spends more time doing than I ever know before. I start worrying maybe Mambo's gonna come back and find him. If she ever gets a notion about what they doing to me, she's gonna find herself swinging in two parts, ain't no mistaking.

Nellie tells me I've got my strength and I need to be using it. Trouble is, I ain't feeling strength at all. Seems I don't know what she's talking about. I just need to hear her talking to me and singing her sad song. That's what's seeing me through.

When Safi comes over we're s'posed to be spending time learning, and her folks say they's happy giving her time for it so she can get on. Truth is, we spend as much time fooling as we do learning. Mambo goes crazy as an old coot when she finds us all done up with her rouge and the new bangles she just picked up in the Brouillette Saturday market stall. She falls about laughing when we show her how we're learning to wiggle, though.

Sure is good having Safi over at our cabin.

When the travelling book wagon starts coming through our parish every two weeks, I get to borrow from it. Pretty soon I'm asking if I can take two instead of just the one we're s'posed to take. I still got time to fill like nobody else.

'Sure ya can, Arletta. I never saw anybody read as much, I swear. Ya must know everything there is to know about the Civil War, Little Bighorn and General Custer and all.'

Late one Saturday afternoon Mambo's dolling herself up for stepping out and I curl up in Pappy's shabby chair. I wanna see if some of my French is getting good enough for translating *The Mulatto*, seeing as French is something I took to learning right away. I hear Cajun folk ain't even allowed to speak French at their school, and that ain't right, 'cause they ain't able to speak nothing else. Mr Parker don't think that's right at all, though I find out he ain't s'posed to be teaching it, neither. But he comes by a copy of *The Mulatto* and says I oughta read it. He gives me that raggedy old book to keep as my own and straight off says I can borrow a French dictionary from him. I'm about as keen as anybody could be to set about practising my French. And *The Mulatto* is the first book I ever had to call my own.

'Why don't ya just get on down to Mamou and have y'self a real good time 'stead of all that goddammed reading,' is what Mambo has to say about it. 'Learn some of them Cajun songs and ya gonna be all right with French, and have a fine time to boot with it. Ya know what having a fine time is, Arletta? That's what the rest of the world is doing when ya got that head on ya shoulders stuck inside of books. Time ya started getting y'self about, find out what having a life is all about, honey.'

'I'm happy reading.'

'How the hell is anybody happy reading?'

'I am.'

'Well, I gotta real good friend, she's French, and I'm gonna see if she's able to come on over, because I see ya serious about it. Like I said, she's real French. Madame Bonnet came right on over here from Paris. Imagine that? All the way from Paris, France. Lord, she sure knows how to throw a party. Real French style.'

My head's taken up with the first page of my very own first book, ain't thinking about no party.

'Madame's able to teach ya proper French, Arletta, instead of spending time sitting there and ain't even talking it. Honey, sometimes I don't understand ya at all. If I ain't sure as hell that I bring my child into this world right here in this room ... and with us looking like we sharing the same pea-pod ... like two peas in a pod we are ...'

'Have a nice time, Mambo, I like learning, that's all. Ain't wanna be going to no party with no Madame.'

She's gonna talk to Madame Bonnet about it anyways, she says. Then she's wiggling down our track and I don't expect to see her for the rest of the weekend. I don't expect to be seeing Madame Bonnet at all.

'Don't go burning oil with all that reading after dark. Ya hear, Arletta? I marked that oil. Ya hear me?'

Somebody's whistling from the end of the road and Mambo's off for her lift into Brouillette, or Mamou, or wherever she's going for her good time. She only does that at weekends these days, and I gotta say, I'm glad of the peace and quiet. The day feels still and quiet after she's gone, ain't a breath of wind, and I settle in, happy spending it just the way I please, reading and learning. Me and Mambo just different, I guess.

It don't last long. In a little while I hear a noise outside on our track and my stomach turns right over. I shove *The Mulatto* outta sight under my cot and run out back to hide in the corn patch. I peep back at our cabin, sure I'm gonna see Mr McIntyre side-step over Pappy's fence like always.

'Don't let him touch ya chile. Ya has ya strength now. This about time ya need to be using it.'

'Nellie?'

Nellie is sounding different, like she just rushed here from someplace else. She's right up close in my ear.

'Use ya strength Arletta. Use ya strength. Don't let him touch ya at all. He's a-comin' chile, and don't let him be touching ya at all. Ya hearing Nellie chile? Ya hear?'

'I hear. What do I do, Nellie?'

'Ya's able chile, ya's able.'

Nellie's always telling me about my strength but that's something I ain't ever feel. I close my eyes and sink to the ground 'cause all I have is fear.

'This time he's gone, and y'all need to be listening to me. Don't let him lay a hand on ya nowhere. I'm right here. He's gone chile. He's gone ...'

Mr Seymour is out on our porch, drunk and jiggling his coins.

'Hey Fifty Cents, where are you?'

'Use ya strength Arletta, this time he's real gone.'

I creep flat on my belly along the ground between the rows of our corn and catch sight of Mambo's fish knife, sharp as a razor, sticking up out of the can by our washtub out back. I dash outta the corn, grab it and hide it behind my back. Then I take the biggest breath I reckon I'm ever gonna take and climb the back step up into our cabin. Mr Seymour hears me coming and pokes his silly head round our front door.

'There you are, Fifty Cents. Here, come and get it.'

He's jiggling coins in his podgy hand.

'I want a dollar.'

'Oooh,' he says, puckering up his lips. I can tell he's right pleased with himself. 'A dollar? What are we going to have for a dollar then?'

I keep that fish knife well hidden and back myself into the bedroom so he follows. My eyes are fixed on him, real steady. Mambo's knife got a thing it needs to be doing. A mambo's knife's got a power in it. A mambo's knife kept razor sharp for more than gutting fish.

He follows me like a fool.

'Will that be fifty cents for one thing, and fifty cents for another thing, eh?'

'Maybe.'

'I get a lot for my fifty cents now. Ooooh, you are a naughty, naughty girl.'

Sounds like he's talking to a dog.

Mr Seymour's already got his jacket off and waggling his dirty fingers my way. His breath is smelling rank and he stinks like he ain't washed in days.

I hold steady 'cause my time has come.

'That's ya strength chile. Ya got it, ya got it now, and Nellie's right here.'

I point at his pants.

'I wanna do that first and then y'all do whatever ya want but I ain't taking no fifty cents. I reckon on getting a dollar for it.'

He sniggers, like he's feeling right pleased with himself. He pulls out a wad of dollar bills from his jacket pocket like I never seen before, and waves one right in front of my face. I grab it. He unzips his pants slow, swaying from side to side and humming a stupid kinda tune, like he just hit jackpot on his birthday. When he drops his pants I swallow so I don't throw up before I do what I gotta do. I need to be keeping him off his guard. I don't know how I smile the way I do, I guess I just knows I gotta, and it gets him giggling like one idiot child, standing there naked like the day he's born.

'This time he's gone chile. He's real gone.'

I hear Nellie.

Seymour leans back on Mambo's dresser and gets himself steady for it. When he closes his eyes and starts his moaning I move outta my corner so I'm sure on having a clear run outta there. I move real slow, keeping check his eyes stay closed, then slowly, real, real slowly so he don't get no wind of it, I get myself outta the side of Mambo's dresser. He's gone for sure, lost in his pleasing I'd say, ain't seeing nothing. Then I'm ready. He gets a hold of my hair and forces himself so far down my throat I start gagging. Time come and I got my strength. I raise my Mambo's knife, careful like, with my heart thumping and bumping like it's never been. Then I take one long slash at the side of his private part and run like hell.

He starts screaming more than I think a sound could ever be coming out of just one man. I ain't never hear that sound before. Even on the dark moon, when I hear all kinda stuff, I ain't never hear nothing like I hear coming outta Mr Seymour when his private part takes my slashing. I ain't stopping to pay it any mind though, 'cause I'm outta there saving myself. I just ain't taking it no more and Nellie says he's real gone too, that's all I know. Soon as I reach the trees out back my ankle turns in with my rushing and I stumble. I'm starting to feel terrible scared about what it is I just done to cause Mr Seymour to be bellowing worse than a mad bull.

I just didn't wanna do it no more.

Inside of our cabin Mambo's bottles are rattling on her dresser and then I hear them clatter to the floor. I squeeze my eyes shut, thinking about all the trouble there's gonna be if any of that got broke. Mr Seymour is crashing through our cabin and I guess our clothes are all over the place too. I wanna be running just as far away as I'm able, but I gotta stay close now for clearing up once he's gone. All that mess is gonna need fixing up before Mambo comes home, that's for sure.

'Bitch! Bitch! Bitch!' Mr Seymour is yelling as he gets stumbling out onto our front porch. I just don't know what I'm gonna do next. I know I've hurt him bad already, but I keep Mambo's fish knife real handy in case he gets minded on causing more trouble. I'm shaking from top to toe, and my chest sure is pounding like a drum, but I run round to the front of our cabin 'cause I need to be seeing what's going on with all that bellowing. He's out there trying to keep steady on his feet, ain't a stitch of clothes on him. He takes off, limping and hopping up our track, holding on to his bleeding part. Seems blood is just pouring outta that man. I never got to thinking about blood before I took Mambo's knife to him. I never thought about much except this was gonna be the last time I ever let him be doing to me.

He points fat fingers my way and his eyes are near popping outta his head. I ain't sure if he's planning on coming back at me or not, so I hold up Mambo's knife high. My own face is wet with crying tears, and I reckon I'm howling too.

'You little bitch! You'll pay for this,' he screams, limping off butt-naked, trying to cover up his parts. 'You wait, you little piece of trash …'

I wave Mambo's knife one more time and then he's gone.

I gotta set to clearing all that mess up before Mambo finds out something's gone down. Seeing that blood all over Mr Seymour had me thinking it was gonna be everywhere, but I'm glad to see inside ain't so bad at all. Mr Seymour crashed out onto our porch, so seems that got most of it. Mambo's string is down, but her clothes and my uniform look fine, ain't no blood on them at all. I stand on one of our stools and get that string tied back up on its nails. Everything gets hung back over it, the same as always. I'm scared as hell, dashing in and out of the place in case Mr Seymour takes a mind on coming back. If he gets a hold of Mambo's knife, I'm gonna be done for myself. Glad to say there ain't no sign of him, though, 'cept for that trail of blood. I fix things up and find the dollar he gave me.

Most of his blood is out on our porch and up our track; I soon get done with that. By now our bucket and rain barrel are both dry and I need to be tearing up and down to the pipe for more water. Mr Seymour ain't nowhere at all, he sure got outta here real quick. I'm used to seeing Mr McIntyre up the gov'ment road a ways, waiting for the bus after he gets his doing, but ain't nobody up there now at all and I start reckoning Mr Seymour's bleeding to death in the cane.

I cover up the last trail of blood on our track with earth and check our porch. Inside, the cabin floor ain't so bad, that gets done quick too, and then I start wiping up inside the bedroom. Ain't easy cleaning up bad blood and I'm back at that pipe three more times with my gut turning over and swallowing back on my own retching.

I check Mambo's bottles are just so, like they're all s'posed to be. She's right particular about that, so I sure am glad nothing got broke.

I check one more time that everything is done right and there ain't no blood left at all. Then I spot a splash of it, though it's near dried out already, right there on Mambo's dresser next to where I slashed him. I get down to wipe it, feeling feared to death for myself 'cause by now I'm sure as hell the law is coming for me and I'm gonna swing. That's when I see the mighty wad of money outta Mr Seymour's pocket rolled way back up under the dresser. And that's when I stop and get to feeling doggone tired out.

What I just done to some big-shot white man is starting to sink into my stupid head. I don't even know how bad cut he is, there sure was some blood outside on our porch. I just know when he was forcing himself on me I had no mind at all what might be happening to him, I was too busy caring what was happening to me. But I start thinking then about how bad cut he is and if he's lying flat out in the cane with me put an end to him. I start wondering if I need to be telling somebody about what I just done. Maybe I oughta get over to Safi's folks and tell them Mr Seymour is laying up bleeding to death in the cane 'cause of me. Then I get to thinking about how I once saw the law come for one of Pappy's pals. He was called Big Marcus. Pappy and me were over that way, 'cause he was looking for work, and I saw Big Marcus get his hands tied back and marched off with a state marshal and a dog 'cause he stole something to buy his grandson a pair of shoes to go to school with. Big Marcus had shiny tears on his face and said he was sorry for it. Next time anybody saw him he was smelling bad and swinging from the branch of a tree. Folks said he was so big that branch near enough touched the ground and if he was wearing a pair of shoes himself he ain't never have swung.

Ain't nobody ever ask how Big Marcus get from that marshal marching him off to them finding him hanging outta that tree. Everybody scared and living in fear of saying anything about it. All of them talked a lotta noise about a riot, but it ain't never happen.

I reckon it's best that I ain't tell nobody about what I just done to Mr Seymour, 'cept Nellie.

I add up all them dollars and get to 405, counting the one I just got. I always chucked the fifty cents he gave me after every time into the washhouse, I never kept a dime of it. I hear a bunch of kids got caught poking about with a stick, thinking they's always gonna keep finding money, and all of them got a right licking for playing in other folks' shit.

He sure never looked like it to me, but Mr Seymour gotta be some kinda wealthy white man if he's walking about the place with all them dollars, 'less he stole them from someplace. He ain't no thief though, too soft for that, and sure as hell he gonna be easy to catch. I'm thinking he probably just been to the bank, and that must be how he knows Mr McIntyre. I take one long time checking all that money sitting in the lap of my frock before I need to give up thinking on it.

Our cabin looks the same as it always does after I'm done giving it a good clean. Mambo likes everything just so, and she's gonna be pleased I set to it instead of reading *The Mulatto*. I do one last check all over – the porch, underneath the dresser, and up our track. Then I take the bucket and fish knife up to the pipe to scrub them clean.

I'm finishing up when Claudette Benoit comes with a basket of mucky roots she's getting ready for peeling.

'Hey Arletta. I hear ya doing great at school. And look at ya. Now ya cleaning for Mambo. Ya just a honey Arletta. That's what ya is chile, just a honeychile.'

Mambo's fish knife gets put back in the tin can out back of our cabin, and I feel a whole lot better when it's outta my hands. One way or another Mr McIntyre's gonna find out something's happened to Mr Seymour and I'm sure I ain't gonna be seeing him no more neither. I get to feeling so happy I stop feeling bad about the slashing I just give Mr Seymour.

I wrap the wad of dollar bills in Mambo's black newspaper; ain't nobody gonna ask what's in that packet. When it's dark I creep into the trees and dig up Pappy's tin. I suck on Pappy's pipe like it holds the finest baccy in America, then hide the dollars on top of his sent'mental papers. I put the pipe back, close the lid tight, and place the King of England back in the ground. The last thing I gotta do is get up to the pipe and fill our rain barrel out back same as it was before I started my cleaning. Best do that while it's dark too, 'cause folks ain't s'posed to do it at all, and somebody's sure gonna shout about it if I get spotted. After that's done, I creep up to the washhouse and throw his white suit in the shit.

The fried chicken Mambo left tastes good and I fall asleep with a full belly, thinking I ain't never gonna have to be doing with Mr McIntyre or Mr Seymour again.

When Mambo comes home she says Madame Bonnet is gonna come and give me lessons in French. Well, I gotta be pleased about it, I guess, 'cause I wanna learn, but there ain't no way I was ever gonna be tagging behind Mambo or wiggling about the place for it. Madame Bonnet must be real nice if she's thinking on coming all the way out here to be teaching me my French.

Then Mambo tells me about how she got word to go see Mr McIntyre and he's gonna give her a job cleaning the bank office in Brouillette. She's mighty pleased about it.

'Well, I just says I'm gonna do it right away Arletta. I mean, of course he don't let on we knows one another, him being white and all.'

She winks my way.

'Some of them white folks just get a taste for a bit of good old black soul loving. On the side, like.'

'That right Mambo?'

'Sure, always been, and I ain't never foolish enough to be thinking he was laying down with me for anything other than a piece of good loving like he ain't never gonna get outta that skinny little white wife he gone get himself.'

'Well, ain't something oughta be going on Mambo, him being married and all.'

'Married ain't mean he get good loving.'

She looks at me like I oughta know it.

'Honey, ya gonna find that out for y'self one day. I always set about giving good loving. He get himself one good time and just look now how it pay off, Arletta. Look how it just darnit pay off for us. We gonna be fine now honey. I got me some work outta that.'

Mambo's about as happy as I've ever seen her. She drags a brush through her hair and looks in the mirror like she's seeing a whole new person with a whole new life out there.

'I got me a job Arletta, we gonna be fine. All that sneaking about, giving him what he wanted, just right darnit paid off.'

'Well, I'm glad Mambo, real glad about it.'

Mambo's so happy she wraps her arms around me and hugs my breath right out. I hold onto my Mambo real tight. Feels fine. I love my Mambo and it sure is good that we're gonna be okay.

It turn out to be some kinda day.

Five

M ambo gave up thinking I'm ever gonna be following her ways. 'Ya ain't got it girl.'

Simple as that, she reckons. Too much schooling put paid to it, she says. Ruins the gut, takes away what she calls instinct. All that reading up on other folks' instinct sure as hell kills ya own, she says.

'I knows it, and ya grandma knew it too, when she was living here in this world.'

She blames Pappy. That he taught me different, did it to spite her and grandma, so that I ain't ever gonna be mambo. He always said he was gonna do it, and ain't it just what come about. That was Pappy all over, she moaned.

I tell her she's sore 'cause she ain't never get no proper schooling herself.

'I ain't ever want no schooling. Schooling get folks thinking too much about stuff ain't nobody's business to be thinking. White folks' business. A mambo need her gut.'

'Most folks need reason.'

Days past, I'd be sure on getting a thwack for my cheek and answering Mambo back like that. Last time she thwacked me I could see she knew it ain't right, and ain't working neither. Seems me starting to learn took the whole wind of thwacking right out of her.

I got my period round that time too, and she laid a power on it.

'Blood gives a woman power,' she says, giving me my rags and telling me to be private about them and never find cause to use them for anything else.

'And don't ever let nobody get a hold of ya rags honey. I'm warning ya and ya best listen good. Them rags holding ya own blood, ain't nobody else's. Blood from outta ya belly and that ain't nothing. That's life.

'There's some woman over Pawnee way and I hear she's counting on taking up being a mambo. Going round asking folks to call her Queen Something-or-other, priestess, or some damn rubbish. Lord Almighty. That kinda stuff going on, Arletta. And that half-bake shit is bad stuff. I'm telling ya that.'

'What's that got do with my rags?'

'That's what I call it. Half-bake shit.'

'Ain't nothing to do with me.'

Well, that start her off about how I ain't never learn nothing and telling me to listen good. A woman gets power in her moon-time and all that power is able to be turned back on her if she goes getting careless. Course I know that's just Mambo's crazy old stuff talking.

'Ain't no crazy stuff. Ya just ain't got it, ya ain't never got it. That's exactly what I'm telling ya. And that Pawnee woman is going after some of my folks too. I ain't wanting her finding no way of getting nothing over on me, so always go minding what I'm saying and watch ya rags.'

Then she laughs right out loud and says, 'Hey, y'all grown up now girl. Ya need to be getting on out there and find y'self a young man for popping that cherry.'

Anybody would think that was the funniest thing she ever said. The way she set to laughing all over our cabin about popping my cherry. Well, I tried telling her about that one time and got me nothing but a mouthful. And none of it was anything to laugh about, or worth a mouthful neither.

Madame Bonnet is just about as flighty a person as I ever saw in my life, and a right sight for sore eyes too. The first time she comes flouncing, and that's the word for it, down our track with a bunch of pink feathers round her neck and a pair of dainty slippers on her tiny feet, she's cursing the good earth she's walking on for having the affront to be dusty.

'*Mon Dieu, c'est un désastre! Je vais devoir en faire quelque chose tout de suite.*'

She rolls up the gov'ment road sitting up front of a fancy wagon ain't nobody ever seen the likes of, with a set of red covers on the seats and a black box to rest her dinky li'l feet on. She calls the driver – ain't much outta being a boy – 'Tout de suite', and he's about as plain and quiet as to say he's probably dumb. The sight of them on that road picks up a trail of nosy kids thinking who the hell coming to see Mambo and Po'bean now.

With all the giggling going on later, I find out that box under Madame's feet is just the right size for a heap of real French wine. Tout de suite fetches two fine glasses outta it, them's so thin I wonder they don't snap in half, and gives them a right good polishing before he fills them up with dark red wine. It's plain to see he's doing that every day of his life. Then he says, '*Excusez-moi*,' because he ain't dumb at all, and ain't no Creole neither. That's the first time I ever hear proper French spoke. He starts picking up all them feathers Madame let fly down our track, he don't look this way or that way, and when he's done picking up feathers, he stands guard over Madame's fancy wagon.

Course I don't learn anything at all that first time. Well, no French to speak of anyways. I learn what it is to be drinking fine wine and get to giggling about nothing. And I learn what it is to be real nice to them that's serving on you, 'cause Madame sure treats Tout de suite like he's somebody worth something. Matter of fact, that's exactly what she says.

''E worth ees weight een gold. *Le garçon d'or.*'

Before she comes flouncing down our track again, two young fellows help Tout de suite lay wood planks down so Madame and her satin slippers don't get friendly with dirt. Mambo says it's just on account of her being from Paris, and I guess they probably ain't got no dirt tracks over that way at all.

I ask Safi to come on over 'cause she could do with the learning too, and we set to translating the Paris newspapers Madame brings. She and Mambo just get tipsy on her fine French wine, ain't no kinda real teaching going on at all. Madame rocks to and fro in Pappy's rocking chair with Mambo sitting on our front step listening to her talk about what happened to her before she came to Louisiana. She ain't never known no family of her own on account of her being passed through a hole in the wall as soon as she come into this world, with nothing more than a piece of cloth they said was worked by her ma, so she was going to know her when she came back. She ain't never come back, though. Madame's still got that piece of linen and says she carries it with her all the time.

'Look, I show you. Ees 'ere.'

That got Mambo all choke up.

Safi and me get out there to take a look at that piece of old linen, gone turned yellow with all the time of Madame's life. We feel right sorry for her 'cause she ain't got nobody, she just got a piece of cloth. It's worked up fine with coloured threads and all, but it ain't family and it ain't real folks. I guess there's some on this earth got it worse than me.

Like I always say, one thing I know about is good teaching and Madame ain't got that at all. She got patience and she's real kind, what with all our asking, but truth to tell, the most we learn is how they talk in Paris and we start wondering if folks down in New Orleans gonna be caring anything about that. I s'pose I got myself a nice French accent and I know more than anybody else about the Great War and all the trouble going on in Europe. Knowing all that goes down well in school, though, so I guess that's something.

When Madame finds out I like cocoa and ain't never hardly had it, she brings a tin of it done up in shiny paper I can see my face in. Tout de suite ain't used to ever saying much, but when I bring him hot frothy cocoa, like Mambo's real good at, he's right pleased.

'That's very nice of you, Miss Arletta. *Merci beaucoup*.'

'Ya ain't go calling me no Miss.'

'Well I surely must, on account of you ees working with Madame Bonnet.'

'She's teaching me French is all. Well, she s'posed to be teaching me French, but her and Mambo just getting on all the time. It's going okay I guess though.'

Tout de suite takes to whittling sticks when he's waiting for Madame and the kids hereabouts are all right tickled with it. I get outta there as soon as them kids show up for fear they start calling me Po'bean and he starts calling me Miss.

Then Safi stops coming for French lessons 'cause of her grandma saying Madame needs to come to Jesus, and I gotta ask her what that means.

'Well, I don't rightly know, Arletta, but that's what she says, and he'd be right forgiving of her too.'

Her grandma and my Pappy, them's the same kinda folks, all for Jesus, and that ain't ever go down well with my Mambo. It's about that, I guess. I see Mambo's always mixing and pounding up before Madame gets here, so something's going on all right. She fixes up some kinda gri-gri and Madame takes a bag of it away with her every time she's over here. Safi's grandma is big with the church and all, like Pappy was, so maybe she just don't like Safi round Mambo's stuff no more.

So I just carry on by myself. Madame reckons she's teaching me French and Mambo gets a taste for fine French wine. I keep up with all my studies though, so I do well at school. Mr Parker was teaching me for a couple of years before Mrs Lee Hem took over 'cause he ain't able. He says he's just getting old and wanting to see more sunsets 'fore he ain't able to see no more of them at all.

English gets to be my best subject but I love geography too, and start daydreaming about going travelling to the new Republic of China Mrs Lee Hem is fond of talking about. She's from north China someplace, says it took her two weeks to get all the way over here, and a firm down in New Orleans has published a diary she wrote about the Chinese Boxer Uprising. I borrow it, on account of it being something to read, and she seems pleased 'cause nobody else ever asks her anything about it. Then she takes to standing up on an old soapbox over in Brouillette shouting about a revolution in Russia. I find out what a Communist is and Mrs Lee Hem gets minded on being one. Mr Lee Hem takes himself right on off to Georgia and she's left shouting about all us black folks taking up as Commies. I ain't rightly see much wrong with it, but Mambo goes mad about that.

'Keep ya big mouth shut on it Arletta,' she screams, like she hit the roof and it gone and blow right off. 'One time girl! Do as I says and keep outta it.'

'Well, I'm just saying I think it's all right to be sharing out among folks ...'

'Goddammit, Arletta! I swear I gonna take to thwacking ya outta them big ideas! This Commie shit is just the next big trouble and ya gonna leave them white folks to sort it out among themselves. Ain't gonna let ya even think on it. Ya hear Mambo girl?'

'Okay Mambo, I was only saying ...'

'One more word and I'll be thrashing it outta ya. Them whites gonna chew that poor Chiney woman up and spit her out into a penitentiary one way or the other, and that's if she gets lucky. They's all gonna get worked up about Commies now, same way they was about black folks. And what the hell ya know about sharing? Ain't no white folk ever share nothing with any of us.'

I ain't saying nothing.

Course, Mrs Lee Hem loses her job at the mission and her diary on the Boxer Uprising goes too. She's kind enough to search me out first and make sure I ain't been seen with her diary. Everybody is talking about them taking her away on account of her being a Commie, but the truth is I feel sorry about losing her from school.

Crinkly 'old Guffy' takes over our class after she's gone. His real name is Mr Guthbertson and we learn nothing more than that before Mademoiselle Ledoux waltzes into our school and every man and boy in the place falls right in love with her.

I say 'waltz' because Mademoiselle puts me in mind of Mambo, except she's got a proper education, and even though she wears tight little dresses, her chest is covered up to the neck and her wiggling is kinda decent, like what they call a waltz. She asks if we have boyfriends and we blush up. She wants to know what songs we like singing and then we learn a couple of old-time tunes because that's what she calls poetry, though Mrs Hampton sure don't agree with that at all. Then she starts telling us about helping poor folks in Africa so we can learn how to come like 'citizens of the world'. She's Cajun, only white face we got in our school now Mrs Lee Hem's off someplace, so she's right impressed that I'm learning French by myself. I learn more French with her in a month than I did in nearly two years with Madame Bonnet, though I'm right fond of Madame and Tout de suite, and of them coming out our way.

My cot gets moved.

'Arletta, I moved ya cot. Now ya's a woman it ain't right we still sharing a bedroom.'

Ain't never been right; Mambo's got a new beau, that's all. He's called Quince and she's going for him big time. I ain't never seen anybody fluttering round somebody the way she fusses round him. Bosoms all pushed up, wiggling and pawing one another like I ain't even there. He's tall, dark, handsome, they say, and stupid. Quince is out here all the time now and I guess he don't wanna be showing off when he's doing to Mambo. That suits me fine, because he's the biggest grunter she's ever had.

'Fine by me Mambo, long as I can use the bedroom for homework, 'cause I got a whole lot of that coming up and they say I'm gonna be doing real well at my exams.'

Mambo says that's fine but I need to be thinking about getting work someplace, start helping out round the place, says she's been putting food in my mouth long enough.

'No. I'm staying at school Mambo.'

'Don't go getting all worked up and full of y'self now Arletta. I work hard cleaning that bank, and I tell ya it sure ain't easy putting up with that creepy McIntyre breathing down the back of my neck like he own it. And I'm telling ya, he's getting worse than he ever was. And all ya's thinking about is books, books, books. Stupidness.

My hands cut sore with bleaching and cold water. I'm all worn out looking after ya.'

Mambo ain't never looked after me right in her life. I been looking after myself most of the time since Pappy passed away, with her stepping out all over the place. And well she knows it too. I tell her just that.

'Ain't taking ya talking back at me Arletta. All that blasted learning got ya thinking ya something ya ain't girl. Sure is.'

'Well, I just wanna stick with school.'

'Ya just about right for getting a job, so think on it now, Arletta. More money coming in ain't gonna go wrong, and ya got an education so ya's able to earn good. Ya worth something with all that learning.'

Mambo gets a ride into town with Bobby-Rob that afternoon and I rock out on our porch thinking about that 405 dollar bills I got buried 'longside Pappy's pipe. Ain't no matter how much I think about how all that money gonna help us out when we get short, and that's most of the time, I'm so scared of all the questions it's gonna raise, soon as anybody knows I got it, that I start shaking like it just happened yesterday. Thinking of it makes me feel like I'm gonna keel right over. I ain't even sure folks gonna believe what I gotta say about it neither. Most of the time I just get on with my learning because that stops my mind dwelling on what Mr McIntyre and Mr Seymour did to me all them years. I ain't saying it works all the time, I'm just saying that's what I do, and it gets me by, most of the time. If I didn't have me my learning, I sure as hell would be floating face down in Sugarsookie Creek and well on my way to the mighty Mississippi.

I never hear it, but I'm pretty sure Mr Seymour bled to death someplace in the fields round here and my slashing be the cause of it. Ain't no reason us folks down the end of our track ever gonna hear about any butt-naked white man coming to his sorry end bleeding in some field, back end of no place. Maybe his folks hush it all up. I guess that's what they need to be doing, anyways. Hell, if they ever get any kinda notion about him being a dirty pig and meddling with kids, they sure as hell gonna be hushing it up. Especially since he was slashed good in his parts and all. I reckon they know all about him and think he got caught red-handed, so some mad-as-hell daddy done for him.

One thing for sure is plenty folk gotta know Mr Seymour weren't no good. Mr McIntyre knows all about him anyways, and he's running a bank. Ain't no decent sort ever gonna look at Mr Seymour with his dirty-smelling self and think him decent. He ain't ever came back for that roll of dollar bills, I know that much, and it seems to me if he was out there living, somebody sure would have come for them, even if he don't want to show that nasty face of his in case that gets slashed too. And I sure would think nothing about doing it. I ain't sorry for nothing.

If he's still living, I figure somebody would have got themselves on out here, turning our place upside down looking for that money. It never happened, so I reckon he's done for and I ain't about to be marched off like Big Marcus and swinging from no tree 'longside Mambo for it. Ain't worth telling folks nothing.

If Mambo ever finds out what Mr Seymour and Mr McIntyre were doing to her daughter, him being her boss and her thinking she got herself that job for giving him a few of her good times, she's gonna go outta her mind, for sure. I never thought it wise to go telling her how she really got that job for fear of what might come crashing down on my head, and all of Louisiana cursed to high hell at the next dark moon. Anyways, folks ever hear that Mambo and Mr McIntyre were rolling so he could get from a black Mambo what his wife ain't up for, they's maybe gonna believe it, but ain't nobody ever gonna swear on it.

That's just the way it is, always been, and jobs for folks round here sure are hard enough to come by. Whites are out all over, marching and hiding their faces like we care a tooting who they are and like we don't know, anyways. Saying we're taking white folks' jobs because we're trying to get out of service, like we ain't got no right to be getting on the same as anybody else. Only hanging needed round here is Mambo hanging on to that job of hers, 'cause she might be damn good at cleaning the bank, but there ain't no way she's ever gonna be up for reg'lar old-time service. Bowing and scraping to white folks? My Mambo ain't got no style for that at all.

I'm just leaving Mambo with no clue why I figure she got that job the day after I slashed Mr Seymour. I'm plenty feared on telling her anyways. She'd sure find some way of turning his wife into a widow on account of that. I've already got white man's blood all over my hands, one more time's gonna take me over the edge and I been just about hanging on already.

I'm scared folks'll just find some way of making what happened to me my own fault anyways. And I know stuff like that ain't ever gonna keep itself quiet neither. All them folk I know are gonna find out, sure as day follows night, that Mr McIntyre and Mr Seymour were doing to Po'bean for years. I guess some folks even gonna say I was happy doing it for money and that I was liking some white man taking a shine to me.

I'm done feeling dirty enough already and as soon as it's dark I take myself off to the King of England and cry myself blind thinking on it. Ain't no matter which way I think about how we could make good use of that roll of dollar bills, I know there's gonna be a mighty scene over it, one way or the other, and I'm gonna end up coming off worse, same as always. I been keeping stuff to myself a long time now and the way I see it, that's still the best way. She don't ever say it but I know my Mambo, and I reckon she feels guilty about leaving me in our cabin when she took to having herself a good time all over the place. I think she's gonna go stark raving crazy if she ever finds out what was going on, and that just means more trouble. Worst part of it is, if marching white folks ever find out, then me and Mambo ain't even gonna make it as far as the branch of no tree. We gonna wake up one morning with the flaming cross of Jesus stuck right up in our front yard and a bunch of white sheets feeling righteous about roasting us alive inside Pappy's cabin.

I walk all the way to Sugarsookie Creek in the dark and don't even know how I get there. I find myself sitting on the bank staring at silver moon-ripples flowing to the ocean, makes me feel kinda peaceful. I think hard about the day I let Mr Seymour have what he got coming and I shiver through to my bones thinking on all the times he was doing to me to be deserving of it.

'Nellie?'

It would be real nice if Nellie had a mind to tell me everything is gonna be all right and I'm able to stay learning. Pappy got me good and ready for learning so I can get on in this life, and that's what I wanna do. But I don't hear Nellie now like I used to. Sugarsookie Creek is still hearing me the same old way though. Seems I been crying tears into Sugarsookie Creek as long as I can recall.

'I'm done with it Nellie. Even when I feel I ain't able to be thinking on it no more, it stays right here, holding on to me like it ain't never gonna let me go.'

I wish I could still hear that voice of hers, deep and sweet, and singing through the wind in the trees. But the night is just cold and dark, and my mind is just full of remembering Mr Seymour's smell and filthy fingernails all over a frightened little girl like me with nobody looking out for her. The churning in my gut reaches right up in my throat when I get to remembering Mr McIntyre and how he always placed his hand over my mouth till I learnt I ain't s'posed to make a sound. I throw up right there till it aches so much I fall over and just lie down shivering. There ain't nothing I can do about what I got inside of that tin. I got a hold of all Mr Seymour's dirty dollars and they ain't worth nothing. I'm just gonna leave the King of England buried there in the ground till I can figure things out.

'I don't know what's gonna happen if I leave school Nellie. I ain't even sure about Mambo's new beau. He's gonna get rid of me and that's for sure. Ain't no way he's taking on some little *pichouette* Mambo had with some other man we ain't even know about, because she ain't ever say nothing.'

It would be right fine if Nellie was there listening like she used to, but she ain't. There's just the sliver of a moon, with a wind coming up. I wash my mouth out in the creek. The water is real cold but it tastes sweet, like all that blood of old sure did give it something special for making me feel clean and wholesome.

Back inside our cabin I curl up in Pappy's chair and think I'm just about as scared of that roll of dollar bills as I've ever been of anything. Don't seem wise or right throwing a mighty roll of bucks in shit for other folks to find. Don't seem right floating them down Sugarsookie Creek neither, so I ask Pappy if he's able to take care of it all, 'cause I sure as hell don't know which way is best on turning. That was one long night.

Quince moves in with Mambo the day after my cot is set up, and I reckon he's nothing but a lazy layabout. Ain't ever hold onto no job for any time at all, ain't got no education neither, 'cause he ain't ever get no schooling. Lord, he's some kinda sight, tweaking his hair like he's somebody, and checking out how he looks in Mambo's mirror. It sets me off laughing, seeing him wondering what folks see if they look sideways at him. Ain't never seen a three-way mirror in his life.

He's right on top of Mambo every chance he gets, and one time when he throws a wink my way, I swear I get scared as hell in case he starts thinking on doing to both of us. He's got a habit of staying out all night with his drinking buddies too, and Mambo don't take kindly to that at all. One time she walks the floor of our cabin all night till he comes back, just as I'm getting myself off to catch the school bus.

'Y'all have a nice time in the classroom now sassy,' he says, kinda drunk. I shoot one of my stares his way, 'cause he's a fella and I ain't sure about any of them. He kicks Pappy's gate shut and I walk away, just about as mad as if he kicked at Pappy himself. I ain't taking to Quince at all, and he ain't treating my Mambo right neither. Can't figure out what's happened to her since she's taken up with him. She's all over the place, and from what I see, he ain't worth nothing.

Madame Bonnet is still coming over with Tout de suite though, and he's still calling me Miss. Ain't nothing I can do about it. Quince fits right in with all that giggling and before I know it our place is full of his pals hanging round Madame Bonnet like she's the queen of the bees. Ain't no learning French with all that flirting and giggling going on, ain't no learning at all, so I take myself off over to Safi's place to help out with her chores. Ain't got nothing else to do.

'S'pose Mambo feels if she keeps them partying in ya cabin, then Quince ain't gonna go staying out all night and straying.'

'I guess, but it sure is noisy. Tout de suite been telling me he's carrying Madame outta there half the time, she gets herself so full of liquor.'

'Well, she's used to all that fine wine, moonshine's gotta be knocking her sideways.'

One day I come off the school bus and find Mambo sitting out on our porch wearing that look she takes on when I'm in big trouble.

'Arletta, it's time for ya to leave.'

'What? I ain't leaving school, I told ya that already Mambo.'

'I ain't talking about no school Arletta. Ya leaving home, gettin' work and starting ya own life.'

'Leave home? I'm only fourteen.'

'Ya nearly fifteen Arletta, and that's plenty old enough to be getting out there and finding y'self a job, finding ya own way. Most kids wanna be getting off and leading their own life. Like they's wanting to find out about life in this world and ...'

'What ya talking about? How the hell ya know about it Mambo? Ya ain't never leave home.'

'I ain't taking none of ya cheek young lady,' she says, raising her voice. 'I'm telling ya and that's all there is to it. Ain't no conversation we having here, I'm telling ya. All of us gotta work and put food in our own bellies.'

That layabout Quince got her head turned good and proper. She ain't nothing but miserable since he started coming round here. And I ain't hearing her telling him to get on out there and be putting food in his own belly. Course, that ain't something I oughta have said to Mambo.

'Ain't long ago I was washin' ya mouth out with carbolic for talking like that,' says Mambo.

But my mouth's already off running.

'He's too busy preening and pruning like he's one of them screen idols. Ain't nothing in his head but jumping on ya, and like he's getting his belly filled up and paid for doing it too. That's the way it seems to me ...'

Thwack.

My mouth got me heading for that I guess. Mambo ain't raised her hand to me in years and I see it don't come easy.

'Can't ya see Mambo, he ain't good? He ain't gonna stick around here …'

'Okay, enough Arletta.' Mambo flops back down in the rocker. 'I ain't wanting no fight.' The chair creaks, the boards creak, and the colour drains outta her lips. She's looking tired. I ain't paid it no mind till now, but it looks like something's wearing her out. That Quince is just bleeding her dry.

'I'm gonna have a baby.'

'Not his! No, Mambo.'

'Arletta, I ain't no spring chick and I'm taking what chance I'm getting here. Quince already got himself a job on a wharf in Baton Rouge with United, so we's gonna be all right. There's plenty work goin' down on the river in Baton Rouge.'

Oh, that's what he says, I bet. Like he knows anything about working. I ain't saying nothing but I reckon my face is saying plenty.

'Hell, Arletta, at least be happy about the baby. Why ain't ya?'

'Ain't the baby I ain't happy about, it's him. He's no good, he's just full of himself, and full of lying round the place, combing his hair and preening himself in that mirror. Looking at other women too; I seen him do that when his pals bring them here. And hanging out till all hours of the night with all them good-for-nothing cronies he's got. And they're all just like him, lazy as hell. Mambo, he ain't never gonna look after no baby. Ya can't see that's the way it's gonna be?'

'Well, what I'm gonna do? I'm having a chile and that's all there is to it. Arletta, I'm glad I'm having another chile, I'm wanting that, and he says he gonna stick around for it. That's what he wants too, he's ready for it. That's why he's gone got himself fixed up with work. Quince ain't no bad man, Arletta. Ya wrong about him honey.'

I offer to help. I figure between us we can look after the baby. I can carry on at school so I can get a real good job when I finish, not cleaning or darning. Folks like us are getting educated now, we're getting on, and up till then Mambo can go part-time or something, work after I get home and I'm able to look after the baby. And I can even sneak into the King of England to help out without her ever having to know about it.

She don't go for that at all. Says she gotta clean when they tell her to clean. And as soon as she ain't able, they gonna find somebody else and she's gonna be outta there for good. That's how it is. She don't think I oughta be expecting to find a good job neither.

'A good job? Where ya gonna get that exactly Arletta? Ain't none round here. Girl, ya gonna be telling me ya wanna be a doctor next. Look around y'self Arletta, look who we is round here. We ain't able to go on out there telling folks in this world what we wanna be and what we ain't wanna be. That ain't our world honey, and learning is fine, ya done good, that's for sure, but ain't no time for dreaming ...'

'We've gotta stick together, Mambo. Just don't throw me out for him. He ain't worth it.'

'I ain't throwing ya out. It's time, that's all. That's all there is to it. Ya come of an age, Arletta.'

Well, maybe so, but I ain't gonna go mentioning them dollar bills I got buried with Pappy's pipe in the King of England, though we sure could manage on that for a while. I'm holding back on that 'cause I ain't sure at all how things are with Mambo right now. Ain't just her and me like before, now I got Quince to think about, and another baby on the way. I think all that money is just gonna tangle things up worse instead of making it better. Could be Quince just takes it all and we ain't never see a nickel. Maybe Mambo got herself so tied up she's gonna let him do it too. Looks like she might even buy him off to stay with her 'cause of that child she's got in her belly, or something just as stupid. What's clear for sure is that she ain't herself right now.

Course that money's gonna bring all them questions too.

My gut rolls over.

Mambo starts speaking, quiet-like, and I know I ain't telling her nothing about Seymour's wad of dollar bills.

'I'm taking this chance with Quince, Arletta, and I reckon, with times so hard and all, that ya old enough for gettin' work. Setting out on ya own, starting up on ya own life honey. Everybody gotta think about it sometime.'

I flop down on the porch step.

'I reckon he just don't want me around in my own house. Boy, he's trouble Mambo.'

'I ain't able to keep y'all in schooling when I ain't earning with the baby. Ya go on, get a job now Arletta, find a young man to take care of ya.'

'I don't wanna leave school Mambo.'

'I ain't got nothing more to say on it Arletta. Ya all grown up now. That's all there is to it. Time come, is all.'

Seems I ain't got no say in it at all. Mambo and Quince done work it out already. Ain't no easy way of putting it: I gotta leave Pappy's cabin. I've grown up, though I can't surely say I's feeling it, and I gotta start making my own way, same as everybody else.

'I wanna stay learning Mambo.'

'They's got classes starting up all over for learning.'

'Ain't the same Mambo.'

I figure Quince just don't want me around, and there ain't no way he's gonna be feeding me when Mambo ain't able. Ain't nothing I can do except go find a way to feed myself, like Mambo says. I just never figured on starting out on my own so soon. I can see Mambo looks tired and I don't want to be fighting anyway.

'Ain't like we goin' no place Arletta. This is still ya home too, ya able to come see us anytime ya want. Hell, I ain't throwing ya out first thing in the morning Arletta. Ya go on, find a job first. Quince says there ain't none round here, so when ya does, ya gotta live close by so ya able to get there. Make sense, don't it?'

'Makes sense Mambo.'

I guess it makes more sense to Quince than it does to me, since I wasn't planning on leaving Pappy's cabin at all, that's something I sure never thought about in my life. Truth is, I can't see me living here with Quince anyhow, and once that baby comes, we gonna be falling all over one another, ain't gonna be no peace here at all.

I take off over to tell Safi and right off she says she's coming with me. Boy, that sure does put a different light on things. They got so many kids inside of her grandma's cabin, her pa had to cut down wood and build up right next to it. Still ain't room for all of them and her grandma too, so Safi tells her ma it makes sense for her to be leaving and get to earning. It's been hard since, just like her grandma said, that last baby came too soon and ain't right on it. Her grandma says Safi's ma got herself all spent out having babies and, sure enough, that's just what happened. Her ma ain't exactly happy about her leaving at all, but she sees the sense in it and glad we gonna be together.

Me and Safi get jobs at the cotton mill just outside of Marksville.

Mrs Dolly Archer-Laing put notice of her private boarding rooms up in Safi's grandma's church. She wants 'young ladies, pure of body and mind, who attend church on Sundays', something Safi and me ain't exactly got a habit of doing, but we promise to get started on it right away. Mrs Archer-Laing takes a shine to us, 'cause of Safi's grandma being good-living I guess, and says we can have the room, since we're happy sharing it. She's thinking we're sixteen too, 'cause we're both tall, so we're hoping nobody gonna be telling her different.

I ain't happy about leaving my Mambo. Quince is out on our porch slugging from a bottle of strong-smelling liquor wrapped up in newspaper and stinking of crawfish. The parting in his hair has moved to the other side of his head these days, he got his leg cocked up like always, and it seems to me he's looking more smug than any decent man oughta be, seeing young folks outta their own home.

Mambo helps me fold the few clothes I got and ties them up in newspaper. My uniform's already gone back to the mission. I ain't sure how things gonna be in Marksville, so I dig down deep and leave the King of England right there in the soil till I work it out.

'Ya take care now in Marksville. And ya ma wantin' ya back when ya can,' Quince slurs.

I feel his eyes studying us when Mambo and me walk down our path. Pappy's gate don't shut properly since he started kicking at it 'stead of using the latch like everybody else, and I throw him one of my hard looks when it ain't closing behind me.

He shrugs his shoulders like it's none of his business. And he's the one shoving me right outta my own Pappy's cabin.

Mambo's wiping her eyes like the whole business is tearing her up.

'Ya come on back soon honey?'

Her sobbing catches in her throat, so I make out like I'm happy starting out on my own.

'I will Mambo, and I'm gonna help with the baby when it comes. It's gonna work out fine, I'm gonna be earning like ya said. And it's gonna be real nice having a brother or sister of my own.'

'That sure is fine, ain't it honey. We gonna be a family, ain't just us, ya wait and see honey, we gonna be a family. Go on now and get y'self back here to see us just soon as ya's able, y'hear?'

I meet Safi at the bus stop like we said. Ain't too far from her place, so her ma's seeing us both off and she's all cut up about her little Safi leaving home. Seems hard for her to reckon that time come, but she's glad we're both setting off together and able to be looking out for one another.

'Y'all come on back soon, y'hear? We gonna be home here same as always, we ya family and we wanna hear all about how ya gettin' along.'

'Mom, we're only going a few miles down the road, ain't no ways at all. Ain't far to Marksville.'

'Ain't how far ya goin', Safi, it's that ya goin' at all.' Her ma's eyes are filling up. 'When our boys go working on the levees I feel just the same. That's how a mom's gonna feel.'

Safi promises her ma she's gonna be back most weekends, and she's gonna have wages to be helping out. Safi's always thinking of her kin and wants to bring them presents and make it feel like Christmas.

'No, Safi, I ain't wanting ya thinking on taking nothin' back here for nobody.' Safi's ma stands straight up and looks her right square in the face. 'Ya gonna put away every last dime ya earn Safi, if ya's able. That's money ya earn for y'self. Hear? Ya gonna be working hard for it in that mill and I'm wanting y'all to be getting off to one of them night-school classes, learn something and be getting a certificate. That's what y'all need to get on. Them classes. Now I done told ya that already.'

'Yeah Mom. I'm gonna do that.'

'Ya hearing me too Arletta? Because ya gonna do the same thing. Ya get y'self straight on off to night school, both of ya. Ya hear?'

'Okay, we gonna do that, I promise.'

Her ma is dusting down Safi's old frock like it's a right piece of finery 'stead of some cut-down worn-out old pinny.

'Not that I ain't wantin' to see y'all home as much as ya's able – I want my girls home just as often as ya can – but ain't no ways I'm having y'all spending hard-earned wages doin' it. Ain't gonna go spending on no silliness when y'all oughta be getting on with it. Y'all promise me ya gonna get on. Promise me Safi. That's the only thing making my mind easy about ya leaving. Same thing I tell my boys. Ya gotta get on any ways ya can.'

Safi's ma sniffles into her wash-rag then tucks it back into the string tied around her waist.

'Don't go getting tied up with chile like me. Ya gonna get work in some kinda office one day, ya gonna see. Something clean, and then ya gonna get nice young men fit for taking good care of y'all. So make dammit sure ya get a little saving put aside. Get certificates at something, and go get a good set of clothes. Just make something outta life, like I'm saying.'

'I will Mom.' Safi is wiping her own tears now.

'And that goes for Arletta too. Ain't no stopping a girl like ya. That's for sure chile, that's clear as day to all us folks. Time's coming. Times gonna be changing, Safi, and young folks like y'all need to be ready for it.'

Safi hugs her ma tight, they're both weeping right out loud 'cause the bus is already honking and if we don't get on board it's gonna be outta here without us on it. Ma smacks a long kiss on Safi's forehead and breathes real deep, like she's smelling her daughter for the very last time.

'I love ya Safi, and I want ya go make something of ya life for me. That's what's gonna make me happy. I wanna say my daughter is working in an office 'stead of cleaning boots and scrubbing pans for white folks. Arletta, ya's well able. Go on now. I love y'all, and go get on. Go on now.'

I wish Mambo thought about coming to see me off too. Watching Safi and her ma is making me miss my Mambo already.

It don't seem right. Quince left right there rocking on Pappy's porch and me off on the bus to Marksville. I hope he cares something about my Mambo, 'cause he sure don't care nothing about me, and I'm her flesh and blood. I don't know what Pappy would have said about it, but I reckon even Grandma would have put the back of her hand on Mambo for packing me off before I got to be fifteen years of age. Even school says I oughta be staying on 'cause I'm doing well and right at the top end of their marking.

Safi gets so upset about leaving her folks that I just ain't gonna think on it no more. I set myself on being strong for both of us, but driving down that road I ain't able to drag my mind from Pappy's old cabin and how he fixed it up for his own kin to be living in.

Mrs Dolly Archer-Laing seems like a nice little English lady, still kinda good-looking for a widow, I guess, and right well turned out. She ain't got a hair outta place neither, it's pulled tight back and done up with as neat a bow as I've ever seen in my life. She's got two black guard dogs in the yard and they howl like nobody's business when we pull her bell-chain.

I ain't ever seen a place like that house, and Safi sure ain't neither, 'cause we ain't never been into Marksville before last week, and then we only come as far as the mill on the outside of town. That house has two floors and shades they call awnings up above windows fitted with glass, and wooden shutters. Like they gonna be needing both, and we ain't seeing no reason for it. It's done up all over in yellow paint, with red round the windows and the roof. Her railings are painted blue and it sure is 'mighty colourful', as Pappy would have said.

'Errol? Errol, the gate please.'

Mrs Archer-Laing's got a right funny way with that voice of hers. Ain't easy getting a grip on it 'cause of her being from England and all. She's got education, that's for sure. That's written up all over her.

Errol shuffles up and opens the gate with a bunch of keys near big enough for keeling him over. Safi and me hold hands and give them black dogs plenty space.

'Come in girls. Do.'

Do what? Ain't rightly sure.

'Errol, these are our new boarders, Safi Sucree and Arletta Johnson.'

Well, by now we sure ain't got no clue about what the right thing to do is at all, so we just give a little curtsey, polite-like, and Errol's eyebrows raise right up at it. He's the quiet type, that's plain as day already. Must be the help that does round the place.

That house always smelled like church wax. Safi's nose takes to wriggling 'cause that gonna make her feel like she's living in the mission, but I was right fond of being at the mission, and that smell puts me in mind of Pappy's Bible.

'This is my front parlour, the one I use myself. I'll show you the one you can use later on. It's at the back of the house, so it gets the long afternoon sun. I prefer the shade myself.'

We can use a parlour?

We don't know what a parlour is; ain't clear what it's for, neither. It's got one big set of shelving holding fine china and fancy dishes on one side of the room, and them chairs of hers got so much stuffing, and cushions and lace hanging all over them, I get to thinking folks must need permission to sit down. Not that we're thinking on getting that, so we just hug up the wall like we ain't supposed to be there at all. Ain't clear why that room needs so many lamps. There's three of them and all got fancy shades. Like Mrs Archer-Laing is wanting light but then goes halfways changing her mind on getting it. It don't make no sense why she's gonna be fixing up a fine lamp just for hiding half the light under a fancy shade, so then she's gonna go needing another one.

Don't make no sense.

We follow Mrs Archer-Laing outta her parlour to what she calls the hall. It's twice the size of our cabin and that set of stairs sure must take some polishing. It's dark and shiny and looking like we's the first living folk ever to lay a foot on it.

'Please always use this bathroom. Mine is the one on the ground floor. I confess, like everybody else, we have problems with the water supply and the pump, so there is a tap in the yard for when that happens. The water truck is hardly reliable, so we just make the best of it.'

We got a bathroom? A tap in the yard? Me and Safi never figured on this kinda style at all, so I check she knows the little we gonna be earning and paying.

'Yes dear. Now, please take the water up yourself if there's not sufficient for the pump to operate. I won't have Errol exhausting himself up and down stairs too much. I won't have young ladies attending to private business out in the yard, either. Whenever there's a problem, please take sufficient water up to this bathroom, or to your room, and please do perform your daily ablutions in private, as befitting young ladies.'

We gonna need a dictionary.

'You do, of course, have a chamber pot. I will see to it that you have two, one each.'

Then we gonna figure out what for.

She's got three rooms and a 'landing' big as her parlour on the top floor, 'underneath the eaves', she calls it, and all of them painted white. That keeps them cool and airy, she says. We're gonna be sharing the bathroom with Agnes Withers, that's Mrs Archer-Laing's other boarder in the back room, and we got eyes near popping outta our heads at the sight of that white bowl and 'flushable chain'. There's a brass tap straight over the washbasin and clean towels folded up neat, except for the one hanging on a rail, must be for Agnes Withers. The tin tub's got a big jug for filling up and a plug in the middle for letting water out through a pipe in the floor. Errol calls that plumbing, and I know about that 'cause folks round our way are sick and tired of shouting for it and nobody ever paying no mind.

Mrs Archer-Laing says Agnes Withers has got the big room and we sure are wondering how big it is when she shows us where we're gonna be boarding.

'You can decide between you who gets the proper bed for the time being. I've put up the small camp bed until the other one arrives; I have ordered it for you. But there are the two wardrobes, and the water basin and jug over there in the corner. I have some dressers in the basement. You can choose which one is suitable; Errol will arrange for them to be brought up, of course. He arranged to have the small sofa brought up for you to make the room cosy. I thought it was a good idea. Don't you?'

'Yes,' Safi and me say so at the same time.

'This is the laundry basket. We change the sheets once a week, I insist on it, and you must take the basket down yourselves every Saturday morning. First thing, please. I like you to have all your washing done on a Saturday. The Sabbath day is our day of rest and worship. You must arrange to do all the cleaning yourselves. I don't think it gracious that Errol is in and out of young ladies' private chambers. I'm sure you agree.'

We nod. Ain't sure what about.

'I don't use what's in the basement, so you're welcome to arrange to have anything else taken up.'

She speaks about arranging like she's thinking we gonna know how to go about doing it. Sounds like she ain't sure how things get done round here at all. I guess, as long as things get done, folks like her don't pay it no mind.

'So that seems to be it for up here. Let me know when the rest of your things are arriving so we can arrange with Errol to let them in. It's best to be careful about security. Remember that, girls.'

We just nod. All we got in this world is wrapped up in newspaper, tied with string and tucked under our arms.

'Come along now, girls. Let me show you to the guests' parlour.'

Safi grabs my newspaper packet and throws it on the bed 'longside her own.

I ain't never been in a place like that house, with all them rooms and windows and two sofas in what she's calling our parlour. They're a little worn out, but there ain't no horsehair sticking out, and I'm real happy with all them books stuffing up the shelves. First proper thing I says is, 'I'm gonna read all them books if we's able to, Miss.'

'Of course, Arletta. That is why the bookcases are here. I take it you like reading.'

'Sure do, Miss. I love reading and if y'all don't mind ...'

'Of course not, Arletta. The books are here to be read.'

Out back is built in a U-shape round what she's calling her courtyard. Across the ways from our parlour is a kitchen like I've never seen, and the first I've ever seen inside a house, though I sure ain't been in any of those, as I recall. She's got that many plants growing in pots in that courtyard, the place looks just like out back of our cabin.

'I do breakfast for you myself.'

That's when Safi's jaw drops about as far as I ever seen it. Ain't nobody ever hear of no whites 'do breakfast' for us black folks.

'I don't do a cooked breakfast, actually. I organize it in the evening before I go to bed and set the table out for the morning. You help yourself from the refrigerator and in the evening Errol prepares dinner. You'll find he's an excellent cook. If you want lunch then it's extra, and you must arrange it in advance with him directly. Of course, you must also pay him directly for it.'

She waves her hand like taking money for lunch is right beneath her.

'How we pay ya, Miss? I mean, for our board and all?' I ain't rightly sure who we gonna be paying and arranging what for.

'I'd like to see you at the end of each week for a little chat. I'm sure Saturdays will be fine?'

'We gonna be working right up till twelve o'clock. We got all day Sunday off. Well, except for church ...'

'Meet me in my parlour at one o'clock on Saturday afternoon for a nice chat, then, and you can tell me all about your first week at the mill.'

She smiles and leaves us right there on our own.

'Ya okay, Arletta?'

'She sure ain't like no white folk I ever seen.'

Before we left, Safi's grandma told us Mrs Archer-Laing was real nice and kind, and gonna be looking out for us. Said she was right godly, but of course I ain't really got the hang of that. Pappy was godly, but he ain't never have nothing.

I reckon we're lucky she was looking for boarders same time we needing it. And I'm reckoning she's gotta be big on church and needing to be kind with all this house and stuff. That got me thinking what it must be like to find y'self able to be kind to strangers just walking on in outta nowhere.

'Don't see why not,' says Safi. 'That's godly, Arletta, being kind to strangers. And she's got a refrigerator.'

I ain't never heard the word.

The mill is just about a mile away from where we're boarding on Main Street, and they have more folks crammed up inside that barn of a place than I've ever seen in my days, and all of them busy working, shouting and moving about like taking it easy gone out of fashion.

The place is full of so much folks and noise, we just stand by the door till somebody comes to tell us we s'posed to be reporting to the foreman, and he's that man sitting on a high stool halfway down the mill. He hardly looks our way at all, just pulls a face when he sees we can sign up for ourselves. Then he sends us off with somebody else who says he ain't got no time for telling us twice, so we gotta make sure we listen up good first time about what we getting paid for.

We're put at what he calls the 'end of the line' and told we're lucky to be packing bales ready for taking down South and shipping overseas.

'There's a pile goin' overseas right now, but they got a mill down South too, so y'all need to be paying attention on what goes where. Ya got that?'

We nod, but truth is, we ain't making no sense of it.

'Then what don't go down South goes over the state line for Dockery, but that don't go through the cotton gin, that go straight off. Packing that ain't easy; y'all come up lucky and get one of the best jobs. Ain't messy like far end, neither. Them's got machines creakin' and turnin' and makin' noise, and we already get one boy catch himself in the axle shaft. He lose half his arm and half his wage for soilin' the cotton with his own bleeding, but ya gonna be fine here. Ya both gotta wear these, and this is ya station. Station M: y'all remember ya station. Station M, right?'

'Right.'

He hands us thick cotton aprons and I ain't sure I'm gonna bear all that heat from head to toe, and with all that noise going on. He shouts like a horn over it, telling us where we gotta start and what we gotta do. Then he's off and we're left trying to work it out for ourselves. It don't go too well with us fumbling about with them needles big as spoons and bales piling up for stitching. We ain't getting the hang of it at all, so them bales start piling up till there ain't no room left for more. Then a boy, looking like he ain't more than ten years old, comes to sort us out.

'Ain't go lettin' thems pile up nah. Dey's gotta be outta here right off. Gimme dat needle an' I gonna get dem movin' on, and den ya's on ya own.'

'We ain't sure about nothing, we just get started.'

'Well, I start same way an' ya gotta get shaped up nah, or ya goin' get dragged on over to Li'l Skivvy on account dem bales ain't outta here.'

'Who's Li'l Skivvy? He that foreman?'

'Nah, de foreman okay. He ain't say much, and what he say, he says wi' that cane a his.'

'Ya saying he gonna cane us?'

'Jus' a pokin', ain't hurt nothin'. Nah, Li'l Skivvy de badass round here, an' ya goin' know when y'all come up 'gin him. I's called Chester, an' I start on darnin' 'em bales too. I'm on loadin' now an' we jus' 'bout got none left fo' loadin' on de wagon, an' y'all don't want Li'l Skivvy findin' out we's idle 'cause a y'all ain't darnin' and stampin'. Nah. Us neither.'

'We just ain't sure what we s'posed to do.'

'And we ain't hear half of what he said in all this noise.'

'Look, I show y'all one time an' it gotta be quick. Grab a bale like dis, okay? An' roll 'em edges round like dis, tuck 'em edges in. See? Den get a hold on it an' stitch up tight. Y'all gotta be quick 'bout it. Ain't always busy, but when it like dis, ya need a keep 'em movin' fo' us loadin'.'

Chester sure can chatter, but we listen up good.

'Some dem bales goin' to a mill down South. Wi' a waterwheel an' cotton press, I seen it, an' folks waitin' on us a keep 'em busy wi' sendin'. Ain't worth forgettin' dat, we gotta keep 'em all busy. We load a wagon, wagon load a train an' off South wi' it. Rest get shipped out. See? Roll 'em edges and get darnin'.'

Chester slips back outside before Li'l Skivvy catches him, and we're left struggling with the big curved needles and the hairy string tough enough to cut through flesh. We start rolling the burlap edges over, but it ain't as easy as Chester made it look. Then we get the stitching in place so the cotton don't fall out before it reaches where it's going. Sure is tricky, with keeping the cotton in as well. We gotta work fast, 'cause them bales keep coming and we need to be watching out in case folks see them piling up. Then they all get stamped with black paint saying 'Export' or 'Homeland', and we hope we get that right too, 'cause we gone forgetting what line is what. Every fingernail I got is broken on the rolling and I don't know how many times them needles stab into my flesh with all the rushing. But the bales start moving out and we're glad about that.

I'm just about feeling my back is gonna break when a hooter goes off and I near jump outta my own skin. Everbody files out, ain't no orderly fashion to it. The foreman gets down off his high stool and walks about pointing his cane like anything he can reach is descrving of a poke. He don't come our way and that's fine 'cause he's walking about with a skinny weasel we hear folks say is Li'l Skivvy, and he don't look wholesome. He's asking questions and taking notes and we just know, like Chester says, he ain't somebody we gonna be getting on the wrong side of neither.

Li'l Skivvy is making sure folks ain't smoking their baccy near the mill and bales of cotton. Women smoking it same as men. Even with them dirty aprons and hair wrapped up in old cotton rags ya can see they's all thinking high on themselves and making eyes at menfolk. Later on, back in our boarding room, we gonna be copying how they get on, how they take in smoke and hold them long, long breaths. They're passing round a pot of bright-red lip colouring that makes their teeth look whiter than Mambo's.

'Ever hear of outer space, Safi?'

'Course I has.'

'Well, them's all like they come from outer space.'

'Might be, 'cause ain't nothing in they heads but smoke.'

The way them womenfolk talk seems they mean that whole yard need to be hearing about the weekend just past. Next one coming gets spoke about like they don't have no care at all and don't know nothing about having private business and keeping stuff to themselves. They don't notice us at all; we're feeling lost anyways. Then the hooter goes off again and we're back at our M Station finishing bales bulging out with cotton.

First thing I do with my rushing is drive that needle deep into my own flesh. Safi runs off for Chester.

'One ting dem go crazy 'bout is ya gettin' blood all over de cotton, so ya ain't never let that happen nah. Get on stampin' 'fore y'all get Li'l Skivvy dockin' wages. I seen him dock a man dat much he ain't got nothin' a feed his kids fo' a week an' we's all feedin' 'em fo' him. Ain't right nah.'

The new sacking already has dark stains where it soaked up my blood, so Chester heaves it over, stamps 'Export' to cover it up and tumbles it onto the trolley for moving out. He winks and takes off with it for loading.

I leave Safi on sewing bales and get on stamping for the rest of the day. Every bale we finish needs to be hauled onto a trolley for wheeling out to loading. That's man's work for sure, but we gotta do it. We jam the trolley up in the waiting pile of bales and Safi holds it steady. I push with all the might I got till each bale topples onto the tray and then we roll the trolley out for Chester and his pals loading the wagon.

That day feels like it's gonna just last for ever. One bale is done, then another, and another. Ain't no let-up. Safi lets tears go and even though I'm feeling the same way, I hold back. Ain't no point two of us bawling like babies.

At the end of our first day of working, Errol hands Safi a cloth for drying her eyes.

'Have yersel' a good nose-blow now. Day gone, sun down on it. Ain't never gonna be bad as that again.'

He serves up stuffed crab and boiled shrimp with rice and turnip greens just like Pappy's. Then we fall asleep, tired out like drains. Been one hard day, but we got full bellies.

We try signing up for shorthand and typing evening class. We get told they have a waiting list but we're thinking that ain't right, 'cause all the girls we see in there are white. We're just on our way out, I'm feeling kinda mad, when one of them girls' ma comes straight over and spits on the side of my face.

'Niggers need to be staying behind whites and oughta know that's their place.'

We walk back to our boarding room, ain't no word spoke.

When we tell Mrs Archer-Laing on Saturday, sitting right there in one of them fancy chairs, she takes off her hat and gloves. She says she's gonna see somebody at the Presbyterian church, and then the National Association for the Advancement of Colored People – that's something else we ain't never hear of.

A couple of weeks later they find us space to learn office work inside a crowded church hall where girls are able to go twice a week in the evening with no charge at all for it. Seems that crazy old bat of a white ma did us 'niggers' a favour, because now it ain't costing us a dime, and Mrs Archer-Laing is right proud about it.

Safi goes for all that learning shorthand, she takes ready to it, but it ain't holding me at all. I start thinking about what else they might be teaching down at those college evening classes and how I'm gonna go about getting in there. I start my daydreaming again, about getting a certificate in English, and what it would be like teaching it, like Pappy did. That's the best teaching I ever got. It's just a dream, I guess, and, like Mambo says, I ain't got no business dreaming.

Truth is, I don't feel inclined to be going off on my own and learning in a room full of strangers without Safi. We been doing stuff together ever since she got me on scotch at school and I took to helping her with lessons and chores. I stay put because she's so keen on it, but I know there ain't no way I see me sitting with folks like Mr McIntyre and Mr Seymour, taking notes and looking after their business. Can't see me doing those folks' bidding at all. I guess I'm more like Mambo than I ever thought. Anyways, I feel glad we got a place learning something, and if I bide my time, that gonna lead to something else. That's what learning's like.

Except for Saturdays, soon as we finish our time at the mill, and taking us to church on Sunday, Mrs Archer-Laing keeps herself to herself. That's the way Errol puts it. And we don't see much of Agnes Withers, neither. Errol says she's what he calls 'a loner'.

'Them type ain't gonna be mixing. Since she come here, she ain't mixing. Just that sorta girl.'

Across the courtyard, other end of Errol's kitchen, Mrs Archer-Laing's got a room she works in every weekday on sewing she takes in from folks. She's a 'Fine Seamstress' it says on the board next to that bell-chain out front by her gate. She sure can work up a rhythm on that treadle when she's flat out and, boy, is she good with a needle, fixing up smart suits of fine cloth like we ain't never seen.

I've already started on all them books she got in our parlour. Them's mostly what they call classics. I learn that later of course, right then there ain't none I ever hear of, except Mark Twain, and he sure did write a classic. R.L. Stevenson, Sir Walter Scott, Victor Hugo, Edgar Allan Poe and Henry James. I'm gonna work my way through them all. I already read *The Adventures of Tom Sawyer* from our travelling book wagon and I ain't got no preference on them others, so I start up in the left corner, reading *What Maisie Knew* by Henry James.

That leaves me thinking I'm lucky I just ever gotta deal with my Mambo and her beaux, because Maisie's ma and pa sure were all over the place and that had her stuck right in the middle of them both. Ain't right, but she turn out fine. I curl up my worn-out mill bones in the parlour every night till it's done and I'm nodding off. Next book I read is *Treasure Island* – that got me up late another few nights, then *Kidnapp*ed, then *Les Misérables* (that so full of rambling, I reckon I get two for one) and a real fine set of short stories with drawings by Edgar Allan Poe. I finish *Uncle Tom's Cabin* and turn right back to read it again. Second time round is easier, too. And I cry tears on my own reading about Celia, a slave, and how she buried her master in the hearth 'cause of all his doing to her that she ain't able to take no more. Well, I know just how she was feeling, and I'm glad I never said a word to anybody about what I did to Seymour, 'cause she ended up swinging.

Course, I'm nearly falling asleep at the mill, and I lose count on how many times that needle poke itself sore into my flesh, drawing blood. Me and Safi keep rags just for soaking it up and wash them every Saturday out back of our yard. She gets a better hold on stitching than I ever do and most of that blood is mine. She keeps me awake at work too and tells me to leave off reading or I'm gonna be outta there.

'Ya give it a rest, y'hear, or we gonna get hauled up by Li'l Skivvy. I seen him looking our way already, and y'all slacking off with that head full of nothing but reading. He don't wanna be knowing nothing about no reading, so leave it be.'

If I'm caught slacking we're both gonna be for it, that's for sure, and Safi don't deserve no trouble. I need to be keeping her company more anyways, so we start getting out in the evening, watching folks going about their business in Marksville, or walking over to the mill village where stuff's always going on. Over there's what folks call lively. Safi's keen on being out among folks; she's from a big family anyways, so down that way suits her fine, but I'm always thinking about what I could be curled up reading instead.

When we find a run-down hardware store at the far end of Marksville selling all kinds of second-hand stuff and giving away all sorts of pamphlets, on a wobbly old trestle table resting out on the sidewalk, Safi takes off right away.

'Oh no, I'm gonna leave ya right here with all that rubbish, Arletta. Meet me when ya good and done at Coco Corner, about half an hour? I ain't wanting no books on my day off! I'm gone.'

I hand over a few of my hard-earned cents to buy a big old battered atlas from a table so shaky it near falls over soon as I pick the atlas up. That table's only holding up 'cause the store boy tied it up with string, and I'm glad he did the same with my atlas. His boss – I guess that's who he is – catches me fingering a few old shabby pamphlets from the start-up days of the abolitionists and he says them's free. I ain't ever had cause for buying much of anything, and I reckon maybe he can see that. He throws in a pamphlet on the war going on in Europe and tells me I oughta be reading up on all them folks perishing in trenches. He bundles them all up with the atlas and I feel about as happy as I've ever been with anything, till I catch up with Safi at Coco Corner.

She's all over the place on account of some white man ordering her off the sidewalk so his kids can see niggers know they need to be making way for white folks.

'Well, I stood my ground just as long as I'm able to, Arletta, and he gets red as hellfire in the face on it.'

'Ya did right.'

'He gets on, huffing and puffing, with folks turning round to see what's happening. Well, I think I need to be stepping aside for fear them poor kids gonna end up one parent short of a pair, 'cause somebody's gonna start a fight or he's gonna give himself a heart attack.'

She sure is mad now, though, for giving up her ground, but she couldn't stand looking at them kids getting lessons on thinking the same way as their pa. The way I see it, they gotta be thinking that way already. Ain't right, but that's how it is. Folks wanting a change to come but sometimes I ain't so sure on seeing it coming at all.

Mrs Archer-Laing is entertaining a gentleman she calls Monsieur Desnoyers from Quebec. He's passing notice on every move she makes, so it looks to me like he's taken a shine to her.

She sees my tied-up bundle from the trestle table and reckons I've read my way through the whole bookcase in our back parlour already.

'Oh no, Miss, not yet.' Then I think about Mambo always telling me I ain't to be using up oil for reading after dark. 'I'm using up lamp oil, I knows it, but I'm gonna pay for it, Mrs Archer-Laing. I will. Just say what I got owing.'

Safi looks like she's wondering what I got be paying up with.

'Don't be silly, Arletta. You read as much as you like, my dear. Next Saturday I'll let you have a look through the other books. Mr Archer-Laing was an avid reader, you know. There's an old trunk in the basement you could ask Errol to arrange to be brought up to your room to store your books in if you like. Safi wouldn't mind that, would you?'

I like the sound of that trunk, but Safi don't understand books at all.

'Why ya saying ya gonna be paying for reading, Arletta? Ya wanna be doing scrubbing so ya can be doing reading?'

I guess I was thinking of pulling one of them dollar bills outta the King of England back at Mambo's, but I ain't saying nothing. Matter of fact, I need to be fetching him up out of the ground anyways. We been here in Marksville for months and he ain't got no place being someplace I ain't.

The mill workers say they wanna be holding what they call a 'social' for Christmas coming up, and folks sure do get excited about it, except of course all them bosses strutting about, and Li'l Skivvy. They say the mill ain't no place for it, and it gotta be down in the mill village. Folks say there ain't no room down there for no social and Chester comes to tell us we gotta work slow.

Li'l Skivvy gets mad and hauls a couple of men up to see the foreman, and that puts an end to working altogether. The whole place gathers round to look up through the windows of the office on the gantry. Nothing comes of it, can't say I rightly follow it all, but next thing we hear is that 'social' is set for holding inside one of them empty mill barns and everybody is right cheery about it. Anybody able to get a tune outta anything gets asked if they wanna play and we get told we can bring one guest each. Well, me and Safi ain't got nobody except Agnes, ain't no surprise when she says no, and Errol laughs into his chest and says 'social's for young folks'.

Our wages don't go far past our board and lodgings and the few cents I spend on what Safi calls 'old rubbish' for reading. She gets on back to her folks more than me, 'cause I still ain't taken to spending any of my time watching Quince rocking out on my porch in my Pappy's chair. Safi always leaves something where her ma is able to find it after she's gone, 'cause her ma's got pride and don't take nothing put straight in her hand. And with her still on about saving, Safi gets an earful next time she goes home too. By the time that mill social comes round, we ain't got much set aside and it's plain as day, looking through our closet, that we're both in need of something. All we got hanging in that wardrobe Mrs Archer-Laing was thinking we were gonna fill are worn-out frocks maybe one day showed some kinda pattern, way faded out before we ever seen it.

All them young ladies at the mill gonna put us to shame if we don't do something about our lack of finery. We ain't no laughing stock, and I been thankful nobody's called me Po'bean, but we sure would be struggling to put on any kinda show for a social. Me and Safi ain't ever buy a stitch of clothes in our lives, we're still washing and wearing, and don't know where to start on it. We move our sofa over to the window to see what's going on up and down Main Street while we talk over the ins and outs of purchasing new clothes.

We tell Mrs Archer-Laing we gotta be cutting short our Saturday chat for trawling through Marksville and Mansura looking at frocks ain't no way we're able to afford. Then one shop door is slammed shut as soon as we get spotted looking through the window, and we just about give up on it. A 'No coloreds' sign flips over, so we take off for the bus station and the row of seating set aside for us 'coloreds'. A bunch of young men dancing with nails in their shoes and folks 'da-da-dadding' out a tune soon lifts our spirits except, truth be told, by now buying clothes for a social is starting to seem flighty.

Looking at the state of our frocks gets us back to it, but all we got by late that afternoon are a pair of canvas slip-ons with shiny black buttons and a pink hair band each. I see right away the boy selling slip-ons takes a shine to Safi. I catch him setting his eyes on her sideways, and she starts fussing and flushing all over. They end up smiling and giggling at one another like a fine pair of clowns.

With the price of everything, we start worrying we ain't gonna have nothing fit for a social at all. Then, in the nick of time, as folks say, and just when they's already starting to pack up, we see something on one of them nickel-and-dime stalls in the market. Something we're able to afford, anyways. We get ourselves a brand new shift made outta thin cotton each, and that's the first stitch of clothes me and Safi ever wore that never got handed down from someplace. Safi gets a pink one that matches her hair band and I have to get a lemon one because of how tall I'm growing, it looks like it's the only one gonna fit. We're about as happy as we ever been and laughing over how that lemon frock is gonna clash with my pink hair band. Buying new clothes sure feels good, like we ain't got a care in the world. Errol feeds us rabbit stew and yellow corn biscuits he's been keeping warm for us. Tastes fine.

Soon as our bellies are full, we wash down in the tub and put on our new cotton frocks. With our new hair bands and slip-ons we look like we're gonna pass fit for that social. Safi says she's gonna buy a lipstick.

'Ain't nobody buying them card pots, they're outta fashion. Colouring comes in a stick now. I see them sirens with lipsticks.'

That's what we call all them young ladies at the mill since I started my classic reading from the bookcase.

She pretends she's pasting a stick of coloured grease on her lips and we end up sore with laughing, thinking we're young ladies.

'Ya gonna be smokin' next Safi. I can see ya gonna be just like one of them sirens.'

'Sure will be. I'm gonna be smoking cigarettes just like this. Look.'

Safi walks the floor with a wiggle Mambo's gonna be right proud of. Reckon that's where she got it from.

Right then I catch myself in the mirror. Mambo's always telling me how I grew up pretty and don't even know it. She's keen on saying we're like two peas in a pod too, so I ain't ever been sure about wanting to know it. This is the first time I see a mirror say she's right. I ain't ever seen it before now, so I reckon lemon got to be my colour. By the time Safi buys that lipstick she sure is gonna be doing something for men with that wiggle of hers too. Wiggling works fine on men. But I get my head outta that mirror fast on account of feeling like I'm gonna pass right out. I ain't wanting no pretty face telling no men it's fine to come at me for nothing. No way. I've had enough of men to last me a lifetime.

'Hush ya mind chile, with that thinking, ya's the one gonna be all right. Hush now.'

'Nellie?'

'Hush chile. It's gonna be all right.'

'What ya say?' Safi is still pretending she's blowing siren smoke and tossing her head like she's been doing it all the days of her life. I'd go as far as to say she's a natural.

'Nothing. Ain't nothing ...'

'Who's Nellie, then?'

'That's one of them sirens. Ya put me in mind of her, ya just like her, Safi.'

I ain't heard Nellie's voice since I don't know when and I'm wondering why I'm hearing it now, even if it's just a whispering. But she says I'm gonna be all right and that takes the fear of looking fine right outta me. I got my strength and I used it good. If I need to be using it again, well, that ain't gonna be nothing.

'I hope that Nellie is getting ready for the competition,' Safi says. 'Look at us. Heads gonna turn, Arletta.'

'They sure will if ya get a hold of that lipstick.'

'Uh huh. And ya gonna be the prettiest picture there wearing it too Arletta.'

I ain't.

Errol hires a cart and takes Mrs Archer-Laing with her big suitcase all the way to the new depot in Plaquemine. She's off visiting her kin, and he ain't happy she's gonna be sailing the ocean in winter when war's getting worse in Europe. We hear all the menfolk over there been called up for fighting and ain't much chance of them getting home again neither. He's back in time for serving crusty meat pie with fried beans and onion. Our evening class breaks up for Christmas and that old trunk gets hauled upstairs outta Mrs Archer-Laing's basement so my growing heap of printed pamphlets and shabby books have someplace Safi ain't falling over them and cussing. Soon as I see it's got a padlock, I set my mind on bringing the King of England to Marksville.

We find out what a social is all about. Music plays on and on, and me and Safi learn dancing alongside them sirens till my feet sure are worn out and it's long past midnight. Ain't nobody wait to be asked up for dancing like Mrs Archer-Laing said it was gonna be like at all. Nobody knows who's dancing with who half the time, and it don't seem to matter neither.

Everybody is talking about jazz and the fresh-faced happy jailbird up from New Orleans playing trumpet on the makeshift stage Chester and his pals fixed up. Gossip says that trumpet player's got a ma working as a prostitute down in Storyville, and even though he sure is tiny and I'm just about the tallest girl in the place, he's got the happiest smile I've ever seen and he keeps it looking my way half the night. I smile back like we're long-lost pals 'cause dancing sure does make me feel nice. I'm hoping it don't have me looking like I'm foolish too. Chester does a fine turn with his nailed boots, I reckon he's full of liquor, and I find out why my own Mambo was gadding off to have herself a good time when she was just about my age.

The mill shuts down for Christmas after that, so me and Safi get on home to our folks.

We get off the bus and I see Madame Bonnet must be visiting Mambo. Ain't nobody else gonna be out this way in a brand new crimson velvet trap looking about as out of place as any damn thing could. Tout de suite is looking mighty pleased with himself, and wearing a smart new tunic.

'Braiding and epaulettes, Miss Arletta. That's what they call these. Epaulettes.'

He looks fine, real smart, and I tell him so.

'*Bien. Merci beaucoup*, Miss Arletta, you a fine sight too. Good to see you 'ome.'

'Stop calling me Miss Arletta. I ain't no Miss.'

Madame Bonnet has a broom out on our porch and dust is flying all over the place. That's enough to tell me something ain't right. Mambo's right fussy who touches her broom on account of it being what she uses for pointing at folks and pounding the earth up at Lamper Ridge mule barn.

'What's happened Madame? Mambo okay?'

'Arletta? *Mon dieu. Viens, un plaisir* seein' you 'ome, *ma chérie. Bon.* You come. Mambo need *la joie, le bon mot. Elle est très fatiguée avec l'enfant. L'enfant* come soon. You help, *non?*'

Madame's brushing out our cabin best she can I s'pose, but it's easy to see she gotta be better at something else to get her that brand new fancy trap, because dust is flying up one minute and falling back down the next. Looks like Mambo ain't doing so good since it's near her time, she's all sour-faced and droopy-eyed. Don't seem like my Mambo at all. Soon as Madame takes her leave, I get down to proper cleaning and cheering Mambo up.

'Mambo, I been thinking ya oughta paint this cabin.' All that newspaper's been up so long it's turned yellow and peeling off all over. It don't feel much like Pappy's cabin these days and now Quince is living there and got work, he oughta be putting something aside for doing stuff round the place. Ain't right he don't seem to be doing nothing at all.

I tell Mambo all about our shopping in Marksville and dancing at the social because I'm trying to get her spirits up. Must say I get a little smile outta her when I tell her about the trumpet player smiling at me in my lemon frock all night.

'Ya ain't gonna have no trouble getting hold of men honey. I'm sure as hell there wasn't anybody inside that place looking like ya, and he got sense enough to see it.' Her voice sounds like it's hard to get the words up out of her throat. 'Ya mind ya find a good one though, 'cause that's all ya needing.'

That sure makes me wonder why she chose Quince. It's clear he ain't no kinda help and Mambo all borne down with child. Our cabin ain't looking good and clean at all, like Mambo's always been fussy about, and our land looks like it ain't been touched since I was back the last time. I reckon the place ain't kept proper since I left. Ain't right, and sure don't seem like my Mambo.

I reach Mambo's broom up into the grey cobweb hanging from the rafters above her bed. Never seen cobwebs up there before now. Mambo lifts her belly outta the rocking chair on the porch, saying she wants to come in and lie down.

'Can't be much longer, Mambo, the baby coming.'

'Feels like anytime.'

'Well, it look like it oughta been last week.'

Something shifts out of the rafters. Looks like a chicken wishbone bound up with red twine and a small wrap of leaves hanging from it. The leaves split apart and a dark red powder is spread all over Mambo's bed. It's a voodoo fetish and it ain't one of my Mambo's.

Next thing I know, Mambo is screaming like she's gone lost her mind. Her eyes are sticking way outta her head and she's yelling like she wants all of Avoyelles parish knowing about it.

'Get it out! Get it out of here!' Mambo is clawing at her throat like she's sucked in some of that powder and it's burning. 'Out! Out!'

I pick the fetish up and throw it out the window. I ain't ever seen Mambo scared of anything.

'It's gone, Mambo. I threw it out. Stop yelling.'

She's gasping for breath and down on her knees. I'm fearful for that child she's carrying.

'Mambo! Stop it! This stuff's only gonna work if you let it!'

'You don't know. You ain't never know nothing about it girl.' Her voice is raspy, it don't sound like her at all, and she's looking like she's gonna be falling into one of her trances it ain't ever possible to get her out of. I shake her hard on account of that child in her belly. She's looking like the spirits are taking her over and I know for sure if that child gets to thinking it's coming now, we're all gonna be in a heap of trouble.

'Help me. Please help me, Arletta.'

'How Mambo? I ain't know nothing about it!'

'Open the closet. Here, take the key.' She fumbles round her neck and I help her get the key to Pappy's closet. She ain't ever keep that key round her neck before now, but I guess that's because she was sure of one thing. I was never gonna touch it.

I open Pappy's closet, first time I seen inside that since he's gone. It sure is orderly, like I'd expect from my Mambo, and filled to busting with dried leaves, roots and berries, powders in old tins, and all kinds of strange shapes I'm thinking I don't want to be knowing about. One box is flowing over with coloured ribbons, some old and faded from Grandma's time. Most of all I notice Pappy's closet has a Mambo smell that stayed with me every day of my life till I left our cabin.

'Quickly, Arletta.'

'What do I do? What ya want?'

'Bottle … white bottle, the small one, second shelf. Quickly, Arletta.'

It looks like she's gonna stop breathing.

There's several white bottles; I pick up the smallest.

'Bring it.' Mambo clutches it tight to her chest. 'Hog hair – get me hog hair.'

I fumble where she's pointing and bring the hog hair in a black wrapping I probably painted myself. She's down on all fours and gasping for breath, telling me to get outside for a big leaf. I do as I'm told and she empties black powder from the bottle and folds the leaf up; she's gasping for breath all the time. Then she pierces it through with hog hair so it stays put.

'Cotton, any cotton. Hurry!'

I grab the box of cotton reels. Mambo, quick as a lightning strike, binds the leaf up and makes a loop at the end. When that loop is strung round her neck, she holds the leaf tight in to her chest. Her breathing gets slow and deep and normal.

'Oh Lord, child. Oh Lord.' Mambo leans against the wall wiping sweat from her neck with the hem of her frock.

'Mambo, what happened?'

'It's a curse, somebody's cursed me, Arletta. Ain't no wonder I been feeling so bad. I should have guessed it, I should know, I sure should, but it got me. This is bad stuff and it got me. First time.'

'Mambo, don't go talking that kinda nonsense. This ain't real. Ya let all this happen, this is just something ya let happen. Ain't real stuff.'

She ain't listening. She raises herself up from the floor and I see the old anger flash across her face. I see that old Mambo look of hers fill her right up till she stands straight. She was stiff with fear a few seconds back, now I'm starting to feel kinda sorry for whoever it is thinking they were gonna put that wishbone up in Mambo's rafters and get away with it. Seems to me only Quince ever gonna get the chance to do that, so I reckon I been right about him all along. She's gonna find him out good and I sure am glad about that.

'Arletta – y'all go on doing as ya see and please. I'm gonna go on doing as I see and please. Some damn *vaudoux* got in here and bring me a heap of trouble. Right here in my own cabin.'

'Maybe Quince …'

'Don't be stupid, Arletta. He ain't got no clue about nothing of it. He good for one thing, and one thing only is all he's good for. Only thing he got is right there between his two legs. He ain't got nothing else.'

I wince. I been living alongside Mrs Archer-Laing and her fine manners for just about the length of time Mambo's been with child, but it's got me right outta Mambo's way of talking.

'Mambo, don't talk that way. Ain't ladylike …'

''Cept he's starting to earn, that's something. Come on, help me, girl.'

She grabs the red-stained bed sheet and marches outside, pushing her big belly in front of her. She's got herself in fighting mood and I gotta watch it don't come my way. I'm wondering where the hell Quince has gone on Christmas Eve with Mambo just about to drop his child. I'm glad I come, but birthing babies ain't something I been figuring on.

She gets a fire started out front so quick it looks like she just snapped her fingers.

'Get a hold on that wishbone and don't let ya skin touch it. Go on, use this leaf and get it over here. Don't let it touch ya skin now. That powder gonna burn.'

It's Christmas time, so I reckon on doing like she asks for the sake of peace on earth. I left the world of Marksville a few miles back. That's the real world. Out here is Mambo's world, the old world with the old ways. Back in Marksville they're gonna be singing carols and ringing bells. Down our track Mambo's mumbling and growling and stamping the earth, heading on down the warpath, same as always. I see she's gone when her eyeballs start slipping and she starts shaking. I throw the wishbone and what's left of the red powder packet onto the flames. All that old-tongue chanting takes me right back someplace I ain't so keen on being any more.

She throws herbs and all kinda stuff into the flames till a yellow cloud of smoke lifts up, thrashing daylight and sounding like thunder. She starts out with one mighty wailing I know gonna be heard all the way over at Safi's. Mambo's old terrible self is right back where it belongs. I watch the flames get a hold of her stained sheet, then I help her back to the porch where we watch it burn.

'Ain't no wonder I been feelin' worse than some old goat. Just ain't no wonder, but I'm gonna be fine now.'

Mambo falls asleep in the rocker and I get back to cleaning like it never happened. Still no sign of Quince turning up. When I'm done I sit out on the front step and close my eyes till I hear Mambo's chair start rocking. The smell of that sulphur cloud is still hanging in the air and up my nose.

'Want something, Mambo? A drink?'

'No honey. I'm fine.'

I ask her who she reckons got inside our cabin, and tell her it looks like they gonna be needing locks, in case somebody's taken to creeping about when she and Quince ain't here.

'Ain't no lock gonna keep that out.'

The rocker is going full length on its runners. Mambo is mad.

'I reckon, sure as day follow night, on some upstart bitch working over La Pointe and Pawnee way being inside of here. She's been after my people for a long time, I know that for sure. Thinking they's gonna go her way 'stead of where they's always come. I knows all about folks round here and that's strong medicine, that's good stuff. Arletta, sit down girl, I'm gonna tell ya somethin' ya don't know.'

I do as she says, but she knows I'm only gonna be listening to keep her in fine humour.

'Pappy make it so ya ain't ever get any faith in me and Grandma's ways. He go way out so ya ain't never gonna get it at all, but I'm wanting to tell ya something, and I want ya remembering it all ya whole life. Ya understanding me, Arletta?'

She reaches over and takes my hand. I sure don't recall her ever doing that before and it strikes me if I had ever spent time learning her ways, I was maybe gonna know a different Mambo. She taps her bony finger in the palm of my hand. Can't say I'm gonna be understanding her mumbo-jumbo, but I'm gonna listen anyhow.

'Ya see, Arletta, when folks get off to one of them doctors in Brouillette or Marksville they say, "I got a sore head, or a sore leg," and that doctor's gonna treat them for that. That's his way, he trained up for it. Out here, when folks come to me with something ailing, I remember some old uncle, he had this same thing. Maybe my Mambo told me some great, long-gone uncle have that same thing too, and she know'd it from her old Mambo, way back. This thing is in this family and it gonna grow out in its own fine time. Nature taking its own way and heal it out in time. It's gonna die in the blood. Sometimes that take one generation, maybe it take two, three. Maybe it just gonna take that long. That's their own blood pumping through them folks and we watch that blood do what it gotta do to make its own healing. Blood is strong stuff, I always telling ya that, and the best healer this world's got, same as water. Ain't no business of ours meddling with this and meddling with that unless we knows it. We been mambos round here for a long time, till y'all take to learning, and we know all that stuff about folks coming to us.'

I look away then because I ain't wanting to see that look she gets when she's mad that I ain't gonna be Mambo.

She just carries on talking, says sometimes a family gets a weakness in the mind and that goes way back in them too. Ain't nothing gonna stop it till that grow out and nature gets done with it. That's when the spirit moves on, and that family's always gonna be stronger for it, able to fight that thing off if it comes again. Sometimes folks got a weakness for liquor on account of that spirit feeling tired out and needing to sleep, but life comes, wakes it right up and it ain't its time. Them's old spirits, she says, and them's just tired. Some folks soft, ain't strong enough to be standing up for what's right because it's set out in blood that they gonna be like that. All that stuff set out in spirit and blood and a mambo needs to be learning how to know which one they're dealing with.

'We mambos keep folks' record about all that in our mind. We knows about all them folks and families, and how we been helping them, father to son, mother to daughter, over time. We keep track on all them cousins and even all them cousins' cousins, some they don't even know they has. That get handed down to us, like a family telling us its own story. I learn all that, Grandma taught me all them lines on folks and how they cross over with one another. We keep all that in our head, Arletta, it goes from mother to daughter, generation to generation, so what look like mumbo-jumbo to you and Pappy make good sense to us. That's our business, to be remembering the spirit line in all them folks that come to us, remembering how the blood is flowing in the family, when they don't even remember it themselves. Sometimes they get a lot of pain outta remembering stuff they don't wanna be remembering, so Mambo remembers it for them, so they get a release from that pain. That's the way a family make sense to us. And we hand down what we learn, about what heals what and what works with one person and ain't no good on another. We of the old ways gotta learn us all that. We help how we been told, but we gotta find ways of facing up to all them changes when bad blood takes to moving out when its time comes. That sure is the tricky part, sure is hard work for a mambo. And we got the gut for it. That's old voodoo ways, Arletta. That's our old ways and we proud of them. We don't get ourselves all this pride for nothing.'

Seems I got some of my learning ways from Mambo's blood, same as Pappy's.

'This woman over Pawnee way ain't from no family, she got Indian blood, I hear, and there sure ain't much of that in her that I knows about. She been mixing Indian ways with our ways and that ain't ever gonna work, ain't real stuff, she just mixing and choosing whatever she take a fancy to, ain't no blood-learning in her, ain't no memory of folks, and there ain't no Tunica shaman taking her on at all, either. They came all the way out here one time, way back, warning me, telling me all about her. Tunica got ways just as proud as our ways, just as good as our ways. We respect one another, even help one another out sometimes, 'cause I know all them Tunica and Biloxi shamans same as they know me.

'Confusion and mix-up stuff is all she got and selling it for some price too, from what I hear. Them ways are old ways, them's pure ways and ain't no mixing unless ya real smart with it. It don't serve them and it don't serve us. Times be that a mambo and a shaman talk about stuff, there sure is, but she just start up on her own, 'cause she take a fancy it something she wanna be doing.'

'Why?' I ain't able to figure anybody wanting to be a mambo. 'Money?'

'Well, I say that's about it. But she gonna get big trouble from some shaman out there. That's for sure, I knows that. They ain't looking kind on her at all. She's one stupid mamma, and she got too much of what they's calling ego. That ain't pride. Pride a different thing altogether. A mambo don't just start up, Arletta, a mambo get born that way, even if they don't know about it. And she gonna find out we ain't always get paid, neither. Good folks take care of their mambo no matter what, and a good mambo take good care of them. Always been.'

She leans back in the rocking chair and closes her eyes.

'A mambo always looked after.'

It's more than I ever hear her speak in my life. She sure had a lot to teach me if I'd been born a mambo.

'I know her, know who she is, but I don't know who's telling her about our ways. Somebody learning her something, but she ain't got no memory of my people. If ya gonna teach, ya gotta teach it all the way. Grandma spent her whole life teaching me, since I was born, and I knew that was all done when y'all come along. That's why I ain't never start with it. I knew ya ain't never gonna be no mambo.'

'I'm sorry, Mambo. Seems I always knew I ain't no mambo neither.'

'I knows it, Arletta.'

Maybe I ain't no mambo, but I sure like hearing about my own people. She tells me how our people come from Africa, but they came to Louisiana from Haiti. My great-great-grandmother went by the name of Celia Dessalines, and she says them Dessalines were powerful folk in Haiti. They were powerful folk in Africa a long time before that.

'"Fon", they called them back in the old country,' she says. 'And Celia Dessalines' ma was what they called a "botono". That's what they called a sorceress. My Mambo told me that before we ever set foot on this soil it got handed down from mother to daughter, once to a son 'cause ain't no daughter born. The Dessalines take it in spirit, and blood, that's our memory, from Africa, before we were even called Dessalines.

'And like I say, Arletta, I don't know who might be talking to this Pawnee woman about our ways, but I know for sure that ya just found bad stuff. Mambos deal with bad stuff all the time, cursing and devils and all kinds of stuff. Mambo knows a good spirit and Mambo knows a bad spirit. Ain't no bad spirit, ain't no devil, ever gonna heal no folk.'

She opens her eyes and looks at me.

'That was bad stuff. I know devils, Arletta. Ain't no healing in them.'

'Is that what you are, Mambo? A healer?'

Ain't what I ever thought.

'Sure. But a mambo can be lot of things, Arletta. Healing ain't always gonna come on how outside folks think it's gonna come. They don't know what a mambo knows and no mambo ever gonna be talking other folks' business. And a mambo don't pay no mind to what folks spouting out their mouth, neither. We taught to listen past them sounding words. Most times words just noise for foolin' folk.'

She laughs.

'Lord, Arletta, the nicest-sounding words I ever hear come outta the worst kinda folks I ever meet, and that's the truth.'

She gives another little laugh. It's good to see her smile.

'What ya gonna do about that Pawnee woman?'

'I's near my time, and that's a powerful time for a woman. Y'all get on over to Safi's for the night. I gonna do what I gotta do.'

I ain't leaving so close to that baby coming, so I tell her I'm just staying put.

'Next weekend, that's when the baby gonna come. Next weekend.'

'I know ya need to be doing something, Mambo, but I ain't leaving.'

I'm thinking about Quince working down on the wharf and wondering if he knows that Pawnee woman. Could be she got her eye on him. Lord knows the ladies take a shine to him, though for the life of me I can't figure out why. I'm wondering how that stuff ended up on our rafters and Quince needing to be right here and he ain't. Mambo is quiet. I hear her breathing for a long time before she speaks again.

'Get y'self on over to see Safi, Arletta. I'm gonna do what I need to be doing and tomorrow I'm gonna make cayenne pepper chicken just how ya like it and put a fire in the grate, just like Pappy did at Christmas. We gonna spend time together. Today starting to get real chilly now, so y'all get on over to see Safi or take a walk down by Sugarsookie Creek before the weather closes in thick on the bayou. Ya ain't been down Sugarsookie Creek for a long time. Then ya can stay right here on ya old cot and we's gonna talk again.'

I get on over to see Safi and tell her Quince is off someplace and Mambo just about dropping that child. I need to be staying till her time comes if Quince don't come back, so I ain't gonna be back on packing at that mill till then.

'Well, I gonna stay too. I ain't sleeping in that big old room on my own.'

'Don't be crazy, Safi. Ya don't need to be losing no wages on account of me staying with Mambo.'

And I'm thinking that if I have the King of England with me when we get on the bus back to Marksville, she's gonna be asking me stuff I ain't keen on answering at all. I tell her she can have our boarding room all to herself.

'I got it all to myself enough when ya down in that back parlour reading. I'm staying home till ya get done and I'm gonna have me some more of my folks. I got my own folks here, but down in Marksville you's my folks, Arletta.'

Safi's gonna get her pa to send word to Quince about Mambo being so near her time and to tell him he needs to be getting his ass on back here.

'That sure is a good idea. But never tell Mambo we have to do that.'

'Course not. Pa knows all about Quince.'

'What does he know?'

'Well, ya just get on back to Mambo now and I'm gonna tell ya what I hear Pa say after the baby comes.'

'I ain't waiting that long, Safi.'

'He reckons Quince been fooling 'round, but Pa says I ain't ever got to say nothing about it 'cause once my ma hears she's gonna be straight over to Mambo and he don't want no trouble. He don't think Mambo needs trouble, neither. He's looking out for her good.'

I knew it. Mambo ain't needing no more trouble, so I'm gonna keep that to myself right now. Down at Sugarsookie Creek I get to thinking about the stuff Mambo's been telling me. First time I ever think about it. Turns out Mambo's head is full of learning after all; ain't no wonder she never had time for schooling.

'Nellie?' I whisper. Dusk is coming down quick and the only sound I hear is creek water flowing hard. Rains up north have it near busting its bank, and there ain't a leaf on a tree with winter.

'Nellie?'

There's no sound from her at all, so I start making my way home, singing her song. Trouble is, she can get the sound of that voice of hers to start right down in her boots and I ain't got no kinda singing in me at all.

I never laid down my load, Lord
I never gave Jesus my yoke
And on both sides of the river
Blood fed the roots of oak.
Deliver, deliver, deliver my soul
Rest my head on your pillow
Lord, I never grew old.
Hmmm, hmmm, hmmmmmmm ...

I speak to her anyways.

'Ya probably out there Nellie, singing ya song and bringing comfort to some child just like me someplace else. I just wanna say I'm doing fine now. Ya hear, Nellie? I'm doing fine, like ya said.'

I toss and turn on my old cot all night wondering what Mambo's doing. She made me swear to stay put inside, but I get to thinking about how I oughta be out there helping her fight off the woman from Pawnee. That's what she'd have done for her ma. That's her world, and it's my right place.

Seems I abandoned my Mambo the same way she abandoned me when she was no more than a child herself.

I suppose Quince been fooling with that Pawnee woman. Maybe she's just one of them, 'cause from what I ever saw, he's the kinda man who likes flirting all over. Worst of it is, it sure does looks like she's been inside of our cabin putting her bad stuff up there herself. Best I can hope for is that she got him doing it, maybe she told that fool it was some kinda charm gonna make him more manly, since that's all Quince ever got in his head.

Thick rain down our track turns the night cold, and like it's got no air in it. Mambo still ain't back in our cabin. It's quiet, there's no sound from her at all. I shift in and outta sleep all night, tossing and turning in my cot.

Next day Mambo is back and looking like her old self again and I reckon there must have been a curse on her all right. Looks like she's sorted things out good and proper, though. Outside the rain is coming and going, but inside our cabin is warm and glowing with the fire she's lit in Pappy's chimney.

'Come Arletta, we got pepper-floured chicken and this child sure is makin' me starving.'

We eat our chicken watching the flames in the fire. She places a wrap on my shoulders before tucking one round her legs. Strikes me leaving home has done wonders for Mambo and me, and there ain't nothing like the smell of wood burning in my Pappy's cabin.

She starts talking.

'If this world ain't got no bad folks, ain't got no bad thinking in it, there would never be bad spirits, Arletta. Always gonna be simple as that. My Mambo always say, "It take a dog to meet a dog," so sometimes when we seem like we's acting evil, that's 'cause we dealing with evil. One minute that Bible say turn the other cheek, next it say an eye for an eye and a tooth for a tooth. Old ways say an eye for an eye, tooth for a tooth all the time. Old ways are fearless ways. We learn from the time we small there ain't no other way but meeting fear straight head-on. Do what we gotta do to get the upper hand on it and a lot of folks don't like that way of thinking. Especially all them white folks round these parts. They want all of us full of fear, fear of God, fear of white folk, fear of lynching. Fear of any darned thing. Just as long as we're all feared up.'

'But Mambo, I was always scared of ya.'

'I knows it, Arletta.'

'Ya always seemed to have too much ... I don't know what to call it, power I guess, over me, over everything. That's what I reckoned when I lived here.'

She leans forward to poke the fire embers. Sparks fly against the black soot in the chimney. She stares at the fire and tells me about being fearless. How that makes her powerful and folks are scared of a fearless mambo. That's the way it's meant to be, she says. That's how she was taught.

'I just never knew how to be a ma when I was no more than a child myself. I'm real glad ya turned out fine and all, 'cause I should never have been steppin' out the way I was.'

'It's okay, Mambo.'

We fall quiet and smell that sweet wood burn in the warm hearth. She reaches out for me and I rest my hand in hers. We stay like that, watching the flames and hearing the wind. And breathing deep and easy. She lays down in the early afternoon and Quince finally gets himself home.

'Where ya been?' I ain't even looking him eye to eye.

'Ain't ya business.'

'Smelling of liquor and Mambo just about dropping ya child. Some kinda big man ya sure ain't.'

'Ya ain't know nothing about it and I wish ya'd get a civil tongue in ya head, Arletta. Ya sure oughta learn how to mind ya own business. But I been doin' overtime, if ya wanna know, tryin' get us what we gonna need. And then I had a Christmas-time drink with my pals till the rain gave up. Anything else ya wanna be knowin' madam? 'Cause I'm just as ready for sleepin' as ya is for bleatin'.'

I take the long way round to the King of England. I dig it up for the last time and then check back on Mambo. She's still sleeping, with Quince passed out right next to her, mouth open and catching flies. I borrow a piece of old burlap so I can hide the King of England from Safi and her folks, because there ain't no way I'm spending any more of my Christmas time listening to Quince snoring and the place smelling of sour mash. I sneak up on Mambo to kiss her goodbye.

'Ya look after y'self Arletta, we's gonna have a new baby next week, so come and see us both. Okay honey?'

'Okay Mambo, but ya gotta send word if ya need me before then. I told Quince he gotta come if ya need me.'

'If I needs ya. Go on now.'

'And Safi's ma and pa just over the track. Same as always.'

I leave, glad to be hearing the strength back in Mambo's voice and wondering if Quince got any kinda clue what's gonna hit him when he wakes up if he's been messing. I'm sure he don't and that brings a smile all over my face crossing the muddy fields in my bare feet to Safi's folks' cabin on Christmas Day. I'm just smiling all over thinking on it.

I get the King of England safely into Marksville; Safi didn't ask about him at all.

She tells me her pa used to see Quince out all the time. Flitting and flirting he calls it. Quince been flirting round all kinds of other women since Mambo got with child and her pa knows the trouble that can cause. When he told Safi's ma about Quince's carry-on, she marched straight on over, when she knew Mambo had gone off cleaning, and she gave him a piece of her mind. Safi says he took a right offence, claiming none of it was true. She got mad and just went at him.

'So now ya calling my good man a liar? Like he just making up a conversation? Like we ain't got nothing else to be doin' but talking about y'all?'

'Hell, woman, y'all got so many kids, ain't no time for no talking.'

'Just be minded, real minded, what ya dealing with, Quince. She's my good friend, and ya know she's more than that. If I tell her what I'm thinkin', ya gonna be history round these parts. Gonna be like ya ain't never happen, child or no child. 'Cause in case ya ain't noticed, Mambo already done rearing a child fine on her own. Last thing she's needing round here is somebody messin' about.'

Safi say Quince just laughed.

'I ain't telling her nothing this time. Just this one time, ya hear me, Quince? Next time I'm telling her all about it.'

'Ain't my fault if all them women want a piece of what I got. And it's *qualiteee*. Man, I'm thinking ya just over here wanting some of that *qualiteee* for y'self. Ya old man ain't doing nothing for ya no more, so ya just in need of some fine loving y'self.'

Safi says her ma slapped his face right then.

'Ya kidding!'

I'm feeling real pleased somebody is standing up for my Mambo.

Quince was mad as hell getting a busted lip from Safi's ma, and from a woman too. She marched right off feeling fine about it.

'How did he explain that busted lip to Mambo, I wonder?'

'Well, Mambo told Mom Quince bust his lip fixing out back of ya cabin.'

Couple of days later Quince turned up apologizing for talking to Safi's ma that way and promising he ain't messing at all.

Following week Rochelle is born, just like Mambo said.

Six

Working at the mill sure is hard work but boarding with Mrs Archer-Laing feels easy, and Errol is one fine cook too, so we're eating like we never did before. Matter of fact, I never knew folks ate so well; we ain't ever hungry at all. Course, we attend church every Sunday like we're supposed to, unless we get on back to see our folks, and we're making fine progress at evening class. Safi's happy studying office work, but I change to studying for English, even though I gotta do that on my own. I ain't able to take much more of all that clacking and typing, that just don't seem to keep my attention for more than two minutes.

The young man who sold us our canvas slip-ons for the mill social last year is called Ainsley; we see him from time to time when we're down that part of town. Then one Saturday when we're passing his shoe store, he runs out after us, asking Safi if she wants go on a date.

'No!'

It's like she was taken with some kind of shock that he could be so bold as to ask. He winks at me, like meaning to say, 'she would wouldn't she?' and I nod because I know my friend Safi and it seems to me that under all that fussing she's right happy he's asking.

He's a handsome slip-on seller, we know that already, and he seems like a fine young man too. Nice-looking, that's a good start I'd say, and he's got a job that ain't building levees or shining shoes.

Safi takes a fit of giggling every time he opens his mouth though, and that sure does have a way of clouding things, but I reckon he's worth a date for her. Seems that's just what she's been pining for. Every Sunday he's in church handing out prayerbooks and showing folks to their seats, that's how we know he's called Ainsley. Being church-going is gonna keep her grandma happy anyways, I reckon. I don't see much wrong with Ainsley at all, so I says she oughta be thinking about it.

'Ya think so, Arletta? I ain't never been on no date. Ya ain't neither.'

'No! But who gonna want me? Most boys smaller than me anyways. I want somebody taller than me. I wanna be looking up to my beau.'

That rules out most of the population, so I'm thinking I just find my first excuse for turning down menfolk.

'Y'all gonna find some nice beau too,' she says, coming over all dreamy. Safi's already in love I reckon.

And that's the way things go. I stick to reading and Safi starts sticking with Ainsley. I hear all about them, and how they're getting along fine. I hear how he moves from a peck on her cheek to kissing her full on the mouth.

'My lips all puckered up like I'm kissing Grandma! Arletta, I ain't never hear how kissing gets done. It's *sooo* nice.'

Safi sure is taken with it all, so I just let her mouth go on running.

'It goes on for ages. We must be the longest kissers in Louisiana, and the world!'

I hear every little detail and we giggle till Agnes Withers knocks on our door to tell us we need to hush up.

I get on back to see Mambo and little Rochelle as much as I can now Safi's taken up with Ainsley, and I must say Quince looks like he's taken to being a father. Course, I feel sure Mambo's got something to do with that, but Rochelle is just so beautiful it ain't hard to take to her at all. Feels fine having myself a little sister in this world, even if Quince is her pa, though watching him humming and fussing over her gets me thinking maybe he ain't so bad.

We get pretty desperate about finding work to take us outta that mill. It's been hard grafting on account of good harvests and shipping that much cotton for the war in Europe, so we're kept busy all the time. In between harvests they get us fixing and cleaning and sewing up bale sacks cut from heavy rolls of rough burlap ready for filling. Then the field carts start coming back in and we end up choking on all the cotton floating about in the air of that mill. That floating cotton makes plenty folk sick; it's killing off old men for sure, though Li'l Skivvy says that's just a load of rubbish and the mill ain't forking out for nobody.

I don't ever get to not stabbing my flesh with rushing them needles. Even Safi gets cut up, and she's pretty neat with a needle, but it looks like my hands are scarred for life. One time when I start coughing on all that cotton, the needle sinks right into my thigh, feels like it's scraping bone. Chester pulls it out, but Li'l Skivvy is over in a second to send me home with a nasty earful because of the bleeding. Errol fixes it up tight with a warm poultice of ointment and cayenne pepper, but ever since, soon as it gets cold, I feel that hole hurt bad.

Every girl inside that mill is thinking they're gonna get themselves outta there as soon as they 'bag a fella'. They're just throwing themselves at fellas, far as I can see, and some don't even pay no mind whether he's already spoken for or not. They're like bees round a honey pot, lookin' fine and foolish a lot of times too. They get hell bent on telling me I ain't dressing right for a fella and that's gonna be the cause of me staying in this 'dump mill' for ever.

They parade themselves all over town, smoking cigarettes and touching up lipstick in little mirrors from the five 'n' dime. Looks like they're all taking their style from Mambo and there ain't no way I'm gonna go for that. Then comes a craze for loosening up hair with Madame Walker's hair straightener. That takes the Negro right out of it and I reckon Madame Walker is making herself a heap of bucks, 'cause black folks want hair looking like white folks.

I ain't got any interest in it, straightening my hair or bagging a fella. I don't want no boyfriend. I've had enough of men already, but I'm glad Safi and Ainsley always get along fine. They're what folks call stepping out, and that makes all them sirens treat Safi like she's one of them.

I see that cheeky-face with the big smile up from New Orleans playing his trumpet at the socials, always making big eyes at me. He even set his trumpet down one time and asked me for a dance. He laughs like his teeth are winking.

'Ya's one big mamma, but ya sure is pretty as a summer day,' he says.

My belly is tickled pink with that, and we jive so hard Mambo would have been right proud of it. His lips press hard on the back of my hand when we're done, then he jumps back up on stage and gets bugling again. The whole place is jumping and clapping.

That night he leaves me feeling fuzzy, like I got a glow all over, and I get on off to sleep with a smile on my face, wondering what life is like for folks living with a good man's loving.

Later that year Safi gets a new job. One of the new plantation bosses asks the National Association for the Advancement of Colored People if they can recommend a clerk with shorthand. Mrs Archer-Laing tells us about it and Errol pours us all a glass of sweet lemonade.

'Both of you young ladies are to go along now. I insist on it.'

'Sure, Mrs Archer-Laing, that's real nice of you. Thank you for thinking about us.'

I've forgotten most of what I picked up on shorthand anyways, so I only pretend to go along for it, because I want Safi getting that job. I want Safi able to help her ma and get nice clothes for stepping out with Ainsley. He's right smart, with a lot of ladies looking his way, so I reckon she gotta be smart too if she's gonna be keeping him keen. Anyway, that kinda work just ain't something I wanna be doing, and I gave up shorthand when I started my English, I just didn't tell Mrs Archer-Laing.

I think about the King of England, now safely locked away in my trunk. So many times I get to thinking about the heap of good all that money oughta be doing, but there ain't no escaping how I came by it. The smell of Mr Seymour's dirty money is all over Pappy's pipe and papers and that's one thing I sure ain't able to deal with at all.

I dug it up in good time too. Mambo gets mad as hell telling me they're gonna get a new tar surface laid down near the end of our track for all the traffic coming to cut trees down for new gov'ment projects all over Louisiana. Most of the projects are down New Orleans way, but rail tracks are sprouting up all over. I don't know why she comes over all surprised at that, like it ain't been written all over our cabin walls for years. As I tried telling her and got thwacked for.

'Right strangers gonna be movin' up and down all over. Ain't none of us safe no more.'

Some of us ain't never been safe.

'Ain't got no damn business takin' timber that ain't even gonna be used round these here parts. It all gonna get hauled off to make things better for folks dammit better off already. Don't make no sense to us. Plenty sense to them, I s'pose.'

'There's gonna be jobs in the lumber company though, Mambo. Maybe Quince oughta get a job over there and be closer for Rochelle growing up.'

The benefit of having complete strangers moving up and down all over is that the electric wiring comes out our way, and about time too, after all the hollering folks been doing. Big black ugly cables get hung right past our cabin, but Mambo can switch a light on and Quince can pay for it because he gets a good job at the lumber company alongside the rest of his pals.

The world is changing like folks always say it would, that's for sure, and right then is when I recall it coming about, like Old Man Time woke up and rolled out of bed. US soldiers are back from the Great War in Europe and it seems things ain't never gonna be the same again. Mambo knows these changes coming too. She's been full time with little Rochelle, except for her potions and black-painted packets still coming and going outta Pappy's closet. Madame Bonnet is out there regular for her packets, but from where I'm standing, it's clear from the start that Mambo is in two minds about whether little Rochelle is gonna be learning all that stuff she's got locked up in her closet and inside her head about folks.

One time I get out there and Quince is lounging out on our porch with his leg cocked up as usual. Ain't ever get used to seeing him living in my Pappy's cabin. Don't ever seem right.

'I see ya busy fixing Pappy's gate, Quince. 'Specially since ya the one who broke it.'

He moves his cocked-up leg like he means to give me a poking, thinks that's funny, but I swerve out of his way. He's looking as glum as I've ever seen him, kinda doe-eyed and heavy-lidded, and I'm wondering, like I been for a while now, if Mambo's teaching him a lesson about that phoney Pawnee bitch with a dosing of stuff from inside of her closet.

I reckon I'm probably right when she comes out with Rochelle, looking like she's glowing all over. Rochelle holds out her little hands and I take hold of her. I've taken to loving my little Rochelle like I loved my Pappy.

'Walk with me, Arletta, I'm gonna go get water from the pipe. Y'all take a hold of Rochelle now, so she gets air. Quince waitin' for the ice truck. He got us an icebox out back so we's gonna have a cold drink soon as it comes.'

Quince throws her a look when she waltzes past, and she shakes him a wiggle. I guess they been having words. It's good to see she has the upper hand on him. When we're out of earshot, she tells me she's thinking she might even throw him out as soon as she gets back to cleaning the bank. The bank says they're happy taking her back when Rochelle starts school.

'I says I need work before then on account of my husband saying he's gonna leave, and me with li'l Rochelle and all, just like I was with you ...'

'Quince ain't no husband.'

'Well, I ain't tell them that. Anyways, I asked to see Mr McIntyre and he was right friendly. Well, he's right creepy is the truth, but he says ain't nobody ever done that cleaning like me and they've had nothing but trouble since I been off with Rochelle. Hell, it's fine being good at something other than being a mambo.'

My heart sinks. I ain't heard much about Mr McIntyre since I did my slashing and I sure don't want to hear about him sniffing back this way at all, especially with my little Rochelle gonna be getting just how I know he likes them. Maybe that ain't as likely as I'm fearing, since one thing he knows for sure is just what I'm able to do when I get pushed over the edge. Still, I'm gonna be on red alert about him and he needs to be real careful on account of it.

'Rochelle going to school is ages away, Mambo. Ya able to stand living with Quince till then?'

'That's all the time I'm needin'. I wanna stay with Rochelle, and I'm wanting y'all to help me teach her what Pappy taught us so's she can have a good head start too. Ya good at that sorta thing – better than me, for sure.'

'He's been okay since Rochelle though, ain't he?'

Always looked to me like Mambo was making sure of that.

'Well, he's earning okay, and he ain't foolin'. Sure has taken to Rochelle, I gotta say that, so maybe I just gonna see how things go.'

I'm glad Mambo's thinking about doing for herself. Now I'm work-ing, I can dip into the King of England and no question asked about my business. Just as long as we can figure it so Rochelle ain't ever left out here on her own. That's something I'll be paying a lotta mind to.

Rochelle is quiet in my arms and I'm hoping Mambo is gonna be more of a mother for her than I ever knew. Truth is, ya don't ever know it all with Mambo, but I'm sensing she's gone through some changes and Rochelle's gonna have a different sort of life from me.

Instead of treating Quince like she just told me she's feeling about him, Mambo starts flirting all over him, and of course he goes for that. Evening time comes around and she's back in one of them tight dresses with her bosoms all propped up in her corset. When they're both full of iced moonshine, she's running her fingers through his hair and throwing me a wink.

My Mambo is one big mystery to me.

Safi's been dating Ainsley all year and meeting up with him after he finishes at the shoe store a couple of nights every week now that she don't have to do classes in the evening. He's got skin like chocolate, 'handsome chisel cheekbones' they say, and a smile that sure can light up a room. When he first started coming for Safi he got a right royal grilling from Mrs Archer-Laing and Monsieur Desnoyers, but he's got an easy way about him. He's always telling them he's got plans for getting on and that's the sorta thing that wins folks over.

'Things ain't always gonna be like now; there's gonna be breaks for blacks comin' up, and if ya ain't able to find them, ya gotta make them. See me inside of that store? Ain't nobody walking out empty-handed; I'm gonna sell y'all something. Half the time that's just bootlaces. I seen times I just sell one bootlace at a time, but that's something, ain't it? That's called getting on when the boss starts counting up bucks at the end of the day.'

Ainsley sure could talk a cat out of a tree. Safi's doing fine in that clerking job of hers, too. Her boss out at the plantation must be a far cry from them in the old days. He's taken a shine to her good nature and treats her fair and nice, like he does everybody. I'm glad things are going fine for my friend.

One time though, when I was on our sofa curled up with a book for the night and looking down from our room to watch Safi and Ainsley stepping out for the evening, I think I hear Nellie's voice again. Just faint, like she's out there someplace, but I reckon she's there for sure. I've been feeling happy for Safi because Ainsley always turns up looking like what any sighted woman is gonna call handsome. He wears light cotton shirts and smells clean. I wasn't expecting him to turn round and catch me like I'm spying on them from our window. He winks and that gets me flushing hot. The only thing about Ainsley is I get the feeling he's the kind that goes in for a bit of flirting and that's something I don't ever take to. I sure saw Mambo practise that plenty, and I don't like Ainsley winking my way at all. Ain't fitting.

I get on with reading *Essays and Sketches on The Souls of Black Folk*.

In the new year I hear the NAACP has a place on one of their English-teaching prep classes and I take to studying that like it's just made for me and nobody else. Time's going by with Safi and Ainsley giggling and grinning like a pair of Cheshire cats and Monsieur Desnoyers spending most evenings sitting with Mrs Archer-Laing in her parlour. Errol and me end up spending time out back in the courtyard or in the kitchen. I help him shell peas, he's always shelling peas, and we don't hear much from Agnes Withers at all. I never met a mouse as quiet as she is.

I feel easy with Errol. He gets ready for the following day and turns in early. I read or get on with essays from class and wait for Safi to come back from seeing Ainsley.

Safi's ma is as pleased as anyone can be over Ainsley because he's got a fine job and Safi is working in an office. I swear her ma is looking taller these days, there's that much pride in her.

'Ain't it the way things gonna be,' she says when I see her over at Mambo's. 'Ain't no sayin' when for sure, but one day we's all gonna be living here in this country and ain't nobody gonna be tellin' us where we oughta be and what we oughta be doing, like we don't know what to be doing for ourselves and we's all in need of telling.'

I reckon she and Mambo been sipping Quince's moonshine.

I'm lucky when I get on back to see Mambo and Rochelle these days, because Bobby-Rob picks me up at the mill. It's been that busy, they hired the use of his cart and it don't cost me a thing to be swinging off the end of it when he heads out there, and heading back too. Says he likes keeping company with Pappy's li'l girl, tells me some of their old stories, though I already know them all and he sure does have a habit of repeating them; even sings a few tunes from the old days. Can't say singing is one of his strong points, but it gets me humming along – course, that's out of tune, too.

My Rochelle is one gorgeous little child and I stay over sometimes when Mambo and Quince go dancing. She's so funny and so full of laughing that I forget that wasn't how it was for me. I swear I don't remember all of Pappy's baby-tales till they come tumbling out at bedtime. I'm never in any rush getting her off; I'm happy spending time showing her what Pappy showed me. She knows all her numbers long before she sees we're not playing games. I tell her how Pappy built the chimney on the side of our cabin when Mambo was born so they could be warm in winter, and how folks from hereabouts would come over to keep warm too, and bring food for sharing when times were tough. Men used to go out cutting wood and keep it dry for Pappy's fire so they could cook their rice and beans together and have more for everyone. That's how folks looked out for one another in days gone by. I tell her how he planted corn and looked after his fig tree, and how he built our fence to teach me my numbers.

'Pappy was real clever, Arletta, wasn't he?'

'Oh yeah, he was real smart, just like you're gonna to be.'

When she gets drowsy I hold her just like he held me. Her little body feels warm on my chest and I think about how I must have felt to him when I was her age, like a little warm glove.

One night, just as I think she's dropping off, I softly sing Nellie's song into her hair. When I reach the humming part, because I never heard Nellie sing a second verse, Rochelle takes a deep breath and then lets out a long sigh. Sounds like she's thinking as deep as a little one can.

'That's a sad tune, Arletta, but it's nice. Sing it ag'in for me.'

'Okay.' I kiss her curls. 'One day I'm gonna tell you all about Nellie. She's a good friend of mine. I haven't seen her in a while though, but she used to always sing this song for me.'

'Well, she's real sad Arletta, she's real sad. Sing it ag'in.'

When Rochelle is four years old, Mambo gets around to baking a cake and telling me the woman over Pawnee way has no folks going her way at all now. She's been ailing, and getting worse for years, she says, so folks have come right back to Mambo. She's doing better than ever from it because now everybody got into the habit of paying, though she turns it down outright if she hears folks ain't able.

Quince sure is looking different these days, too, like the fight in him just gone and withered away. He's still got strong arms, with all the lifting he's gotta do in the lumber company, but he's stooping a little now, like he's always carrying a heavy load. Looks like his old cocksure swagger has left him behind, even starts wanting to know how I'm getting along in Marksville.

I think about Mambo telling me how blood runs through families and I figure that's what I'm seeing in my own. Mambo and Rochelle stick together as close as Grandma was with her. Pappy and me were never part of the world they shared and that's how Quince is starting to look now. I don't know if he's strong like Pappy was, 'cause Pappy took to Jesus, I guess, and I wonder how he's gonna deal with living out there at the end of our track, and folks dealing with Mambo. The good thing is he's working hard and bringing in wages. He's back in Baton Rouge, at the lumber depot down there, loading barges on the wharf. I don't know if he's wandering or not, but it ain't none of my business and that's something Mambo knows how to deal with anyhow.

We even strike up some talk these days. He's in his usual place, outside on our porch, leg cocked up and glassy-eyed with liquor.

'Quince, I was thinking it's gonna be something nice if the place gets a lick of paint. What you think about that?'

'Eh?'

'Some folks are painting their cabins now and I was just thinking how that would brighten this place up. And it's good on wood, they say, helps with weathering and all.'

'Paint? That sure takes time and dollars. Though I sees folks doin' it.'

'I think it would be nice. Like a whole new place, and they say it guards against termites too. I think Mambo would like it.'

I jiggle Rochelle on my lap.

'Ya think she gonna like it?'

'Oh sure. She said something about it one time. I s'pose it's getting round to things, with Rochelle and all. I heard her say she would like living in a painted cabin like those other folks are doing.'

A little while later, and a few drinks, he asks what colour I think Mambo would like and I say pink.

'Pink? I ain't livin' in no pink house.'

He does now.

Rochelle puts me in mind of Pappy sometimes. When she laughs she stops right where she is and giggles just like he used to. It's the sweetest thing I've ever seen. I wish he was around helping me teach her the same way he taught me, so she's able to get on. When I find a well-thumbed copy of L. Frank Baum's *American Fairy Tales* on one of the trestle tables in Marksville, I splash out more than feel I should to buy it for her.

'Ain't that lovely, Arletta,' says Mambo. 'Come on now, Rochelle, see what Arletta got for you? See all them pictures? Ain't that something? That's real pretty, Arletta.'

She points that finger of hers and tells me off as soon as Rochelle is sleeping.

'It's real nice and all, but ain't what ya need to be doing with hard work and earnings. Go on and be getting for y'self Arletta.'

'I want her learning early though, that's all.'

'I know that, but listen to me girl, and take care of y'self. Quince is seeing to Rochelle, he sure has taken to that. Ya just need to be teaching her and don't go spending no more earnings over this way. Ya hear?'

'Okay, Mambo.'

Me and Mambo, even Quince, we all got something to see eye to eye on. Our little Rochelle.

Seven

Safi and Ainsley start talking about getting married. I figure it's about time.

'I don't know when Arletta, I mean, he ain't asked me outright, but we're talking about it.'

Half the mill stepping out the same time as Safi and Ainsley are already married and started a family. He says he wants to take it one step at a time, wants to talk about where they're gonna live, says it 'ain't gonna be no rooming house', and when they're gonna start having kids, all that kinda stuff. Sounds like too much talking and not enough doing to me, but I ain't saying nothing.

'Arletta, when ya gonna go out on a date?'

Safi, and everybody else it seems, asks me that every now and again and my funny talk of waiting for somebody taller than me sure is a long time worn out.

'Well, I've been thinking of somebody from my class.'

'Ya never said a word! Ya thinking about it? That's some news Arletta.'

I tell her about Red Benson. We've got examination papers coming up and he's been helping me out with my prep. We started English class at the same time but he's smarter than me, that's for sure, and been doing all kinds of other classes for five years now. Safi can't believe I ain't never said a word about him, calls me a dark horse. Truth is, he ain't exactly asking me out, he's just suggesting he comes over here and we can help each other out with revision. Course, she reckons that's just a cover for him taking a shine to me.

'Tell me all about him. Go on.'

'Well, he's tall, like he needs to be of course, and clever. He's already passed math and history; that's what he wants to do, history. He wants to study at college and go on to teach history. There's nothing else on his mind but getting to college, and his folks pushing him hard for it too. Fancy that Safi. College. Nobody in his family ever been to college.'

'Oh my, Arletta.'

His pa's working flat out on the highway for it, and his ma's doing domestic for two families. He's got three sisters, all of them older than he is, and from what I hear, all of them in that family are hell bent on Red getting into college. I can't see any doubting it at all. I like Red Benson on account of his good manners, for one thing, and he can sit in a room for four hours reading without saying a word.

I can tell that ain't the kind of information Safi wants to be hearing about so I say, 'And he takes size ten-and-a-half in shoes, in case Ainsley wants to know …'

'Oh Arletta, ya know all about him. So what does he look like?'

'He's tall, and he takes size ten-and-a-half in shoes.'

'Stop it.'

'He's just as good looking as Ainsley, thank you very much. I guess I'm just gonna say he can come over here so you can check him out for y'self.'

Well, with Safi pushing for it, there ain't no way I'm gonna be able to get out of it at all. I'll have to introduce him to Mrs Archer-Laing and Monsieur Desnoyers too. He ain't gonna get through the front door and into that parlour unless he gets the okay outta them. They'll be needing to know if he's a churchgoer and it ain't no surprise at all that I never thought of asking.

But Red Benson's fine manners get him through all of that without a hitch.

'He's just ya sort,' says Safi when she meets him. 'I mean, he's what ya call the studying kind, and that's your kind too, for sure. Ainsley ain't ever read anything but a price tag. And ain't Red got a fine set of teeth?'

'A fine set of teeth?'

We laugh about Red's teeth till Agnes starts banging.

Red truly does like his studies, and he's what I call a gentleman. I'm right pleased with that because he only ever pecks my cheek when he's leaving. I sometimes think he might have a notion about my nerves.

Errol is always asking us if we want to try something new he's just cooked up. Safi and Ainsley seem to be out all the time, over seeing his folks or down at the mill village, jiving and talking, so it's just me and Red sitting in the back parlour reading and tasting for Errol. He's baking all kinds of stuff from the *New English Cookbook* Mrs Archer-Laing brought back from her last trip, and we must have tried a slice of every tart and pie placed in front of the real King of England himself.

'Lord, Errol, I swear my beau is just round here for some of that cooking, some of that pie.'

'Sure am.'

'So, ya not round here thinking I'm the finest catch in class?'

Errol is dishing up fruit pie covered in white sugar and saying, 'I reckon ya is, Arletta.'

'Ya ain't seen the rest of that class, Errol. Ain't two legs matching in it.' Red gets one of Mrs Archer-Laing's cushions slapped over his head for that. But we're easy.

It feels so fine I don't even notice Safi getting quiet till after everything happens and I look back on it. I'm so full of thinking about the first boy I ever really got to know that I just don't notice she's piling on the pounds till it gets like she can't fit in her own clothes.

'Ya getting porky Miss Sucree, that's what that skirt is trying to tell ya.'

'I know it. I'm gonna have a word with Errol about the size of his plates, and how nice and tasty all that baking is. Especially molasses pie. He gotta stop making that.'

'Oh no, don't ask him to do that.'

'Well, maybe he should stop with that sugar pecan topping of his.'

'Oh, not that either. Please.'

'Well, I'm sure getting to look like one of his pies.'

I go home to see the pink cabin. Mambo is still growing her herbs in the front yard and the plot out back is yielding good since Quince started doing things round the place. He ain't exactly what I'd call altogether his old self, but whatever Mambo is giving him sure seems to have got the devil in him tamed good and tilling soil. Even wrapped up Pappy's fig tree; told me all about it. She's still winking and wiggling, and he looks stuck on her again, so I reckon they've worked something out. Rochelle's got a bit of me and Pappy in her with all her reading, and I see Quince is right proud of her.

'I'm tellin' ya, Arletta, he's talking about his li'l girl gettin' good learning from y'all, and he's right happy with how ya keep bringing her on.'

'He ain't never been happy with me at all Mambo, never been.'

'Ain't true honey. He come to his senses and right fond of ya, just took him time, is all. Proud of all ya learning, tells folks about it.'

At least the place looks like he's doing something with it at last, and he doesn't smell of liquor. Mambo told me that's on account of him getting carried back to the cabin one time, ain't even able to stand on his own two feet with boozing. Rochelle bawl and cry and don't want nothing to do with him for days. That just about do it. He lay off it from then, got grown-up senses. Just took him a time, like Mambo says.

Soon as get I back to Marksville after that visit, I feel something is wrong. Safi is curled up in bed; it's not even five-thirty in the afternoon.

'Hi Safi. How the folks? I was thinking I might meet ya on the bus, to tell y'all about Quince quitting liquor. Lord, he's changed, holding conversations and sticking about the place, ain't a weed left alive out there. Ya must have left your folks early.'

No answer.

'Mambo says your ma's rheumatism is much better with whatever she's giving her. Lord knows what she's putting in it, but if it works, it works. That's what I always say about it. Ya ain't sleepin' already? Ya okay?'

I only notice then that Safi is shivering in the bed, drenched in sweat with a fever coming out all over. Her eyes are rolling up in her sockets and she's looking like Mambo in one of her trances. My heart sinks low.

'Safi? Safi what happened? Ya burning up. Oh, poor Safi, you sure are looking ill. I'll go get Errol. He knows about fevers and colds, he'll have something …'

She grabs hold of my blouse.

'No. No Errol.'

'Don't be silly, Safi, ya looking terrible. We might even need a doctor. Errol's gonna know what to do.'

'No. Please no …'

Safi sounds like a bucket of stones are rumbling round the back of her throat. She's shaking and pulling at her belly. Like she's having some kinda fit is all I can think of.

'What's wrong, Safi? Ya hurting? Ya belly hurting?'

'No Errol … doctor. I'm burnin', burnin'. Please … stay with me Arletta, don't get no doctor. Read that … please read that …'

'Read what?'

Safi is slipping away.

'Read it, Arletta, read it, please, please.'

She passes out right then. I stay awake all night mopping her sweat and wiping her down, but she's just going from bad to worse. She comes to a couple of times, but I can't make any sense of her mumbling. I tell Errol we're both down with heavy colds and need a couple of days off work. I sniffle like it's true, and make out I'm feeling groggy, so he says he's gonna send word to her boss and over to the foreman at the mill so we don't need to be worrying about that.

I bring hot milk for Safi, but she just about manages a sip and no more. Next thing I know she's thrashing all over the place and I'm struggling to hold her down. I keep thinking the fever's gonna pass soon, but then she starts throwing up. Her vomit is dark like treacle, thick and foul-smelling, and it keeps coming like it's never gonna stop. It's all over Mrs Archer-Laing's sheets, and her mattress.

I'm pacing in and out of the bathroom filling our jug with fresh water to keep her wiped down and as clean as I can. When all the throwing up stops, she lays there, eyes cloudy, and I don't think she's even hearing me speak. On days like these, when the heat lasts long past dark, water ain't for running the way I've being doing and I just hope nobody hears me in and out of that bathroom. I hope Safi comes out of this before that tank runs out.

But it does run out and the pump pounds through the house for the whole world to hear.

I'm sitting on the floor feeling ready to give up when our door opens and Errol pops his head round. He takes one look at Safi, comes in and lifts up her eyelids. Then he feels for her pulse.

'What's happenin' here, Arletta?'

I let the tears go because of his soft voice and me past knowing what's happening here at all.

'I don't know, Errol, she's been like this since I come back from seeing my folks yesterday. When I got back she was laying here all done out like this and sweating all over. I thought she must be having some kind of fit, and the last thing she said is don't get Errol, don't get no doctor. She made me promise no doctor. I don't know what to do and she don't seem to be getting better at all.'

'Hush. We don't need Agnes hearing nothing about this. She's feelin' hot, but wrap her up all the same. I'm gonna come back just now. I'm gonna fetch something. Maybe it helps, maybe it don't, I ain't sure. But I'm gonna try.'

I wrap a fresh sheet from my own bed round Safi and lie down next to her crying quiet tears so Agnes won't hear me. Then Errol comes back carrying a glass of what looks like milk but smells like something else.

'She gotta drink this right away. Lift her head up now. We need to be sure on gettin' most of it down her throat. It's gonna help.'

I lift Safi and hold her head back so Errol can spoon-feed her. My heart is breaking to see Safi this way. Her eyes are open but I know they ain't seeing a thing. We're speaking to her but there ain't no sign she's hearing any of it either. Her jawbone hangs slack like she's never had a thought of sense in her life.

Errol is slow and patient. He gets most of it down her throat, says this is something he's seen before.

'Poison.'

'What?'

'She gone and taken somethin', Arletta. I's sure of it. I reckon she gone and got herself with child and now she's taken somethin' to be shot of it. Ain't the first time I seen this, Arletta, but I never thought I was ever gonna see it again. She's gone got herself in a heap of trouble.'

I don't know how that can be at all. She never said a word to me, so that just can't be what's wrong. But then, when I think of the weight she's been putting on for months, she's about twice the size of me now, though I'm sure skinny still, I start to fear he might be right.

Errol lifts the sheet and feels Safi's belly.

'She gone and left it way too late. She clean outta time on it. This sorta thing needin' to be done in the first few weeks, if folks thinkin' on doing it at all. I ain't no doctor, Arletta, but I say she's gone over six months already. Ain't no child that much on comin' away easy. Any child that far on is bed-in hard. That child holding on strong and waiting to be born.'

'What we gonna do, Errol?'

'Where she get it, Arletta? What she took?'

I look at Safi. She's calm now, awake it seems, but ain't nothing going on in her head at all, I can see that. She's staring blind, like there's nothing out there to look at. Then she blinks, real slow like it's hard work. I get minded of the first day I ever set eyes on her, when she come over our way to pick something up from Mambo to help her ma get her pa back home from wandering. I reckon she's been to see Mambo.

'I'm not sure about it, Errol, but maybe she got something from my ma. It's hard to think my ma would give her this, but Safi, well she don't know anybody else ... and my ma, she's ...'

I'm sick at heart thinking my Mambo would do this to my best friend, and kin to her own best friend. It don't seem right, but I always wondered if one day my Mambo might go plumb crazy.

Errol puts a bony arm on my shoulder and lets me weep.

When I dry my eyes, he goes to the window and looks down Main Street. I guess there's a world out there carrying on like nothing happened. Inside our room underneath the eaves, Safi's in trouble and he don't reckon she's ever coming out of it. If any sheriff finds out what's happened here, they're gonna come down hard on it. Mambo could end up with a lynching, no question about it.

'That baby need to be comin', Arletta. It likely to come too soon, but it gonna come.'

'How? How can a baby be all right when she's like this?'

'I ain't saying the baby gonna be all right. I saying it gonna come.'

I don't know what to do. I'm just so worried about her, and her folks. Her ma's gonna fall apart, ain't no question about that. She's gonna go right over the edge if she sees Safi lying there carrying a child and not a bit of sense in her head. Errol is gonna start her on fresh milk to line her insides. Might be, when evening comes around, she's able to start taking fresh custard. That sure would be a good sign and I'd be happy to see her eating something. Maybe that's gonna start pushing some of that poison on through.

'What are we gonna do, though? We need to be telling Ainsley and her ma, don't we? Oh my Lord, this just gonna put an end to her ma.'

'Well, I reckon ya oughta go get Ainsley. Ya know where his folks biding?'

'Yes, yes. I'll go get him.'

I sneak downstairs, though I don't think Mrs Archer-Laing is home, and slip out to fetch Ainsley. I don't know what I'm gonna tell him. I've got no proof at all that Mambo gave Safi whatever it is she's gone and taken. With so many old brews supposed to get rid of babies, we hear about them all the time at the mill, and so many old wives and young fools willing to hand them out, I get to thinking I ain't gonna mention Mambo at all right now. Outside the two-roomed cabin where Ainsley lives with his family I put a full brace on myself and pray he answers the door himself.

He don't. I started praying too late in life, ain't got no knack for it at all. One of his sisters asks me in; she's right cheerful.

'Well, see, it's just that Safi ain't well and says she wants Ainsley over right away.'

Ainsley's real happy to see me, but I never saw a smile wipe off a face so fast in all my life. He speeds on ahead like a bolt of lightning and it's all I'm able to do to keep him in plain sight. By the time I get there, he's already cradling Safi in his arms.

'What's wrong? What happened?'

'I don't know anything about it Ainsley …' My voice don't even sound like it's my own. Errol sits next to Ainsley and puts a hand on his shoulder.

'Son, I think Safi took something.'

'Took something? What?'

I start to tell him but Errol puts his hand up, asking me to say nothing. He used to see this happen all the time back in the old days, so I take his advice. I'm about as shocked as he is, though, when Ainsley says there ain't no chance of Safi being in the family way.

'Well, I'm just as sure as sure can be Ainsley. I'm guessing well over six months. I ain't no doctor, mind you, but that's what I'm gonna say about it, that's what it's sure feelin' like.'

'And y'all thinking she took something to be rid of it? Safi, Safi, it's me, Ainsley. Look at me, Safi. She ain't with no child, no way.'

Ainsley is raising his voice but Safi's poor head just rolls around stupid.

'Okay,' says Errol, 'but when I've seen this, stuff taken when the child gets so far on, that baby always comes. Whatever she took, she took too late. That baby still there, Ainsley, ain't been no blood or nothing. Eh, Arletta? Ya ain't seen no bleeding come away?'

I shake my head.

'It ain't mine, we ain't never, we ain't never done it.' Ainsley's voice is low like a whisper. 'Safi always says she's gonna wait till we get married, that's what she wants. We been thinking about maybe getting married, we just start thinking about it. Ain't that right, Arletta?'

Errol turns my way, eyebrow raised up like I might know something I don't. Safi never told me anything about having a child and I don't know about no father if it ain't Ainsley. The whole business don't make any sense at all and I'm starting to feel like I'm accusing somebody of something, though I ain't sure what of. It's just that feeling. Safi never said a word about sleeping with anybody – not Ainsley, not anybody.

'Ain't legal, taking something, is it? I mean, folks get … folks get hauled up for it, don't they?' Ainsley starts to shake.

'We sure gotta be thinking what's best to do here, boy. The law don't get nowhere with this sort of thing anyhows.'

Errol throws me a look that makes me feel better. It sure ain't legal and we all know that. One good thing is that everybody will close up ranks, ain't nobody gonna say no word to the law. It's gonna be like nobody knows nothing. Trouble is, they'll just pick on somebody and turn the whole thing into some kinda circus. Some folks don't ever get to court: they're gone, and the next thing you know they're swinging. Ain't none of that gonna help Safi, or Ainsley.

'I'm tellin' ya, son, say nothin' to the law.'

'I ain't saying nothing to no law. I ain't answering no questions. I ain't got no answers for this, Errol.'

But I need to know what we're gonna do about Safi. What is Mrs Archer-Laing going to think is going on? I'm asking because I'm not following what exactly we s'posed to be doing here, and we sure need to be doing something.

Errol takes a deep breath.

'I'm gonna make sure the missus goes out in the morning and the two of y'all gonna get Safi back to her ma. Ya gotta hide her before the law gets on it. If Monsieur Desnoyers finds out, he's gonna get the law in, that's for sure.'

Errol's voice gets quiet and he shoots one of his side looks my way. I got already that Errol knows who Mambo is.

'Nobody gonna say this chile ain't yours, Ainsley,' he says. 'Ya say no – well, whose chile is it? Eh? I believe it, I right here a witness on this, and I know ya some, but take my word on it, 'cause nobody gonna give ya better. Take Safi to her folks, tell them what's happened, and then ya gotta walk away. Ya gotta go get on with life. Ain't no helping Safi now. That's the truth of it, son.'

'I ain't gonna do that.'

'Ain't no better advice, son.'

I know Errol is right. This is gonna drag Ainsley down and if he ain't the father of that child, it ain't his fault. I tell him Safi must have done what she did so he would never find out about it. She was trying to keep a secret and I know she would never have wanted to hurt Ainsley or her ma. I know she wanted to marry Ainsley, she was talking about it, and she never spoke about anybody else in her life at all. I figure something happened to Safi, something she didn't want to happen, and she got desperate when she found herself with child over it. She risked taking something, whatever it is that got her like this. She didn't want me or anybody else knowing about it, that's for sure. That's about as much as I can figure.

'She's gonna come outta this,' says Ainsley, tears rolling down his face, 'and we gonna carry on. I don't care who fathered the child, it's gonna be like it's my own, anyways. I see we ain't needing no sheriff here, but that's all. No way we need no sheriff …'

'We gonna take this one step at a time, son. Tomorrow morning Safi's gonna get on back to her ma,' says Errol.

This is going to kill Safi's ma.

'No. I'm gonna ask Mrs Archer-Laing if she's able to stay here till I find a place for us. Me, Safi and the baby,' says Ainsley.

'Stay here?'

'How's that gonna happen, son?'

'She's a good Christian woman, ain't she? It ain't gonna be for long, just till I find a room someplace that gonna take us in. And I know Safi's gonna get better.'

I know she won't.

Safi's head flops in Ainsley's arms like it's just not part of her body at all. He rocks it to and fro and I turn away. That's a sight I don't like to be looking at.

The front door closes behind Mrs Archer-Laing. She's back. We all know we're never gonna get Safi out of here without her knowing about it. She's gonna find out about this one way or another. Ain't like Safi can just disappear off the face of the earth with no word said.

'She'll let Safi stay till I find us a place. I know she's gonna do that. I'm gonna ask her …'

'No, son …'

'I'm gonna ask Mrs Archer-Laing if she can stay till I get something fixed up, or I'm taking her home to my folks.'

'You can't walk out of here with Safi, look how she is … and she needs to be with her own folks.' I'm reckoning already that I can get Bobby-Rob to pass by here with his cart for taking Safi back to her folks.

Ainsley starts picking her up off the bed.

'No, Ainsley,' I grab his arm. 'Leave her be.'

'Shush now …' Errol holds his hands up to stop us arguing about it.

'She needs to be with her own folks, me and her ma. Errol, don't let Ainsley take her, please.'

'All right, son,' says Errol. 'This all coming out one way or another, like Arletta says, so best Mrs Archer-Laing ain't left in the dark in her own house. Like Arletta says, ain't like Safi can just disappear and no one say nothing about it. And she's right fond of her, too. She gonna ask anyways. I'm gonna go tell her what's happening here. Maybe that's best. Let me go.'

Errol shakes his head and leaves to tell Mrs Archer-Laing about Safi. In no time at all I hear her gasp as she rushes upstairs. She looks like she's just got one of these electric shocks, but then I see her face soften when she catches sight of poor Safi looking limp and lifeless on her bed. Mrs Archer-Laing holds her floppy head in the palms of her hands and Safi's lifeless eyes blink, like maybe she knows her. A tiny flicker of a smile curls up on her pale lips and I turn my head away. It's the smile of a child. That's when I know for sure that I've lost Safi.

'Oh you poor, poor girl. What on earth could she have taken? Arletta, you must know something.'

But the truth is I don't know anything about it.

Mrs Archer-Laing has a good friend she says we can trust. He's a doctor, a man of the church too, but he knows about these things because it used to happen all the time. She wants to send for him right away.

Errol nods at Ainsley.

'If there's a chance he's gonna help Safi, but we ain't wanting no sheriff, Mrs Archer-Laing. That's just big trouble for all of us.'

'Yes, Ainsley, I know that. We can trust him.'

The doctor says the same as Errol, that Safi's over six months gone and she's full of poison. I start wondering if there's one of Mambo's black newspaper wrappings hanging round someplace that I need to be getting rid of.

'I've seen this too often,' says the doctor. 'More often than I care to think about. Fortunately less and less these days, but I have never seen anyone ever come out of it entirely.'

'But Errol says these babies are often born,' says Mrs Archer-Laing.

'Yes. Though the girl is alive, she's catatonic, but the baby will continue to grow.'

We should not move her, we have to make sure Safi has nourishment, feed her like a baby, but she must have food for the sake of the child. She might improve a little in time – the doctor is kind and says he's sure in this case she will – but then he says there's some that would advise something else.

'Terminating the pregnancy, Dolly,' he says to Mrs Archer-Laing. 'In the circumstances.'

'Good heavens, we can't do that!'

'Well, it is against my faith too, Dolly, and at this late stage it would involve surgery, but I can think of nothing else. Nothing that I have ever seen work, and of course there are no guarantees it would benefit the mother or the child.'

Mrs Archer-Laing thanks him for his time and offers to see him out.

'Forgive me for suggesting it, Dolly, we've known one another a long time. It would not bring her back. It would just terminate the pregnancy, that's all.'

So it comes about that Mrs Archer-Laing lets Safi stay. Ainsley comes less and less, and Safi lies there with the child growing inside her belly. The rest of us take turns looking after her. It's no task at all because she just needs spoon-feeding and walking as far as the bathroom when Agnes is out, though getting her to put one foot in front of the other ain't exactly that easy; she just shuffles, a little like Errol does himself. The rest of the time she stares at the ceiling and I keep wondering about her secrets and why she kept her trouble from me. I'm her best friend and never once did she say anything about it.

I tell Mambo Safi's hardly gonna be able to see her folks right now because she's working hard and saving up to get married. I know Mambo will tell Safi's ma and she's gonna be proud her girl is getting on. She's gonna be happy Safi found herself a hard-working husband able to earn money and get a better life. I pray hard in church, and every night, first time ever, that by some miracle Safi will come out of it.

Mrs Archer-Laing sure is the good Christian Ainsley thought she was gonna be.

'We must keep ourselves to ourselves for the next few weeks till the baby is born. I've told Agnes that Safi has gone back to look after her mother, and since Safi makes no sound, well, that should be fine. Arletta, use the chamber pot when Agnes is in. I'm sure she doesn't suspect a thing.

'Arletta, I forbid you to tell Red, enough lives have been ruined here, and the more people that know about it, the more likely it is to leak out. And remember that we have chosen not to tell Sheriff Clusky, and that's a burden we share together in order not to hurt those we love. I am praying; I have faith that Safi will come out of this. If it's in His will, then she will recover, but remember, Arletta, we are not privy to God's will here on earth.'

I hear her put Monsieur Desnoyers off when I got class and she needs to be sitting with Safi. For a good Christian woman Mrs Archer-Laing sure is some kind of fibber.

'It's the usual with my back, when I have trouble with it the doctor says nothing but rest for a few weeks. I'll certainly be at the service on Sunday to see you.'

Red comes over, same as usual too, and we keep studying but it's hard and I tell him I have a few aches and pains myself to get him to leave early. He don't seem to notice anything different. We were never used to seeing much of Safi in our back parlour anyhow, and he's so taken up with studies, nothing else means much. I start thinking he ain't even particular about being with me.

One night when Red ain't over, Errol knocks on the parlour door. 'Ya all right, Arletta?'

'Sure. Come in.'

He brings the kitchen smell of the past half-hour on a small plate in the form of a steaming fruitcake slice he places in front of me. He's been thinking about Mambo. It never crossed my mind that he'd know about her till Safi happened and it was clear he did.

'I know about our old ways, Arletta. Them old ways were goin' on all over when I was growing up – ain't no ways but the old ways back then. Even where I was raised down South, everybody was always speaking about the mambos in ya family. Ain't thought of then the way it is now, and ya grandma was the best there ever was. From the Dessalines your mambos. Ain't no beating the Dessalines.'

'You never believed in it, though?'

But he did, that's the way it was in his time, till getting an apprenticeship changed his mind. Took him out of the old life.

'I got me one of them apprenticeships they had goin' on back then. When we become free men, my folks got lucky. We found us a strip of earth for working. Plenty folks ain't even get that; some folks even stayed on at the plantation for the sake of a wage – ain't nothing else for them to do – so we sure were lucky. I was just a young man then and still with my folks, but there were plenty with li'l uns and it was hard on them. Them were hard times, Arletta. My pa, he learnt carpentry on the plantation, his father teach him that good. He was able to make fine tables, fix chairs and cabinets and all that, so when he got work fixin' something, he'd take me with him and that's the way I got me that trade. I got to be a carpenter's apprentice. Gov'ment help gave us a start with it, so I was earnin'. I ain't know about nothin' before then. I been pickin' cotton since

I start walkin', but I get taught carpentry by my pa, and I learnt to be good at it too.'

He takes a dusting cloth from his pocket and starts wiping furniture. He's got that habit. That's why the whole place is shiny as a new pin.

'We all get outta them old ways and take to the Holy Bible. We used to sing in praise, but nobody was able to read on the plantation back in them days, they ain't let us read, we learnt our praising off by heart. We start learnin' how to read when we got to be free men, and that was from the Bible, ain't no other book about. Only book there was then. Anyhow, the only folks teachin' us were church folks. I got to thinkin' it was God's own book, and got a hold of one of my own from my pastor, a right fine man. Still using it every morning and every night. Pages ain't holding no more, so I got a new one for taking out to church, but I'm still using Pastor Abraham's for myself.

'After I was taught to read, I was able to hold the Holy Book in my own hands and make my own mind up on stuff. Then they started building up all them new churches. I found plenty work to feed my kin and took to a God-fearing life along with it. God, and working on His churches to spread His word, gave us a good life when I think on what went before.'

He stops polishing.

'That sure was a good life and we were lucky. Some ain't so lucky, that's true. But when my missus gone to the Lord 'fore her time, and my kids all grown anyways, I come here, start lookin' after Mrs Archer-Laing and doin' about the place. I been here all that time since. I know Mrs Archer-Laing from our church, and I knew her good husband well too, he was a fine, clean-living man. I knew him from all the building goin' on down South. He was part of all them buildings goin' up in them days. Come over from England to supervise stuff goin' up. Folks were real sorry when he passed away. Them's good folks.'

The fruit slice is gone. I flatten crumbs on the plate and suck them off sweet-tasting fingers.

'Mrs Archer-Laing is a fine sorta woman, that I can say for sure,

Errol. Look what she's doing for Safi. And for me. You think she knows about Mambo too?'

'Nah,' he says, 'she ain't never think about that. Ain't her world. White folks don't pay it much mind. Just something else to beat black folks up with when they get to feelin' like it. Mrs Archer-Laing ain't one of them kind.'

'She's been good to us, and Agnes, and you too, I guess.'

'Well, she sure got some stick back a-ways, for taking in coloured folks as boarders.'

'Did she?'

That's why she got the dogs in the yard. Makes sense. Some folks even took to writing her nasty letters, that's why Errol opens her mail first, to make sure none of that sort of thing is in there to upset her. One time they were throwing stones and broke her parlour windows. One time somebody even spit on her.

'And she's still taking us in? And we're all better off here than anyplace I ever seen.'

'The church got onto it. She never went to the law, though they showed up wantin' to cause trouble. She sent them packing, though, and over the next few weeks Reverend Franklin preach one fine sermon after another on it from the pulpit, sayin that kinda carry-on ain't nothing to do with Jesus at all. He wouldn't let it go. Folks started callin' him Reverend Holler over that, for a while.' Errol laughs his quiet laugh. 'Yeah, they called him that for a while. But his sermons and them dogs sure put paid to it.'

'Ya have a lot of children of your own, Errol?'

'Four of my own, and six grandchildren, still countin'.'

His family are down in New Orleans, all good-living folks, and doing all right for themselves, it seems. He's rightly proud-sounding of them all. Two of his boys doing the carpentry he taught them, another one building levees, and he's got a daughter cooking for somebody called Mr Maestri.

'Mr Maestri's got a fine furniture store down there and we worked 'longside him and his pa for a long time. Mr Maestri always after us for doin' something.'

Errol laughs into his chest and picks up my plate.

'You taught her cooking too, I guess.'

'Nah, my good lady missus do that.'

'Thanks for the fruitcake slice.'

'Maybe it ain't ya ma at all, Arletta. I mean, we don't know for sure and it ain't right jumping to thinkin' things. I been thinkin' on how in the old days a mambo always wanna know how things workin' out. If it go this way or that way. Ya ma gonna wanna know, I's sure about that. If ya ain't heard nothing, like she ain't asking, then I'm thinkin' this gotta be somebody else. Ain't no way ya ma gonna do this, anyways. That's what I'm thinkin' now. I never hear about this bein' part of her ways at all.'

'Maybe something went wrong. Maybe Safi was to take it in two stages instead of one, or maybe my ma got distracted by something, and put too much of something in it.'

'Well, them's a lot of somethings, Arletta, and ain't any kind of messy mistake I hear ya ma ever make. And I sure know her make a few, but ain't ever as Mambo. That's a fact.'

Errol chuckles in his chest. I guess he's seen my Mambo wiggling. I just thought, because Safi knows Mambo so well, that's where she'd go, but it might just as easy be the reason she didn't. Errol's maybe got it right.

'I dont know who the father of that child is, Errol. I've been thinking about all the folks we've met since we came to Marksville, all the folks we know back home and I'm stumped good about it. I never got no sign at all she was seeing somebody else. Never. Sure shocks me the same as everybody else.'

'Neither did Ainsley, Arletta, neither did Ainsley.'

'And I reckon she'd have told me. Me and Safi never been ones for secrets.'

But that ain't exactly true neither, because I never told Safi any of my secrets.

I go visit Mambo. I know her better than anyone and I feel sure I'm gonna know if she's given Safi something. Mambo's a woman full of big pride, she's all for flaunting her pride; like Errol says, that's a mambo.

Rochelle is growing up fast, and pretty. She's got Quince's way of looking in mirrors and combing her hair till it's been every which way hair can be, and never the same way twice. And she's right proud of the new frock he's bought for her in Baton Rouge, twirling and dancing with a little rag doll Madame Bonnet brought on her last birthday. She's still sharing a room with Mambo and Quince and that brings bad stuff right up in me now she's getting older.

Mambo tells me she's got paint for inside the cabin, just like I said.

'Quince brought it. Some of his pals got work paintin' steamboats. I don't reckon it's extra, but he bring it home so I ain't askin'.'

'Quince goin' get off his ass and do it,' says Rochelle, and it's like I'm hearing myself at her age.

Mambo's chipping ice out back and popping it in new tall glasses with pretty yellow pineapples painted on the sides. Good to see Mambo getting nice stuff for herself and the cabin. She pours fresh orange juice and hands me a glass.

'Guess what Arletta? I'm gonna build me a kitchen out here.'

'That's great Mambo. Who's gonna put that up?'

'Everybody clamourin' for work these days. We got men round here askin' all the time and some of them doing fine stuff along here on them new cabins. I got us a price, nothing fancy mind you, with a little room for Rochelle right 'longside it.'

'That's great, Mambo. Quince able to afford it, then?'

'Well, we's on our feet a bit Arletta, with all my people comin' back again, and Quince getting on so well in Baton Rouge. Got some men answerin' to him now, he's what ya call an overseer. We ain't got a lot spare, but we doin' okay, and I reckon we best do something to the cabin while we have it. Ya never know what's round the corner.'

'You'll be having piped water and a bathroom next.'

'People say the gov'ment gonna get round to laying pipes. Ya remember what things used to be like? Lord, we ain't never have money when Pappy was alive.'

Neither did anybody else, but I'm saying nothing.

'So how things goin' with y'all, Arletta? Ya still got that beau, eh?'

'Yes I do.' Though wouldn't exactly say he was a beau.

'I bet ya studyin' and readin' like crazy. Well, I hope Mrs Archer-Laing don't mind ya burnin' up her oil.'

'Well, that worried me 'cause I'm always up reading, so I asked her. I offered to pay for it but she says she's pleased having a boarder reading all her dusty books. That's why she put them in there in the first place, she says. It's fine.'

'Well, I'm glad ya gettin' along. And how ya helpin' Rochelle. She wants to learn. She's just like y'all with learnin', learnin', learnin'.'

'That's great. They've started printing lessons on paper now. Even got a book shop in Marksville, can you believe that? Selling nothing but books. Used to sell hardware and household, now he's just selling books.'

'Well, I ain't wantin' ya spending hard earnings on any more of them books for our Rochelle, like I already said. Ya just tell us what ya reckon she's gonna need and we gonna go get it.'

'Okay.'

'She's gonna have to learn all she can. Things changing, Arletta, and I knows it. Seems ya always know it. She's gonna need more than I'm able to be helpin' her with. And he ain't able to be helpin' her either. Me and Quince ain't got that kinda education to speak of, not like folks need nowadays. He still best at rollin', far as I can see.'

I wince. She laughs.

'That's all he do. Like some kinda wild animal. No sweet-talk, no nothing, just goes like one of them runaway steam trains.'

'Shush, Mambo he's gonna hear, and Rochelle too.'

I lower my voice.

'I thought you were gonna ask him to leave after all the trouble with that Pawnee woman. He's still here, Mambo, and it looks like he ain't going nowhere.'

'Well, I thought about it good, for a long time too, y'hear. And I reckon with Rochelle needin' stuff, and now that she got herself ambition like y'all got, I figure I need him round the place. I need all the help I can get 'cause I want her to have what she needs.'

'I guess that makes sense, if you can put up with it.'

'Then when I gave it up and all, he was about busting outta his pants and I had me the time of my life. What the hell. He let me do my thing. Then he quit liquor anyways. Scared as hell of them chickens, mind you. Won't even feed them chickens, and clears right off when we go to the mule barn. So I still get me my bit of variety up there, if ya know what I'm saying.'

She throws her head back and laughs. I gotta laugh myself. I'm not sure we're laughing at the same thing, but we're laughing together and that's something, even though I once busted the ribs on one of her variety.

When we're done she nods her head and gives me a wink.

'I'm gonna stop that, though. Now Rochelle comin' on so good, I'm gonna give up on my variety.'

Things sure are changing, even down our track.

'Scared of the bloody chickens,' she says. 'And how's Safi? I saw her ma last week. I think she's taken to goin' to that new church for sure. She ain't gonna be wanting much outta me no more. That's how it's goin'. Folks leavin' old ways behind.'

'Safi's okay. She's picked up some bug but she's doing fine. Her beau, he's a fine hard worker and seeing to settin' up home for when they get married. Seems just work, work, work, with them.'

'About time they got married. Ya best be tellin' her it ain't no good lettin' him slip through her fingers. Good men ain't thick on the ground. I'm tellin' ya that for sure.'

She spends the rest of the day trimming out front and planting new corn out back. I read with Rochelle till Quince gets back, then head back to Marksville on the bus.

'It wasn't Mambo, Errol,' I say when I see him taking the air in Mrs Archer-Laing's courtyard that evening.

'Where else she gonna go then?'

'I don't know.'

Safi started to give birth early, on a day the Louisiana rain had streets running like rivers. It's roaring down on our tin roof, the wind is howling through the eaves and the shutters are rattling outside our windows. The sky is dark, there ain't a living soul leaving home and Marksville Main Street is like a ghost town.

I wake early with the noise of the storm and the leaves lashing against our windowpanes. The rain is pouring down and Safi starts moaning softly in her sleep. She's soon wide awake and moaning loud enough for Agnes to start banging the wall. I get myself downstairs to wake Mrs Archer-Laing, then out back for Errol. He gets water on to boil right away, and by the time we're all back upstairs Safi is wide-eyed, tossing and squirming and moaning in pain.

'Here, Arletta,' says Mrs Archer-Laing, 'help me put this rubber sheeting underneath her. I bought it for the purpose.'

The pains are coming quick. Errol reckons he can see the baby's head and it probably won't be a long labour. Mrs Archer-Laing says that's a blessing at least, and I just hop from foot to foot, watching Safi's agony. There's nothing for me to do but wait.

Agnes is told Safi's got appendicitis and the doctor is on his way over. Mrs Archer-Laing tells Agnes she needs to be going to work and it's clear to see Agnes thinks she's clean out of her mind, given the weather. Errol says a hurricane is coming, so Agnes stays put in the back parlour all day and says nothing about it. Mrs Archer-Laing wraps up and walks out in all that thunder to fetch the doctor.

The only one who knows anything about birthing is Errol. He's delivered a couple of his own before now, and he says Safi needs to be pushing, but she won't. She starts screaming and Errol doesn't look happy about it.

'That baby ain't moving 'cause she ain't pushing, it's stuck in birthing. Ain't good Arletta.'

We're thankful when the doctor arrives and rolls up his sleeves, because by this time Safi is flailing about, that's what Errol calls it. We get warm towels and boiled water at the ready but I feel sure Safi's baby must be dead and gone already.

She starts pushing – the doctor says instinct has taken over – but then she falls back on her pillow and he looks worried. Suddenly she arches her back, it looks like a crab walking on all four legs, and lets out a long low groan I know I'll never forget. I don't know how it happens quick as it does, but suddenly that baby slides out of her belly and the doctor is holding the tiny little thing in his arms. Mrs Archer-Laing is ready with the towels, so I've got the only pair of hands left doing nothing. I end up the one holding that newborn child in my arms because the doctor needs to be attending to Safi.

'She's convulsing. Cardiac arrest. Errol, hold this towel to stop the bleeding, quickly, the afterbirth should come. Her heart's stopped.'

He pushes on Safi's chest.

'One, two, three, push. Come on, Safi. One, two, three …'

She never took another breath. She's gone. The doctor looks defeated and my heart nearly stops too. I hear him say there was nothing more he could do. Not even a hospital could have helped. He did all he could, so did Mrs Archer-Laing and Errol. Nobody could have done anything more.

'I'll need to get the death certificate, Dolly.'

I push past him.

'Safi? Look, this is your little girl. She's just a beautiful baby. Look, Safi. Please look.'

'She's gone, Arletta.'

I don't know who's speaking.

'No, there's no way she's gone. Safi? Look, it's your baby girl. She's so beautiful, please Safi … please …'

I hear my own voice fade away because I know my friend is gone. Somebody takes my shoulders and turns me away. Safi's baby girl is lifted out of my arms and I think somebody bathes her, then wraps her up in a cotton shawl before she gets handed back to me. I sit on our sofa holding the child and whispering her name, 'Safi, Safi.' The rain lashes the street below and thunder rolls above Louisiana.

Mrs Archer-Laing cleans Safi and dresses her in the white nightdress she asks Errol to bring from her laundry. It makes my friend look like she's wearing a shroud. One thing I can say is that Safi at last looks peaceful and she ain't looked that way for months, long before she even got that poison inside of her. Looking back, it was all probably for the best, 'cause it's likely she was never going to be the Safi we all knew anyhow, that's how the doctor put it. But it sure is hard to think my friend is gone and I'm left holding her child.

'Say goodbye, Arletta dear. You must be tired. You can stay in the guestroom downstairs till we ...'

But I'm not tired at all. All I can think of is what we need to be doing for Safi and her baby. The first thing we have to do is tell Ainsley, and I just can't think of what we're gonna do for food to feed the baby. The child needs food and now Safi is gone, I've got no clue how we'll come by that.

'Errol and the doctor are seeing to all of it, Arletta dear. We have to contact her people now. Go down to see Errol, have something to eat and I'll stay with Safi and the baby. You need something to eat; we've already had breakfast.'

I sit and watch Errol pour me a glass of milk. It's all I feel like. He tries to get me to take more, food being the best thing for bringing folks round from shock that he knows of.

'Well, I'm full of plenty shock. I just lost my best friend. She's gone, Errol.'

He insists I try to eat creamed crab and cornbread with pepper. I can see he won't be taking no for an answer so I force myself.

'There's gonna be some explainin' to do here Arletta. That doctor, he needs to be tellin' the sheriff's office 'bout the death.'

'What?'

'The death certificate gonna just say Safi died in childbirth.'

'She did. Ain't no business of no sheriff.'

'And he's gone to see about a wet nurse. He delivered a baby a few days back. He reckons they'll be willing to help out till Safi's folks get here, with milk and all, if we run out in this weather. Don't know how long this howling gale gonna last.'

'Is the baby okay Errol? She's okay, isn't she?'

'A baby girl, and she's real fine, so far, anyways.'

'Why the sheriff then Errol? We oughta go get her folks ...'

Doctors have legal ways to follow if they want to carry on practising. That's the law. Now Safi's gone, the doctor's gotta go by it, that's the best way of making sure no questions get asked that nobody inside of this house feels inclined to answer. I hear Errol say folks die in childbirth all the time and, as far as the law goes, that's what happened to Safi.

Monsieur Desnoyers comes with a priest but I stay right out of it. When they're done, Mrs Archer-Laing takes the baby downstairs. I unlock the trunk and open the King of England. I count fifty dirty dollars and sit next to Safi in her shroud. Then I wait in full dread of Safi's ma and pa coming to Marksville.

The storm raged on for twenty-four hours and no word could get to Safi's ma and pa. But then they came, looking all wrung out with pain and sorrow. They want to know why they were never told about Safi getting with child. And they want to know what happen to Ainsley. Seems I get to do most of the answering.

'Safi said she didn't want y'all knowing she got with child.' That much is true. Tears spill down my face and I'm finding it hard to speak at all. 'She and Ainsley, they split up and the child, the child ain't his. She said she didn't want ya knowing about it.' That's true too. 'She wanted to tell ya, she was planning on telling ya, in her own time. The baby, the baby, came early so …'

'They split up? They were talking about gettin' married. That's what Safi said, that's what he says too, last time I saw him in church.' Safi's ma's voice just trailed off to nothing, like there's no point in saying anything at all about it now Safi's gone.

'It didn't work out.' I can see they're struggling, so I say, 'He let her down badly, y'know. He let her down badly.'

Her ma is holding Safi's baby in her arms like it's her own child and I cry again when they're ready to leave. I press the fifty dollars into her hand.

'Take this; it was Safi's savings, it'll be a help with the baby. It's for … for the baby.'

Her ma hands it to her pa.

'This her savings?' he asks, looking at the roll of bills. 'She was saving to get married and get started with a home of her own. But this much?'

I'm wishing they'd just get on their way.

'She wanted to surprise y'all, her folks. Have a nice wedding and a real good start.' I'm lying straight off now. 'She's been keeping a bit back ever since we got here, and she kept all that overtime she was doing, never spent a dime of it, ever. She was going hard at it, working too hard sometimes, I think, for a better life. She was always working. That's how y'all didn't see her so much, she was working hard all the time.'

'How much is this?'

'That's fifty dollars.'

'Fifty dollars? Safi saved fifty dollars?'

Then the sheriff came and wrote down all about Safi's passing in childbirth for some stuffy record.

Eight

With Safi's folks going to the new church now, her service is to be held over there and it's a real nice send-off for my friend. Though it's still hard to think she's gone.

Mambo and Rochelle come dressed in purple sashes. I wait for them then we sit together right behind Safi's family. When Mambo reaches out and pats Safi's ma on her shoulder, she grasps her hand and holds on tight. Neither is able to look at the other, there's too much pain between them. Even though they've taken to church-going, the old ways are still strong, I can see that. Come time of trouble, the old ways are still there and I see Safi's family are glad Mambo came. Rochelle's a real good girl and sits quiet. She's not like me at that age at all, she's been well trained that way, but I wonder what she's holding in that tidy little basket in her lap. Next time I look, she's handing it to Safi's ma.

Mrs Archer-Laing sure turns heads when she walks down that church aisle arm in arm with Monsieur Desnoyers and a bunch of flowers all tied up with pink bows. She walks straight up and lays the bouquet on top of Safi's box. Then she steps back and gives a little curtsey. I remember the day we arrived at her boarding house for the first time we did one just like it. I reckon she must be remembering. The whole place is as quiet as a mouse. Everybody turns to watch Mrs Archer-Laing and Monsieur Desnoyers take a pew. Then the singing starts. The singing is the best thing about the service before folks take to the road for the march to the cemetery to cut her body loose. They sing an old mournful Creole marching song that has my heart as low as I ever knew it, but, like I says, it's a nice farewell for my only friend.

Errol tells the family, 'It's just one sorry shame it ain't work out with her and Ainsley. We sure was sorry when he stopped comin' round and they ain't courting no more. It happens that young uns get themselves caught out like that. I'm sorry for ya loss.'

Ainsley doesn't come. That was one of the saddest days I ever recall and he didn't even come and say a right goodbye to Safi.

'We told them you split up or they're gonna think that's your child. They found it all hard to believe, that you split.'

'That's 'cause we were talking about gettin' married.'

'I said you let her down.'

'I let her down?'

'I'm sorry, Ainsley. To tell the truth, I had no idea what to say about it.'

'That's okay, Arletta. Ya did it for the best, I guess.'

'I hope her pa don't come looking for you, Ainsley, if he gets to thinking about it. I hope they move on and think of that child like she's their own.'

'Arletta, I ain't able to figure it. How my Safi, my girl, get herself knocked up with somebody ain't none of us know nothin' about. Ya's living with her, Arletta, ya must have seen something ain't right? She must have said something, the way y'all talking all the time. Y'all as close as any folks can be.'

Safi never said anything about it, and that's a whole lot stranger to me than it is to Ainsley. I press on him again that it's best he moves away in case her folks come looking for him. Her pa and her brothers are gonna get over the shock of it all and I reckon that's gonna leave them wanting to come asking what happened with him and Safi. Errol reckons the same thing and Ainsley needs to be moving on, starting over someplace else.

'Yeah. Yeah, I'm thinking about it,' he says.

When I next go to see Mambo I sleep with Rochelle in her new room out back. It's small and we share the tiny cot Quince paid one of his pals for. My old cot is gone. I don't ask about it, but I sure wish I had that back room when I was growing up. Rochelle gets me telling stories and she stays awake till we both fall asleep at the same time. Her arms find their way round me anyhow I turn. Rochelle's the best thing that ever happened to me; she's got Pappy's love in her.

I wake up in the night with Safi on my mind and can't get back to sleep. When daylight starts coming up I head over Sugarsookie Creek way. It don't look the same now that loggers been up and down the tarred road and out there felling trees. The banks of the creek have been cleared and now there's a new track beaten all the way alongside of it. Across the bayou new cabins are going up, some already have folks living in them and there's a man fishing out of a canoe. It's not a place Pappy would ever want to be going to smoke his baccy by himself, and I can't see Nellie singing her sad song out here, neither. Things, and times, have changed.

By the time I get back Quince has already left for Brouillette. He's off fishing with his cronies, Mambo says. He don't have time to see much of them these days, everybody's got families and mouths to be feeding now. I smell eggs cooking out back.

'Where ya been?' calls Mambo.

'I woke early, so I went to Sugarsookie Creek.'

'Ya see all 'em changes?'

'Yeah, they sure did take a lot of trees, and I see folks setting up home on the bayou.'

'Thank goodness they ain't takin' no more from round here. Tree management, they's callin' it. That's what rich folks call fellin' trees these days. Tree management. They gonna start thinning out over Florien way, so we gonna get a bit of peace and quiet. I'll be glad when they get themselves outta here. Them folks moving in on the bayou are Cajuns. Don't mind that, folks say they's filling the water up with good fishing. Some of them even coming my way, too.'

She's serving up eggs with fresh pancakes and grits in pig fat.

'Rochelle, come get ya eggs.'

'It was a nice funeral for Safi, wasn't it, Mambo?'

'Yeah, Arletta, it was a nice funeral.'

Mambo says Safi's ma asked for help, something to get her through the day, and there's no way Mambo was gonna say no, church or no church. I'm glad Mambo did that, and glad Safi's folks asked for it. I feel for Safi's good folks now they're left with one more mouth to feed. Like that's just what they were needing. And now I know what was in Rochelle's little basket. I didn't think it was eggs.

'Arletta, who the father of that child?'

'I'm glad you gave her ma something to help her.'

'I fix some herbs for keeping her calm, that's all she's needin' right now. Just 'cause folks take to church ways, Arletta, ain't mean they gonna start mixing up what raises the spirits and what fixes the soul. Us folks know the difference. First time I ever been inside one them churches Arletta. Ya still go with Mrs Archer-Laing?'

No chance of getting out of that.

Mambo's pancakes and fresh eggs taste nice. Rochelle reckons they're the best pancakes anybody makes.

'Rochelle, finish ya swallowing and then speak. My Mambo never let me speak with a mouth full of food when I was your age and I never let Arletta do that neither.'

'I ain't speakin'.'

'Yes ya is. Well, it sure was a right fine send-off for our Safi, with all that singin' and all. Right fine. They did her proud. Ya ain't answer my question, Arletta.'

'I don't know who the father is.'

'Safi ain't never struck me as free an' easy.'

Years gone by I would have said, 'You would know,' and we'd get one almighty fight going on about my cheek. Now I know when to bite my tongue. Leaving home taught me how to deal with Mambo. She's glad I'm not pregnant and hopes I'm wise enough to keep it that way.

'Ya gonna get over this, Arletta. Life ain't easy. Never was, never gonna be. This world kickin' folks all the time. Ya gotta learn how to kick back.'

'I want to tell ya something, Mambo.'

'Girl, don't ya go telling me y'all get y'self in the family way now?'

'No Mambo, it's about Safi.'

So I tell her. I tell her Safi took something, nobody seems to know what, and how I didn't even know she took it till after she'd done it and I came back and found her flat out like she's one of those zombies who can't do anything.

Mambo's lips turn pale. That happens when she's fearsome, and I start fidgeting with my grits.

'Errol thinks she wanted to be rid of the child. You should have seen her Mambo, it was just terrible ...'

She grabs me clean off my stool and shakes me hard.

'Why ya ain't come on straight out here and tell me girl? She gone get herself with child and y'all thinking she come to me to get rid of it? Arletta, I wish ya ever learnt something. I don't touch that shit, that's bad stuff, Arletta, bad stuff.'

She drops me and gets herself head first into Pappy's closet, shouting mad as hell back at me. I sit over my half-eaten plate of food, holding my head in my hands. Rochelle looks like she's frozen to death. Mambo comes out wrapping a blue cloth round her head, still shouting about why I didn't come straight out here for her.

'What for?'

'To save her life, ya damn fool! Where did she go? Who gave her that shit? Who?'

Mambo is screaming, so I scream right back. It's just like the old days after all.

'How the hell do I know? I don't know where she went, I don't know who the father of that child is and, goddammit, I don't even know how any of it happened. I didn't know anything about it except I came home and found her flat out. Only thing says she ain't dead is that she's breathing. Ev'rything else looked dead to me!'

Rochelle has never seen me and Mambo fight, but I'm not stopping. Mambo finishes tying up her head and I follow her back to Pappy's closet, where she's throwing stuff into a basket.

'And yeah,' I scream at her, 'I thought it was you! Where else was she gonna go? You're the only mambo she ever knew, seems she knows somebody else now, though. I'm sorry, Mambo! Who else did she know?'

'Nobody else. I am the only mambo she knows. They've always lived round here and come to us. They ain't ever go no place else. We knows them. She been harmed bad, that poor girl and y'all gonna come, right now, and help her lie peaceful in her grave. I knew as soon as I hear it that she ain't resting. She's walkin'. I knows it.'

My head is spinning with all her shouting, and my own. She grabs Rochelle and starts striding out towards the mule barn with her basket full of whatever she's taken from Pappy's closet. Power is rippling through the air behind her. I don't seem able to move a limb.

She doesn't even turn round; she just stops and calls my name.

'Arletta!'

Rochelle looks back and her little hand tells me I oughta come. I'm frozen to the spot, scared of what Mambo is going to do. Scared of facing up to what I didn't do. I didn't come for her.

Mambo knows I still haven't moved.

'ARLETTA!'

Rochelle comes running back.

'C'mon Arletta, we gonna help Safi now. Is all right. Come. Mambo do it good. C'mon Arletta.'

We walk. Nobody says a word. I can hardly think about what I should have done to save Safi. Mambo's right, I should have come straight home to fetch her. Safi would still be living if I had.

At the far end of the mule barn, Mambo places her herbs, roots and potions in what is left of the old fireplace built into the wall. It looks now more like a stone pit, black with years of burning. She lights a small tallow candle to burn the herbs. I watch her in silence and think about how everything is always cleared away after the dark moon. There's not much sign of what goes on ever left up here at Lamper Ridge mule barn. Mambo takes no part in setting up or clearing away, and that's the first time I ever thought about it. I was always too busy thinking about how folks must be thinking low of her for being a mambo, but all the time they were always looking out for her, preparing for her to arrive and cleaning up when she left. I just never saw that, never got to thinking about it.

It never mattered what Pappy thought of it, folks believed in the old ways and looked after her good for it. Anybody passing would never guess what goes on in that place. It doesn't even look cleaned up, it looks like a place abandoned long ago, a place left idling for years, birds chirping in trees, honeybees buzzing. I look over at Rochelle sitting on a rock fallen from the wall, the same way I used to. That makes me smile through my tears for Safi. She shrugs and grins like a little imp from one of her storybooks.

Mambo pulls me to my knees.

'She's ya friend and the daughter of mine. Help her now like ya never did when she was needing it.'

'Don't say that Mambo, please.'

'For crying out loud, stop bubbling girl. Bubbling the last thing she's needin' right now.'

Mambo turns then and our eyes lock. She holds me by my shoulders; I see her face soften.

'It is what it is, Arletta. This gonna help ya too, else this gonna lie inside ya spirit for the rest of the days ya got on this earth. Do as I say now, and get it out. Ya gonna find her walkin', because that's what she's doing, tell her ya sorry and ya right here, and listen for her tellin' ya whatever it is she's gotta say. Tell her it's gonna be fine, it's gonna be okay.'

I nod to agree. There's not much else I can do. Mambo has got me up here to make things right, to help Safi the way I didn't when I should have. I bury my head in my Mambo, hoping she can help me make things okay for Safi walking.

Mambo starts chanting and burning, and marking the air till I start thinking what I always think about it. She sure is crazy, looks crazier than she's ever been, and I must be too, for being here alongside her. I watch all she does with smoke curling round us both. Her face is serious, set hard.

I don't know what makes me feel I need to be speaking. I guess I'm feeling that my friend is gone and here's my Mambo doing all this for her when I did nothing but listen to other folks and watch her die. I reckon I owe her, big time. Lamper Ridge mule barn smells of Mambo's herbs in the smoke.

'Safi, I miss you,' I hear myself whisper, like it's coming from somebody else. 'Please be at rest. I'm sorry. I'm sorry I never came for Mambo and I never got the right help for you. I'm sorry I didn't do anything right when I know I should have.'

One time Mambo called that talking to thin air. Right now she's going into one of her trances. Doesn't look like she's gone all the way over yet, though, that's when she's terrible, so I'm glad for that. I don't understand her old-tongue talk, so I just listen and tell Safi she needs to rest peaceful in her grave and don't take to no walking. I tell her over and over again till there's nothing in my mind but telling her I'm sorry and trying to make it right. I start rocking and swaying with Mambo, she's holding me tight and that feels safe. I listen to her chanting and the sound of her rattling, and breathe in the smell of her herbs and sulphur smoke. That's all there is, the smell of Mambo's burning, the sound of the old country, the rocking and the swaying, and the spirit coming up in my belly.

'Call her name Arletta, call her.'

'Safi, Safi, I'll find out who did this and then you'll be peaceful. Help me please, Safi, if you're able, I want to find out who took you away. Safi, my friend, I miss you, and I'm real sorry I never went for Mambo. Be peaceful, please be peaceful and I'll do what's left in this world for you to do. I promise my friend, my Safi, my lovely Safi, my friend ...'

Grief pours out alongside my tears, and all the guilt I feel for leaving Safi how she was. I don't know how I could have left her that way, listened to other folks and not come for Mambo. My mumbling tumbles out, Mambo chants and holds me up, her breathing feels hot on my cheek. Then she wraps her arms closer around me and we're both rocking and swaying, like I always saw her. That takes me, and I'm walking with my Safi one more time. Like she finds me and I find her, and we're both walking.

That's the last thing I know till I come back and find I'm leaning against Mambo and she's wiping my face with something cool and fresh-smelling. She draws me closer and my head rests on her chest. Her heartbeat is strong.

'Ya my flesh and my blood and we're using our own ways. Y'all be thinkin' of Safi now, so she don't walk. That holds her close. She's gonna show ya what she needs doing for her restin'.'

I smell musty sweetgrass and sulphur on her clothes. The smell is so familiar I feel like I've really come home to Mambo and our own old cabin.

We walk back in silence, no need for words.

I lay down on Rochelle's little cot and Mambo brings me a bitter draught. My sleep won't be for long, but it will be good and deep. Like a child, I do as I'm told and sleep for a couple of hours. When I wake up Rochelle is sitting at the foot of the cot reading. I know she's been there watching over me because Mambo told her she had to do that.

'Ya feelin' better Arletta?'

'Yeah, I slept good. I feel fine.'

'I'm glad. Ya been tired 'cause of missing Safi. She gonna be resting soon, though. Mambo's real good at that.'

She comes snuggling up. Mambo comes in and sits next to me, folding a teacloth in her lap.

'Ain't gonna feel different right away honey, just 'cause ya feeling better about things. It's gonna take time. When folks go over 'fore their right time they take to wandering and that ain't settled. They don't mean no harm, but when ya ain't nothing but a spirit, ain't got nothing to hang onto, all kinda things gonna happen. That's why ya need to be calling her name, so she remembers it and hangs on it. Hanging onto her name keeps her safe, she's protected, and she's gonna appreciate ya doin' that for her, Arletta. Look after Safi's spirit till she gets ready for restin'. Y'all guard her good. Do that for her because ya got life and that's good strong medicine for somebody walkin'. She's right 'longside ya now, ya called her and she's come, so guard her good.'

I don't know how exactly, but I'm going to do that.

'I expect she gonna make ya feel like needin' to know who give her that poison. Safi connect up now, real strong, like she was since young.

Me and her folks, we always been connected, and way back before that too. So if ya need to be findin' stuff out, then be sure on tellin' me so I know what's goin' on and able to help. Ya got that Arletta?'

'Yes I will. I know it now. I just can't figure out why she never told me what was going on with her, who the father of the child is.'

'Well, that's what I'm talking about. So remember it, Arletta, ya ain't doin' nothing without telling me. Promise me, and just once in ya life let me do what I'm real good at.'

'I promise, Mambo.'

Nine

Red gets himself a scholarship and leaves for California. He's going to be studying for four years and I know he's never coming back to Louisiana. He's going to meet some new girl on that California campus and, being what they call a gentleman, he's probably going to write letting me know he's met her. He's going to tell me how much he thinks of her and how he hopes I find somebody else. I reckon all that's going to happen before she even gets a second kiss.

I hope she's good for him and his fine set of teeth. He'll make a fine husband. He'll be a good father too, and that's something I know I'd never be able to make him.

I've started working in administration at the NAACP offices since Red left, thanks to Monsieur Desnoyers, and there's plenty of shouting these days every time somebody gets a lynching; even white folks are turning against it.

Cotton-mill workers send representatives to the NAACP office, wanting union rights, but as soon as the bosses hear about that, eight people get laid off. The whole place is on edge, wondering who did the whistleblowing, and Li'l Skivvy is found badly beat and bleeding. That's the last anybody ever sees of him. Monsieur Desnoyers says it's just a matter of time before everybody living in the USA gets equal rights.

Even though I'd already been moved to overseeing in packing and finishing bales at the mill, and got a pay rise to go with it that nearly covered my rent since Safi's gone, my hands are thick with callouses from working rough hessian. The needles always scarred me on account of my rushing so nobody could ever say I'm slacking. I can't say I ever took to it. The NAACP got me out of there and Mambo is right proud of it, telling Rochelle she's going to get a 'fancy job' too if she sticks with her lessons.

'Ya done good for y'self, my girl,' Quince says. 'Ya ma's all high 'n' mighty about it, telling folks all over the place about ya new job and how ya talking so fine now after all them lessons. Right proud of ya. She reckons our Rochelle's gonna make college.'

I let him know that I think the same thing and she just needs the chance to do it. She's as smart as anybody else and he needs to get behind her for it. Once I tell him there's a new college opened up north of Grambling for coloureds, I can see he's starting to think things are changing, even in the South.

'Changes coming fast; no stopping it, Quince.'

'Ya keep outta them changes girl,' says Mambo. 'I ain't saying none of it gonna happen, I'm saying white folks gonna start thrashin' it out of coloureds trying to get on. There's plenty out there taking a mind to round us up and get us onto reservations. That's what I hear some folks thinking. Want to do to black folks like they do to Injuns.'

'That's not going to happen, Mambo.'

'Sure as hell it ain't, but they gonna try. They's gonna try, girl.'

I wonder sometimes about getting properly qualified for college myself, because I still dream of teaching. That's what I reckon I do best. The Anglican Church lets me help out with their Sunday school teaching and I plan every lesson to make sure these kids have a nice time learning. I don't know that I've got what it takes to go trailblazing for coloureds getting an education, but I sure know how children learn and that's fine right now. I make sure Mambo knows what reading Rochelle needs to be doing. She's attending the same mission school I did and she's smart too, even good enough for Grambling, and I press her to get Quince thinking about sending her there.

'Ya really thinking she's able Arletta?'

Mambo's voice is full of hope, and doubt.

'I think we all need to be getting right behind her on it,' I say. 'Find a way of helping her get a good life. Only thing going to stop Rochelle is money Mambo.'

Same old story for us folks. A pot of free paint to brighten up the cabin is one thing, paying for a college education is something else. I see the older kids at Sunday school going up for scholarships and some are not as smart as our Rochelle. That's what Red got so he could go to California, though in truth he was smart enough. Plenty of coloureds are getting scholarships for Grambling, and other places, too. They've got black colleges starting up all over.

'The other thing is letting Rochelle go, Mambo. Setting her free of the old ways. Maybe she doesn't want to be a mambo.'

Mambo stays quiet for a while before she speaks again.

'Maybe she don't want free of the old ways.'

I leave it right there.

Safi's little girl is called Martha. I see her as much as I can and every time gets me thinking about Safi's secrets. Ainsley moves away. He doesn't come to say goodbye, but I hear he met somebody and got married. The following Christmas I come across him when he's back seeing his folks.

'Things ain't the same, Arletta. Just ain't the same.'

'I'm sorry about that, Ainsley.'

I tell him about Martha, and how she's growing, how she looks just like Safi. He's been wondering if what Safi did caused the child harm and I have to say it has, for sure. Martha is the sweetest, loving little child, but she's going to be slow, no question about it, everybody can see that. She stays on in her cot long past the time she should be walking, but when she finally takes her first step, a mighty fuss is rightly made of it. Mambo says it's just as well she turned out good-natured, because trying to get rid of a child with poison leaves no telling how they're going to grow up.

Even when she's still a toddler, she likes being with Mambo.

'She likes to be mucky in the soil with Mambo,' Safi's ma says.

'Ain't slow with that sort of thing at all, she sure got it,' says Mambo.

Mambo still keeps her herbs out front and vegetables out back, so when Rochelle starts getting marked top of her class, and Mambo says she's gotten too precious for getting her fingernails into the good earth, little Martha is already keeping the weeds down. When she's talking, she starts telling Mambo when things need picking and pruning.

'Mambo, need a pick dis. Long time growin' ain't good, 'erbs get old an' hard get in 'em.'

'Soil needs rest,' she tells me one day. 'Soil needs rest to get strong, jus' like us when we sleepin'.'

Sitting on our porch watching little Martha get mucky, I tell Mambo Safi is still on my mind all the time. I know she's not at rest, and I know I'm dwelling on it too much, but I still miss her. I look at little Martha, glad she's going to be okay, she's just going to be slow. 'Ain't nothing,' says Mambo. She wants to be over here at our cabin with Mambo all the time, in and out of the pots and herbs.

'She's got it, Arletta, she got her gut.'

'Don't tell me you're thinking she's going to be Mambo!'

'That's for her and her spirit, and y'all gonna stay right outta it. Might be Safi's watching over her child and she's gonna find something for her to be doing in this life. I'm watchin' for it. Right now I only tell her what she wants to know, then I watch that she goes about it the right way.'

'I'm not angry Mambo. I'm glad you've got Martha. I'm real glad about it.'

I'm deep down happy for Mambo. She lost me and Rochelle from learning the old ways – we wanted to be learning something else – but one thing I know by now is these old ways will always want to be staying alive in this world. Mambo is always saying this world needs these ways real bad and they'll always find a way to be here.

'But I'm wishing y'all could meet somebody else since Red gone, Arletta. Somebody nice, maybe have children of ya own to care for. Ain't nobody ya liking?'

'I don't want to get married.'

'Don't be talkin' like that, Arletta. Ya need somebody to talk to, ya need company, someone to help out, do things with. That's just nature's way. Who wants to be alone for ever? Who wanna be lonely?'

'I don't feel lonely.'

'Don't take this the wrong way but, honey, ya starting to look lonely. Ya getting that look.'

'I don't want to fight, Mambo.'

'I know. It's just there ain't no joy in ya at all, and that ain't good, ain't healthy for no girl. Hell, ya ain't no girl, ya done with that. Ya come up like a young woman and a beauty, same as always. What's wrong Arletta? Ya ain't ever tell me what's wrong, and I know there's something. All ya life it seems something ain't right.'

'There's nothing wrong, I'm happy by myself.'

'That sure ain't happiness I see in ya face at all, and whatever it is, been goin' on long before Safi passed away. I knows it honey.'

I shrug. Being happy never figured in my life. What she doesn't know, and I'm already sure of, is that I'll never bear children because of what was done to me as a child. I sometimes get a bleeding, but it won't show much, and I know I'm not fertile enough for bearing children. My periods are coming less and less anyway. Last time was three months past and hardly showed at all. I don't need a doctor telling me what I already know, and I'm not going to start telling no husband why he's never having children of his own. That's why I'm glad Red found somebody else.

'One of 'em days, Arletta, I want ya telling me what's wrong. I been waitin' a long time. I know I ain't no kinda ma when ya were a child, and I'm real sorry for it too, but Pappy drive me crazy and I did everything to make him crazy back. Ya grandma and me were always close, and I don't recall she was ever nice to Pappy, I don't know the cause of that. I reckon he had one helluva life with her; she sure was hard to deal with. And I'm sorry I ain't never able to give ya what I can give Rochelle.'

It came years late, that she's sorry about me, but I'm glad it came anyways. I reach out across our porch and get hold of my Mambo's hand. When I look up I see she's wiping tears.

'It's okay, Mambo. I grew up okay. Don't cry about it, Mambo.'

'And look at us now, holdin' hands out on our porch and me all full up of emotion. Ya got plenty to be forgiving me for, Arletta, and I knows it. And I know things take just as long as they take. Just like I always saying.'

Ten

M rs Archer-Laing has a new kitchen put in. The new floor lino-
leum is nice and bright and there's a sparkling-clean Corwith
sink that makes Errol a happy man.

'"Efficiency kitchens" they call them, Errol,' she says.

'Suits me whatever they's callin' them, ma'am. All sure is easy, ain't
no scrubbin' wood and bleaching. Just wipin' easy.'

Though I've never been one for much company, I am glad I'm not
living on my own. The way things are set up at Mrs Archer-Laing's
suits me fine. She eats in her posh dining room every night (never
seen yardage like the curtains she ran up for that room), three times
a week with Monsieur Desnoyers, and if I feel like talking I go eat
with Errol instead of on my own, because Agnes isn't around here
much these days.

'Don't you ever take a night off, Errol?'

He's serving up gumbo z'herbes with plenty of tomatoes on
account of it being Lent. He only makes that for himself and the
boarders; Mrs Archer-Laing eats English food all the time. She tells
everybody she taught him, though that raises an eyebrow or two,
and says he's got a knack for it and bakes the best Victoria sponge
she's ever tasted.

'Girl,' he mumbles, 'since I give up carpentry I done have the rest
of my life off, I tell ya that's what it feel like. I got church, I got me

169

my grandchildren, and I sees them as often as I'm able, and that's me fine, Arletta. That's life just fine with me.'

I met his family when Mrs Archer-Laing asked them over one Easter time. They all came, smartly dressed in their best clothes, and had what she called perfect manners. They brought homemade dainties; seems all of them got what it takes in a kitchen. She insisted he take the day off, though he didn't want that at all. She laid out what she called a 'buffet' on a table in the courtyard. We found out why he never wanted to take that day off, and I for one was right grateful when he got himself back into the kitchen.

I dip my fried cornbread in the steaming gumbo. Errol is studying me over his spoon, like it's the first time he's ever noticed I got a face.

'What? What are you looking at? The gumbo tastes fine, if that's what you want to know. You're a great cook and you know that fine and well, Mr Errol Simpson.'

'I knows it.'

'What then?'

'Something I been thinking about a long time. Ain't like it's any of my business, mind, but I figure I gonna ask it anyways. Figure I know ya well enough by now for it.'

'I reckon we know one another fine, so be my guest. That's what they say.'

'Like I says, ain't my business but ...'

'What, Errol?'

'Where ya get all that money ya give Safi's ma when they come pickin' up li'l Martha?'

Well, he's right about thinking on it a long time and it being none of his business. My taste for gumbo's gone clean off; in fact, I just about fall over.

'Ain't none of my business, like I says, but hell ...'

'No it ain't, but that was her savings.'

'Well, that sure is odd Arletta, 'cause I knows she ain't never had none.'

'What you mean? She was saving to get married, you know she was doing that.'

'And y'all telling them she done overtime. She ain't never done no overtime for no pay in her life 'cause the mill don't pay none and plenty men out there lose jobs tryin' to start a union for it. Tell ya that. I know's 'em. Plantation sure as hell-shine ain't never paid no overtime neither. Not in two hundred years.'

Errol's spoon is wagging in my face.

And I'm saying nothing.

'Even if she get herself some of that fanciful overtime of yours, ain't no way she gonna manage fifty dollars in all the time ya been here, let alone the length of time she been clerking in that office. Hell, Arletta, I ain't got the time to work out how long it gonna take for her to save that kinda money.'

'Well, maybe it's none of your business. Like you say.'

'That's true, like I says. But that's one big set of cash and I'm sure they found a good use for it.' He starts spooning gumbo up into his mouth. 'Right good of ya, givin' it.'

We finish eating without another word said.

That kept me awake all night wondering if Mr Seymour is dead or alive. I know Mr McIntyre left the bank, because since Rochelle started at school Mambo's been back in there and she's got a new boss who treats working folks fair and square. One thing I know about Mr McIntyre, wherever he's gone, is that he's raping little girls. I've never forgotten any of it, not a second of what was done to me, and I'm right upset with Errol asking questions it's none of his business to be asking. I fret so much my belly churns over like it used to and I end up heaving gumbo all over Mrs Archer-Laing's bathroom floor.

'Oh, Nellie.'

I'm down on my knees cleaning up my own mess and back talking to thin air. There's times I don't feel any strength at all and this sure is one of them times.

Mambo's asking questions, Errol's asking questions, and here I am remembering the smell of stale sweat and sour liquor. It stays that way till dawn and for good or bad I make up my mind I'm going to tell Errol about Mr Seymour's wad of money. It's about time I told somebody, and since Safi's gone, I'm about as close to Errol as I am to anybody, and I reckon he's somebody I can trust knowing it.

Agnes is home the next evening, so he serves up in the small parlour. He nods when I enquire if he's not busy and free to hear what it is he'd like to know about.

After we finish eating I wait in the courtyard for him to finish clearing up in the kitchen. Light from the lamp flickers through the leaves; the air smells of oranges and warm jasmine. I breathe it in deep to steady my nerves. He brings two glasses of cold lemonade and sits next to me. There's no place good to start, so I just tell him right out.

'I was raped when I was a child.'

He says nothing.

'It started as soon as Pappy, my grandpa, was gone. He died when I was eight years old. It started with Mr McIntyre. He was stepping out with Mambo; not much, only a few times I recall. Well, with him being white and all, I'm not exactly saying they were stepping out, going out properly, he was sneaking down our track is more like it. Mambo said he had a pokey wife someplace, but some white folks are just like that.'

'Black folks like that too, Arletta.'

'That's how he started coming. Our cabin is right out on its own, so he was able to sneak out there. It's an easy place to be sneaking in and out of, the bus only came maybe half a mile away around that time. There was no tar road and the nearest cabin to us was well out of sight, at least half a mile away then, too. They've taken down a lot of trees out our way now, and folks are putting up more dwellings, but back then trees were growing thick round our cabin. The clearing we live in was made by my Pappy when he settled it.

'Mambo likely picked Mr McIntyre up in one of them dance joints on Mill Cross or Big Sky, she was always hanging out over there when she was young. Running wild all over and couldn't stay put anyplace. Always out, dancing all night in juke joints mostly, but I know she and her girlfriends sometimes went to dance halls, not that he'd be a white face inside of there, but somebody must have known him. I can't exactly say how she got familiar with him, but I know he started

sneaking out our way, having himself a good time with nobody knowing anything about it. Anyways, he dumped her pretty soon after he
saw me all the way out there at the back of no place on my own, and
with her out all the time.

'Back then the banks had some scheme going, from what I been
told, trying to get us poor black folks paying into something, anything. Anything that was going to part us from our hard-earned
cash. Nothing short of stupid, because nobody had a dime, but he
was going round on the bus collecting in a black bag and trying to
sell insurance for this and insurance for that, talking about pensions.
Nonsense, my Pappy always said. As if anybody out our way was
ever able to afford it. As if anybody had anything worth any kind of
insuring. Most folks out our way didn't even have floorboards – they
were living on packed dirt. I wonder if there ever was any money in
that bag at all, not from anybody round us, anyway.'

'I remember,' says Errol, 'trying to get us signed up for insurance.'
His voice is quiet. 'Wantin' money for nothing, that's all that is. Goin'
on all over, a dime here, a dollar there. Folks gettin' rich on that.'

'Well, we sure never had insurance, we never had nothing. Everybody
out our way was living hand to mouth, out of the bayou and root
crops, rice and okra, and the only thing they ever bought was rice,
flour, maybe a bit of oil and soap, running up bills at the Brouillette
commissary when it was still standing. Anyway, he got to know when
Mambo was going out some place, what time she was getting on the
bus or the back of Bobby-Rob's cart. If you knew Mambo back then,
that was nearly all the time. Every day, near enough.'

'I know Mambo. I tell ya that already.' Errol smiles, seems he's
kinda fond of my Mambo.

'The first time he came I was feeling mournful, real sad about Pappy
dying. Mambo had left me all alone and, like I said, there was no
other cabin out our way. Only folks I ever saw were coming to see
Mambo for something, and folks at the pipe, or the washhouse. He
told me not to make any noise, that he was going to make me feel
better, comfort me for losing Pappy. I knew right away something was
wrong, couldn't have said exactly what then, being the child I was,

but I knew it was wrong. So when I pushed him away he got rough and said, since I lost Pappy, how did I feel about losing Mambo too? I got scared then, wasn't able to say anything at all, like my throat dried up and I was struck dumb. But I got away from him, ran out back to hide in the trees.

'I was no match for him, though, and he got a hold of me in seconds. That was the first time. It happened every week on his rounds after that. He knew what Mambo was doing, where she going and when. He seemed to know where she was enough of the time and there was nothing I was ever able to do about it.'

'Ya ain't never tell her?'

'I tried, but she thought I heard it from somebody else and I was trying to get her attention, seeing as that was something I didn't get enough of. I only tried telling her one time, because she said I was making it up and we were likely going to get lynched if anybody heard me talking that way about white folks. He was always so polite to her, and downright charming, and maybe she can't see past a white man working in a bank flirting and having time for her. Don't know, but she was young then.'

'I seen 'nough of that foolishness in my time,' says Errol.

'One time Mr McIntyre brought somebody else and I screamed so loud this other fella got cold feet in case anybody heard it. They left that day, but the next time Mr McIntyre pitched up he got real nasty, telling me I had to do it with this other guy too. If I don't then Mambo was going to get hurt bad round the back of one of those juke joints, or on her way home. Said he'd see to it. The other guy's name was Mr Seymour, and he said Mr Seymour was going to pay me for it. Like both of them were doing me a favour or something, and I ought be grateful.'

The cool wind rustles in the leaves of Mrs Archer-Laing's potted plants. Telling Errol has got me choked up. I close my eyes and keep my face out of the lamplight. Errol says nothing, just keeps his head bent low.

Then I hear it.

'Ya has ya strength.'

The deep, low voice rustling in the leaves makes me gasp. I wasn't expecting to hear Nellie at all.

'Y'all okay Arletta?' asks Errol.

'Sure. Sure, Errol, I'm okay.'

He can't see that I'm smiling a little, even telling him my sorry tale. I have strength for it now that Nellie is near.

'I hear enough, Arletta. Ya don't need to be tellin' …'

'I want to, Errol. I'm going to tell it all, about the money, it's what you asked. I've never told anybody what I did to Mr Seymour, till right now.'

'I sorry I'm hearing this. I sure am.'

'Well, it just went on and on for the next few years. And now I had the two of them it was happening twice a week, sometimes more with Mr Seymour being the pig he was. And them full grown men, one with a wife that I know about. Mr Seymour was rough, he was right cruel and nasty, always making me take liquor, thought that was funny. It got so I couldn't take it any more. So one day when I was feeling that way and I heard Mr Seymour coming, I got hold of Mambo's fish knife and hid it behind my back. I didn't think about it, I didn't plan it or anything like that, I just couldn't take it any more. When he forced himself on me I slashed at him, at his privates, and ran like hell out of our cabin. His blood was all over the place. On the floor, the dresser, his suit, and he was screaming like I never heard anybody scream before. When he ran like blazes out of there, he left a trail of his blood on our path too. I don't know how he disappeared so quick, but I never saw either of them ever again.'

'Lord have mercy, Arletta. Lord have mercy.'

'After it happened I was always thinking he must have bled to death in a field someplace. I still think, though I never hear, and I don't know if I was ever going to hear, that I probably killed him, Errol. I don't know.'

I look at him. He's sitting forward so the kitchen light glistens on his forehead. He's sweating and his face is set hard.

'Mr Seymour was a real bad man Errol, he used to throw me fifty cents every time, and I'd just dump it in the washhouse next time I went. I don't know how much money I dumped over the time he was raping me. And Errol, we were folks who didn't have a dime.

'That last time, the day I grabbed Mambo's fish knife, I asked Mr Seymour for a dollar. I wanted him thinking I was bold, got brazen, that he was going to get something more for his money this time, put him off his guard, and he pulled a dollar bill from a big wad of money he had in the inside pocket of his jacket.'

Errol nods.

'With all the trouble and shouting after I cut him, that wad of money fell on the floor. He was busy trying to stop the bleeding and cover himself up to get the hell out of there. I found the money when I was cleaning up the blood before Mambo came home.

'I hid it and I never touched it again till I gave Safi's ma and pa fifty dollars for little Martha. I haven't touched it since. Still got it. Makes me want to throw up every time I pay it any mind. Even if I find myself thinking about it in church, in the middle of the day, in the office, I feel like I'm going to keel on over.'

'How much was it?'

'Four hundred and five dollars. Three hundred and fifty-five left. That's including the dollar I ask him for that day.'

Errol whistles.

'That's it Errol, that's the story of that money you wanted to know about. I couldn't sleep last night because it seemed to me the time had come to tell somebody. Seems the right time for it.'

'And ain't nothing ever done about it?'

'No. Nothing's ever been done about any of it. I never told anybody, though, not even Safi. I try not to think about it, but then something pulls it up and it feels like it just happened yesterday.

'But the thing is, Errol, when I do think about it, I know Mr McIntyre is doing that to some other little girl someplace else, that's what those folks are like. And Errol, I don't know what to do about it now, any more than I did back then when I was just a kid myself. I don't know if Mr Seymour is alive or dead, but if he isn't dead he's still doing it too, if he's able. I slashed him good, I think. Well, I know I did.'

My voice starts cracking. I've been talking a long time about something I've never talked about in my life. Errol hands me a handkerchief.

'Errol, I've got all that money hidden and I don't know if it's earnings I got for murder or not. And more than anything else in this world, I'd do anything to see people like them stopped. I sure would like to do it myself, but I don't know how. I know for sure Mr McIntyre is still out there doing it, there's nobody stopping him. He even gave Mambo a job, right after I slashed Mr Seymour, that didn't feel like she was going into domestic service with white folks.

'I reckon he heard something happened, or that Mr Seymour was found, I don't know. Mambo was right pleased with that job. Cleaning the bank office was different, she thought, and she liked that plenty. Domestic family service was never going to work for somebody wild, like Mambo was back then. Wouldn't work for her now, either. She's got one big mouth for talking back.'

'Ya want water?'

'Thanks, yes.'

I stare into space till he returns, exhausted from telling him my story.

'Ya ever hear about Celia from Calloway County up in Missouri? Ya ever hear about her, Arletta?'

'I hear she got hung for killing the white man that owned her and kept raping her for five years.'

'Well, don't go thinking nothing crazy.'

Though I've already been crazy. But that doesn't mean nothing should ever be done about Mr McIntyre. Mr McIntyre and Mr Seymour didn't buy me anyplace, like Celia was bought. Mambo was born free and so was I. They were out there looking for kids who weren't able to do anything about them, and nobody ever did do anything about what they were up to. And oh boy, somebody sure should have done something.

'Mr McIntyre is easy to find.'

'What?'

'I'm saying Mr McIntyre is easy to find.'

'You saying you'd do something about it? Help me? Thing is, I've never wanted folks knowing what happened to me.'

Errol's just saying they ought to be found, see what they're doing now. But I know what they're doing. If Mr Seymour's alive, that is.

'Mambo still at that bank office?'

'Yeah, she's gone back cleaning there, she got her old job back, though he's gone on to another job someplace else. She's going to go crazy if she ever finds out what Mr McIntyre was doing.'

'Maybe that ain't no bad thing.'

'How can men do that, Errol?'

'I don't know, chile. I don't know. How old ya reckon they were then?'

That's hard to say when you're just a kid, but as far as I can recall, they were perhaps early thirties, something like that. I wouldn't have said they were in their forties, but it's hard for a kid to judge. But they were organized, knew all about one another, and how to find out who was all alone, and when. Errol surprises me with what he says next.

'And maybe ya ain't the only one on them rounds out there.'

'You don't think Safi …'

'It's possible, Arletta.'

Oh Lord. That's it. That could be Safi's secret. Maybe they were raping her, too, or somebody was. That would make sense, and maybe it carried on, went on even after we started living in Marksville. Poor Safi, she would never do anything like I did, so I guess it just carried on. I was always studying, thought she was with Ainsley.

'Except she ain't no child by then, she'd grown up. She got too old for them sort of vermin.'

'That's true. But maybe, because of them being organized, they sort of hand you on over to some other bunch, something real seedy, like a prostitution ring or something.'

'Safi ain't no prostitute Arletta. Not that girl.'

Imagining Safi a prostitute isn't easy, I admit, but I get up and start pacing the courtyard. I feel sure we're right: this was Safi's secret too. Errol is cautious, that's just his way.

'Well, maybe not that it carried on, and the prostitute part of it, but we just don't know, do we, Errol? Something was going on with Safi that I knew nothing about. You have no idea how I have turned this over and over in my mind about her. Nothing ever makes any sense. Maybe this does. I don't know how or where it was happening but I'm willing to bet you anything that somebody was messing with Safi. She was pregnant, Errol! Pregnant!'

I stay out in the courtyard long after Errol turns in, my mind turning over like wildfire. The wind comes up. I always like hearing it rustle in the leaves.

> *I never laid down my load, Lord*
> *I never gave Jesus my yoke*
> *And on both sides of the river*
> *Blood fed the roots of oak.*
> *Deliver, deliver, deliver my soul*
> *Rest my head on your pillow*
> *Lord, I never grew old.*
> *Hmmm, hmmm, hmmmmmmm ...*

Eleven

The following Saturday I knock on Mrs Archer-Laing's parlour door to deliver the rent, same as always. One of the best things about my new job is that I don't have to work Saturdays at all.

She lays her embroidery down. She's made a new name for herself embroidering tablecloths and cushion covers for wealthy folks. Houses are going up all over and folks are filling them with that sort of thing. She's right handy with it.

'Well, my dear, Monsieur Desnoyers tells me you're doing very well at the NAACP, and helping out with Sunday school.'

'Yes, I'm doing fine.'

'I was thinking of Safi and Red, both gone, and how you're faring on your own.'

'Oh, I get lonesome, same as everybody else sometimes, but I was always used to being by myself with no brothers or sisters growing up. I've got Rochelle now, but I left home and came to Marksville before she was born.'

'It's wonderful to have a sister, at least,' she says. 'I would love to be closer to my family. Perhaps we can invite your family next Easter when Errol's family comes too.'

Thinking of Mambo sitting in Mrs Archer-Laing's front parlour making some kind of polite talk and drinking from one of her fine bone-china cups sure does makes me smile.

'Has Agnes told you she's leaving? That she's getting married?'

I didn't even hear she had a beau.

'Someone she met at Bible class, a nice young man. I'm very pleased for her. They're moving to Chicago; there's plenty of jobs up there and I believe he's already been lucky enough to get something.'

Everybody is moving to Chicago for the jobs.

'I will have to advertise her room, of course, so we will have a new tenant. I take it you are quite happy in your room, but you are welcome to change, if you prefer something fresh. Or perhaps you'd prefer to be at the back of the house, too. It's quieter ...'

'No, thank you. I like my room. I like the front of the house, y'know, seeing the street and folks going out and about. If that's okay.'

'Of course, that's fine. I also wondered if you would like to take over her Bible class.'

'No. No, thank you, Mrs Archer-Laing. I'm fine just helping out with Sunday school sometimes.'

But of course now that Agnes is leaving, they have an opportunity for someone like me, according to her, and I should consider it. It means I'd get out among folks and meet new ones too. Everybody seems to be concerned about my life these days.

'You can choose what evenings you'd like. You wouldn't want to do Sunday school as well, so you could get over to see your family a bit more. You can do an evening in the week. Two if you like.'

I don't know I'd be much good at teaching from the Bible at all, that's different from Sunday school. I sure love teaching, but we were never much of a Bible family to speak about, except for Pappy, and that sure is going to show in no time.

'To be quite frank with you, my dear Arletta, what we need is a good reader and a good teacher. Somebody who can encourage the class, the way you do when you take Sunday school. The children love you, Arletta, how you make it such fun for them. Bless Agnes, she's a good Christian girl, and a believer, but she's not the world's best teacher. I think you'd be excellent, Arletta. Teaching seems to be for you. Everybody says so.'

'Oh, I see. Well ...'

By the time she's finished explaining how much of an opportunity it is, how it could count as teaching experience as far as the NAACP is concerned, and how things will change, even here in the South, I'm about won over.

'And you are such a clever young lady. I'd like to see you get on.'

'Mrs Archer-Laing, I guess you're talking me right round to it.'

'I thought I might. And remember, it would give you time to spend with your sister at weekends too.' She smiles and picks her embroidery up. When I leave I hear her softly singing with satisfaction: 'Angels from the realms of glory, Spread your wings o'er all the world …'

That's how it came about that I, the daughter of a mambo, started teaching Bible class two nights a week at the Anglican church in Marksville. I know more than I thought because of Pappy and his stories and, after all, I've been attending church with Mrs Archer-Laing long enough, though truth be told I never listened half the time. Still, the other half turns out to be time well spent. Of course I take to teaching, no matter what the subject is. Then I reckon I'm going to start reading the Good Book from the beginning for myself. I settle in the back parlour, curl up on the sofa and start reading the Holy Bible. I believe that's impressing Mrs Archer-Laing, but Errol doesn't look sure at all.

'Enjoying the Good Book?'

'I enjoy teaching it.'

'Ain't the same thing, and ain't what I ask.' He laughs into his chest. 'Lordy Lord.'

Our new tenant, Sadie, moves in and I get company in the back parlour. She seems a quiet girl, and does sewing for a seamstress friend of Mrs Archer-Laing. She's hand-stitching every night, and I've never seen a bodice full of embroidery like she does for some rich folks' weddings. She's not one for reading and asks me to teach her. Her folks needed her about the place, so she never had any schooling to speak of.

I think it's a good idea for her to come to Bible class. That way she's out in company too, since she doesn't seem to know anybody and I think it's easy learning that way, with everybody else.

She doesn't seem to mind being in a younger class at all, she's happy sticking with me. I've got fifteen in my class and we're spread out over two pews, at the back right-hand corner of the church. I begin every lesson with a story I've just read myself in our back parlour; sometimes I knew it from Pappy and he had a way of telling it that I follow. I tell the story before we read anything, get them interested, since that book sure has got a style hard to fathom for kids, and then they take turns reading a verse each back. We work out what's happened after every verse and they get points for it. Sadie doesn't manage a verse on her first day and every little ten-year-old hand shoots up to help her out.

Seems Sadie is only coming to our church for two minutes before she gets herself a beau. It isn't long before he's taking up space in our back parlour and I start feeling like a gooseberry. I take to spending more time in the kitchen with Errol. I perch myself on top of one of Mrs Archer-Laing's new stylish high stools and read. Can't say these stools are easy for sitting on; Errol calls them 'a fad' and says they're in his way.

'Ain't for no kitchen, them's oughta be in a bar someplace. Ain't leaving them in here for me to be perchin' like a parrot and peeling potatoes, with all of them slidin' off my lap. Foolishness. Ain't practical at all for no workin' kitchen.'

'I want to be right there hearing you tell Mrs Archer-Laing all about that, Errol.'

He laughs into his chest.

He fixes food, polishes silver and crystal, sometimes I help. He de-ices the refrigerator and reads yesterday's newspaper. Mrs Archer-Laing always leaves her daily paper open at the crossword till Errol tidies up her parlour early the next morning before she rises. In the evening he hums and haws over it, filling in here and there. Sometimes she says, 'Errol dear, did you manage to get six down? "Hot and cold spelling".'

'"Spice" fit fine.'

'Yes, of course.'

Sadie and her beau go out every Saturday to see his folks, so I get our parlour back. He's one of those giggling childish sorts and I find his jokes wear me clean out. Of course, she thinks he's just the thing and hangs on every silly word he says.

So that's how life goes on and I feel easy with it. Always folks about, but nobody bothers anybody else much, and there's never a voice raised. I just get on, get top grades with my geography certificate and start thinking about college more every day. I've got my own bit of funding from the King of England and that's what I'm going to do with it. Quince says he's going to see right by Rochelle, make sure she gets a scholarship, and I start figuring me and her could go to Grambling. I'm going to set my mind on nothing else, make Mambo and Rochelle right proud.

'Ya gonna go for a scholarship honey? I'm sure y'all gonna get one of those with how smart ya always been.' Mambo is pleased with my news, and that the NAACP can help me. Of course, she doesn't know about the King of England.

'Quince, ya hearin' that? Arletta's thinkin' about getting herself off to college. I know ya can do it honey, ya just smart as smart can be. Ain't she, Quince?'

'Hell, I always reckon ya for a smart kid.' He laughs, seems a happy man these days. 'Now I knows ya just smart. Ya need help wi' that, Arletta? My hand gonna go straight in my pocket to give ya whatever ya needin'.'

I look straight at him in surprise – speechless, I reckon I could say. Never figured on Quince putting his hand in his pocket over me at all.

'Well, Quince I'm working myself, too. That's real nice of you and I don't want to be a burden …'

Mambo touches my arm to stop me, so I say nothing else.

'Ain't gonna be no burden. Nobody got much, but ya gonna need more than that scholarship and I'm gonna make sure ya has it girl,' he says. 'Ya just tell Quince what ya needin'. Y'hear?'

Well, I don't know why, but that lifts me right up and has me feeling like I'm part of the family. Mambo winks.

I'm taking the King of England to college and life sure is fine. I got it planned.

❁

Then, one Saturday afternoon, Errol pops his head round the parlour door. That's when everything takes a different turn altogether.

'May I come in, Arletta?'

'Sure. Errol, what's happened? You all right?'

In all the years I've been with Mrs Archer-Laing, I've never seen Errol shake and his face looking grey like it does today. I missed him out of the kitchen when I got breakfast this morning; he's usually about someplace.

He wrings his hands and wipes his brow with his cloth.

'It's just, well, Arletta, it's just a heap of trouble. I don't know. I just don't know ...' His eyes are tearful. He wipes them. 'It's a child, a little girl I know, a friend of mine, his daughter, she's in a heap of trouble.'

And I know exactly what's coming next.

'She's hurt bad, Arletta, real bad. She's in the hospital now.'

She's just eleven years old and I don't think I can bear to hear about it. I can't speak for a while. Errol sits by the dining table and sniffles into his rag. Her folks are friends of his, he's known them a long time, and her since the day she was born. She's hurt bad. Real serious, and been in the hospital since they found her bleeding at the side of the road outside Marksville a few days back.

'What do they say? In the hospital?'

'It ain't good. Her folks are Cajun, living down between here and Mansura, and her pa's with the police. He sure is all cut up about his li'l girl. Ain't able to figure how anybody can get a hold of a child and hurt her so bad, never mind his own child. It's terrible, Arletta. The hospital ain't sure she was gonna pull through at first but she's started comin' to a bit now. Her folks are real good folks, I knows them all from church. We got close way back, and they started coming to us, been coming to our church a while now, so maybe you seen them sometimes too. Truth is, he don't go much himself 'cause he got duty times, being with the law, and four kids and all. He got his hands full enough.'

I wish with all my heart that I was not hearing this at all. That it never happened, that I could block the whole world out. That's how hearing about that little girl got me feeling, like this whole world was too much for me to bear living in.

'Arletta, will ya go talk to her pa? Tell him what happened to ya?'

'Oh no, Errol, I'd be scared he ever found out ...'

'Him being the law and all. Go tell him about it.'

'No, Errol. You know what I did. Please don't ask.'

'It's something she said, something she tell her pa.'

'What?'

'Was a white man done it, she says somebody else was there too and call his name, kept telling him to stop, that he was goin' crazy and gonna be killing her. They's called him Seymour.'

The room spins just before I feel myself falling. Everything is black and the world is gone.

Next thing I know Errol is returning from the kitchen with a glass of water.

'Ya pass right out Arletta. Drink this lemonade. Sugar is good for ya when ya get a shock.'

All I can think of is that Mr Seymour is still alive. I didn't kill him. I didn't even stop him and now a little girl has been left at the side of the road, heaven knows what he did to her.

'I figure on telling ya 'cause I think ya oughta know that anyways, he ain't dead. And maybe ya's able to help with somethin', 'cause they gonna go after him big time now. I figure ya might wanna help them out. What he looks like, stuff like that. Y'all seen him good. I ain't tell them nothing about ya, though, I figure I gonna come talk with ya about it first. Ask ya to go speak to them. Ask if ya gonna wan' do that.'

'I can't, Errol, you know that.'

'Well, I reckon ya ain't ever know what to do about them kinda folks and this just might be ya chance. He ain't dead, so ain't no murder hanging on ya at all.'

'But I slashed him good ...'

'Arletta, that's called self-defence, and this sure might be the time to be doing somethin' about it, like ya wanted, to help all them other li'l girls, 'cause one thing we know for sure now – he been at them.'

'But I don't want folks to know …'

'Ain't how it's done, ain't nobody gonna know but me and her folks. Ya wanna do something, ain't nobody ever do nothing, and I been thinking about Safi too.'

When I start thinking about Safi walking I reckon I start to change my mind right there. The room is real quiet; Errol stops talking. My world is turned upside down thinking about Safi and that little girl in the hospital.

'Errol, can you tell them about it, about me? I don't know if I could manage it.'

'I'll tell them, Arletta. If ya say so, then I'm gonna get on over to see Albert and tell him, and I'll say ya coming. That okay? We gonna get him, we gonna stop him, Arletta and that's what ya want, ain't it?'

Albert Gaudet is a big man to see weeping. He lives in one of the new cottages going up, all lined in a row with not much land between them, and right up close on the sidewalk. Soon as we climb the front steps I smell home cooking and new wood. A woman opens the door. Her face is purple with crying and she doesn't manage a smile at all.

'Errol, thank you for coming.' Her voice is trembling.

'How y'all doin' Bette? This here is Arletta. I tell Albert maybe somebody gonna help, and she's come. Wasn't easy for her, but she come.'

The hallway leads straight onto a room where three kids squeeze up on a sofa together, faces all glum. They're younger than their eleven-year-old sister. I guess two of them are twins. These poor little frightened faces sure are hard to look at.

Albert Gaudet is wearing his police uniform. He gets up and comes towards me. He's one big size of a man and that uniform makes him look even bigger. The big man says nothing. He's fighting back his tears and I can't find any words to say either. Then he gathers me right up and holds me tight to his chest. Great sobs wrack through that man, like his heart broke clean in two for his little girl.

'*Merci*. Thank you for coming. Sit down, Arletta,' he whispers; his voice is rough with choking back emotion. 'Can we get you something, *ma cherie*? Something to drink? Eat? Anything?'

'I'll bring some lemonade, sit down Arletta. I'm Bette, Eveline's aunt. Her mama is my sister, she's staying overnight with her in the hospital since it happened. Come children, let's leave Papa talking to the lady.'

There's a knock on the door.

'I'll get it. That gonna be Jackson,' says Errol.

Jackson Ortega is a broad southerner with a drawl about as thick as Albert's Cajun accent. He's just a little smaller, and I figure they're the sort of men who get respect from folks just for being themselves. I'm not sure why, if it's the uniform or just the way some white folks come. I know if I was guilty of something, there's no way I'd want to be coming up against the pair of them. Can't say if that makes me feel any good about not being guilty of killing Seymour or not.

Jackson takes his cap off.

'It's good of you to come, Arletta,' he says in a voice full of hurt, so I guess he's a family friend as much as somebody Albert goes to work with.

Errol sits down next to me. Albert and Jackson pull two chairs up and sit right in front of us.

I'm scared. I'm scared that folks are going to know what happened to me, that they're going to know what I did to Seymour, and I'm scared that I don't know what's going to happen next.

'My little girl is not doing too good. They say she'll survive it, and that's the important thing to us right now, but she'll never bear any children after it …' I see he's struggling with that. 'She was brutally attacked. The doctors never saw anything like it before. It's internal … *pauvre t' bête*.'

He breaks down, unable to carry on. He sucks air in through his teeth like that's going to keep him steady. He's finding it hard keeping a grip on himself and it's breaking my heart to see.

'Tell us about the man you know as Seymour,' says Jackson.

I thought he was called Mr Seymour, but I called everybody 'mister' back then. That's his first name or his last, I never knew, never thought about it.

'He … he was brought out to where I lived. I was just a kid, about nine years old when he started, though Mr McIntyre started long before him.'

'When did Mr McIntyre start?'

'When I was eight, right after Pappy, my grandpa, passed away.'

'Jesus Christ.' Albert squeezes his eyes shut, nips the bridge of his nose with his huge fingers and shakes his head.

'Arletta,' Jackson says, 'We know who Mr McIntyre is. Errol told us about him and we've traced him.'

My back shoots straight up.

'He transferred to Baton Rouge a few years ago.'

'He's a married man …'

I knew that.

'With children of his own.'

I didn't know that at all.

'One son, he's twelve, and a younger daughter, not quite ten years old.'

'Ya okay, Arletta?' asks Errol.

'I hope you're watching Mr McIntyre? I mean, he doesn't look like a beast, but I'm telling you, that girl is not safe. Not at all.'

They promise me Mr McIntyre is being watched. I know he's raping his girl, daughter or not, and I sure do doubt if they're able to be watching that.

'So you know who Mr Seymour is too?' I ask. I feel right weak with it all.

They haven't been able to trace him, that's where they need my help. They're sure about the name: Eveline heard the name Seymour, she's sure about it. I'm wondering why they don't just pick up Mr McIntyre right now and find out who Mr Seymour is that way. The smell of warm food wafts through the house.

'Now, Arletta, we gotta get this right,' says Jackson. 'The law states quite clear what you can do and what you can't do. Right now we got no evidence other than a whispered name corresponding to the one you gave Errol. They seem to match up. That's all we got.'

'When we get these men we need to put them away for good,' says Albert. 'Arletta, that's my daughter inside that hospital. If it was left to me, I'd set about killing them both with my bare hands, put a bullet through their heads. I'd happily go to jail for the rest of my life for it, but what I really want is these men put away for a very long time and me left right here bringing up the family that needs me. Let prison deal with them. Prison is no good place for their sort. Believe me on that.'

'I just don't understand why you don't get Mr McIntyre right now. At least one of them is taken away and his girl made safe.'

I sound, and feel, like I'm losing my mind, but I know they need as much evidence as they can find to have a watertight case. They want them put away for good as much as I do.

'If we don't get it right, they walk, Arletta. They walk away and nothing happens to them at all.'

'But if we can put the two of them away, it sends a message out to the rest,' says Jackson. 'There's more than these two vermin at that nasty game. We need your evidence, Arletta. We need you to tell us everything you know.'

'We need to find other victims, get as many of them to come forward as we can. Do you know of anyone else they've done this to?' asks Albert.

I look at Errol.

I tell them about Safi.

'I can't know for sure, she never said, but she died. She ended up pregnant and she died giving birth to the baby. She never told me she was ... a ... a victim. It was after she died that I suspected, because she never said a word about getting pregnant, who the father was, who she ...'

Albert reaches out and pats my hand.

I got my strength and I need to be remembering it.

'You've waited a long time, young lady. Have a little more patience and do this our way. I know that's hard, but it's how we'll get them, put them away for good.'

I've never seen a man so full of sadness. Pappy looked sad sometimes, especially when Mambo started up, but he never looked like Albert Gaudet. I guess if Pappy was alive right now and he was hearing about me, he sure would look just like him. I don't know how I can help, but I'm going to do all I can. Now they know all about me.

'Can you give us a description of Seymour?' asks Jackson. He opens his notepad.

'He was younger than Mr McIntyre, but more portly, he wasn't small like Mr McIntyre. He was a full head and shoulders bigger than him. Blond hair, dirty, always sort of tangled, never used a brush or comb, I would say. He never went much on hygiene, and he drank all the time. Always full of liquor already, and still drinking. I guess he was what you'd call a heavy drinker. I remember how he talked too, it was different. It's a long time ago now. but I never heard anybody speak like that. It was different.'

'And you hurt him. Arletta.'

I remind myself that I'm sitting with friends. They need my help and I'm glad to be giving it.

'I wanted it to stop. I never planned it or anything like that, it's just when he turned up that day I was feeling like I wasn't able to be taking any more of it. I got about as desperate as anybody was ever gonna get.'

I don't look up at them. My life feels like it could be sliding into an empty shell and I start wondering if things are going to be different now folks know about me. I go through how I heard him coming and hid out back, then I saw the fish knife.

'I just knew it was going to hurt him, enough to make sure I wasn't going to have to do it with him right there and then. I never thought past that. They'd got me so I couldn't think straight at all. I thought I'd killed him – I mean, I thought he was going to bleed to death. I never saw him or Mr McIntyre after that, but I didn't know if that's because Mr Seymour was still alive and told him, or if he was found dead out our way and Mr McIntyre put two and two together. I just didn't ever know.'

'It was a very brave thing for a little girl to do,' says Albert. 'Why did you never tell your parents?'

'I don't know who my father is and when I tried telling my ma about it, she never believed me. Well, she never heard much about it because of Mr McIntyre being a white man, and working in a bank, and black folks likely to get lynched just for accusing someone like him.'

The room is very quiet, it seems for a long time.

'That's the way it was for us folks.' I whisper.

I reckon everyone is glad the silence was broken.

'Thank you, Arletta. That wasn't easy.' Albert takes my hand again. 'Arletta, would you go see Eveline sometime? See if she says the same thing about him?'

'I guess so. We've both been through the same thing. I want to be sure about Mr Seymour too, if you think that's okay. I want to be sure it's him. When she's well enough, and ready, yes, I guess I'll go see her. I'll help.'

Jackson plays with his hat, saying nothing. Errol pats my shoulder and Bette brings lemonade. The kids are silent someplace. Albert brings a cart to take me and Errol home.

I'm grateful to be back in Mrs Archer-Laing's new kitchen and sitting on one of her uncomfortable 'fad' stools. I play around with Errol's catfish and fennel and never manage to put as much as a spoonful into my mouth. He watches it get cold, then takes it away. I climb the polished staircase up to my room and sit at the window all night. Long after dark Errol knocks on the door and brings me hot milk before he turns in. He doesn't say a word. I stare down Main Street all night and not a living soul is to be seen out on the street. It was the longest night I ever had.

A couple of days later Albert and Jackson pull the bell-chain at Mrs Archer-Laing's front gate and set the dogs off. That's a couple of days when I can say Errol never managed to get a morsel of food past my mouth.

On the road over to see his daughter in the hospital, I sit up front with Albert. Jackson and Errol sit behind us.

'She'd just finished school on Thursday and gone round the corner to see Grand-mère in the old house.'

I close my eyes and listen. I'm finding this world hard to bear and that's the truth.

'We lived there till last year, in the old house. We've only been where we are in the new place for eight months. She's always popping back to see her grand-mère and grand-père, it gives her time to get spoilt. She's good with the rest of the kids, being the oldest by a long chalk, and she's a great help to Brigitte and me, so we're happy for her to be the favourite back at Grand-mère and Grand-père's. She got, she got … grabbed on the way home.'

His cheeks are running wet. He runs his hand under his nose and sniffles.

Then they realised she was missing. Only took them half an hour or so because her ma popped round to their grandparents' house with the rest of the kids. Nobody saw or heard a thing. The force was out, all over town, the sheriff's office had empty warehouses checked, back of the shops, into the fields. No one in the neighbourhood slept a wink, and then she was found at the side of the road by a couple of guys on their way to the cotton early next morning. She was hurt real bad.

'They operated, did what they could,' his voice is cracking, 'so we're hoping for the best. What else can we do?'

The hospital is a long, single-storey building on the edge of town with the smell of disinfectant hanging in the air. A long snake-like corridor, painted two shades of green, dark on the bottom, light on the top, has wards leading off on both sides. Inside the wards rows of tidy beds and flowery curtains line up on each side. Nurses walk about wearing stiff white uniforms and soft white shoes that squeak on the rubber flooring. Apart from the squeaking, it's quiet and it strikes me if I'd thought about carrying Safi here myself she would likely still be alive. Trouble is, the only black face I see is my own.

Albert's daughter is in a room by herself, a side ward, with a nurse sitting outside her door flipping through a copy of *Life* magazine. She gets up when she sees us coming, gives Albert a solemn nod before she opens the door.

I gasp out loud when I see that little girl with her mass of white curls tumbling over the pillow. How young she is, how small, makes my knees just about give out. Her ma stands up.

'Arletta, this is my wife, Brigitte. Brigitte, this here is Arletta, she's come to see Eveline.'

'*Merci beaucoup*, thank you for coming.'

I cover my mouth to keep from screaming. Jackson is holding me up and I lean back on him. I've got to be strong. I have my strength. I've got to find my strength, she's just a child and I need my strength for her.

'Praise God, Albert. He's going to answer our prayers. Now that God has found another witness, they'll find him,' says Brigitte. 'It's in His hands.'

'Ya all right Arletta?' asks Errol. His steady hand has taken hold of my elbow. I reckon Errol knows better than to be thinking I'm any kind of a sign to be praising God for, but he can see I'm shaking.

I don't know what I was expecting. I thought her face would be bruised, or cut, or that she was going to have a black eye or something, that there would be some sign of what she's been through, but there isn't a mark that I can see on her. She looks like a peaceful sleeping child, her pink cheeks framed with white curls, about as different from myself at her age as it's possible to get.

I hear Albert moan in his breathing.

'Eveline's on morphine,' the nurse says, 'so she's a little drowsy. The doctor is monitoring the pain but she's coming along now.'

Albert moves next to her bed and runs his fingers through her curls as she stirs. When she opens her eyes they are glazed over, she's drowsy from the drug.

'Papa?'

'*Je suis venu te voir*, and to sit with you awhile. Me and Jackson. *Tu t'en sors très bien*, just great, baby.'

Eveline manages half a smile for her pa.

'This is Arletta. She's come to see you too. She's a real good friend of Errol's. Come and say hello, Arletta. She's come all the way out here to see you, Eveline.'

Though my legs have turned to jelly, I cross over to her bed without falling over. I want to bawl out loud but I'm going to be strong.

I've got my strength.

'Hello Eveline.' My voice breaks a little but I'm holding on. 'I've come to see you, and look how you're doing so fine now.'

Jackson pulls a chair up and I sit. When I take hold of her little hand a voice I know so well whispers close beside me.

'Ya have ya strength, chile.'

I nearly whisper Nellie's name out loud, but I stop myself on account of that room being so full of folks. Instead I smile at Eveline's pretty baby face. She looks like a young version of her ma, like a little blonde angel. Her eyes are deep blue, and the morphine has made her lids heavy, but she manages a faint smile.

'*Bonjour*,' she whispers.

'We're going to be strong, you and me. You feel how strong I am? Feel it in my hands? I'm holding you, Eveline.'

She nods.

I just have no idea what to say. I wonder why they wanted me to come, but then I notice my shaking stop. Looking at her and knowing all she's been through is making me strong. I'm able to keep control of myself and gulp down on the nausea swelling up in my throat. Someone, Errol or Albert, places a firm hand on my shoulder, but I could swear it was Nellie standing right there beside me.

'You and me, we're both going to be fine, aren't we?'

'Yes.'

I just let the words come.

'We're going to help each other because I know he's a bad man. He got me too, Eveline, and look how I'm doing fine, same as you're going to be, because we're both strong. Okay?'

'Okay.' She whispers softly and smiles so beautifully. How could anybody hurt this child? A part of me nobody can see is standing behind my strength weeping tears not shed for years.

'Eveline, that pa you got is just the best I've ever seen and he's going to find him, and we're going to help him do that. That's what we've gotta do and we're going to be okay.'

I turn to Albert and whisper. 'Should I ask her about him?'

'He was fat, fat like a pig,' Eveline says softly without being asked at all. Tears fill up her lovely blue eyes. I wipe them away and raise her soft little hand to kiss it.

'We're going to be strong,' she whispers.

'He was like that? A fat and smelly man?' I ask.

'He was like that.'

'His hair, what was that like?' I ask again, since she's talking.

'Like mine, but smelly. Maman brushes my hair every day, and at bed-time, so it don't get tangled up.'

Then I hear it.

Nellie's voice is low and close by us. I lay my head closer to Eveline and sing along with her. That's how I really know for sure that Mr Seymour's been at Eveline.

> *I never laid down my load, Lord*
> *I never gave Jesus my yoke*
> *And on both sides of the river*
> *Blood fed the roots of oak.*
> *Deliver, deliver, deliver my soul*
> *Rest my head on your pillow*
> *Lord, I never grew old.*
> *Hmmm, hmmm, hmmmmmmmm …*

Eveline grips my hand tight and speaks softly.

'She says don't go in the river.'

'What?' She can hear Nellie too?

'She says don't go in the river.'

'You listen to Nellie, Eveline. Don't go in the river. Stay with Maman and Papa.'

'What's her name?'

'This is Arletta, Eveline,' Albert says gently.

'No, Papa, the lady. She has a nice voice.'

'What lady, bébé?'

I beckon to Albert and say, 'It's okay, Albert.'

Then I turn back to Eveline.

'Nellie, she's called Nellie, and she's going to take the best care of you, just like she did with me. You listen to Nellie, listen and stay out of the river. She's going to say, "Stay with us, child," and you're going to listen. Eveline, listen to Nellie.'

'She's nice. She's a real good singer.' Eveline closes her eyes and I feel her drift. Nellie begins singing her song again and I hum alongside her.

'Stay, chile, stay.'

Suddenly Eveline stirs and opens her eyes wide.

'She says she's going to bring me a little puppy and I can call it Nellie. I'd like a puppy.'

'I'm going to bring you that brand new puppy called Nellie first thing tomorrow morning. I am.'

Her smile is so beautiful, I'm not thinking about how I'm going to fill that promise, I just know it's going to find a way of doing that for itself. It's going to be fine. If Nellie says so, it's going to get done.

'Think about all the things you're going to do with your new puppy. That puppy is going to need looking after, though, so we both need to be strong for that, won't we?'

'I'll be strong if Nellie's here. Will she stay with me till the puppy comes? I'd like her to stay. She's nice.'

'Oh, sure she will. She just asked me if she was able to stay with you all night. To take care of you, along with your maman. Isn't that funny?'

'That's funny.'

'She looks after folks real good. She looked after me real good when Seymour came and he was never able to come again. Never. Ever. That's the way it is with Nellie. Real safe. You just got to do exactly like she says. Okay?'

'She says you must come back. She wants to tell you something.' Eveline's voice is weak but her hand is gripping me strong.

'Arletta and Nellie will both be here when you wake up, first thing,' says Albert. 'I'll be here and we'll all be together, you, me, Arletta and Nellie, Maman, everybody. It's going to be fine.'

His voice is breaking up so he stops.

Eveline is looking sleepy. I reach over and kiss her forehead.

'Get to sleep now, and rest. Get your strength,' I whisper. 'Stay with us, don't go in the river, child. Promise.'

'Promise. Thank you, Nellie. She'll tell you tomorrow, she says she'll tell you something …'

Eveline closes her eyes; the morphine brings sleep.

I tiptoe out and Errol takes my arm. I'm glad I've got something to lean on. Albert closes the door to Eveline's room behind us.

'Thank you, Arletta. I don't know what you just did in there, but my little girl doesn't look so bad,' he says.

I remind him we've got to find a puppy before the morning. I turn round and start walking with Errol close behind me.

'Who the hell's Nellie?' Jackson whispers behind me.

'Don't know, Jackson, don't know,' Albert replies.

'Hope this ain't none of that voodoo shit …'

Errol swings round to face them. Quickest I ever saw him move.

'Maybe it is and maybe it ain't, Jackson, but I'm telling ya, I'm thinking that little girl's gonna make it and I sure as hell didn't think nothing on the chances of that 'fore now.'

I touch his arm gently because this is not the time to be getting mad.

'I'm sorry, Miss Arletta,' says Jackson, 'I didn't mean …'

'It's all right, Jackson. Let's go find a puppy and I'm going to tell you who Nellie is.'

I know Eveline is going to make it. They don't, so I'm not blaming anybody for anything.

Jackson speaks first, once we get back on the road. He knows where we can get a puppy, a little beaut, he says.

'One of those little lap dogs, a poodle sort of a thing, cute as hell.'

'Yeah?' Albert brightens up. 'Where's that? Can we get it now? Before tomorrow?'

We follow Jackson's directions and hang a left out the Old River Road towards the oak grove.

'You remember that French lady friend of everybody, Albert?'

'Oh yeah. Hey, yeah, she's always carrying that little white curly poodle tucked under her arm. *C'est beau.*'

'Think they're completely pointless myself, but I guess we found a use for one of them now.'

I turn in my seat so I can see them all. I want to tell them about Nellie. Jackson apologises, says he feels like a fool after all I've been through and what I'm doing for Eveline. He shakes his head like he doesn't want to be looking me in the eye right now.

'That's all right, Jackson. First time I hear Nellie sing happened one day down by Sugarsookie Creek, a little ways from where I was raised. My ma had left me on my own; she knows that was wrong, but these were different times, I guess, and looking back, well, she wasn't much outta being a kid herself. She was leaving me alone like that all the time, anyways. Mr McIntyre watched for her coming and going so he knew when I was by myself. I'm never going to have kids either.'

Nobody is looking my way.

'This day, I was hurting, I was bleeding from Mr McIntyre and, well, it just made me cry like the child I was. I was like that more days than I care to remember. There was no other folks living nearby, nobody I could tell. This day it felt so bad, real deep-down bad, so I head off on my own, like I did all the time, missing my Pappy. And then I hear somebody singing the saddest song I ever heard. I thought at first maybe somebody had followed me out there, so I got real scared. But it was Nellie.

'She told me then just what I told Eveline today, and that made me strong. Every time it happened I'd go talk with Nellie and she always told me what I had to do, and she'd sing her sad song. When it got real bad, when Mr Seymour started coming round, she said she was going to give me a gift. She was going to make me so strong I was going to be able to stop it happening and, I swear to you all, I heard her voice just before I slashed Mr Seymour.'

They stay quiet so I carry on.

'Well, not only did I save myself, but my ma decided it was about time to start sending me to school. She started worrying about hearing me talking to what she called "an imaginary friend". Actually, she called it the fresh air, but that's what she meant. She thought I might be going a bit loopy because I never had any friends, never even saw many folks back then. Living where we were, there was nobody close by, but that's when my life started to change. Nellie really did give me a gift. Mr McIntyre and Mr Seymour stopped coming and I got to go to school.'

I look at Errol.

'And I even made me some real friends.'

We're about halfway up Old River Road. Once upon a time it was the avenue leading to a big old plantation house, but that burned to the ground years ago. Flames never took a hold on the oak trees lining either side of the avenue, so it still looks grand. The first golden orange of evening light is dappling through leaves busting out of their buds.

'I swear I heard Nellie in that room with Eveline and that isn't going to do her any harm. That's just the way it is. And I swear she heard her too. I swear.'

I don't reckon there's anybody sitting in that cart going to say any different.

Albert pulls off the Old River Road and stops by what was once the slave quarters and storehouses of the old place. The buildings are all in the way of being fixed up now, housing a forge, a hardware store, a bakery and what looks like a general store, with seamstresses sitting in the windows. They're starting to clear up for the day. The other side of the road has a lot of construction going on, looks like more new housing is underway.

Albert helps me down from the cart.

'You're a good woman, Arletta, and I see what you're doing for my girl.'

Jackson takes my other hand. 'We'll get them.'

That's the only time I was ever inside of a bordello.

'Jackson, I ain't going to ask how you know they got puppies here. I ain't going to ask.' Albert shakes his head.

Jackson laughs and reminds him they raided Madame a week ago. He raps on the shutters till a voice comes screaming back.

'*Silence! Arrêtez! Je viens maintenant!*'

Tout de suite opens the door.

'Miss Arletta?'

'Tout de suite?'

Madame Bonnet comes bustling down the hall, shouting in French.

'*Mon Dieu*! *Encore*? *Non, non, non*!'

She sure stops dead in her tracks when she sees me.

'Arletta?'

'*Bon soir, Madame. Je ne sais pas* …'

'Is Maman well? *Qu'est-ce que c'est*? *Petite* Rochelle?'

Madame looks about as shocked as Errol, Albert and Jackson. I assure her everybody is fine, that I didn't know we were coming to see her, or that this was where she lived. I'm stumbling over just what to say when I notice the poodle Jackson meant at Madame's feet, yapping and making a right noisy fuss. She picks it up and Foufi wags her tail at me, probably about as shocked as everybody else to see me.

Foufi's puppy is going to be perfect.

'You know Madame?' asks Jackson.

'One time Madame Bonnet taught me French. She's a friend and … we know each other that way …'

'*Entrez*! *Vite, vite*. What ees going on 'ere?'

Madame pulls me through the door like she doesn't want anybody seeing me there and orders a bewildered Tout de suite to go tell the girls they must be very quiet.

'We have the law 'ere again. *Vas*.'

Tout de suite takes off and Madame invites the rest of us to come in and sit down. I sit on a chair painted a bright red like I've never seen. The whole room is that colour, in one shade or another. Drapes, lamps, even the carpet under my feet is dark red and full of big pink roses. Madame smells as nice as ever. I always liked her perfume – she'd give some to Mambo sometimes. It fills the room just like it would fill our cabin, even long after she'd be gone. She's looking more puzzled than I ever saw anybody about why I've turned up with the law, that's for sure. Jackson, hat twirling between his fingers, speaks first.

'Madame Bonnet, this is my colleague, my friend. The little girl who was attacked – I'm sure you've heard – the little girl who was assaulted … this is her father.'

Madame's face changes.

'*M'sieur*, I am so sorry, so sorry for you, and your family. *C'est terrible*. How ees *l'enfant?*'

Albert shakes his head.

'But why you are here? What can I do? Anything, *m'sieur* … anything. I do anything for you and your little girl. Maybe you think I know who do this? Arletta, *ma chérie?*'

'Madame, you have puppies …'

'Ah! Oui, *je vois* … I see, *oui, venez. Si l'enfant veut un chiot*, a puppy … *oui, oui* …'

One of these puppies takes to me like it's been waiting for me to come since it was born so little time ago. It's a little female pup and it's licking my face clean.

'*Oui*, yes … a little girl, so sweet,' nods Madame Bonnet. When she nods, more perfume fills the room.

'*Une petite* fluffball d'allsorts' is what she calls the puppy.

'She have no pedigree. Part poodle we know about, but what part what else? *Je ne sais pas*. Ees enough to be watching my girls. Watching the dog ees too much.' She laughs a little. 'Nobody see anything at all, but then she's carrying the puppies. Who knows?' She shrugs.

Jackson asks how much for the pup, but she refuses payment, hoping it brings comfort to the little girl. She thanks Albert for coming to see her, for letting her do something for the poor child. Madame has tears in her eyes, she dabs at them with a sweet-smelling lace handkerchief.

'Madame Bonnet,' I begin, 'please don't mention I was here to Mam— … my ma, anybody, not yet. Please. I promise I'm going to explain. I promise you.'

'Of course, *ma chérie. Je t'aime. J'espère que tu* …'

'*Je suis très bien. Ce n'est rien.* I know the family from church, and Errol, he does for Mrs Archer-Laing, that's where I have my boarding. That's all. Eveline, the little girl, she asked for me, she wanted to see me, isn't that right, Monsieur Albert?'

Madame doesn't look like she believes me at all, and Albert's awkward assurance that he knows me from church sure doesn't leave her convinced, either. Her eyelashes flutter.

'I will tell nobody that you came 'ere, *m'sieur*. Now go. *Allez, vite*, so no one can see you are 'ere. I will tell my girls to say nothing.'

'Madame Bonnet, I will tell everyone that I came here, and I will tell everyone of your kind gift to my daughter. Thank you.'

'No, *m'sieur*, there is no need, *l'enfant* keep the puppy and you, you keep your reputation.'

Albert wags his finger at her.

'I will keep my reputation, Madame, and make sure you gain one. Thank you. Goodbye to you.'

Madame looks right bashful, like I've never seen her, when Albert kisses her cheek. We get a shaking of more perfume.

'I will pray for 'er. *Au revoir, m'sieur*, and thank you. *Merci, merci beaucoup.* You come to me, I do something to help, *merci. Merci.*'

She takes hold of my hand.

'*Je t'aime*, Arletta. *Nous aurons reparlé demain …*'

'*Non*, Madame, I will come back.' I lower my voice right down and plead with her to say nothing to Mambo until I have had the chance to tell her what's happened, and why I'm here with the law. Then I'll come back. I promise her everything is fine.

'Let me tell Mambo,' I whisper, 'please, then we can talk. Everything is fine. Really, I promise. I must speak to her first.'

My head is spinning. Madame is no fool: she knows for sure I'm not there because I know them from church, and I never had any idea that she was running a whorehouse, either. I never thought, even when Mambo was at her worst, that she was ever tied up with that kind of business at all. I think about Pappy and how his heart would be broken if he knew that about my Mambo.

I ask Albert if I can keep the puppy for the night.

'Anything you want, Arletta. I'm going to drop you and Errol and that new pup home right now and I'm going to pick you up in the morning to take little Nellie here to meet her new mistress.' He smiles and ruffles the puppy's ears.

'Thank you. Errol, you think Mrs Archer-Laing is going to mind? We don't really need to be telling her, do we?'

'No, we don't, but I'm sure gonna, 'cause I know this li'l mite's gonna be yelpin' and pining all night. Don't go worrying none about it. I gonna fix that. Ya sure done all right here, Arletta. Ya done good today.'

It's just as well Mrs Archer-Laing and Sadie are told about little Nellie, because she yelps and skids across that floor making the kind of racket that house has never heard before. She gets chewing on my shoes, sofa cushions, pillows, my only hat, anything she's able to get her tiny mouth around. Errol leaves a bowl of milk and finely minced pork and she eats the whole lot in between racing round that room like trouble.

When I get myself off to bed she whimpers from the blanket on the floor. I figure this is her first night far from her ma, so I lift her up into the bed. We both fall asleep right away.

Eveline holds her hands out as soon as she sees the little pup next morning. I reckon Nellie's already taking care of her fine, because she looks like she's got what I call Nellie's strength in her.

'Oh I love her, thank you! *Merci beaucoup*! *Merci*! *Merci*!'

The pup is licking at her face and making Eveline laugh; her eyes are sparkling.

'I love her! Look Papa, she loves me too!'

I reckon she's found a moment to forget what happened to her, and Albert's face is wet at the sight of it.

'Nellie told me she would be a nice puppy, and she said she would always be my strength. I'm so happy, and Arletta, come, come.'

She beckons me close. I put my head right next to her and stroke her curls. She's going to be fine. That much I know, even after all she's been through she'll find a way to be fine. Like I have.

'Nellie says she will help you.'

Her little face is real serious. Our eyes lock on one another.

'Help me? Help me how? To do what?' I whisper.

'Nellie will help you, that's what she says.'

'Okay, Eveline. Thank you.' I stroke her fine curls and smile because I think she's a kind, quaint sort of a child. But I'm not ready for what she says next.

'Then you will have to go far away. As far away as you can get, where nobody can find you. Ask your friend where she can send you. She will know.'

'What did Nellie say? I don't understand, Eveline. What should I do? Did she say?'

'She says she will give you the strength for it, like she did before, but you must go far away after it, to be safe after it, she says. She says she will help you get it done again. Don't worry, she says you must not worry, it will be all right. But you must do it and go far away once it's done.'

Then she laughs at her new pup. Albert's face lights up every time he sees her laughing. The sparkle is back in his baby's eyes and they're both laughing over that little mite of a half-poodle pup like Mr Seymour never happened. That's one of the nicest things I ever saw.

Errol nods me out of the room.

'What was that, Arletta? What she say?'

'I'm not sure, Errol. She said Nellie is going to help me. Then she said I was going to have to go away where nobody would ever find me.'

'I ain't liking the sound of this at all, Arletta.'

'Well, she heard it from Nellie. She said.'

'Nellie ain't real, Arletta.'

'Not to you, Errol.'

'Arletta, I wish ya'd come to the church.'

'I know I'm going to stop them, Errol. That I know. I just don't know how. With these men in there or without them. I'm going to stop it.'

Errol shakes his head.

'Just take care. Take care, y'hear?'

After we leave the hospital, Albert looks straight ahead and speaks very softly.

'Be sensible, Arletta, this is best left to the law. There's no doubting your feelings, I have them myself …'

'It's all right, Albert, I'm going to help you find Seymour like I said, that's all I'm going to do. I know what he looks like and I know where that scar is. I put it there.'

'That's what worries me, Arletta. That's what worries me.'

Twelve

I open my trunk. It's stacked full of the journals and pamphlets I've been collecting, and what I call my real treasures, half-a-dozen shabby, spineless books. I lift the King of England into the first light of day he's seen since Safi passed away. His ermine robe is trimmed with light rust now, from all those years underground, and his once brightly coloured medals look like a milky magnolia has been poured over them, bleeding the colour.

I open the tin. It still smells of dirty money. The comforting aroma of Pappy's baccy is a long time gone. My own savings come to just $22. That's the paltry sum of all my years of working, but Seymour's $355 are still there. Except for what I gave Safi's ma, that money has never been touched. This is the first time I ever looked at it and didn't feel like I'm going to keel over.

At the very bottom, Pappy's old papers are still there too, tied up with the same old twine. I feel heartsick about Mambo and glad he never found out what she was doing with Madame Bonnet. I lift his papers out and hold them close to my cheek. These old papers, the King of England and his pipe are all I have left of his that I can call my own. The old twine is brittle and falls apart with handling. The contents drop to the floor. Inside the outer newspaper wrapping there's an envelope, foxed with rusty-coloured spots and smelling musty. I feel happy right away seeing my name written in the clear beautiful hand-scripting he was so proud of. That's how he taught me to write too; folks are always talking about my fine hand. The envelope glue has crystallized and I see the folded papers inside. I never knew they were there. He never said anything about it at all. He just said his old pal Jeremiah had to be there opening the tin with me, but of course he passed away too.

Dear Arletta,

    This is for the day that's coming. I will be gone and you're going to need a help. Maybe that you will study; I hope so because you are a clever girl and the day will come when coloreds are lawyers, and more of us sitting in Congress even. I know you will make me proud in Heaven.

    When I was young and working on the cotton, I saved the life of the master's only son from drowning. Your mother and grandma sure never know that I own our land for that day. All the land from the track to the trees, you can see from the deeds, belongs to me, nobody can argue it. When I got to be a free man, the master gave me the land for something to start out with and I was lucky because not everybody round here got a piece of land like some did in other parts. I'd never seen a dollar till after I leave the plantation, but I got the land.

    The land and what little we have on it is yours, Arletta. The legal deeds are put right and proper in your name with Mr Roy Herbert's law firm in Baton Rouge. Don't never put Mambo off the land, she just been young and got no proper direction yet from the Lord, but He will answer my prayers because I been praying for Mambo since the day she's born. But the land is yours alone.

                  Your loving Pappy

I read that letter over and over again. In all those years he never told his family that he owned the land all the way from the pipe to where the track ends and up to the trees behind our cabin. The deeds show it clear as day. Pappy sure did know about keeping secrets. Must be where I get it from. I look at those deeds and what my Pappy gave me that I never saw because I never liked going near that dirty money. I have another night sitting at the window long into the darkness, watching a couple of mangy stray dogs scavenge Main Street in the moonlight. The public works have just started laying a sidewalk down our way because of all the automobiles taking to the streets these days, and it looks like workmen's leftovers must be good pickings. My mind is like it's on wheels, thinking about Eveline and what Nellie said, thinking about Pappy's letter, and my own land. I'm going to do something about it all; I just don't know what.

Now I find I'm a landowner.

The following morning I pass by the NAACP office and tell them Mambo has taken ill and I'm going home to help out with Rochelle for a couple of days. I take a few dollars from the King of England and catch the bus south. It crosses over the Mississippi River bridge and into Baton Rouge. Everyone leaves the bus downtown and I ask the driver where I'm likely to find the Louisiana Planters' Bank. It's just a few blocks away.

The doorman outside the Louisiana Planters' Bank is wearing a uniform, something like Tout de suite, except in green. He looks at me like I'm guilty of something before I even speak.

'Ain't no beggin' here, miss. Go on now. Clear off 'fore the law sees ya.'

That doesn't exactly give me the confidence to ask who the bank manager is.

Baton Rouge is another world. Buses, traps, carriages, horses, new automobiles, are all sharing that big thoroughfare and it's about as noisy a place as I ever heard. A scruffy kid pacing outside the bank is selling oranges and just when the doorman clips him on the ear for it, the blast of a motor-horn takes his mind off doing it again. He opens the door of the shiny black Ford and a woman wearing a fancy coat and high-heel shoes steps out of the plum-coloured leather interior. She walks inside that bank like she owns it. Maybe she does. This world has Marksville ladies, and ladies like the one that steps out of that car in Baton Rouge. I don't know what to say about her at all, except she's rich and beautiful and never been down a track like the one leading to our cabin.

I've never been one for getting lucky, but right then, as the doorman opens the outside door for her, and she waits for that, I see a big wooden plaque with shiny brass lettering next to the frosted-glass doors inside the lobby.

Louisiana Planters' Bank
Manager: Mr Charles McIntyre

Then I head back to Florida Street, near where the bus let me off, looking for Mr Roy Herbert's law firm. They don't want to let me see him till I show them the deeds to my own land.

'That's some story, Miss Arletta Lilith Johnson,' he says once I'm inside his office and talking. 'I sure expected to see you in here a long time ago, but I guess that letter gave you some kinda surprise when you got around to opening it up.'

'Yes, sir. It sure did.'

'Well, I can tell you it's right. Right above board. Mr Johnson came in here himself to do it. I heard he passed away. Here are the original deeds; what you have is a copy,'

'Is that how it works? You have the real deeds and I have a copy?'

'That's a safeguard. In case anything happened, you lost the deeds, or they were stolen. We keep the original here in our safe. Mr Johnson was a smart man. And of course you are the legal registered owner ...'

'If I want to change, pass the land on, what do I do?'

'Well, Miss Johnson, I hope that you will not be requiring a will for a long time yet, but we would attend to that here ...'

'How much would it cost please, Mr Herbert?'

'A few dollars. You want to make a will, Miss Johnson?'

'No, not yet.'

I spend most of the day watching workmen on the new levee and all the bustling down on the riverfront, keeping my eye out so I don't bump into Quince. I walk one way and then the other, buy steaming hot cornbread and gumbo wrapped in waxed paper, and eat it watching barges drifting up and down the Mississippi River, loading up and loading off. Two steamboats are lined up, sounds like one is throwing a party, and I think about my little upstream creek and the blood it washed away into this mighty flow of water.

When I make my way back to the bank, the scruffy boy is still hollering, 'Orangest oranges! Bes' colour and bes' taste this side a Mississippi.'

I pick a couple and toss him a whole dollar.

'Thanksee, Miss, thanksee kindly, Miss.'

I eat them out of sight in the narrow garbage alley across the thoroughfare and watch the big clock hanging in the bank window. At exactly four o'clock Mr McIntyre comes out and starts walking. I'm out of that garbage alley and mixing with folks on the sidewalk till I see him running for a bus coming his way. I dodge the traffic and jump on board before the doors close. He's sitting up front with his back to me, but I've still got to tell myself that he hasn't seen me for twelve years and it isn't likely he's going to know me at all.

He shakes out a newspaper and doesn't even glance up once when the driver starts arguing with some mulatto using the front door of his bus.

'Well, I's a bit of this and a bit of that and ain't no door for me.'

'Y'all ain't be starting no trouble on my bus again or I'm gonna get the law. Ain't got no place usin' that door and well ya knows it. Makin' trouble, that's all ya doin'. Same as always. That ain't ya door.'

'That's what I'm sayin', massah, ain't no door for me.'

The mulatto swaggers up to the back of the bus with everybody laughing except white folk up front tutting and twitching, all tight-lipped over his nerve.

'Well, there sure is a damn law for ya.'

Seems there's nothing but law all over Baton Rouge.

'I ain't black and I ain't white and that's 'cause a all ya white folks messin' wi' my ma.'

That gets the back of the bus clapping. Mr McIntyre just pulls his hat down and reads his paper like nothing is happening. I've got to keep in mind what kind of man he is, because he sure does look every inch a fine respectable bank manager, with what Mambo used to call a reputation.

When we get out of the city centre, he looks up once or twice to check the streets and I figure he's looking to get off soon. A few minutes later he folds his paper and I get ready to hop off too. I hold back with the folks boarding till he gets ahead a little then, as soon as he turns a corner, I speed up and reach it just in time to see him turn up a tidy path about halfway up the block.

That whole area looks more well off than I've ever seen, with nice neat lawns out front and frilly curtains stuck on the windows. Folks even have carports and across the way I see a garage. It's hard to think a man like Mr McIntyre is going to be leaving someplace like this to make his way down our dirt track because he needs to be raping a kid in a dingy shack with nothing but newspaper and flour paste up on the walls. Not so long ago thinking about that would have had me baulking.

I walk about the place, hoping I look like I could be the help inside one of those homes. I've never been in the habit of coming across folks who live in tidy streets like these. One thing I get to thinking is that somebody must be brushing inside and out, because there isn't a leaf out of place on the lawns, hardly a speck of dust on the sidewalk. I come across one of my own kind wearing a crisp blue dress with a white collar and pushing a shiny new cream-coloured pram. She smiles when we pass and I get the feeling she's looking back at me, wondering whose new help I'm going to be, since she's never seen me round that way before.

I keep on walking till dusk is past falling, then I make my way back to Mr McIntyre's. Except for a dim light from the porch, the garden is in darkness. It's a single-storey property and I creep round it to get an idea where the rooms are.

I get a bad feeling right from the start. That house is too quiet, especially since I know there are two kids living in it. I sneak, quiet as a mouse, round the back to what I reckon is the kitchen with the lights on. Must be Mrs McIntyre fixing dinner, and right there, with workbooks on the table, his two kids sit doing homework. Creeping right round, and from where I take my stand underneath the cover of a tree, I see Mr McIntyre in his front room still reading his newspaper. When he gets up, I follow from the outside and see him enter the kitchen. The children move right away and clear their books before setting plates down while he watches from the head of the table. He sits, folds his hands to say grace and they eat with not a word spoken between them at all. They don't even look up at one another, they just eat. When they finish he gets up and leaves, Mrs McIntyre starts clearing up and these two kids just slide out of their chairs and disappear. I creep back round and see Mr McIntyre turning on a wireless in the front room, like he's settling down for the evening. He pulls the window drapes across. I shiver, because that family hasn't spoken one single word to one another the whole time I've been watching and I reckon already that I'm right about his daughter. I was hoping he'd be treating her different, being his daughter and all, but I already know he's crazy enough for it.

I move around the house, spying through lace curtains. In one bedroom I find the boy sitting at a small table looking like he's back on his homework. He looks the studying kind.

I go looking for his sister. That's who I crossed the Mississippi river to see.

She's got a real nice room, it's spotlessly clean, with pretty pictures of flowers on the walls and a neat row of dolls lined up on a painted basket-chair in a corner. She's just sitting there on her small, neatly made bed, holding one of her dolls and swinging her legs as she rocks to and fro. Her poor little face is all I need to see. I see she's waiting and hoping it isn't going to come tonight, and I see she has nobody looking out for her and no place ever feels safe. I see all that fear, and hurting in her that she doesn't know what to do with. I see all that wondering why her mother doesn't ever come in the middle of the night to stop it.

Mrs McIntyre opens the back door and empties a bucket into the trash.

Albert says we need evidence: well, it looks to me like this little girl's got some of it. I don't know if she's ever going to give it up against her daddy, but one thing I do know, and she doesn't know it yet, is that I'm going to do for her what nobody ever did for me. I'm going to make it stop, make her safe.

I creep away and get back to the main road. I have more luck, I guess it's one of those days, and a bus pulls up in five minutes. Back downtown I catch another one home to Marksville and make it up to my room long before midnight.

The time has come to tell Mambo.

It's pouring with rain next morning, but the deluge has stopped by the time I pitch up at our cabin. I know Quince is off working and Rochelle is already at school, so Mambo will be alone.

Our cabin hasn't been that dull old place I grew up in since Quince quit liquor and Mambo got back earning. It's still a simple kind of place, never going to be anything else, but it's got two bedrooms now, even if they are tiny, and with Mambo's green fingers there isn't a yard growing like it all around. The pink paint is cracking on the outside, but it's still looking fine, and all that old newspaper we stuck up a long time ago is gone from inside. Mambo told me Quince cursed and cursed for a whole weekend trying to clean the flour-and-water mix off the walls before he could paint it white.

Mambo is out front picking fresh mint.

'Arletta! I's pickin' all this mint 'fore it takes right over round here. I'm gonna be giving it away 'cause it's growing like nobody's business. Take some when ya go, Errol do somethin' with it.'

'Bit wet for gardening Mambo.'

'What ya doin' here girl? I ain't expecting to see ya at all.'

'We alone Mambo? Quince working?'

'Ya poorly?'

'No. But I need your help. I came out here to tell you about something, and then I'm going to need your help sorting it out.'

'Hell, that sure do sound serious. Let's sit outside, it's clammy. How the hell it so damp and clammy at the same time? Huh?'

'Humidity. A breeze would be nice.'

'Hey, ya ain't working? What's up? Ya notice that gate got fix?'

I didn't even notice that. Too much else on my mind.

'You've got that man trained good Mambo.'

'What's up Arletta?'

Mambo's got her hands full of fresh-picked mint. I think right then that I'm always going to remember the smell of Louisiana's good wet earth and mint dripping with rain.

Mambo cocks her head. She's wondering what I'm doing out there in the middle of the working week.

'Sit down, Mambo. I've got something I need to say. Something that happened a long time back.'

'What girl? Ya frightening me.'

She sits in Pappy's old chair out on the porch – it's still rocking – and fans herself with the bunch of cut mint. The fine water spray off the leaves is as refreshing as the smell.

I lean on the doorframe and start talking. No point in putting it off, been doing that long enough.

'It happened when I was alone out here, and I got left out here a lot …'

'I knows it Arletta. I look back and I don't know how I gotta be crazy like I was; I was just flying high bein' Mambo round here when Grandma passed on. I was too young to be knowing so much 'bout other folks' business and be telling 'em how to fix it. That make me crazy, I reckon.'

That's the way it was for Mambo. Everybody came and listened to her anyways. Everybody took her stuff because it's always been the best there is.

'Having Rochelle teach me what being a ma is all about, and I'm gonna go to my grave feeling bad about the way I was when y'all were just a chile.'

'You were young too, that's all.'

'I was crazy girl …'

'Let me speak. Please.' I take a deep breath. 'First time it happened was when Mr McIntyre was kinda taken with you.'

'Mr McIntyre?'

'What he really wanted was to get at me …'

'What ya say?'

I see she's dreading what all at once she guesses might be coming. I waited a long time for today, it's what's always been wrong and she's about to hear what she could never figure out. Her lips turn pale and draw back. Her eyes stare wide and unblinking at me.

'I'm telling you now because what was going on with me has just happened to somebody else. She's just eleven years old Mambo, and they weren't even sure at first if she was going to survive it. She said a name I know about, so the police got in touch with me. Errol told them about me, I had told him just …'

'The police? What ya telling police that ya ain't tell me Arletta?'

'When I was left out here, Mr McIntyre used to come out all the time, he was always on his rounds, watching for you leaving. They do that, that's how they know …'

'Who Arletta? Ya ain't telling me …'

'Mr McIntyre was raping me for years Mambo, since just after Pappy died.'

The scream coming out of my Mambo sounds like heaven split open and let go of its thunder. Like her soul is rent apart with it. Roosting birds empty out of the trees with a great whoosh. The earth beneath the cabin is shaking.

'Mambo, stop, listen …'

'No! No! Not that Arletta. No, not that. Pleeease no, don't tell me that.' She's up and clinging to the porch for support because her knees have given way. Her face is twisting with tears and fury. 'No Arletta, please no. I knows something wrong, I always knows something gone wrong, but not this!'

She throws herself down on the wet ground.

'Not this Arletta! Please not this! I let this happen to ya? My own chile. No! Please, not my chile, my baby girl!'

She half rises out of the mud and staggers, almost on all fours, towards her crop of herbs. Her hands reach into the wet dirt and she starts rubbing great clumps of it into her hair. Her eyes are wild and red like fire. Suddenly she straightens up, throws her arms up to the dark heavens and screams at it, like I never heard.

'MA-A-A-MBO!'

I fall back with the power of her voice calling her own Mambo. That scream is reaching way beyond the grave. That scream is reaching back through all our Mambos, the Dessalines, back to Haiti and all the way back to the Fon in the old country.

'MA-A-A-MBO!'

I don't know if I'm just thinking these dark clouds are coming down low with all her bellowing, but I know it's frightening me.

'Mambo, stop this and listen to me.'

'No Arletta, please no! Don't tell me this.'

I've never seen my Mambo this way. Except for the time she got wind of that Pawnee bitch, and when the spirits take a hold of her up in the mule barn, she's always been in charge of herself, as far as I ever saw. She's been in charge of herself and everybody round her all her life. Now she's going right out of her mind, seems clean out of control, more than I ever saw anybody, about what happened to me when she was leaving me alone and wiggling off like this world was nothing but what she could make of it. I guess all that guilt she was too young to feel at the time finally got a hold on her.

She lurches about in the mud, I don't know what she's saying or what tongue she's using, but the clouds sure are rolling down lower in the sky. I don't understand any of the old tongue, never could. She gets as far as the trees at the edge of Pappy's land and starts beating herself with a stick so hard I see blood coming with every strike, still mumbling. When I try grabbing it we do battle till we both fall down. She's looking as wild as any madwoman could and breathing deep, like a mad bull.

'Mambo, it's in the past …'

She looks up at me with those eyes red and crazy, dirt and blood covering her face, hair tangled up with grass and twigs, white teeth snarling. She looks just like one of those evil spirits I've seen her raise up at Lamper Ridge mule barn.

'No, Arletta, ain't in no past. I'm gonna kill him.'

'Mambo, get up. Listen. I need your help. Listen. Please.'

She pulls herself upright, eyes full of hatred. Mambo is terrible, but I never saw any hatred in her till now. She staggers a little, then reaches out to pull me close.

'Arletta!'

When she says my name it sounds like a hurting is let out of her belly. Her grip is so tight I feel I'm going to smother on all that muck clinging to her clothes. She starts swaying like she's going to go slipping into one of her trances.

'Mambo, let me go. It's all right. It's all right.'

She keeps swaying. Mumbling starts up again.

'No Arletta, it ain't all right. Ain't never gonna be all right.'

'I want to tell you everything about it. I want to tell you something I did. Mambo, will you listen?'

She lets me go and I wipe her face with her skirt. She nods but tears are coming now and they don't stop all through my sorry story. Her mumbling goes on, a low sound like Mambo is only halfway listening to what I'm saying and halfway gathering fighting forces from someplace else.

We sit down, past caring that the grass is wet and rain is falling again. When I ask if she remembers that I tried telling her about Mr McIntyre just after it started, her voice doesn't sound like my Mambo at all.

'Yeah,' she says. 'When ya go telling me, I thought, with all them newspapers ya always reading and all, that maybe ya just making it up. I s'pose I was thinking ya just wantin' attention, since that's something I ain't never give ya enough of.'

She's sniffling and wiping her nose in her skirt.

'It's okay, Mambo. That's all a long time ago, I just want to tell you everything. It's time, Mambo. It's time.'

'Arletta, I was real scared somebody was gonna hear ya talking that way. Back then talking that way was gonna get us a lynching. Still could. Folks lynched for a lot less honey. Him being at the bank and all. I was scared for ya honey.'

The rain pours down. Her hair sticks to her forehead and her beautiful face is washed clean. She's staring into nothing and looking like a woman who just found out she's been conned her whole life. I guess that's about right. And I'm counting my Mambo isn't going to go for that at all.

I tell her all about what they did to me and she weeps, mumbling into the rain on her face. I tell her about Mr Seymour and what I did with my slashing. I tell her about Nellie, and about how she used to sing, and how I heard her singing to Eveline in her hospital room. I tell her about what Nellie told Eveline to tell me.

'I've been carrying this with me every day of my life, Mambo, and I don't want to be carrying it no more. In all these years nobody ever stopped them, they ain't never been caught.'

'Well, now they's caught good. Net closed in. Law and Mambo.' She gets up. 'And I'm telling ya this, child of mine, Mambo is getting there first. I hope they ready for what's coming. I hope they ready for it.'

'I'm ready Mambo, ready for what we need to do. You should have seen that little Eveline, she's lucky to be alive. They need stopping, and nobody else is doing it. And like Nellie says, I'll go away as soon as I've seen it done.'

Mambo is wiping her face.

'One thing at a time Arletta. Ya ain't going nowhere. I'm gonna take care of this. Don't be worrying about that. Arletta, ya my flesh and blood and I's gonna take care of this. This here about payin' for all that shit done to my child, my li'l girl, this here about revenge, and Arletta, ya know how good I am at revenge.'

Mambo dries her eyes, the heavens rumble. I sure know what the fight looks like when it's coming up in her. Here it comes.

'Hell, I ain't ever done nothing else for ya. I even asked ya to leave at fourteen years old,' she sniffs. 'And look at ya now. Come like a young lady I'm right proud of. I sure am proud of my own daughter. Look at ya, honey, a lady now. Ya turn out a lady who knows how to talk right and I toss and turn some nights feeling the devil's own guilt about how I was with y'all, and Pappy. I sure do.'

'You feel guilty, Mambo?' I say that quietly because I never got round to thinking she ever felt guilty.

'Well, hell, if I didn't before, and believe me girl, I did, I sure feel sick about it now. I feel sick on hearin' this, Arletta, and Mr McIntyre better start counting his happy sunrises, 'cause he ain't got too many of them to be lookin' forward to. No he ain't.'

She wipes herself down and straightens her shoulders. Mambo and me are both tall, and she is up to her full height now, dress covered in wet mud, hair tangled up with dirt and leaves. She looks like she's just spent a fortnight up in the mule barn and that suits me fine, because I don't care what she's going to use, how fearful she's going to get, just so long as we do what needs doing.

'Mambo?'

'Eh?'

'You know Mambo, we finally found a real use for one another. We're going to be doing what we got to do for one another.'

She nods and a little smile curls up the side of her lips. She's madder than I have ever seen her, but I know she's pleased about that.

'That may well be,' she starts walking back towards our cabin, 'but this is my trouble. I'm taking care of this.'

'No, Mambo. Because of Rochelle. We've got to think of Rochelle.'

She stops right there and turns her head to the side, in that way of hers.

'Whatever happens Mambo, we've got to make sure everything is okay for Rochelle. I want to take care of it so nothing is blamed on you. You can help me, Mambo, I need your help, there's no way I know what I'm doing without you, but I'm going to take all the blaming there is if it starts going round. I get a feeling it's going to, so whatever happens, whatever we do, I'm going to be leaving, for China, England, anywhere, someplace nobody knows who I am. You're going to stay here and do right by Rochelle.'

Her neck stiffens. I can see she's tearing apart.

'Do right by Rochelle, Mambo. That's the thing. Do right by her.'

Her head hangs down in front of her.

'She's going to college, I'm going to see to that, and when she gets a good life, she's going to give you a good life. I'm seeing to that too.'

'Now, how the hell ya goin' be doin' that?' Mambo turns to look at me, hands on hips, head cocked to the other side.

'Have a wash, Mambo, and I'll tell you. We're going to talk. You look like an old ju-ju queen covered in all that dirt.'

She points at me.

'That's 'cause I am girl. That's 'cause I really am.'

The old wiggle is still there as she turns and walks off. She lifts her head up to the dark clouds and throws her muddy hands in the air.

'And I'm the best there is McIntyre.'

She reaches the cabin before I do and comes back out holding up her old fish knife. After years of sharpening, the blade of that knife has gone deadly thin. I shiver at the sight of it.

'This it?'

'Yes Mambo, that's it.'

'Well, Mr Seymour ain't seen the last of this. It's still got his name all over it. Crying out for more of his blood, I'm telling ya that. It's bellowing for blood!'

While she washes herself with water from the barrel, I fix a couple of moonshines with plenty sugar and a bunch of freshly picked mint. It's been a long time since I tasted liquor, the first not pushed down my throat. Sometimes I'd have so much forced on me that I'd be staggering to Sugarsookie Creek – even fell in a few times. I chip at the icebox and take the drinks out to the porch. Rochelle will be back on the school bus and I have a lot I need to be saying before she gets home.

When Mambo comes back out onto the porch she's wearing fresh clothes.

'That's better Mambo.'

The rain is coming down in sheets. We stare into space and listen to the din it's making on the tin roof. I notice the porch doesn't leak like it used to.

'How is Quince doing?'

'He's changed, settled down, I guess, even doin' more round the place, like that gate. He's fetchin' wood for putting the fence all round, he says. Even gettin' himself out there, making noise about them laying water pipes down this way. Says it ain't gonna happen for years, mind you, but ain't never gonna happen at all if folks don't get on out there shoutin' for it.'

Seems they're getting on okay, like they're going to stay together.

'Sure we are. We're used to one another now. He's a man with his own ways.' She shrugs. 'Once he started gettin' on at work, things got a whole lot better, things good. Quince likes a bit of money in his pocket, he got used to that, and he wants Rochelle to get on. I mean, he don't earn a whole lot without overtime, but he does as much of that as he can get since they pay it there nowadays, and we gettin' by okay. I'm sure as hell he had a fancy bit someplace, a woman knows that sorta thing, but to be honest, Arletta, long as it wasn't that phoney voodoo bitch out Pawnee way, I ain't care nothing about it. He ain't messin' now, I's sure of that, so, long as he brings home the bacon and don't get on with arguing and all that, we're fine.'

'As long as you're okay, Mambo.'

'Shoo Arletta. I'm more worried about my daughter than I am about Quince. We sticking together now, me and Quince, but I sure wish ya'd go get somebody to care for ya.'

'I look after myself. That suits me fine.'

'Well, ya sure ain't handling Mr McIntyre and Mr Seymour by y'self.' She half empties her tall glass in one long mouthful.

'What I didn't say before, Mambo, I've got so much to be saying, is that I have money. The day I lashed out at Mr Seymour there was blood all over your room. On the dresser, the floor, and I needed to get rid of it before you got home. I was real scared about what I'd just done and the last thing I needed right then was you getting on about it. I don't really know what I thought, other than what I did was wrong and there was blood everywhere to prove it. He had a wad of money inside his jacket pocket and it must have fallen out, because when I was clearing up all that bleeding before you saw it, the money was right there underneath the dresser. I mean, it wasn't like I was able to go looking for him and be giving it back, so I just kept it. I hid it away. I didn't know what else to do with it. Nobody ever came looking for it either. Never did.'

'How much?'

'Over four hundred dollars.'

'What?'

'Yeah. I hid it in that old green tin Pappy gave me, the one I used to hide his pipe in as well.' I look at her sideways.

'Ya took that pipe. Knew it. What tin? I ain't never seen no green tin with Pappy.'

'Probably because he kept it hidden from you and Grandma, because of what he hid in it.'

'And what the hell he ever have to be keeping hid from me and ya grandma? He ain't never have nothing. Ain't never ...'

'Mambo, stop that.'

First time Mambo ever listened to me.

'The trouble with Pappy was he give me too much rope. Ain't ever raised a hand to me and, boy, I sure needed it, as I recall. I started dealing with Pappy the same way I seen Grandma deal with him 'fore I was even past his kneecaps. And I tell ya, that lay heavy on my mind, too.'

She looks sad and I believe her. I let her be and say nothing for a while. That's between her and Pappy in his grave. I guess it's time she started talking to his spirit; reckon she will.

'So what he got in that tin?'

'The deeds belonging to this land.'

'Ya kiddin' me Arletta.' Her head cocks sideways.

'No Mambo. Pappy owned this land, from the edge out front, over there to the tree line and back up to the pipe. That pipe is on Pappy's land.'

'How the hell?'

'I just opened the letter he left for me a couple of days ago. I never knew what he put in there, thought it wasn't anything much, really, like you said, he never had much, never had anything. I thought it was just old newspaper he wanted me to read someday, probably something about Jesus, I always reckoned. I never read it right away anyway, because he said old Jeremiah ought to be there with me when I read it.'

'Jeremiah ain't ever able to read.'

'I guess he just wanted somebody with me.'

'And then Jeremiah died too. Ain't long after Pappy 'fore we put him in the ground.'

'And I was just a kid. I kept Seymour's money in the tin and I never liked opening it because of that. Last time I opened it was when I handed fifty dollars to Safi's ma when she came to pick up Martha from Marksville.'

'Hell, they ain't never believed that was her savings. They figured that come from Mrs Archer-Laing. She's a good woman and everybody figured she'd told ya to say that was Safi's savings. I figure the same thing.'

'No. I took the money from the tin. Only time I ever took.'

Mambo shakes her head.

'Ya ain't thinking Safi was … oh Lord. Ya think this happened to her too, how she get herself with Martha?'

'I've thought about it.'

Except Martha ain't got a look of no white man's child.

'I can't figure Safi, Mambo. Me and Errol thought about that, too. There's no telling about Safi at all, but we sure have been thinking about it.'

'Oh boy. How the hell did Pappy get his hands on this land?'

'Pappy saved the life of his old master's son just before they were all freed, and he got this land to give him a start because of that. I brought the letter. He never wanted anybody knowing he owned this land when everybody else hereabouts had nothing. Must have made him feel bad – I don't know, I guess he felt he had when others hadn't.'

'I tell ya what I know. When he was able to work this land, like he did before ya were born, he was always handing out to folks, corn, sweet potatoes, just a little bit of something. Grandma used to say he was doin' that 'cause he thought a mambo was gettin' something for nothing, on account that he got no faith in the old ways and medicine. He was a kind man …'

I hand Mambo the letter. She doesn't look too sure at first, but then she opens it up and reads her Pa's nice flowing script. He taught her that too, the same way he taught me. Afterwards she folds it slowly and holds it in her lap like it's some kind of holy thing. She says nothing for a long time, just sits in Pappy's rocking chair watching the rain drip down from the porch he built, and holding on to his letter.

'I ain't never think him good for much but, looking back, he just got on like everybody else, gettin' whatever work there was till he ain't able to go get no more. He'd come on home, work this land, ain't bother nobody and, my Lord, could that man keep a secret.' She looks down at that letter. 'Me and Grandma rib him all the time and he ain't never said a single word about it. And this, I tell ya Arletta,' she waves the letter at me, 'this was gonna shut us up good. Ain't nobody round here ever own nothing. Huh!'

She smiles, a great big beam of a smile that makes me grin too.

'Lord, except my Pappy. Ain't that something. Ain't that really something else. Old Pappy. He own this here land we sitting on and ain't never say a word about it.'

'Yup. He sure could keep a secret. I must be like him.'

'That's for sure.'

'Mambo, I've got stuff. I've got all that money, I've got this land, and when I need to be going, I want to take some of the money, then leave the rest for making sure Rochelle gets a good start at her education. She's going to have the life you and me were never going to have. And I want to pass this land over to you.'

'Pass it to Rochelle, she's ya sister, Arletta.'

'It changes everything though, doesn't it? I don't know where I'm going to go. I've got to work that out after ...'

'Ya just stop with all that jumpin' ahead, will ya? Ya hear Arletta? We gonna work out what we gonna do before ya start thinking about what we gonna be doin' after that. And I ain't wanting ya going no place, no how.'

'So you're going to help me?'

'No Arletta. I ain't.'

'What?'

'No Arletta, y'all gonna be helpin' me. That's the way this gonna be.'

'Oh Mambo, I thought for a minute you weren't going to ...'

'Shush, Arletta. I'm thinkin'.'

'The other thing is ...'

'Oh Lord, Arletta I ain't able to take no more. What else?'

'Well, Jackson, that's the other policeman, he knew where to get that pup for Eveline when she asked for it. He happened to know where there was pups. It was one of Madame Bonnet's fancy poodle pups. Foufi got pups.'

Mambo turns slowly.

'Madame knows about ya?'

'I chose the pup. I went with them. I didn't know where I was going but, well, of course she wanted to know what I was doing turning up with the law.'

'I'm bettin' she gone and get herself the shock of her life.'

'She knew about Eveline, everybody down that way heard about it. I said I knew Eveline's family from church, but I could see she didn't believe me. Well, she's never known any of us going to no church. Anyway I could see she didn't believe that was the whole story, or even the truth. She's thinking there's more, that's for sure.'

'Well, well, well.'

'She's going to ask, Mambo. I wouldn't be surprised if she's already told Tout de suite to drive her out here first chance she gets.'

'Well, well.'

Mambo is thinking.

I say no more because I'm about as washed out as that sky, going over all I had to tell Mambo. I let her do her thinking and wait till she feels it's time for her to do her talking.

'So, Mr McIntyre's gone to Baton Rouge. They know where Mr Seymour is?'

'No. They reckon Moreauville way, Mansura maybe, in striking distance of Eveline they called it, but they never heard of anybody with the name Seymour. He's got money, enough to be carrying wads of it in his pocket.'

'And ain't bothering to come and get it back, like it's nothing to him.'

'And he looks like a fat, rich, spoilt-brat sort. I'm thinking, now I know he isn't dead, maybe he's not going to be too hard to find.'

'No, he ain't.'

Mambo drains her glass of sugared moonshine.

'I'm gonna get me a nice suit.'

Thirteen

I take Nellie's advice and ask Mrs Archer-Laing for help. I ask her how I might go about being a missionary overseas. Mambo gets the idea eventually, though she still can't figure the Church.

'Got be good for something – all that dammit shit they's feedin' folks.'

Many mambos have taken to the Church one way or another, mixing one way of thinking and believing with the other. Not mine; my Mambo doesn't go for any mixing at all and says they're doing it just to keep hold of folks coming to them.

'Ain't mean nothin' but dollars to them. Church and all them phoney mambos. Ain't wanting nothin' but dollars.' She laughs. 'Spirit ain't know nothin' about no dollars and it sure ain't gonna get them into that heaven they's always squeaking on about neither. I'm bettin' ya can't buy ya way in there.' Mambo finds that real funny.

I want to be sure Mrs Archer-Laing sees that I have taken to being a serious Christian. I start that right away next time I pay my rent.

'Come in Arletta, dear, I was just thinking about you and how well you're doing teaching Bible class. Everyone is very impressed. I'm proud of you. Tea?'

'Yes, thank you, Mrs Archer-Laing. I always felt teaching children was going to be for me and now I know that it's my vocation, thank the Lord. Teaching His word made me see it plain.'

Her eyebrows rise up and a little smile twitches on her lips. I think she's taking a pride that I'm her convert.

Mrs Archer-Laing is about as shocked as I am when she finds out African Americans are not eligible for missionary work in Africa.

'Good heavens above, wouldn't you think African Americans would be the very first Christians they'd send back to Africa?'

'Yes ma'am,' Errol mumbles.

Can't say he's looking right sure about me being a missionary at all.

The NAACP get up in arms of course, and before I know it they're fighting the cause of a good Christian girl – myself – going to do God's work back in the old country.

Monsieur Desnoyers goes marching off to see what he can do about it too, courtesy of Mrs Archer-Laing's outrage, but I start thinking where else I might go. Right off I make out more disappointment than I really feel about Africa, but later on I find my thoughts drifting and dreaming about what I had heard all my life was 'the old country'. I dream about some far-off village with a small school and a simple life. Someplace everybody knows everybody else but nobody is going to know anything about me, about my past. I dream of some place I can teach children and make sure they're kept safe. Someplace where folks look just like me and I don't stand out different.

I get resigned to the fact that it's not going to be Africa, though, and think back on the yearning I once had for travelling to China when I was reading Mrs Lee Hem's journal and listening to her talking about her home country. There's no great call for missionaries in China these days though, so I agree to think about India and South America. I reckon I need to get taken with India, seeing that's about as far away as I'm able to get.

I set about getting a passport and papers for my 'calling' abroad. Of course, none of that is easy, since black folks get turned down all the time. Like they don't want us here but they don't want us going no place else neither.

'Them's startin' to worry who gonna do cleanin' and polishing if all us black folks take on off back to Africa,' mumbles Errol with a giggle in his chest. 'Them's got no clue on cooking, neither. And we been doin' they washing for hundreds a years.'

Monsieur Desnoyers sure is up on his high horse about my papers, and I've never seen papers like I've got to sign and swear on before I'm free for travelling. I leave Mambo considering the fine details of dealing with vermin like Mr Seymour and Mr McIntyre, because I'm right up to my neck with everything else. Especially since I'm not able to honestly say I got the Lord at all.

'Ya gotta be strong, Arletta. Nellie told ya that. And ya the daughter of a mambo, think hard on it, girl. Think of nothing else but what ya gotta do. Ain't room for nothin' else now. Ya been round this stuff long enough. Get them papers for travelling, get them tickets, and the day before ya put it all to good use, we gonna take care of business. And when it all dies down, ya gonna get y'self right on back here to ya own folks.'

She tells me it's best I don't see Albert or Jackson, except if they call of their own free will. I want to see Eveline, but I know it's best I listen to Mambo. If they get minded on calling round to Mrs Archer-Laing's, I've got to be careful to tell them just what I want them to know.

'Don't be lettin' no friendly white lawman coax ya business outta ya. Like ya says Arletta, ya's a woman able to keep secrets. Keep them till we do what we gonna do and ya well gone. They sure as hell ain't ever gonna get nothing outta me. I ever get asked? Well, I gonna bawl and cry and get on about what happen to my daughter and ain't nobody do nothin'. Way I figure it though, ain't nobody gonna know nothin' about me at all.'

Mambo gets herself that nice black suit, a string of false pearls and takes off for Baton Rouge. I give her fifty dollars.

'Girl, if ya seen them folks when I says I has fifty dollars to deposit. That clerk, he inspect every note I has, and all them white folks lookin' at me like I ain't got no business in no bank.'

She creases up laughing.

'And then,' she can scarcely speak with how funny she thinks it is, 'ya should have seen them snooty faces when I says I need to see the manager. "The bank manager is not in today," that clerk says, all uppity-like, so I says, "Yes he truly is, 'cause I just seen Mr McIntyre walk on in here before me. He's a dear old friend of mine and I needs to be seein' him right away. We done business before. So just go on now, please tell him I'm here. Go on now.'"

I gasp.

'Mambo! I have no idea how you even got past that doorman without landing a clip round the ear.'

'Him? He ain't nothin'. Arletta, if ya'd seen nasty old McIntyre's face when he finds me out front in his own bank in Baton Rouge, all dressed up and all! I shake his hand, polite-like, and I get on so gracious he just ain't able to think what the hell is goin' on!'

'The clerk would have told him you were there to bank fifty dollars.'

'And he knows I sure ain't earning it cleanin' that poky little shed of an office in Brouillette. Lord, it was funny. If I wasn't so set on ruinin' him, I'd be gettin' myself feeling right sorry for him.'

I don't feel sorry for him at all.

'I tells him I'm gonna see him next week 'cause I'm doing real well and gonna be coming to Baton Rouge doing more banking. His eyes near pop right out of his head Arletta. Then I says, real low so ain't nobody else gonna hear, "We need to be gettin' together sometime, Mr McIntyre. I get myself a nice little business on the side, parties, that sort of thing." I give him one of my best smiles, and I winks. Then I says, "Ya kinda thing, if ya know what I mean, Mr McIntyre." Then I parades myself right out that front door like it's my very own, and wiggling my rear end like it's everybody's business.'

'Mambo, you're going to scare him off!'

'Fellas like that? No way. Arletta, ya don't know nothin' about men. Leave men to me: I been leading them on all my life, honey.'

No arguing with that. But I ain't saying nothing.

'Right now that respectable Mr McIntyre, manager of that right stylish bank in Baton Rouge where he's gone got himself fixed up, he's havin' himself a bit of relief in a dark room just thinking about his kinda thing. Men's fools, Arletta. Fools.'

✿

Monsieur Desnoyers reports back on a mission in Nigeria that thinks any African Christian from America is going to be what they call 'a worthy addition to their small school'. I'm not able to go as a missionary, I'd have to go as assistant for the school, but the Church is going to pay my passage and present me with a new Bible. The Lord gets his thanks next Sunday and the NAACP get themselves a winning they're able to print on a pamphlet.

'That's wonderful, Monsieur Desnoyers, that sounds just what I want.'

Once I'm there they'll see what a good teacher I am and he has no doubt I'll be given a class of my own. I hope he's right about that. Sure is pleasing to hear.

'Gosh, Arletta that gonna be fine. Ya goin' home girl. Ya taking care of business and goin' home,' says Mambo. 'And change is coming, coming soon. Y'all goin' be right back here with us soon as it comes. All gonna die down and change comin' on.'

Though they are looking for proper teachers over there, someone must be talking well on me, because in the letter I receive a couple of weeks later, they say they are sometimes going to need me in the classroom anyway and will give me the first-aid training I need for it when I arrive.

It seems things have started to go my way for the first time in my life. My new life is coming and I forget what I have to do before I get there. I've been sending my best wishes to little Eveline through Errol and I hear she's doing well and gone home to her own folks. Her pa and Ortega Jackson want to come and talk again, but I know through Errol they still don't know who Mr Seymour is.

One Saturday, just as I'm leaving Mrs Archer-Laing's parlour, the dogs start howling in the yard and I meet Errol shuffling to answer the bell-chain.

'Good morning,' he mumbles in his usual.

'Good morning. I believe ya must be Errol. My name is Mrs Johnson and my daughter Arletta is boardin' here. I'm wondering if ya might be kind enough to tell her I'm here.'

She sees me and flashes Errol one of her smiles as she waltzes past him looking fine and elegant. That's what a black suit and a string of pearls has done for her wiggle. Mr McIntyre must easily believe she really is running her own business. What sort of business? Well, he's known her a long time and that must be giving him his own fancy ideas about it. That's what we're banking on ourselves. She holds a pretty bunch of flowers from outside our cabin.

'Errol, Arletta tells me she's got a real nice room here.'

Mrs Archer-Laing opens her parlour door and finds Mambo at her best. Looking and behaving like she's been walking in and out of houses just like this one all her life.

'Ya must be Mrs Archer-Laing,' she says, holding out her hand. She's purchased a pair of white gloves and that looks like Grandma's old handbag she's carrying. She once called that handbag 'stuffy old-lady shit', but I see she kept it, polished it up and found a good use for it now.

'I pick this bouquet for ya, Mrs Archer-Laing. I grow them blooms in my own yard. Blooms sure cheer a yard up.'

'Thank you, Mrs Johnson, these are lovely. It's such a pleasure to meet you at last, after all these years. I saw you at poor Safi's funeral but we didn't get the chance to speak. I did mean to, of course, but it was such a sad day, a time for the family. Errol, please bring a vase to the parlour – I'd like to arrange these myself. Would you have time to take tea while you visit your daughter, Mrs Johnson?'

'Yes, of course. That's mighty kind.'

I guess she gets all that brimming-over confidence from being a mambo. She was born beautiful and that goes far with folks, anyways. She takes that seat in Mrs Archer-Laing's front parlour like she's been spending her whole life sitting in nice fine rooms just like it, instead of a leaking, fixed-up cabin stuck out in the fields with sharecroppers.

She's charming, telling Mrs Archer-Laing she's right grateful for how kind she's been to her daughter.

'She's been a wonderful boarder, Mrs Johnson. I'm glad that she stayed with us.'

'And all the help ya giving her, gettin' to Africa.' She's peeling her gloves off slowly; anybody would think she'd been doing that all her life, too. 'Our Arletta is late in coming to the Lord, but I has y'all to thank for her coming now. I sure do.'

What?

'Her pa and me, we right pleased, so I just had to come personally.'

Quince?

Mrs Archer-Laing accepts the vase from Errol and asks Mambo what church she attends. Errol casts a glance my way and raises an eyebrow. We're both waiting to hear how Mambo deals with that.

'Exceptin' Arletta here, she only just come to the Lord, but we're all baptized in the mission out Brouillette way. My other daughter, she's called Rochelle, is studying at school there. And she's doin' well too. We expectin' her to go to college. Arletta's always been teachin' her, so she's real good at learnin'.'

'Well, I believe Arletta is just right for teaching and missionary work. She'll be starting at the mission school over there, as you know, and teaching in no time, I believe, although she will be far from her family. It's a sacrifice for all the family. A calling.'

Mambo takes a white handkerchief out of Grandma's old handbag and dabs her eyes. I've never seen anything like it.

'It's gonna be some pullin' away from her folks, like ya says, Mrs Archer-Laing, but those that want to be doin' missionary work, they's called by the Lord. Sure are.'

I glance at Errol.

'When ya thinkin' she gonna be leaving, Mrs Archer-Laing?'

'Arletta has asked to go soon, as you know, so I think just a few weeks at the most. Lemon?'

'Ice, please.'

Errol shuffles off for ice. He's got both eyebrows raised now. Of course, Mambo doesn't know Mrs Archer-Laing is serving tea hot out of that pot. She's never had hot English tea served up like that before and I don't suppose Mrs Archer-Laing's fine bone china ever rattled with ice neither.

By the time we finish tea, and a slice of Errol's English fruitcake, Mrs Archer-Laing is left firmly holding the idea that I've been the child of a God-fearing upbringing.

As soon as we're up in my room, Mambo says, 'Arletta, we find Seymour.'

'Oh Mambo! Where?'

'St Francisville. Like ya said, turns out he ain't that hard to find.'

I collapse onto the bed. Finding him took Mambo no time at all.

'You've seen him, Mambo?'

Mambo expects the first time she sees him to be the last. I want to know where he is and how she found him.

'Somebody I knows from Shenandoah. And she say he's about as bad as bad can be. Ain't never married; I ain't tell her why that's gonna be. She says he get left a plantation over St Francisville – them's wealthy folk – but he's a lazy coot, and always drunk. She says he been drinkin' and all kinda problem for his ma and pa ever since he was a boy. But they ain't got no more children, so he end up with it all after they's gone. He go by Seymour Hamilton, that's his proper name, and she knew his folks. They were good-living, hard-working folks, and good to all the workers they had too, she says, but he was always the wrong kind.'

'Mambo, we really are sure now that he isn't dead. I never killed him. I never killed him Mambo.'

That's like a ten-ton bale of cotton just got lifted off my shoulders. Mambo goes on speaking about how her friend was saying what a disappointment Mr Seymour was to his folks, how he never took any interest at all in the plantation and it's in trouble since they've been gone. But I hardly hear it. All those years he was never dead. He was doing what he always did.

'And I got us a plan. It's crazy, but it gonna work.'

She spins round right then, like someone just tapped her shoulder.

'Somethin' funny going on in here, Arletta, inside of this room. Somethin' just got me shivering. Ya ain't feeling it?'

It's Safi. I feel her like that sometimes, too.

'This is going to settle Safi, Mambo. I'm sure about that.'

Mambo doesn't like the idea of me sleeping where Safi's walking. That's bad stuff and I know it, but as soon as we've done with Mr McIntyre and Mr Seymour, my friend Safi will be at rest.

'Sure ain't no down-home boarding house ya got here, honey, with washing hanging up all over, roaches and bony dogs. It's like ya's even have a butler with that there Errol. It was a real nice place for ya. Real nice.'

'Tell me the plan. What are we going to do about them?'

'Well, I went to see Madame Bonnet. Y'know, I found out from my friend in Shenandoah that he was a regular of hers, and they sure do all hate him over there. But some girls say they gonna take him on 'cause of him bein' so full of ready cash and ain't caring nothing about it. And some of them girls got plenty mouths to be feedin', too. But he ain't ever nice to them girls and so …'

'Madame Bonnet? He goes there?'

'Uh huh. Used to, mind, some time ago.'

Seems Madame sent him packing when one of her girls got treated so bad she ended up in big trouble. Her girls complained about him from the start that he wasn't right and he wasn't clean. Madame made sure he got bathed every time he walked through her door, like it was some kind of game before he saw a girl. She charged him extra for it, hot water and soap. And he was never happy with just one girl, never wanted to leave, then he started hurting them.

My stomach turns over.

'Ya all right honey? I ain't gonna say if ya …'

'Yeah. I'm fine, just glad we found him. I was always thinking nobody ever suffered like me, and all the time Madame Bonnet was dealing with him too. I wish …'

'Ain't no use wishin', honey. I'm wishin' too. Ain't nobody wishin' more than me, I'm telling ya that.'

'You tell Madame about me?'

She told her. Told her all about him and what he did to her little girl out at the cabin. Madame went crazy, like she was ready to go out there killing him herself. She was hollering about how her girls were one thing but to be going at a child was something else. Mambo says Madame went raging mad over that 'stinking hulk of filth touching her Arletta'.

'What did she do when he started hurting her girls?'

'Got so they ain't want see him no more, because seems he ain't able to do nothin' at all unless he's hurtin' somebody. That getta be his thing. But she sure is real shocked about Mr McIntyre.'

'He goes there too?'

'Hell, no. She knows him because of her banking plenty on account of her business. Course everybody keeps quiet 'bout what kinda business she's in. 'Specially them banking folks, seeing as some of them's her regulars. Talked her right into banking her earnings.'

I want to know how Mambo knows Madame Bonnet.

'Don't ya go givin' me that look. I ain't never got no more than a good time and a slap on my behind for it. We'd be plenty rich if I did. I ain't sayin' Madame ain't ask me to go workin' for her, but ...'

'You never did though, Mambo?'

'No, Arletta, I ain't. That ain't good stuff for a mambo, and bein' Mambo is our bread and butter, that's our blood, our way, and that takes what it takes to do.' Mambo runs her fingers down her long neck. 'She was always tellin' me I was gonna make real good money if I changed my mind and be one of her girls.'

'Thank goodness you never ...'

Mambo turns wild and points a finger right in my face.

'Hey, Arletta, don't y'all ever go gettin' high and mighty. Folks just gotta do what they's gotta do. Ain't nothin' else to it. Most of them girls are feedin' li'l kids and old folks, and both most times too. This God Almighty bullshit is gettin' to ya Arletta.'

'I didn't mean anything. I'm sorry. I'm sorry.'

'Well, just be watching that, girl. Huh?'

I apologize, and feel ashamed. Mambo knows most of the girls working for Madame Bonnet and they're all good and fine folks. Some of them even godly too, she says.

'So, how do you know one another then? You and Madame?'

'Well, she was one of my people, is all.'

'Madame?'

'I fixed up what she was needin' for some of her clients. Some got a little trouble and ain't able to do for themselves. Some of her gentlemen be in need of a little help, is all. And that's one of my specialities. I get that from my Mambo and her Mambo before her too. It's just a little help. All they's needing. Works fine.'

'What?' Mambo sure is full of surprises, always was.

'Aphrodisiacs they's called. That's growin' all over our front yard Arletta, and I know how to put things together right, and that's what she'd be comin' out our way for, and for teaching ya French like she did, of course. But that help I gave her and her business sure did help us out too.'

'And you reckon she was maybe giving any of that to Mr Seymour?'

'I guess that's the way it was honey. She's sure feelin' as bad as I do about it now. She's gonna fix it though Arletta, Madame's gonna help us fix it.'

I ain't saying nothing. I just let her talk.

Seymour took over his folks' plantation after they passed away. Took over the big house and looking after business, but it's running into the ground because he's one useless good-for-nothing at that too, same as every place else, Mambo says. Drained the plantation of every cent it had. Madame Bonnet says he's needing to sell up now, and it's making him worse than he ever was. Nobody is letting him near their girls and she reckons that's making him crazy.

'That's sure pushed him over the edge, Madame says. He's gone.'

'Nellie said that, all those years ago. The day I slashed him, that's exactly what she said. She said, "He's gone this time. He's gone." That's the very word she used.'

'That's what folks are saying. Tout de suite hit him over the head with a bat one time 'cause of how he was treatin' one of them girls so bad, and Madame reckons that ain't do nothing to help neither. He was mad as a dog before that, but he was madder after it she reckons.'

'Tout de suite? He knows about me too?'

'Madame tell him. Ain't something that made him happy at all, seeing as he know all 'bout Mr Seymour. He's gonna help, Arletta. He always been right fond of ya and he's gonna stand by us.'

Fourteen

My train ticket arrives. I will be travelling down to New Orleans and from there on to Atlanta, where I'm going to meet up with another two ladies taking up with the Church in other parts of Africa. One of them is travelling pretty close to where I'm going, she'll be doing missionary work at Christ Church in Lagos, so I feel lucky I'm not heading out that way feeling lonesome. I don't go in for any big talk, but I like knowing I've got folks about someplace. We'll catch another train in Atlanta for New York and our sailing passage from there, on a ship called the *Mauretania*, has already been booked up and paid for. I'm not even thinking about what that must have cost. We sail from England for Lagos on another boat and then I'm going to be taken inland on my own. The Anglican mission has started up a centre in what they call 'the interior' for poor folks and that suits me fine. Looks like the whole trip is going to take the best part of a month.

I get told at church on Sunday that the mission started working where I'm going about ten years ago with makeshift services and a bit of teaching. Then a doctor started visiting once a month and it seems the whole thing went down well over there, so they got funding to put up a permanent building. Now school spaces are so full up, and queues for the doctor that long when he comes, they're short of folks to take care of it all. I think it may well be someplace nobody else wants to go, but that suits me fine, and I reckon that's going to let me get lucky with my teaching too. I can hardly wait to see my new home.

The old country.

The hardest thing of all is saying goodbye to Rochelle.

'Is okay for ya goin', Arletta, and when ya come back ya gonna see how good I get at my lessons. When ya comin' back Arletta?'

'I don't know yet. We'll see.'

'Next year maybe? That sure is a long time Arletta.'

'Yes, maybe next year.'

'Well, I'm gonna need to get on a train to see ya 'fore then, 'cause I sure gonna be needin' to ask ya somethin'.'

I visit Mr Roy Herbert's law firm in Baton Rouge and transfer the deeds into Rochelle's name. I buy her a new tin because I'm taking the King of England to Africa. Mambo is going to keep Rochelle's tin safe in Pappy's locked closet till the time comes for telling her.

Inside I leave a letter, right on top of the deeds for Pappy's land, and I leave her Pappy's letter too. I don't go much on parting with it, but I reckon that's something of his words I can leave her, since she never knew him. I just keep his handkerchief, because I have his memory and she's never going to have that. Pappy is for ever in my heart, and he's coming back to Africa with me.

Dearest Rochelle

I'm writing this before I leave for Africa because I will not be coming back soon. I'm leaving you the letter Pappy wrote to me when he gave me the land, because I have passed it on to you. You see that he says Mambo must stay on the land, so I will leave his wishes in your care and you must look after her. She has always wanted you to have the best and when I offered her the land she said no, that I should give it to you instead.

So look after our Mambo, Rochelle. She did everything for me that she ever could do and she will do the same for you.

I'll always be thinking of you both with all my love.

Arletta

I give her my pamphlets on black history in America and all my stuff about civil rights. I leave her my journals and the few decrepit books I bought from the trestle table tied up with string on the sidewalk in Marksville, and the first book I ever got, *The Mulatto.* Quince says he's going to make a bookcase for them because Bobby-Rob got a new wagon and his old cart still has a few good planks left in one piece. Quince says there's enough for fixing up a set of shelves. He's taken to fixing things these days, and Pappy's old tools are down from the rafters now. The rust that gave them that nice color I always liked has been sanded off and the blades are sharpened up. He's got himself a new set of nails, laid out neatly by size, and it's all padlocked inside a box chained to his bed and nailed to the floor.

And what a different place our cabin is. Pappy would be proud as punch if he turned down our track right now and saw it. I walk round the land that he made mine for so long and I never even knew it.

'Look, Pappy,' I whisper, 'what Quince and Mambo have done with your land. Look how nice they keep it, the best crop all around here, and Quince is even using your old hoe. It's still going strong as ever. Mambo just keeps sharpening it, like she's real good at. And she turned out fine, just like you said she would.'

The leaves rustle in the trees.

'She never came to the Lord though, Pappy.'

I sit down by Sugarsookic Creek for the last time and watch the river flowing towards the ocean I'm just about to cross and never return. I imagine Africa is where it took my blood, washed it up alongside the blood of my people forced to come the other way. I close my eyes and hum Nellie's tune. I don't expect to be hearing her out here any more. I guess she's busy watching Eveline and all those other little girls needing her right now. I sure did find my strength and it's going to be enough for all of them.

I hear a twig crack and turn. It's Quince.

'Ya okay out here Arletta?'

'Yes, I'm fine, just saying goodbye to the old place, that's all.'

'Long as ya okay girl. We sure gonna be missin' ya.'

I start walking back and he falls into step beside me. We hardly speak all the way back to our cabin; seems no call for it. It feels fine just walking beside him: safe, comfortable. I never thought I'd ever feel that way with Quince, but he sure did turn out all right. He's finished the fence Pappy started; it goes all the way round the land now, from the track to the tree line, leaving the pipe outside so everybody is still able to use it, though some folks are starting to have pipes laid down now. When we get to our cabin he tells me Mambo won't let him change the old front part of the fence because Pappy put it up and she wants that left just the way it is.

'It's in bad need of fixin', this bit of fence, but she won't let me make no changes to it so I just gonna paint it,' he says.

'You sure have done a fine job here Quince. The place is fixed up good.'

He looks pleased with that bit of praise.

'Thanks Quince.'

'Eh?'

'Thanks for taking care of Pappy's old cabin.'

'He was a fine man, ya Pappy. Sure glad to know him, though I reckon I shoulda got to know him better. Ya be takin' good care of y'self over there Arletta girl, 'cause I hear some places over there be just like bandit country. And remember to be writin' ya ma. She gonna be missin' one of her girls and she gonna be weeping about it. She weeping about that already.'

Quince kisses my cheek and puts his hand on my shoulder. We come through the trees to our old cabin just like that.

'Ya's a good sorta person Arletta, and take care of y'self. Ya ever need to come home, ya just holler and I'm gonna see to it. Y'hear? This cabin always gonna be here, yours by rights. Just want ya to know that's the way I sees it. Yours by rights when the time comes and ya back home.'

I look over to our cabin and see Mambo leaning against the porch post. Arms folded and smiling. She's been watching me and Quince talk, like we've never done, and that sure is making her look about as happy as I ever saw her.

That's the last time I ever saw our cabin.

☼

Mrs Archer-Laing gives me a suitcase from her basement and I start thinking about what I need to be taking overseas in it. I've already purchased a nice grey pin-striped suit, real smart and nipped below the waist like the fashion is now, some stockings and a pair of low-heeled shoes for the journey. I reckon I'm going to take three cotton dresses, three shirts and three skirts for getting started in Nigeria. I've been told folks in the missions can buy clothes by mail order over there and have it sent to the church in Lagos for collection, so I guess I'm going to be able to kit myself out once I see what everybody else is doing. I don't want to be standing out or looking different. Africa is my new and old home. I'm wanting to dress like my own kind.

I get Mrs Archer-Laing to make me a cotton chemise with pockets on the sides. I tell her it's going to keep my papers safe on the journey, but when it's finished I wrap Seymour's money in Pappy's handkerchief and sew that into it. I'm going to be travelling with over $200 sewn into the chemise after I pay for what I need. The rest of Seymour's money I'm leaving with Mambo to help with Rochelle's education. I try giving her a bit more – after all, I'll be earning in Nigeria – but she wouldn't have it at all.

'I find out Quince been puttin' aside for her classes, and ya gonna be needin' it. What ya give us already is enough. I told Quince about ya giving Rochelle the land and he says ya right good to us all and ya gonna need that money Arletta.'

'Does he know all about me Mambo?'

'Not about what we's planning on doing, but he knows the rest of it. He's thinkin' we gonna be dealing with it all once ya gone. I said we can talk over what to do then. He reckons we gonna get a squad of his pals and see to it after ya gone.'

'Be sure to tell him I appreciate that Mambo. I never thought he was going to turn out fine at all.'

'He's settled. Seeing blacks gettin' on. And since he find out about Grambling State, he been pushin' for his daughter to get there, and she's smart, he knows that. Like I say, Quince turn out fine.'

It feels real strange to be clearing out my white room under the eaves. I haven't got much left since I emptied the trunk, so it doesn't really take any time at all. Except for what happened to Safi, Mrs Archer-Laing's room has been a fine place for me. That's where my life really started, out on my own with my friend, laughing and watching her getting the new stick of lip colour on right. Safi was full of beans, they always said. I'm missing her these last few days in the room we shared. I sure am thinking of Safi a lot, because she's going to be resting soon, too.

I check the small closet: that's now empty, and then the wardrobe Mrs Archer-Laing had brought up from the basement when we first arrived. The freshly cleaned-out King of England fits nicely in my suitcase and I place my flannel and soap toiletries in it, then tell Pappy out loud that he's coming all the way to Africa with me. The trunk is ready to go back to the basement too, so the room can be painted for Mrs Archer-Laing's new boarder.

I'm just about closing the lid when I see something crumpled into where the veneer panel is lifting with age at the back of the frame. Right off I think it's a page from one of my pamphlets, which I've already given to Rochelle.

'Dammit, how did that get torn out?'

Then I see it's not printed at all, it's handwritten. I ease it out so I don't tear it. The writing is scrawled all over the page, but it's Safi's, for sure.

> *Dear Arletta,*
>
> *I'm frightened and I don't feel good at all. I wish you'd come back soon from Mambo. Ainsley wants me to get rid of the baby and he made me drink something from someone he knows that he says will work, and now I come home alone and I feel so bad. He don't want the baby. I loved Ainsley, but he turn so much now I don't know him at all. Ain't my Ainsley. We been fighting and I don't want to take it but he force me and it feels bad, the pain bad now and I think the baby coming away. I'm leaving this note for you so you know it something I took and you can ask Mambo for help if I need. I'm afraid, Arletta. I wish you'd come. I*

thought Ainsley was the one, but he's all wrong and I don't want let Ma down neither, so I just don't know what to do. I thought we'd be married by now but truth is he don't want it. He never let me tell you and I'm sorry 'cause you my best friend. When you find this get Mambo quick and tell her …

I can't read the writing after that; it looks like a spider lost his legs on paper. Right after she wrote that note I must have come home and found her the way she was.

'Errol!'

I run downstairs two at a time and burst into Errol's kitchen.

'Errol!'

Mrs Archer-Laing hears all that pounding on the stairs and follows in from her parlour.

'Whatever is the matter, Arletta?'

'It's this. Look! It was Ainsley: he killed Safi. Errol, look what I found. I was just finishing with my packing up, and closing the trunk when I found this. It's Safi, a letter from Safi. Look, she wrote this.'

Errol and Mrs Archer-Laing read the letter together.

'Oh, Lord above.'

'Where ya get this, Arletta?' asks Errol.

'Stuck in the trunk upstairs, where it's coming away. The back of the trunk is coming away from the frame, and Errol, I remember now. I remember it. Safi was saying, 'Read … read,' just before she got like she did. This is what she was trying to say before she got like, like she couldn't say anything at all. She was woozy when I found her but she was saying, 'Read, read.' She wrote this for me to find and I didn't find it. I didn't understand. She knew what was happening to her. It was Ainsley all along, and I didn't know what she was saying. And maybe we'd have been able to save her too.'

Errol's head hangs low on his chest, muttering that poor little Martha is Ainsley's child all along. Martha is Ainsley's child and he's never even seen her.

'I can hardly believe it,' says Mrs Archer-Laing, 'and what a performance he put on for us. I never thought for a moment …'

Errol folds the letter.

'Well, he's gonna be havin' himself a fine old time explaining that performance to the law.'

'Try not to upset yourself, Arletta, my dear,' says Mrs Archer-Laing. She's holding my shoulders from behind because my tears have started to flow. 'There's no guarantee that your mother could have helped Safi. Don't you go torturing yourself over this. I saw you do everything possible for Safi. You couldn't have done any more and we have no way of knowing your mother could have either.'

Errol and I both turn towards her about the same time.

'It's all right, Arletta, I know your mother has her ways. I believe, that is to say, I hear, that she's the best there is at them, too. As a matter of fact, I know several who speak very highly of her remedies. Errol, take this to the sheriff's department right away.'

'I'm sorry, Mrs Archer-Laing, I never knew you'd ever heard about my ma.'

She just nodded.

Mambo was right about Safi. As soon as I found that letter and Errol got it out of the house to the sheriff's department, I swear that room feels peaceful when I turn in for the night. That room feels like Safi has stopped walking and I lie there listening to the rustling fronds outside our window, thinking about all the good times we had since we first came here. I remember her laughter, and Agnes Withers banging on the wall to get us to be quiet, her kindness to folks, especially her ma, and her out-of-tune singing at church. Safi was just like me, couldn't carry a tune in a bucket. She's off someplace else I reckon, watching Ainsley get what's coming and when she's done with that, there will be just looking out for little Martha and peace.

'Goodbye, Safi.'

My face is wet with tears saying goodbye to my friend.

The following night comes with a dark moon. One of those mists, thick like smoke, creeps round the oak trees out behind the burned-down plantation house and it sure feels like somebody's going to be dead before morning. I've never known a night with a feeling like it.

Madame Bonnet got electric power down her way some time back and Tout de suite has strung up a cable with Chinese lanterns between the trees to light up the fête she's throwing out back of her bordello. It's been going for hours by the time we arrive. The sound of the Cajun band bounces over the expanse of grass between the festivities and where we stand, right back from it all, at the edge of the bayou, with frogs croaking near as loud as the banjos. Tout de suite has already fastened two pieces of rope that hang hidden in the Spanish moss. Mambo and I are both wearing black and we stand silently next to the ropes. I watch her and feel strong. That's what she said about it before we got here.

'Watch, and do as I say. Watch and do. That's all Arletta. This is just what these two men been walkin' into since the first time Mr McIntyre lay a finger on my daughter, or anybody else's daughter. Ain't nobody to blame for it but themselves. Their own doin' – except of course they's wanted to get away with it and we ain't lettin' them. That's all there is to it honey.'

Madame Bonnet's silhouette grows larger as she appears out of the mist. When she gets close I see she's wearing a long black gown finished off at the shoulder with a spray of peacock feathers. She's got long satin gloves that cover her arms to above the elbow. It's not a night for smiling, but I do when I see she's carrying her satin shoes in one hand and holding her gown clear of the grass with the other. She's got that look, like Mambo has. Both of those ladies might have fitted fine in high society, except they weren't born to it.

'*Allons-y*,' she says, '*vite*. We are ready. I have slipped *les diables terribles* what you give me, and you must come, quickly, *maintenant*. Ees working, I think. *Vite*.'

Mambo turns and squeezes both my hands in her own.

'Remember Arletta. Remember all the pain ya feeling 'cause of them, and all them hard times they give ya when I was leaving ya like I'm shamed about. That's my part in it. Remember it this night. Think on Eveline and ya gonna stay strong. If Nellie is out here,

ya listen to her girl, and how she gives ya strength, and ya waitin'
to use it all this time. Feel ya strength, girl. This is it Arletta honey.
Justice, it come.'

I throw my arms around my Mambo's neck and she holds me
close. Madame is rushing us and wants to know everything is ready.

'Yes, everything is ready, and I'm ready Mambo. I'm ready. Madame,
Mambo, go quickly. Go on.'

'Ya my daughter and we do this right. An eye for an eye. All the time.'

'An eye for an eye Mambo.'

'*Vite*, there is no time!'

The grey swirling mist eats them up and their shadows move back
towards the bordello. The Cajuns play and I'm left alone. Something
splashes in the bayou.

Then I see them coming back. Two other shadows are moving with
them, and it looks like they've all been on a barrel of hooch with the
way they're swaying all over the place.

Seymour's wearing the same kind of pale suit he always wore and
it's the first thing I recognize coming out of the dark. An old instinct
makes me want to run. I find myself backing off till I hit the bayou,
my heart just about busting clean out of my chest. It's beating so hard
I hear it thumping in my ears and I feel like I'm right back all those
years ago, and I'm up to my knees in cold water.

'An eye for an eye.'

I know that voice.

'An eye for an eye, chile.'

I think about Eveline lying raw and sore in her hospital bed with
her parts torn so bad no child will ever grow in her belly. Just like me.
I think about what he did that put her there and how he threw her
out like a rag doll when he was done with it. Just like me. That turns
me round good. I crawl out of the water, growling like Mambo at the
dark moon. It's time for me to be my Mambo's daughter.

'An eye for an eye.'

I get in among the low branches and thick hanging moss to wait for
Mambo and Madame. As Mambo says, this is the time of reckoning
and that's the only right they've got left.

Then I hear his voice.

'Oooh, promises, promises, laydees,' Seymour drawls, groggy like he's always been. I wonder how he's still on this earth with all that gut rot he's put away in his life. I clench my fists, breathe deep down in my belly and straighten my back.

I am the daughter of Mambo.

The daughter of Africa.

'I don't feel so good,' I hear Mr McIntyre moaning.

'Here now, y'all be havin' y'self another drink honey, ya doin' just fine,' I hear Mambo say. He doesn't want it, but the next thing I see, she has that bottle tipping over into his mouth and he's about choking on it.

'That's gonna have ya feelin' a whole lot better in no time. Come on Mr McIntyre, I remember ya fine. I remember ya sure know how to have a good time.'

Seymour is giggling like he's stupid.

'Where are the girliesh? Ooh, hoo hoo! Madame, you are a bad, bad woman.' He's wagging that finger of his and just about falling over, except for Madame trying her best to keep him straight. 'Girliesh? Where are you, girliesh?'

My stomach retches sore, but I swallow and breathe.

The music gets louder. It's booming out now and I reckon Tout de suite is playing his part. Seymour is close enough for me to see the white of his eyes.

'Girliesh, come to uncle little girlsh ...'

He's right under the tree. Madame reaches out her dainty foot to trip him up and he falls right at my feet.

'Ooops a daishies,' he says, as hopeless as a baby because he can't get up. I have no clue what Mambo might have ground up from Pappy's closet, or from what's growing right there in our front yard, but it's sure lost them both the power of their legs.

Madame waves her arm for me to bring the rope. I'm ready with it. She sets herself down astride him and the next thing I see she's placing the noose around his neck. He's still giggling.

I move towards them.

'You remember Fifty Cents?' It sounds like every measure of cold in that bayou is taken up in my voice.

'Huh?' He's surprised to hear another adult voice there instead of his little girlies.

'You remember little Eveline Gaudet?' I ask.

My time has come.

'I don't suppose you even know her name, but she's going to remember you and what you did to her for the rest of her life.'

'What the hell …?'

Mr McIntyre is stumbling towards the tree trunk with Mambo holding on to him. That last gulp has done for him.

'What's going on here? Something's going on. Seymour?' His voice fades as his legs finally lose all their power and he topples over. Mambo props him up against the tree trunk and leaves him there to help us with the rope around Seymour's neck. Mr McIntyre isn't capable of going anywhere now.

'What the hell are you doing? What the hell …'

'*Bâtard*,' whispers Madame as she yanks hard on the noose.

Mambo pulls me into Seymour's line of vision.

'This here is my daughter Arletta. Ya remember her? Fifty Cents, ya called her. Ya remembering what ya gone and do to her, ya evil piece of shit? This is MY daughter. Daughter of MAMBO!' she growls.

She draws herself back then launches forward and spits full in his face.

Mambo's eyes and teeth flash menacingly in the dark. She's snarling. She's terrible. She's Mambo. She pulls the fish knife from somewhere.

'Ya remember this knife? Eh?'

'What the …? No, no!' Seymour tries to push away with his elbows.

'No, Mambo.' I grab her arm. 'No. The noose is enough.'

'What's going on? You're crazy …' Seymour is groggy and confused.

'*Vite*! Pull.'

'Goddammit! Stop this, you crazy black piece of shit …'

'This is for what ya did to my daughter.'

Mambo pulls.

Seems Seymour is finally realizing what's happening to him. Too late. He has no strength in his legs to support his own weight; Mambo's closet has rendered him utterly defenceless.

'And this is for that little girl you left at the side of the road.' I sneer and pull. His ugly, blotched face shows panic like I guess he's never had any cause to feel in his life. He just liked making little girls feel that way. Then I help Mambo get the knot on the noose right under his chin. 'And this is what you get for your fifty cents.'

I yank the noose tight. He squeals.

'And this is for all the other little girls you were never man enough for.'

Yank.

'Piece of shit ...' he snarls through gritted teeth. 'Get this fucking thing off me. Who the hell do you think you are?'

'Who?' asks Madame. 'You know me well enough *monsieur*, and if I knew you ever at the little girls, I kill you a long time ago. *Bâtard*. *Merde*!' She spits.

Yank.

Seymour tries desperately to lash out at us, his voice rasping in his throat, but it's wasted effort, he's drunk, his legs will not obey him, and Madame has his arms pinned. Panic spreads over his face and adrenaline surges through his body with one last futile effort to save himself.

We heave on the rope and his body lifts off the ground, swinging round and round, his face redder at every pull. He soils himself. We use our full force to combat the surge for survival only apparent in the unparalysed top half of his body. The lifeless legs serve our purpose, pulling his weight helplessly towards the ground and forcing the noose tighter.

When his body stops jerking we wait a few minutes in silence before dropping him to the ground in a crash. His vile tongue protrudes hellishly and his body is limp.

We turn to Mr McIntyre. He's struggling to drag himself away on paralysed legs and crying like a baby. Madame and Mambo get hold of his ankles and drag him back. He tries to yell, but his voice is feeble with terror, and pointless against the noise from the bordello. I recall when fear of him dried my throat to the silence of sheer terror. Mambo places the rope effortlessly around his neck and then grabs me again. She pushes me in front of him. He is frightened out of his wits, his eyes bulge, his lips quiver, and we hear him soil himself noisily.

'My daughter, McIntyre. Ya take a last good look. This is for what y'all did to my daughter, and all them other little girls ya been raping for years. Even ya own daughter.' She laughs deep in her throat. 'How the hell ya ever think ya gonna get away with this McIntyre?'

'You're crazy, crazy women ... stop this ... stop ...'

'Ya thinking we gonna just let y'all carry on and on like we ain't got our own ways of dealing with rats?'

'What about your daughter, Mr McIntyre?' I ask. 'Does your wife know what you do to her?'

His eyes bulge wider in terror.

'No, I don't ...'

'Yes you do.'

'Yes, yes ... you won't get away with this ... aarghhh ...'

'Do you tell her she likes it?'

'She does, she does, she ... no, I don't touch her ...'

Mambo pulls the noose tight to shut him up.

'Bâtard,' whispers Madame again. 'Nobody going miss this trash, merde ...'

I stand in front of him and wonder how he ever terrified me. He's a small man, insignificant, weak. I have Mambo's fish knife in my hand. He eyes the blade as I hold it up to his face.

'Did you have anything to do with that little girl?' I ask.

'No!' He's struggling for his life without the power of his legs.

'You know what I can do with this knife, don't you Mr McIntyre?'

'No! Yes ... don't ... please ...'

I edge the knife down to his genitals.

'Did you have anything to do with it?'

His face is wet with tears. The man is reduced to crying like a baby.

'Please. No. That's his shit, he's fucking crazy. Let me down, I'll tell you everything. He's out of control ... he's ... aaargh!'

The noose is getting tighter.

'I was going to turn him in. I was. Let me down and I'll tell you … I didn't know what to do … he's crazy …'

'He *was* crazy, Mr McIntyre,' says Mambo in her sing-song voice. 'He's dead now.'

I take the knife and cut through the belt holding up his pants. Madame does the rest with an expert yank of her hand, leaving him naked from the waist down. He stinks of his own smell.

McIntyre struggles for his life while we all heave on the rope. His ankles are bound together by his own clothes and he wiggles like an eel. He swings his legs out towards the trunk of the tree, desperately looking for something to rest his feet on. We give one last heave on the rope and he's spinning aimlessly, grabbing at his throat. He gets his fingers into the noose, but it doesn't save him. A few seconds later he slumps lifelessly and the rope feels like it has a dead weight on the end of it.

Mambo and Madame hold him there while I prop the ladder against the tree and climb up. I wind the end of the rope round enough to keep him raised off the ground. I secure it by knotting it in the crook of a branch. Then we go back and cut Seymour's clothes so they fall around his ankles before hoisting him up and doing the same to keep him swinging off the ground. The weight soon stops them spinning and they eerily hang lifeless in the Spanish moss. Soiled, stinking, evil men the world is better without.

I stand at the edge of the bayou and throw the fish knife high into the air. It disappears into the mist then a second later I hear it splash into the water.

We carry the ladder between us and head back to the fête. It's dropped in the grass a short distance from the back of the bordello for Tout de suite to collect later.

'Bon voyage, Arletta *ma chérie*. Be strong. *Vas*. Maybe one day you come back. *Je t'aime*.'

Madame embraces me and kisses my cheek before rushing back to the party. I watch her link arms with a very well dressed, very drunk gentleman and lead him onto the dance floor, as though she's delighted to have just this minute spotted him at her soirée.

'I didn't thank her. I need to say thank you, Mambo.'

'Come, come quickly, we need to be gone,' Mambo says urgently.

'Miss Arletta.'

'Yes Tout de suite?'

'Miss Arletta, travel safe on the long journey. Madame say to give you this. Take care, Miss Arletta.'

Then he's gone. Mambo pulls me away.

Mambo stays with me at Mrs Archer-Laing's for this, the last night I ever spend with my own family in my own country. I open the small package Tout de suite handed to me. It has $300 in it and a card that smells like roses. Like her.

> To help with your new life, Arletta.
> Madame, your friend always

It is the last night under the eaves. We sleep. Mambo holds me like she used to when I was a little girl sharing a cot with her.

Fifteen

The following morning two carriages take me to the station to catch my train. Errol, Mambo and I are in one and Mrs Archer-Laing and Monsieur Desnoyers follow behind in the other. Errol tells me the police have arrested Ainsley in Jackson and charged him with Safi's murder. He admits he got her to take something, but denies he knew it was poison. I feel sad about it, but I sure am glad I found that letter. Just for a moment of madness, his life is gone too.

'Happen that way sometimes Arletta,' says Errol. 'When folk ain't wanna face up.'

'What will come of it, of him? Ainsley is not a murderer, not like that, not really.'

'He ain't gonna go to no trial. Albert say he admit to what they's callin' negligent homicide.'

'He's still going to be sentenced, though?'

'Can't see no ways outta that. He's gonna get at least five years, Albert says, but he'll get good behaviour, they reckon. If he's smart, he's gonna get on outta there sooner.'

Mambo has no sympathy for Ainsley at all. He ought to have told us right there and then that he had forced her to take something, and where he'd gone for it. If he'd done that right then, in that room, maybe we'd have been able to save Safi. Maybe she'd still be alive.

'I'd have gone for you Mambo. Would you have been able to help her?'

'Well, I guess so. Ain't be the first time I been called in to fix up some hokey-pokey dammit mess. But ain't work out that way honey, and ya gotta put it behind ya. Remember the good times ya had, all them happy socials and livin' in that fine boarding house. And remember li'l Martha.'

'He oughta face up to that chile. Ain't no two ways 'bout it,' says Errol.

'She gonna be just fine. She's got her folks. And we's all gonna take good care of Martha. She ain't needin' no pa like Ainsley. That she don't need at all. We taking care of her fine,' says Mambo.

I smile because I know she will. Errol chuckles too. Martha won't ever be the same kind of old-time Mambo like mine – times have changed – but everybody can see she has her gut and knows about herbs.

Errol carries my suitcase, though it's perfectly manageable for myself, and we make our way along the busy platform.

'Monsieur Desnoyers and I won't board with you, Arletta dear, we'll say our goodbyes here.' Mrs Archer-Laing removes an embroidered handkerchief and dabs the corner of her eyes. 'Let us know when you've settled in, how things are. We'll be looking for a letter from you soon.'

'Thank you for everything you've done for me, Mrs Archer-Laing. And for Safi too.'

'Dolly,' she sniffles, 'please call me Dolly, my dear. And when you come home, do pay us a visit. I have the guest room, as you know, so please come and stay. And write to us, Arletta. Do.'

I'm embarrassed to be using her first name, but I do when she embraces me.

The train lets out a rush of steam. I turn to Monsieur Desnoyers and shake his hand.

'*Merci, monsieur*, thank you too, very much.'

'It's a long journey, Arletta. I trust you have a good book?' He grins.

'I'm still reading it.'

'We look forward to seeing you just as soon as you have leave. *Bon voyage*.'

He has no reason to suspect that I have no plans to return.

Errol, Mambo and I board the train. Errol puts the suitcase in the rack above my seat and holds out his hand.

'Goodbye Arletta. All the best over there.'

'Goodbye Errol, and thank you. For everything. You've been a good friend and I'm going to miss you. And your cooking. I'm really going to miss your cooking.'

I pop a kiss on his cheek. He nods and laughs into his chest. As he leaves he turns for one last look and says he's sure gonna miss me sitting in his kitchen slipping off these stupid faddish stools. He says he knows God is going with me and steps out of the carriage.

Mambo gives me a hug.

'We did the right thing Mambo.'

'An eye for an eye. That's the old ways. And this world sure is cleaner for it this morning.'

The whistle blows.

'I'm going to miss you Mambo.'

I cling to her, breathe her cologne and soap, her other-wordly odour of warm musk and our cabin.

'I have something for you Mambo.'

I hand her Pappy's pipe.

'Lord, Arletta ...' Tears well up in her eyes and she cannot say a word.

'I took it, like I told you, and I want you to have it to remember me and Pappy by.'

'I love ya girl. One day soon ya gonna be able to come home. I'm gonna be wantin' my girl home. I'm waitin' on that day.'

I hold her as close as I can.

'I love you Mambo. My Mambo. My very own Mambo.'

'Ya get on that boat outta here Arletta. Ya get y'self back over to the old country before they get ya honey.'

'Goodbye Mambo.'

'Before they get ya. I keep tellin' myself why ya going. Ya goin' home, ya gonna be safe. I knows it.'

She gets off the train and I blow her a kiss. I see her stiffen her shoulders and raise her head up high. She wipes her nose.

The whistle blows again and the train jerks forward. Mambo places her hand on the window then disappears into the steam as the train shunts off down the track.

I stand up and scan the steam, looking for one last glimpse of my Mambo, but when it clears I see Albert Gaudet at the end of the platform, among the freight crates, wearing his police uniform and walking to keep up as we slowly shunt down the platform. I freeze with horror, expecting the train to come screeching to a halt with half the Louisiana state law department stampeding aboard to clap me in chains.

Albert Gaudet gives me a faint smile and raises his hat. Before disappearing into the next burst of steam he draws his forefinger across his neck and nods. Then he places his hat back on his head and the train keeps chugging on out of the station.

The St Francisville Herald

SEYMOUR HAMILTON LYNCHED IN AVOYELLES

SEYMOUR HAMILTON, proprietor of Brayhead Rose Plantation, has been named as one of the men found murdered near Mansura, Avoyelles Parish. Mr Hamilton, and Mr Charles McIntyre, manager of the Louisiana Planters' Bank in Baton Rouge, were both found early on Saturday morning by local trapper Claude Riems and his son.

State trooper David Lebrau said the motive was likely to be robbery and their investigations were successfully underway, with the police already questioning an unnamed suspect.

Enquiries included the questioning of well-known socialite Madame Bonnet, whose property borders the bayou where the crime took place. Neither Madame Bonnet nor any of her staff saw anything suspicious on the night of the murders and, because of the Cochon du Lait celebrations taking place last weekend, are unable to account for all those who attended. The area around the old Oakland plantation was crowded with partygoers, and police ask anyone who thinks they saw anything suspicious or unusual to get in touch with the police department.

Harvard-educated Mr Hamilton studied law, but had not practised since his return to the state of Louisiana. He inherited Brayhead Rose Plantation after the tragic death of both his parents in a boating accident. Mr Hamilton Snr. was a seasoned boatman and the unusual accident was considered a fluke of nature. Brayhead Rose Plantation has been in financial trouble since the death of his father but Mr Hamilton's suicide has been ruled out due to the circumstances of his death.

Mr Charles McIntyre leaves a wife and two children in Baton Rouge. The Louisiana Planters' Bank has expressed their shock on hearing about the death of one of their most respected managers. A statement from the bank read, 'We are most shocked to hear of the unfortunate and untimely demise of someone in our employ who had such a promising future ahead of him, and he will be sorely missed by all.'

Mr McIntyre's wife, Ella, was unavailable for comment.

The suspect remains in custody and is due to be arraigned before the court next week.

THE AVOYELLES GAZETTE

20 MAY 1923

Suspect In Hamilton Case Released

EARL FRANKLIN, THE SUS-pect held since last week in connection with the deaths of Mr Seymour Hamilton and Mr Charles McIntyre, has been released. A spokesman stated that Mr Franklin was in fact being held in custody on liquor charges the night the murders took place. Mr Franklin is understood to have below-average intelligence, which rendered him unable to fully understand the charges he had confessed to. Mr Franklin's lawyer, Mr Ken Chester of Payne and Charter, is to lodge a formal claim for compensation on behalf of his client.

More details of the lynchings have since come to light. It is understood that both Mr Hamilton and Mr McIntyre were naked at the time they were discovered hanging from the branch of one of Oaklands' largest trees. It is rumoured they had been muti-lated in some way, but a spokes-man for the sherriff's department refused to comment.

'It was a terrible sight for my young son to see,' said Monsieur Riems, who found the bodies. 'I had taken him out to get some experience of trapping. I wasn't expecting to come across this sort of thing at all. I only hope they find these evil culprits soon. It was inhuman what we had to witness.'

Governor Parker has appealed for calm and warns that troop reinforcements could be sent to the parish as unrest spreads.

The St Francisville Herald

24 MAY 1923

THE KLU KLUX KLAN have warned more action will be taken to protect the citizens of Louisiana from law breakers. Last Sunday they marched through Mansura with burning crosses in protest at the lack of any progress in arresting the culprits who lynched Seymour Hamilton and Charles McIntyre.

By Tuesday evening unrest had spread to Baton Rouge, Shenandoah and St Francisville.

Governor Parker paid tribute to state troopers who have been successful in maintaining law and order throughout the state, but when questioned, Attorney-General Adolphe V. Coco was forced to admit there were no further leads in the case. Klansmen have accused law-enforcement agencies of allowing the trail to grow cold in the search for the killers.

Ex-Governor, Pinckney B.S. Pinchback, spoke from his law office in Washington DC to condemn the rumour that the perpetrators of the white lynchings of Louisiana were blacks acting out of revenge as 'preposterous nonsense with a thinly veiled political motive'.

It has been revealed that the Brayhead Rose Plantation has debts in excess of $200,000 and will close its doors at the end of the month. Foreman Elliot Woods says, 'This is a huge blow to us. Mr Hamilton did not inform any of the workers on the plantation that the situation was as serious as it is. We will be hoping for a purchaser able to safeguard the livelihoods of all on the plantation. There is some talk of a buyout later, when everything is settled, and we are all praying for that.'

Enquiries into the murders continue.

Epilogue

M iss Constance has started to think the Nigerian sun must be
hotter than before, the rainy season longer. She never used to
complain, it isn't her nature. Now she asks for air conditioning long
before she would have in the past, or for the fire to be lit, the lights
to go on earlier. She asks for more pepper in her food. Bem's careful
not to cook too much, and to make sure there is something of her
favourites in the dishes he prepares for her each day.

In the past she possessed an unbounded acceptance of life and the
ever-changing fortunes of the people she met at her post at the mission on the outskirts of Ibadan, whoever they were, or whatever, and
her advice was valued. She could be relied on to have a sympathetic
approach, 'I take the broader view,' she would say. It was always a wise
one. Now she's failing. Bem, the houseboy, has noticed the change
more than anyone. She moves slower than before, peers through her
spectacles more, and she's started to lose her once healthy appetite
and keen interest in food.

Bem, although called the houseboy, is barely ten years younger
than Miss Constance, but he has worked at the house since it was
built, shortly after she arrived from America. When the house was
completed, she had a separate smaller building put up at the back to
accommodate her choice of help, only because she took the advice
from the mission. Miss Constance was not at all keen on getting help

in, and for a time she did for herself, but eventually she selected Bem from among the many stray waifs and orphans at the mission. She chose him because of the deep scars on his back that he had no recollection of acquiring. Bem had refused to talk to anyone for nearly a year after turning up emaciated and traumatized, begging for food at the door of the mission.

Miss Constance began teaching him how to read and write, whether he wanted to learn or not, which he didn't at first. She was patient. She never asked him a question about himself, never asked him to speak when he didn't want to, never chastised him for sneaking a piece of extra food.

There was something more than the scars on her hands that he recognized, the scars she covered with gloves each Sunday for service, or whenever she was out in public. She spoke oddly, quietly, and she liked being by herself. He recognized that too, and she never looked at him with sympathy. He'd liked that about her most of all because, against all the odds, it made him feel like her equal and he couldn't figure out why he should feel that way.

She added further rooms to his quarters when he married Adeola and they started to have the children. She taught them, at school and at home, and when they were ill she took them into the guest room in her house, which was rarely used, and nursed them back to health. They all went to college in Ibadan, something that made her hugely proud. They called her Nnenna, the Igbo word for grandmother.

Adeola took over most of the cooking when the children grew up, and she shares the upkeep of the property with Bem. Miss Constance insists everything is immaculately kept, and that the walls are freshly whitewashed regularly. She is very clear about what she wants, and how she wants it done. She is mannerly, friendly, but strangely neither Bem nor Adeola really feel they know her at all, although they are deeply loyal, born of genuine gratitude for what she's done for them and their children. For all her compassion and the care she shows to those less fortunate at the mission, of which there is a perpetual stream, Miss Constance is a very cautious, private individual who keeps her distance. They allow her to. When they feel that distance is encroached upon by over-forward inquisitiveness or lack of tact, they protect her with all the ferocity of the first line in a military defence force many a stranger has felt the brunt of.

She dresses immaculately, with now just a faint trace of lipstick. She was the first person, even before the priest, to purchase a clothes iron, which is still in use, and the attention she asks them to pay to the dusting and care of her library of books fits with the fastidiousness of her nature and her pride in the collection.

Now Miss Constance spends only a little time each day in the garden. Early in the morning, with Bem's help and before she begins to complain of the climate, whatever it is, bushes are pruned and cut flowers arranged in the rooms. She no longer manages the mower and leaves the lawns to Bem. She is proud of her garden and insists the grass is kept well watered in the dry season and well trimmed during the wet season to discourage snakes.

Her scarred hands are only slightly arthritic. She says the heat of the sun helps. If she is expecting company she wears lace gloves, her selection of various colours laid out for ease of choice according to her daily attire in two drawers of her teak wardrobe.

Adeola always rubs her hands with aloe perryi after she does the garden.

'Thank you, Ade. I think tomorrow we should get the ingredients for our Christmas cakes. I'm surprised we still have the brandy from last year. I noticed it in the pantry.'

'How many this year, Nnenna?'

'I think we did ten last year, didn't we? My, we better start right away.'

'Bem was asked by the Islamic high school if they could have one.'

Miss Constance laughs.

'Well, that's eleven. I don't suppose they offered to become Christians.'

'No, Nnenna.'

'Can't keep a cake from them for that. Can I leave the shopping list to you, Ade? And let Bem have what's left of the brandy; we'll get a new bottle to soak the fruit in. I suppose we need two now. He'll know what he usually gets.'

'What about the Islamic school and the brandy?' asks Adeola. 'We can't put brandy in that cake.'

She laughs. 'Oh, I think we can.'

Miss Constance smiles for a long time at the thought of the Islamic school eating Mrs Archer-Laing's English-recipe Christmas cake laced with brandy.

Adeola finishes oiling her hands and turns to leave her as she is, eyes closed, head resting on the wing of the chair. It is time for her nap, which she would normally take right there under the shade of the thatched terrace roof.

'There's a car on the road, Nnenna.'

'I'm not expecting anyone. Thank you, Ade. Can you turn the air conditioning on inside, please? I don't know what the day is going to do. I suspect heat, although it was chilly in the night.'

The dust trail billows high into the still air long before the car becomes visible on the road. When it pulls up at the bottom of the drive, Ade sees it's a taxi carrying a man and a woman in the back. They fan themselves in the heat. The man gets out of the car first and shades his eyes from the sun. He addresses Ade as he helps the woman out of the back seat.

'Miss Laing? Miss Constance Laing?'

'This is Miss Laing's residence. May I help you?'

Miss Constance hears the exchange from the terrace, opens her eyes and turns slowly in her chair.

'Yes? I'm Miss Laing.'

To Ade's annoyance the couple walk past her uninvited and stride enthusiastically towards Miss Constance.

'Arletta?'

Miss Constance hadn't heard her name spoken for many, many years. She had never heard it spoken in Africa. There was something about the way it was said, the tone of voice, something she had held sacred in her memory all those years. She'd have known it anywhere.

'Rochelle?'

'Arletta, is that you?'

'Rochelle, you've come? My Rochelle?'

'Oh, Arletta! I came to see you … I had to, Arletta.'

'Rochelle?'

The world, in an instant, is an entirely different place.

Miss Constance rises from her seat. The two sisters look at one another, studying each face that has changed so much in half a century, since one last look so long ago at the end of a dusty track in Louisiana. They fall into each other's arms. Miss Constance weeps, repeating Rochelle's name over and over again. Rochelle's husband, Neville, stands behind them, twirling his hat in restless fingers. Ade notices there are tears in his eyes and bows her head to leave him in his private moment. Bem appears at the side of the house, tea towel in hand. Neither he nor his wife has ever seen Nnenna cry.

'I'm so glad you came. Let me look at you now. Let me just look at you. My Rochelle, my dearest, dearest …'

'I grew up Arletta. And I went to college, just like you wanted. This is my husband Neville. Neville, come.'

Neville is the first man to take hold of Arletta in over fifty years. His embrace is emotional, warm and strong.

'It is a pleasure to meet you at last, at long last, Arletta. A great pleasure.'

'Ade, Bem, this is my sister Rochelle and her husband Neville. Oh my! Bring us some iced tea. Would you like that Rochelle – or a soda? Neville, come please. What would you like? Bem please, some drinks right away … quickly, please. I'll have anything.'

Bem and Ade had no idea any family existed and it was the most excited they'd seen her in a long time, probably ever. Bem asks Nnenna if he should tell the taxi to wait.

'Oh yes, offer him out of the heat, though, and let him have a drink too. Be sure to tell him we'll pay him for his time if he'll wait.'

Then as Bem turns in the drive to talk to the driver, she changes her mind.

'No, what am I thinking! My guests, my sister will stay. Would you make sure the guest room is properly prepared, Bem?'

'Yes, Nnenna.'

Bem knew Ade would chastise him for calling Miss Constance Nnenna in front of her guests. The excitement had made him forget himself.

'I knew you would never get in touch Arletta. It was time to come,' said Rochelle. 'I had to come.'

'I'm so glad to see you, Rochelle. Come sit with me, hold my hand. Come.'

Rochelle notices her sister moves slowly and deliberately. It is soon to be her time, that is clear.

'You must tell me about the children too, Rochelle. Please. I know Stephen is a lawyer, and Lilith has done so well. You must be so proud.'

'But Arletta, how do you know about the children? My Stephen and Lilith?'

'Mrs Archer-Laing wrote every Christmas till she died.'

The dry season is not fully underway and the grey clouds coming overhead thankfully give them some shade from the sun, although it's starting to make the day muggy. Miss Constance takes Rochelle by the arm and guides her round the path at the side of the lawn towards the shade of a thatched gazebo. Neville follows a discreet distance behind.

'It is so good to see you, Rochelle. How I missed you, watching you grow, watching Mambo grow old.'

'Mambo cried for you, Arletta. When she was dying she asked me to find you and to beg your forgiveness. And I'm so glad I have found you.'

Miss Constance had forgiven Mambo a very long time ago. Even before the thick night mist had swirled round the Spanish moss next to the bayou and she had held her tight as she slept her last night in America.

'She told me everything.'

'Did she tell you about us, how Madame Bonnet helped us. Were you shocked?'

'She told me, and no, Arletta, I was not shocked. She was my Mambo, too. She had to help you. When she told me everything, she started from the beginning, so it was clear and plain why you did what you did. She told me all about it when I finished college.

She never forgave herself for leaving you alone when you were a child. Never.'

'I missed her something terrible when I left Louisiana. You too, Rochelle, but I ached deep down in my bones for Mambo. It never went away.'

'She was hard on herself. About how she was when she was young.' Miss Constance sat down and laughed.

'Rochelle, she was a crazy woman.'

'That's for sure.' Rochelle smiled and a little laugh rocked her chest. Miss Constance noticed her little sister stop briefly in her tracks when she laughed. Still doing that, just like Pappy used to do.

They sat together in the gazebo.

'I look back and I see what she told me once, that Pappy never took his hand to her. He loved her and I couldn't see it because all I ever did was argue. Lord, could we argue!'

'Lord, could she argue?'

They laughed together. They were easy with one another. The years fell away.

'Did she ever stop, Rochelle, calm down, become mellow?'

'Yes, she did. She was proud that you had taken care of business, proud that I went to college and she stopped fighting the world.'

'And the world changed too.'

'And there was something left in it, something to show for her life, something to prove she'd had a life, to be proud of. She was proud of you. She told me that.'

'She was proud of me in the end? Well, she was always proud of you Rochelle.'

'She loved you Arletta. I'm going to stay and tell you all the things she said about you. How she loved you.'

'I know she did.'

'And she never regretted it. She never regretted that night.'

Rochelle opened her handbag and extracted a small pouch.

'Here, Arletta. When Mambo was dying – it was long after she told me everything – she said she knew in her heart that one day you and I would meet again. It's why I had to come. I was to give you this.'

Miss Constance opened the pouch her sister handed her, smiling as she did so. She knew it would contain Pappy's pipe. She put the old pipe to her lips and sucked deeply.

'Oh Mambo.' Miss Constance fingered the pipe. 'My Pappy's pipe. Thank you, my Mambo. I guess Pappy would never have thought of it coming here to Africa. You know, Rochelle, I get the feeling she might have smoked this sometimes, sucked on it just like I used to. I used to do that, to remember Pappy.'

'She probably did. I never saw her, but I bet she did too, because she took up smoking after you left. You keep it Arletta.'

'No.' Miss Constance looked pleased. 'You give it to one of the children. I'll be under the ground soon, and this here pipe has spent too much time in the ground already. Tell them about Pappy, so they know he saved his master's son's life. That he kept the cabin fire alight in winter, and shared what he grew in the ground. Tell them about their Pappy, and about this pipe.'

'I'm so glad I came Arletta. As Mambo always used to say, we's flesh and blood.'

'I knew it was called the "White Lynchings of Louisiana" but I never knew the trouble it caused till somebody sent me the newspaper clippings about it.'

'Somebody sent newspaper clippings?'

'Yes. Somebody who knew I was here.'

'Who? Have you any idea?'

'I think so.'

'It's been one of the great unsolved cases in Louisiana. Never shook off the suspicion that it was revenge, and it got white folks real scared they might start getting a dose of their own medicine from blacks. Lynchings round our way came to an abrupt end with it Arletta. These lynchings became quite famous, you know.'

'Infamous may be the word you're looking for, Rochelle. That won't get me a pardon. Will you and Neville stay awhile? Stay with me here. I cannot go far. Old age, Rochelle, just old age.'

'We'll stay as long as you like Arletta, as long as you like. We're retired now, and with plenty of time.'

'Won't Neville mind?'

'Neville is the nicest, kindest man you'll ever have met, Arletta. He's a remarkable person, and I'm not just saying that because he's my husband. We'll stay if you want us to and you'll find that out for yourself. And he loved Mambo, they got on real fine. Did everything for her at the end. Neville says you need family round you now. After all you've been through, and having to leave everything behind, we want to stay with you if you'd like us to. He knows you left Mambo the money that got me started and off to college.'

'Quince ever help like he promised?'

'Saved like a madman to send me every cent he could. Took to wearing shiny shoes, patent leather, well, you can imagine Mambo ...'

They giggled like girls.

'Wearing her black suit and pearls. My, she looked wonderful.'

'Oh, she got real pearls in the end.'

When they were done laughing, Miss Constance removed her glasses and wiped away tears.

'You know, I never thought much of him, Quince, till he quit liquor.'

'I don't recall his drinking days, but I heard about it, mostly from himself, I must say. He was pretty honest about it, how he behaved when he was a young man. Pretty wild, the way he told it.'

'I remember him changing, Rochelle, the way he was with me, wanting to help me out, asking if I needed anything. He'd stopped drinking by then, grew up a little, I guess. He followed me out to Sugarsookie Creek just before I left. It was real nice, and I always remembered the little talk we had that day. I always remembered it, and how seeing us together like that made Mambo smile, I could see it made her happy.'

'He followed you another time too. On the night you went to see to business. He wanted to be there in case you needed help.'

'He saw us?'

'He was mad as hell. He knew Mambo well enough to realize she was up to something and not telling him, so he followed you. He castrated them, after you left. Took a machete to them.'

'Lord above. Quince. I had no idea, but the newspaper clippings said the bodies had been mutilated. I thought it was just sensationalizing.'

'After you left he always used to say he was loving me for both of us, and I liked that. His other girl was gone. Always said he wanted to come to Africa, the old country, to see her. That's what he told folks.'

'He would say that?'

Miss Constance felt her eyes sting with tears, her heart leap with emotion.

'Yes, always said his other girl was teaching too, back in Africa. They thought you'd be coming home. A couple of years at the most is what they thought, otherwise I don't think they would ever have let you leave. They clung to one another after you left; they found it hard. Later on they wanted to come to Africa to find you, but he got Parkinson's, you know. He couldn't have made the journey. Mambo looked after him, then they came to stay with us. Like I said, Neville's a special kind of man. Put up with them both.'

'Lord, what a day it is today, Rochelle. You know, if I had done it by myself, I might have kept in touch, but I wasn't alone. I had a lot of help and by then a lot of people knew what had happened to me, what these two men had done to me. Can you imagine Mrs Archer-Laing giving evidence in court? And poor Eveline Gaudet. She'd been through enough.'

Rochelle opened her handbag again.

'I have this, Arletta. It's for you.' She handed Miss Constance a letter. 'It's from Eveline Gaudet. She asked me to find a way of getting it to you. It's so much better that I'm able to hand it to you.'

'Do you know her? Did you meet her?'

'Yes. She tracked us down in Baton Rouge. She's fine, she survived, and she's beautiful. Very smart, very high-profile, and a lawyer now, which is why she was able to trace us, I reckon. Everyone in the South knows who Eveline Gaudet is. Although very few will know what you and I do about her. Read it.'

Dear Arletta
I sincerely hope that Rochelle is able to get this letter to you. I have never forgotten you. I have never forgotten how

kind you were when you visited me in hospital, or indeed, our mutual friend, Nellie.

Papa spoke to me before he died, and told me he had gone to the train station to see you off. As soon as he heard the bodies were found in the early hours of that morning, he knew. Errol had told him you were leaving for Africa and he put two and two together, and realized why you never came to see us again. Errol did too. I understand he found a way to get some newspaper articles to you. My father went to the station on the day you left to salute you for your courage. I wanted you to know that, and he never spoke of it to me until his dying day. He said that you had the courage to do for him what was burning in his own heart to do.

I always wondered why I never saw you again. The day my father died, I understood. I know you did it for yourself, but you did it also for me, and all the others, wherever they are. You sacrificed your life and your family for us, and I hope you found peace, wherever you went.

I eventually studied law and practised in Montgomery, Alabama, specializing in civil rights and women's issues, something close to my heart, and which brought me great success, a purpose, and a return to happiness. There are, beyond doubt, extenuating circumstances corresponding to your situation under Louisiana law. Judicial consideration would be given to your then, and present, circumstances, and to public opinion. If you decide to return to the US, I, and my colleagues at Gaudet and Dulac, offer you our services pro bono. Your sister has all my details, so I hope, at the very least, that we can talk on the phone. I know that I will win your case if it is your wish, if, indeed, a case would be brought against you. The mystery remains unsolved; it could continue to be so.

Some years ago, Arletta, in the course of investigating an entirely unrelated matter, I came across the intriguing case of a woman who had been viciously stabbed and left to bleed

to death in a cotton field outside of Montgomery in June of
1908. She had been a popular and wonderful singer during her
lifetime, about to sign an important phonograph-recording
contract at the time of her death. Her killer, whom it took
many years to find, was in fact a rival both for the affec-
tions of her husband, also her manager, and her popularity
as a singer. When the woman was eventually committed to
Louisiana State Penitentiary, she admitted to the crime in
Montgomery, and in her final hours on Death Row confessed
to the priest that she had 'killed her for a song'. She hoped
to launch her own career, but was never successful.

I was able to find a very old first phonograph-recording of
the song, and surprisingly, in the archives, an unaccompanied
original version by the woman who was killed for it. Arletta,
there was no mistaking the voice.

The murdered woman's name was Nell Maxwell.

I remain at your service,

Eveline Gaudet

Miss Constance felt the comfort of her sister's arm around her shoulder. She lifted her eyes to the distant hills and remembered.

'Come, Arletta. Let's go inside.'

'Did Eveline Gaudet tell you what's in this letter, Rochelle?'

'Yes Arletta, she told me.'

'I'm glad she did so well. Let's sit here for a while. I want to hold
my sister's hand.'

Afterword

A t the turn of the twentieth century, much of America's Deep South remained undeveloped frontier where the extensive programme of deforestation, road, rail and levee construction had yet to begin. Lynching continued to be most prevalent in these Southern states, with the associated mob-rule vigilantism and racism reaching its peak from around 1890 into the early years of the twentieth century, although instances were still being recorded even into the 1960s.

Justification for this form of what has been called 'frontier justice' was the eradication of those considered 'undesirable' in the community and the preserving of social order, for the most part the privilege associated with the dominant white class. Lynching could result for as little as a charge of acting suspiciously, or unwittingly having your identity mistaken. Black men were often falsely accused of theft or rape, or of displaying improper behaviour towards a white person or even using inflammatory language, often nothing other than a black man defending himself against a false accusation. Running a bordello and voodooism would both have resulted in lynching.

In the context of the time, Arletta and Mambo are unusual in that they are African American women lynching white men. There were numerous white lynchings for theft, criminal behaviour, even political purpose, *but in the nineteenth century* many were lynched for being sympathizers of the abolitionists.

Prior to any state or federal regulation, fiercely resisted in the South, lynching was condoned by the perpetrators as the process of law. It wasn't until 2005 that a formal apology from the US Senate was given to Louisiana for its repeated failure in the early twentieth century to pass anti-lynching legislation. During that time African Americans suffered the highest rate of lynching in the South.

Acknowledgements

I would like to acknowledge the many people who offered their invaluable support and advice, from writing to publication, of this book. First of all I am grateful to my agent, Julian Friedmann, of Blake Friedmann Literary Agency, Lisa Vanterpool for her observations and also Tom Witcomb. I am in gratitude to Juliet Mabey, Fiona Slater, James Magniac, Ruth Deary, Lamorna Elmer and everyone at Oneworld Publications for their patience and guidance. Thanks also to my editor Jenny Parrot for her wisdom and advice, which I'm glad I took, and to Kate Quarry for going through the manuscript so diligently. They are all a pleasure to know and to work with.

Most of all I'd like to thank my son Damron and my daughter Genevieve for their incredible love and support on the journey, without them nothing would have been possible. Finally, thanks to my sister, Margaret S, and my two brothers, Coilie and Henry, for having endless and immeasurable faith in me.